I0641319

Against All Odds

★★★★★

President
Paul Ronan

Second Edition Revised
© January 4, 2017
© First Edition Copyrighted December 14, 2012

Historical Novel by Larry Flinchpaugh

J L Flinchpaugh Publishing Company
St. Joseph, Mo. 64503

i

Special Thanks

A special thanks to my wife Phyllis and two sons Mark and Steve, Richard A. Little DDS (1939-2014) of Bozeman, Montana, and Robert Stout of Stout Piano Service in Independence, Mo. who inspired me with their own ideas and the many hours of proof reading and research assistance.

This book would have been impossible to complete without their help, patience and guidance.

Larry Flinchpaugh

January, 2017

About the author

Larry Flinchpaugh was born April 16, 1939 in St. Joseph, Missouri. He graduated from Central High School in 1957 and continued his education at the St. Joseph Junior College, University of Kansas, University of Missouri at Kansas City and Tulsa University in Tulsa, Oklahoma.

Larry was a member of the *International Accountants Society* and worked for Phillips Petroleum Company in Kansas City, Missouri and then Bartlesville, Oklahoma. In 1976 he moved to Bakersfield, California to work as *Inventory Control Manager* for "Tosco". (The Oil and Shale Corporation) In 1981, Larry semi-retired to start his own business, with his wife Phyllis and two sons Mark and Steve. They owned and operated *Consign It Stores Inc.* which appraised and liquidated personal property for individuals, the Kern County Coroner's Office and local businesses.

Larry has spent his retirement years learning and writing about the important issues facing our country today and what we as individuals can do about averting a complete economic collapse of our country. He believes we need to abolish our failed "Democracy" and return to our founding fathers' "Republic." established in 1776.

-Introduction-

Benjamin Franklin, at the close of the Constitutional Convention of 1787, was asked as he left Independence Hall, "Well, Doctor, what have we got-a Republic or a Monarchy?" Franklin replied, "A Republic, if you can keep it."

Today, 2016, we are fully aware just how prophetic Mr. Franklin's words were. Since 1787, our so called representatives have either ignored or have forgotten the differences between a Democracy and a Republic form of government. Understanding the difference is essential in abolishing our failed democracy and returning to our founding fathers "Republic" form of government.

The obligations and duties of both a Democracy and a Republic form of government are basically the same. Both elect officials to lead the government through majority vote. Both forms of government tend to use a representational system where citizens vote to elect politicians to represent their interests and form the government.

Unlike a "Democracy", a "Republic" form of government's majority cannot take away certain inalienable rights. In a "Republic" there is limited government bound by the dictates of the constitution. In other words it is a limited government with a constitution adopted by the people and changeable only by its amendment.

In *Against all odds- President Paul Ronan*, a true patriot, Republican Congressman Paul Ronan from Texas, became a major Presidential Candidate in 2016. If elected, he was surely going to surprise even his supporters by methodically and strategically replacing the corrupt status quo which had been purposely destroying our country for its personal profit for over

iv

100 years. The unelected controllers of the United States, the International Bankers, the military industrial complex companies, and special interest lobbyists, were finally on the verge of being dealt a fatal blow in 2016 if Paul Ronan were elected President.

At last the unconstitutional 1913 Federal Reserve Act, which had allowed a privately owned bank to print and control our nation's money supply, was going to be abolished. This private bank had charged the taxpayers unnecessary interest for loaning them their own money even though the Constitution allowed for the United States Treasury Department to print their money "Interest Free." Also to be repealed was the 16th Amendment which had been passed in 1913 that permitted personal income tax to be collected on people's salaries. Few knew that their personal income tax was to pay the private Federal Reserve only for interest and did not pay for any services to the people.

Additionally, President Paul Ronan would only allow fractional reserve banking for those banks owned by the individual states which would benefit the taxpayers instead of the banks. Up until this time, North Dakota was the only state that had such a bank. This change would allow the states, counties, and cities to finance their own local "Public Works Projects" interest free from the bank profits generated and provide low interest loans to the citizens of their state.

Not only would these changes result in the living standard of most Americans to rise 30-35%, there would be almost no need for federal assistance programs like government paid healthcare, food stamps, public housing, etc. Most of the American people could now take back the control of their personal lives by paying for the "entitlements" themselves. This would greatly reduce the power of the government over the people and greatly increase the power and freedom of the country's citizens.

An additional benefit of abolishing the privately owned Federal Reserve was that the chance of a war or armed conflict would be reduced to nearly zero because the financing of war would be done though **transparent taxes** instead of **hidden debt financing** through inflation. The citizens would now be much more reluctant to support an offensive war in a far off country if they were to experience the immediate effect on their personal finances by the increase in taxes.

As President, Paul Ronan and a Congress sensitive to his ideology were planning to make the governors of each state, once again, the "Commander in Chief" of their states' national guards no matter whether the country was at war or peace. No longer was the president of the United States able to usurp the power of the states. Now the states would not be forced to activate their National Guard units to take part in continuous *offensive wars* orchestrated by the President and the unelected controllers.

We would now have a true *"Department of Defense"* instead of a misguided *"Department of Offense."* This effectively meant that the U.S. military's main objective would be once again restored to defending America from foreign invasion rather that creating *"terrorists"* by meddling in the affairs of other countries throughout the world.

None of these important changes would have been possible if presidential candidate Paul Ronan's great grandfather had not emigrated from Ireland to America in the middle of the 19th century and started a sequence of events that would enable these historic events to take place. Up until now, no president had been bold enough to make these changes or to even suggest them.

When Samuel Ronan, Paul Ronan's great grandfather, set foot in America in the fall of 1858, he had no way of knowing how profound he and his descendants' actions would be in affecting the reconstruction of the American dream from a failed *Democracy* back to a *Constitutional Republic*.

Follow the heartwarming and inspirational journey of the Ronan family as Sam Ronan gets a job as a telegrapher for the Hannibal and St. Joseph Railroad in Breckenridge, Missouri and has a chance meeting with Samuel Clemens while Clemens and his brother are on their way to Nevada.

On September 5, 1861, Sam was on the train traveling to St. Joe when the Confederates sabotaged the railroad bridge over the Platte River. There is mystery and intrigue when Sam discovered a hidden message in a picture that his girlfriend showed him from her deceased husband. She explained to Sam that her husband just might have been a member of the *Knights of the Golden Circle* and might have worked with Jesse James in his attempt to finance the Civil War for the Confederacy.

Sam's son, grandson and great grandson were all involved in politics and the legal professions that put them in the middle of the politics of the day which ultimately allowed them to carve out a place in history for the entire Ronan family.

Even though this is a fictitious story, it clearly explains what steps need to be taken to save America from a devastating economic collapse and the complete loss of state sovereignty and individual freedom.

True patriots like Congressman Ron Paul, Senator Rand Paul, Judge Andrew Napolitano, Michael Rivero, and Thomas Jefferson were the author's inspiration in writing this story.

If anything is to be learned from this story, it is to understand what must be done to save our country from ruin. We must (1) elect legislators that will honor their oath to abide by the Constitution, (2) abolish the privately owned Federal Reserve central bank and modify Fractional Reserve Banking and (3) finance our government through *transparent taxes* rather than by *debt financing* which results in a hidden inflation tax.

This Story Follows
Four Generations of the Ronan Family
How Liberty
and
We the People
Triumphed
Over the Tyranny of the Unelected Controllers

Points to Ponder
As Discovered by the Ronan Family

- The real controllers of the U.S., the men behind the curtain, are the bankers, the military industrial complex executives, the controlled corporate mainstream media and the lobbyists; all unelected. And they are not working for 'we the people.'

- To adhere to the United States Constitution, our money must consist of physical gold or silver or our paper money (notes) must be backed by gold or silver. However in reality, paper money need only be backed by the government's willingness to accept it for the payment of taxes and by the value added to a product or service through man's physical effort or investment.

- The people and the states created the Federal Government for their benefit. The Federal Government is the servant of the people-not the other way around.

- The United States Constitution allows the Federal government to print "Interest Free" Treasury Notes for the benefit of the people instead of "Interest Bearing" Federal Reserve Notes for the benefit of the bankers.

- We only have the illusion of a two party political system! They both work for the hidden controllers.

Ronan Family Genealogy:
(Four generations of true patriots)

Samuel Ronan
1840-1923
Immigrant News Boy to
Telegrapher to Lawyer

Jefferson Ronan
1864-1948
Aid to President Woodrow Wilson

Matthew Ronan
1908-1988
Congressman from Missouri

Paul Ronan
1944-2032
Congressman from Texas
45th President
of the U. S.

This historical novel follows the lives of four generations of the Ronan family's quest to save America; from Samuel Ronan's arrival in Philadelphia from Ireland in 1858 to the election of his great grandson Paul Ronan in 2016 as President of the United States.

Part I
Returning to the Republic of our Founding Fathers'

1840-1923
News Boy to Telegrapher to Lawyer

Table of Contents

Chapter One

Returning to our Founding Fathers' Republic................1

Chapter Two

Irish Potato Famine 1845-52.....…...…...………....……....5

Chapter Three

Sam Ronan's Arrival in Philadelphia.......................24

Chapter Four

Westward Ho ...……………………………….............43

Chapter Five

Breckenridge Missouri - A New Beginning....…...............61

Chapter Six

Confederates Sabotage the Platte River RR Bridge...…....79

Chapter Seven
Lawyer's Assistant....………………………….....…......89

Chapter Eight

June Wedding Bells and Secret Society Intrigue................95

Chapter Nine

Reconstruction..105

Part II
Jefferson Ronan
1864-1948
Personal aid
To President Wilson

Table of Contents

Chapter Ten

Jefferson Ronan Graduates from Harvard.................112

Chapter Eleven

Jeff and Cathy's New Home In Washington D.C.........119

Chapter Twelve

Woodrow Wilson Elected President.........................129

Part III- Matthew Ronan
1908-1988
Senator from Missouri

Table of Contents
Chapter Thirteen

Matthew Ronan -University of Missouri.........…….........153

Chapter Fourteen
Marriage Proposal...185

Chapter Fifteen
Matthew's Political Career.....................................190

Part IV

Paul Ronan
1944-2032
Congressman and Presidential Hopeful
45th President of the United States?

Table of Contents

Chapter Sixteen

Early life of Paul Ronan.....................................195

Chapter Seventeen

Paul Joins the Navy..200

Chapter Eighteen

Medical Career or Politician..............................205

Chapter Nineteen

Congressional Candidate...................................219

Chapter Twenty

Presidential Candidate in 2016..........................228

Chapter Twenty One

Conspiracy Theories...236

Chapter Twenty Two

The Election Process...249

Chapter Twenty Three

President Paul Ronan- Acceptance Speech…....................260

Chapter Twenty Four

Are You Better Off Than You Were Four Yrs. Ago?......291

Prolog…….…….…………………………………….…....297

Suggested Documentaries……………………..……….…299

Suggested Reading........……………………….……….....300

Notable Quotes and Notes:

Jury Nullification: "I consider trial by jury as the only anchor yet imagined by man, by which a government can be held to the principles of its constitution." Thomas Jefferson

Jurors Must Question The Law:
In the American courtroom, there are 12 judges who are called the jurors, besides the one with the robe. In fact, one court ruled, "If the jury feels that the law under which the defendant is accused is unjust…or for any reason which appeals to their logic or passion, the jury has the power to acquit, and the court must abide by that decision." (U.S. v Moylan 427 F 2d 1002, 1006, 1969)
Ref: www.FIJA.ORG

Danger of Democracy – "A democracy is nothing more than mob rule, where fifty-one percent of the people may take away the rights of the other forty-nine." -Thomas Jefferson

Banking-*"You (International Bankers) are a den of vipers and thieves. I intend to rout you out, and by the Eternal God, I will rout you out. If the American people only understood the rank injustice of our money and banking system, there would be a revolution before morning."* Andrew Jackson, in an address to Congress, 1829

Banking *"I have two great enemies, the southern army in front of me and the financial institutions in the rear. Of the two, the one in the rear is the greatest enemy. The Money Power preys upon the nation in times of peace, and conspires against it in times of adversity. It is more despotic than monarchy, more insolent than autocracy, more selfish than bureaucracy. It denounces, as public enemies, all who question its methods or throw light upon its crimes."* Abraham Lincoln

WWI, WWII, Korea, Vietnam, Regime Change
"It is no coincidence that the Century of Total War coincided with the Century of Central Banking"...... Ron Paul

Congressman Charles A. Lindbergh, Sr., 1913
"This (Federal Reserve) Act establishes the most gigantic trust [monopoly] on earth. When the President [Woodrow Wilson] signs this bill, the invisible government by the Monetary Power will be legalized. The people may not know it immediately, but the day of reckoning is only a few years removed. The trusts will soon realize that they have gone too far even for their own good. The people must make a declaration of independence to relieve themselves from the Monetary Power. This they will be able to do by taking control of Congress. Wall Streeters could not cheat us if you Senators and Representatives did not make a humbug of Congress...The greatest crime of Congress is its currency system. The worst legislative crime of the ages is perpetrated by this banking bill.

The caucus and the party bosses have again
operated and prevented the people from getting the benefit of
their own government. "

Two opposing political philosophies:
*"A government is best that governs **least**."* Thomas Jefferson
*A government is best that governs **most**. This is not a direct quote by Alexander Hamilton but, all the same, summarizes his beliefs through his actions.*

"All the perplexities, confusions, and distresses in America arise, not from defects in the Constitution or confederation, not from want of honor or virtue, as much as from downright ignorance of the nature of coin, credit, and circulation."
John Adams

"The division of the United States into federations of equal force was decided long before the Civil War by the high financial powers of Europe. These bankers were afraid that the United States, if they remained as one block, and as one nation, would attain economic and financial independence, which would upset their financial domination over the world. The voice of the Rothschilds prevailed. Therefore, they sent their emissaries into the field to exploit the question of slavery to open an abyss between the two sections of the union."
Otto von Bismarck, Chancellor of Germany, 1876

Notes:

Chapter One
Returning to the Republic of our Founding Fathers'

The election of republican candidate Paul Ronan for president of the United States in 2016 marked the beginning of a new era. The unelected controllers of our government and those pushing for a "One World Government" and perpetual wars which enable them to become unreasonably rich at the expense of the common man had been dealt a lethal blow.

Even the rest of the world was experiencing greater freedom by either withdrawing from the European Union or planning referendums to sever relations with the EU. England voted in June 2016 to exit from the EU and several other countries were seriously considering doing the same.

The people of the world had finally awakened; no doubt the result of the increased use of worldwide independent news sources via the internet and social media. The monopoly of the lying, controlled mainstream media had been exposed. The hidden controllers had lost their power as common people could feel the changes and excitement that was building. Truth and freedom was rising! The controlled mainstream media and the unelected controllers could no longer survive in this environment.

President's Introduction

The chairman began to speak. "It is my great pleasure to introduce the 45th President of the United States, President Paul Ronan!"

"Thank you. Thank you Mr. Chairman."

"Thank you Mr. Chairman and America Patriots. I accept this great honor and the trust you have given me. It's a great honor and responsibility, and I am asking you to join me in celebrating the *NEW AMERICA*! We have just begun to destroy the old failed Democracy and return to our Founding Fathers' vision of a Free Republic that represents us all!"

The crowd continued to cheer!

"The next four years will be trying for all us. I pledge to you that the first order of business will be to bring impeachment proceedings against all those legislators who have continually voted less than 50% of the time for constitutional issues. It has been estimated that this could affect up to one fourth of the current legislature."

The crowd continued to cheer!

"Further, Congress is on notice that any bill brought to my desk will be promptly thrown in the trash that is more than 200 pages long and has more than one subject to be considered. A Veterans' Bill cannot include spending one billion dollars in support of the Guatemalan army or 10 million dollars allocated to study the sex life of a turtle!"

The crowd continued to cheer!

"No longer will the U.S. be allowed to replace democratically elected leaders of other countries by using our own armed forces or hired mercenaries as was done in Syria."

The crowd continued to cheer!

The President continued for another hour with several interruptions of cheering and applause... It was truly the beginning of a new era!

Camp David Meeting

Two months later, President Paul Ronan advised his Attorney General to set up a secret meeting at Camp David.

"Are we still on for the meeting Friday at Camp David?
"Yes, Mr. President. I don't believe I have missed anyone. I invited the top people from the CIA, FBI, NSA, Pentagon, Defense Department and the Joint Chiefs of Staff."
"Were they all advised that this was a highly secret meeting?"
"Yes Mr. President."

Some of those officials traveled the 62 mile trip from the Capitol to Camp David by government limousines, but others were taking the underground tram which had been a secret up until now. There were so many attendees that they could barely get around the conference table and many had to stand at the edge of the meeting room. The Attorney General rose to address the group.

"Everyone. Let me have your attention please. We are ready to begin. Thank you all for coming. What is about to happen here today is an historical occasion that President Ronan and I hope you will peaceably co-operate with, and understand the severity of our situation. Listen carefully."

The Attorney General was interrupted as a large contingent of armed Marines entered the conference room and advised all in attendance to put their hands on top of their head. The marine in charge said to the Attorney General, "You may now continue with your presentation."

"The President has just enacted **Martial Law** and everyone here will be detained for at least four weeks or longer under the provisions provided for in the **Patriot Act** and in the **National Defense Authorization Act.** I am sure you all are aware that these acts allow the President to deem anyone a possible terrorist and to hold them without counsel. It will take a minimum of four weeks to determine which of you here today has violated your oath of office to obey the U.S. Constitution. All cell phones, lap tops and other electronic equipment will be confiscated. Your families will be notified that you are currently involved in high level talks with State Department officials."

With a slight smile on his face, the Attorney General said, "You will now be escorted to your quarters."

At last the United States government was once again to represent the people instead of the unelected controllers and lobbyists who considered the U.S. Constitution as merely a relic of the past and an impediment to their socialist agenda.

Authors note: Quote reportedly made by Henry Kissinger. "The illegal we do immediately; if it's unconstitutional, it takes a little longer.

Chapter Two
Irish Potato Famine 1845-1852

The Irish Potato Famine, 1845 to 1852, resulted in approximately one million deaths and one million more to emigrate from Ireland, many to America.

Eighteen year old Samuel Ronan stood quietly at his mother's grave as the bag pipes played "Amazing Grace". A light rain at the small country cemetery contributed to the sorrow everyone felt. Sam and his Uncle Pat and Aunt Mary held hands and sobbed. There were several horses and buggy carriages that could be seen and a group of people were holding umbrellas protecting themselves from the rain.

"Are you ready to go Sam? We best get back to the house before it starts to rain harder."
"I guess you're right Uncle Pat. I'm ready."

Sam's long time school friend, Michael Murphy, approached to offer condolences.

"Sam ole buddy, I am so sorry for your loss. If there is anything I can do for you please let me know. I'll stop by your aunt and uncle's house in a couple of days to check on you."
"Thanks Michael, but I'll be fine."

As they climbed aboard the buggy to make the trip to Uncle Pat and Aunt Mary's house, Sam's mind wandered back in time to four years earlier. Sam and his mother are standing in their potato field sadly, looking at their dying potatoes. The government has failed to do anything to restrain the ruthless mass eviction of families from their homes. The landlords sought to rid their estates of pauperized farmers and laborers like the Ronans.

"I don't know what we are going to do Sam," said his mother.
"With your father gone, we just can't continue. It looks like the government authorities are not going to assist us in any way. Look, isn't that our landlord coming down the road?"

"How do you do Mrs. Ronan? I am sorry to bring you some bad news but I must evict you and your son and find someone who can produce a profit for me. Sadly, there is just nothing I can do. Besides, I think you both will be better off living in town. I'm sure you will be able to find suitable work in Dublin. Times are hard for everyone; including me."

Sam's thoughts quickly returned to the present as they approach the barn next to the house. Uncle Pat opened the barn door and led the horse and buggy into the barn. Aunt Mary and Sam ran to the house trying to keep from getting too wet. Uncle Pat walked briskly towards the house.

"That sure smells good Mary darling. What's cookin?"
"Smoked herring, potatoes and cabbage."
"I don't know how good it will taste but at least it is hot and nutritious. Probably not as good as Sam's mother's cooking. Oh, did she know how to cook. Neighbors came from miles around to sample her fish and chips and cabbage."
"I'm sure it will be fine Darlin. I'm starving."
"I don't wish to appear rude," said Sam, "but, I just want to eat and go to bed. We have some talking to do but it can wait till morning."

The family sat down to eat. There was little conversation. After eating Sam retired for the night.

Sam awakened at first light as the roosters began to crow and the morning sun peeked through the bedroom window. He realized that the decisions he makes today are going to be the most important decisions of his life.

Sam thought to himself, "I am now a man, no longer a boy for someone to take care of. It is up to me to decide my destiny. Thank God for my aunt and uncle who can help guide me in my journey."
"That breakfast sure smells good," said Sam.

Uncle Pat was already up sitting in his rocker reading the Dublin newspaper, *The Freeman's Journal*.

"Good morning Sam. Have you decided what your plans are?"

Samuel Plans for the future

"Yes I have Uncle Pat. I decided I want to immigrate to America. I've been thinking on this for a long time, actually. There's one problem however that I have to figure out."

"What's that Sam?"

"I only have a little money saved and I suppose it won't be enough to even purchase a ticket for my passage. Also I will need additional funds to sustain me while I find some type of work in America."

"Hey, don't you worry about that son. Your Aunt Mary and I will pay for your ticket."

"That's very kind of you but I couldn't ask you to do that."

"Don't you worry about it? We have a little saved up, just waiting for something special and I would say this is pretty special indeed. You can use your own money for other expenses during your trip and to get a start in America. I believe I understand why you would want to do this, but I would like to hear it from you."

"Well for some time now, I have blamed the English government for my parents' early deaths."

"I can certainly understand that," replied Uncle Pat.

"You know, the Potato Famine began as a natural catastrophe but its effects were magnified by the inactions of the Whig government. Not only were people starving, the government did little to help. They should have done something to restrain the ruthless evictions of families from their farms. You know like what happened to mom and me."

"I can't argue with that. The British government was not interested in the well-being of the Irish people."

"My parents were evicted after years of hard work that had greatly increased the value of the land owner's property. This depressing cruel act coupled with a shortage of food caused my

7

mother and father to die way before their time. I am ready to immigrate to America to start a new life in a country that respects an individual's liberty and freedom."

"I do understand Sam. I certainly don't blame you for feeling such animosity toward the English government. I agree with you completely. I just wish I could have helped your parents more at the time, but we were also experiencing hard times."

"I know. Don't blame yourself. For quite some time I felt that Ireland would demand its independence from England; just like the United States did in 1776. I finally realized that was unlikely to happen, at least in my lifetime."

"There's a worker on my fishing boat who just planned a trip to America for his cousin. He explained everything they had to do to prepare. I'm sure he would help us plan a trip for you."

"That would be very good. When can we talk to him?"

"Should be able to tomorrow. I am taking my fishing boat out to see if it might be time to fish for herring."

"I sure hope he can help us. It sure sounds complicated."

"I know he will help. He is a fine gentleman. I remember reading an article in the "Freeman's Journal" a couple of years ago about booking passage to America. The first thing that they emphasized was to take a passenger ship if you can afford it, instead of the cheaper cargo ship."

"Besides the cost of the ticket, what's the difference?"

'They explained that a cargo ship is usually filled with passengers beyond comfortable limits by agents outside the shipping company who are more interested in profits than the passengers' well-being. On cargo ships, passengers are housed in the area usually used for cargo. They hastily construct living quarters that can be easily discarded when they arrive at their destination so that the same area can be used to haul timber, cotton and other sometime smelly cargo back to Liverpool."

"I would never have even thought of that," said Sam.

"Then they discussed whether you should take a sailing vessel, steamship or a combination sailing ship and steamship. The article agreed that a passenger steamship would be a better choice because it would make the trip faster and more comfortable but the cost of passage is sometimes double the price of a ticket for a sailing vessel or combination ship."

"So what do you suggest we do?"

"My suggestion is that we book passage on the combination sail and steam ship even though it is more expensive than a cargo ship. It will be much more comfortable and the voyage time will be less. I can't stand the thought of you sailing on a cargo ship."

"Would I set sail from Dublin or England?"

"You'll first sail from Dublin to Liverpool on a steam ferry, and then from Liverpool to Philadelphia or New York on a combination sailing ship and steam ship. The combination vessels are extremely efficient. They use their steam power to maneuver in and out of the ports and occasionally on the open sea when there is little wind."

"I'm sure glad you are helping me with all the little details of my trip Uncle Pat. I don't know if I would have made the best decisions without your help. What provisions do you think I should take with me?"

"First, I would pack your things in a draw string sack with your name printed on it. The ship will provide most of your food but I think I would add a small sack of apples and a few potatoes. They should last you several weeks without spoiling. Aunt Mary has a homemade wool blanket that will keep you warm, and knowing how you like to keep records of everything you do, you should take a journal book and pen and ink."

"I sure appreciate all this good advice. It's a bit worrisome traveling on the sea for 3-4 weeks. I recall stories about these so called "Coffin Ships" where many passengers died or got diseases due to unsanitary conditions. Did you ever hear those stories?"

"Don't worry about the 'Coffin Ships'. That was a few years ago and most of those problems have been corrected."

"Who fixed it?"

"It was mainly due to the *1855 Passenger Act.* The United States Congress passed the 'Passenger Act' which greatly improved traveling conditions on both steam and sailing passenger ships bringing immigrants to America."

"See what I mean Uncle Pat? America does what is right for the masses of the common people. Not just for the wealthy."

"You're right Sam. Previously large numbers of passengers died on their six to eight week journey because of poor food provisions and the lack of health standards and facilities aboard the ships. Now the ships are required to have more space for passengers and to provide for more services. Hopefully there are no more 'Coffin Ships' left. The Captain of the Alhambra is a close friend of mine and I will give you a letter of introduction. He may even be able to give you some work on the ship that can help defray some of your expenses."

"Look out the window," said Aunt Mary. "That looks like Michael Murphy coming down the road."

"Oh, I forgot. Michael told me at the funeral that he would check in on my well-being. He's a great friend and is sincerely concerned with helping me adjust. We have been friends since our early school days."

"Top of the morning to you Michael."

"Come on in."

"I just stopped by to see how Sam was doing."

"Guess what I have decided to do Michael?"

"I cannot fathom a guess, Sam."

"I'm going to America!"

"Why, in God's name do you want to do that? Not exciting enough for you here in Dublin?"

"As I just explained to my aunt and uncle, I can't help but blame the English government's poor handling of the Potato Famine and for my parent's untimely deaths. I want to go to America to start a new life in a country that's free of England and has a government that protects the common man's rights. The U.S. Constitution even includes a list of rights, in the first ten amendments, that are guaranteed to its citizens."

"Well, it looks like you have made up your mind. When will you be leaving?"

"Probably in two or three months; maybe the middle of April. I expect it will take me at least a month just to get my tickets and provisions for the trip."

"We must throw a *Going Away Party* for you at *O'Reileys!* Why not make it March 17th, St. Patrick's Day? Most of our friends will be there already. What do you say?"

10

"Sounds like fun. I'll be there for sure!"

"Great, I'll check back with you about a week before the party."

The going away party was a great idea of Michael's. All of Sam's friends were there. Lots of drinking and toasting to wish Sam a safe and enjoyable trip to America. Someone shouted out, *May you live to be a 100 and get shot in the back by a jealous husband!* Everybody laughed and screamed in celebration.

A little over a month later, it was time to say good bye. Sam boarded the steam ferry to Liverpool. April 28, 1858.

Time to say goodbye

With a big smile on his face, Uncle Pat said, "Have a safe trip and be sure and write as soon as you disembark in Philadelphia. Be sure to give my regards to Benjamin Franklin and Thomas Jefferson."

"Right Uncle Pat, with a smirk on his face.. I'll do just that, if I can find them."

"Sniffling and with tears in her eyes, Aunt Mary said, "We love you Sam. Stay safe and I hope your voyage won't take more than 3-4 weeks."

Sam arrived in Liverpool, England on his steam ferry in late afternoon. He stood on the gangplank with a crowd of passengers getting ready to disembark. The scene below was noisy and crowded with vendors, travelers, and dock workers loading and unloading ships. Sam purchased a large loaf of bread and began to look for a hotel. It would be three days before the Alhambra would set sail for America.

"Excuse me sir. Could you direct me to a hotel? I need a clean, cheap hotel for two or three days until my ship leaves for America."

"Cheap and clean may be hard to find," chuckled the stranger. "But I would try the Hotel 'Abbot' just two blocks down and then turn right for one block. Can't miss it. They have the smallest bed bugs of any hotel in town. Just kidding lad."

"Thank you sir. I appreciate your help."

Sam set down his bag, blanket roll and loaf of bread outside the Hotel and contemplated whether the hotel would suit his needs. Just then two young urchin boys appear out of nowhere and grabbed his blanket and loaf of bread and scampered down the street. About that time a cop noticed and both the cop and Sam chased the boys into a dead end ally where they were soon apprehended.

"All right you little hooligans," said the Cop "Give the man back his bread and blanket. You two are going to jail."

"Hold on officer. Look at these boys. I think they are just two desperate orphans looking for something to eat."

"They're nothing but thieves!"

"Right sir. Young, poor and hungry thieves! Here is an apple for each of you and you can keep the bread."

"What are doing Sir?"

"I'm taking them to jail."

"Please don't arrest them. They are only trying to survive. Can't you see that they are hungry?"

"Alright, You are very kind young man."

" Boys, this is your lucky day. Don't let me see you around here again."

Sam entered the hotel lobby and looked around to see if it was suitable and affordable.

"May I help you sir?"

"I sure hope so. I need a room for two or three days; nothing too expensive."

"Well a private room is 5 shillings a night which includes one meal. A dormitory room, with 20 other guests, is only 2 shillings per night and doesn't include a meal."

"I think I will take the dormitory room. Is there a place close by where I can get something to eat?"

"There's a small cafe next door to the hotel that has good food at reasonable prices but not much variety. You should be able to get a decent meal fairly cheaply. They do have excellent fruit pies if the fruit is in season."

"Thank you very much; I think I will give them a try."

Sam entered the cafe but all the tables were full except one. He proceeded to ask one of the diners if he could join him. Sam soon discovered that the lad was a happy-go-lucky type of guy, always laughing and joking.

"Excuse me sir, would you mind if I join you? Let me introduce myself. My name is Sam Ronan. I'm from Dublin."

"Of course sit down. I'm Kelsey O'Sullivan. As it so happens I am also from Dublin. I'm sailing on the Alhambra day after tomorrow to America."

"What a coincidence, I am too! What are you going to do the next couple of days? It sure is going to be boring here while we wait to board the ship."

"Why don't we see some of the sites together here in Liverpool while we are waiting?"

"That sounds like a great idea. But first, let's concentrate on eating. I haven't had much to eat since leaving Dublin early this morning. What do you suggest we order?"

"I have no idea; this is my first trip to Liverpool. That table just to your right looks like they have ordered some acceptable food. I was just going to order the same as they did."

"I think I'll do the same."

"Tell me about yourself Sam, and why are you going to America?"

"Well, it's a long story but basically I want to live in a country that respects its citizens' rights. I hold the English government responsible for my parent's untimely deaths and not protecting my family from the ruthless landlord during the potato famine. Now it's your turn."

"My family wasn't too bad off during the famine but my parents worked day and night in their small tailor shop just to survive. The English government wasn't very kind to the lower and middle class people in Ireland. The taxes were high and there were too may regulations to make a decent living. I want to

13

immigrate to America and buy a small farm and have the opportunity to succeed through hard work with little government interference."

"Isn't it exciting Kelsey to think about the vast opportunities we will have in America? I lay awake at night dreaming about what it will be like. What kind of work do you do?"

"Well, I wish to be a farmer but my last job in Dublin was working for a fish merchant. To make extra money, I also worked as an entertainer in the small pubs around Dublin. I specialize in performing table magic, telling jokes, singing, and playing the Harmonica and the Pan Flute. It doesn't pay much but I usually get a free meal and tips."

"I may have seen you perform in Dublin. Did you ever do a show at "O'Reileys?"

"Yes, I believe I did. Let me see, I was there about a year ago. Were you there?"

"Yes! I knew you looked familiar. Hey, you were really good. You had us all in stitches. I liked the story you told about the man dangling a string in a puddle of water outside the pub as if he were fishing. You said you felt sorry for him and invited him inside to buy him a drink. You then said to the old fellow, 'Had any luck catching anything out there?' The old man replied, 'Sure did. You are the third catch tonight.' The whole audience roared. You were very funny and everyone was impressed with your magic tricks."

"Thanks. I really enjoy making people laugh and seeing them having a good time."

Both Sam and Kelsey finished their meal and returned to the hotel. The next day and a half, Sam and Kelsey were busy sightseeing across Liverpool.

Touring Liverpool

"Look at that beautiful church Sam," said Kelsey as they approached the *Church of Our Lady and Saint Nicholas*. I understand it has been a place of worship since about 1257."

"It's nice but I'm getting a little tired of looking at churches. Let's see if we can find a museum and then a place to get a bite to eat."

Sam and Kelsey were having such a good time, they almost forgot the boarding time.

"Look what time it is! We best get to the loading dock to board our ship."
"Good idea. We are only about three blocks from the dock."

Running to the dock, Sam and Kelsey found that they were the last two to board.

All Aboard for America

"Welcome aboard gentlemen. You just barely made it. We will be leaving port in about 30 minutes."
"Thank you Captain."

Sam handed his introduction letter from his Uncle Pat to the Captain. The Captain patiently read the letter and gradually reflected a slight smile.

"I used to work for your uncle Pat on his fishing boat in Dublin. That was many years ago, but I still have fond memories of your Uncle and how patient he was in training me how to navigate. Very nice man."
"Yes he is. He even paid for my passage to America."
"That sounds just like something he would do. Say, I am looking for an assistant or two to cook and take care of some of my personal chores. Would you two be interested in a job on your trip to America?"
"We sure would. I mean, I sure would. What about you Kelsey?"
"Sure. That's fine with me, definitely."
"OK then. You're both hired. Hope you lads know how to cook. Also you can take care of my laundry and maybe add a little varnish to some of the deck railings. Maybe a few other odd jobs."

15

"My friend Kelsey here is quite the entertainer. He is an accomplished magician, singer, and can even play the Harmonica and Pan Flute. I would bet that you could talk him into entertaining the passengers."

"I think that's a great idea. This will work out just fine. The passengers really get bored after about the first week."

"I would be more than happy to do some entertaining Captain."

"That's great. You both go on and board and the Purser will show you around and explain the rules of the ship."

Getting Settled into Ship Life

The Purser met Sam and Kelsey to explain the ship's rules and to show them their quarters. He was very well dressed and displayed a sophisticated and superior attitude…Not very likeable.

"Welcome aboard the Alhambra gentleman. Let me explain the rules. First you must give me any weapons you may have on your persons or in your baggage. They will be returned to you once we arrive in America."

Kelsey O'Sullavan sheepishly reached into his bag and pulled out a large stick of sausage pointing it at the Purser as if it is some kind of weapon. The Purser was not amused. Sam quickly interrupts.

"What about food? We are both starving."

"I was just getting to that before I was interrupted. Allow me to continue please. The ship will provide you with food but you are required to cook it yourself in the designated cooking area. Due to the weather conditions and the condition of the sea swells, a sign will be posted as to the time the kitchen area will be open. Smoking is only permitted on the above deck and only when weather permits."

"Neither of us smoke, so we need not worry about that. But we do eat," said Kelsey.

"Let me continue please. Only a few candle lanterns will be issued to responsible persons. The oil lamps will be lit and serviced only by members of the crew. Keep in mind the ever risk of starting a fatal fire. You are personally responsible for keeping your money and other valuables in safe keeping. Wait a minute. The Captain just handed me a note explaining that both of you have been assigned jobs for this voyage. Instead of sleeping below with the other passengers, you both will have small sleeping quarters just off the Captain's room and the kitchen. You are very fortunate. Very fortunate indeed. Any questions?"

"No questions. Except maybe one. Do we take orders from you or the Captain?"

"Well the Captain is everyone's boss but normally I will be the one that you must answer to."

Sam and Kelsey began unpacking their bags and checking out their beds.

"Kelsey, do you realize what that introduction letter from my Uncle Pat just did for us? If it weren't for that letter, we would be sleeping below deck with all the other immigrant passengers. It's like we have our own private room on the top deck."

"It was my lucky day when I met you. I am looking forward to our voyage and being in the company of such a fine gentlemen as yourself. By the time we arrive in Philadelphia, we should have most of the world's problems solved." Kelsey chuckles.

The Alhambra began steaming out of Liverpool, England on its long voyage to America. There were three loud short whistle blasts from the ship as they left port. Sam sat down to write his first entry in his journal.

"I'm finally on my way to America. Nothing very exciting has happened yet except a brief encounter with a couple of young ruffians near my hotel. While I was deciding on what hotel to stay in, they grabbed my blanket and a loaf of bread I had just purchased. I chased them and got everything back. I felt so sorry for the little guys that I gave them the loaf of bread and two apples from my sack. Uncle Pat's introduction letter to the Captain of the Alhambra really paid off. The Captain gave my new friend Kelsey and me jobs as his assistant. We even got sleeping quarters above

17

deck and next to the Captain's quarters."

Sam blew out his candle lantern and quickly dropped off to sleep. The next morning he awakened early and stepped out on the empty deck. All he could see for miles was the ocean and the sun just beginning to come up in the East. Sea gulls were flying over the ship honking and four dolphins were following the ship's wake. Kelsey soon joined Sam.

"Good morning Sam. How did you sleep last night?"
"Are you kidding? To keep from being tossed out of my bunk, I was awake most of the night bracing myself with both hands gripping the sides of my bed. This is going to take some getting used to."
"Hopefully the sea won't be so rough every night."
"Guess we had better get busy and fix the Captain's breakfast. I hope he isn't too fussy about what he eats. I think he just assumed I knew how to cook a decent meal."

Sam and Kelsey went to the galley to cook their first meal for the Captain. Luckily the Purser was there to help them. After breakfast Sam and Kelsey found a pile of canvas to sit on and discuss whatever came to mind.

Let's Talk

"Sam, we are going to have a lot of time on our hands for the next few weeks to discuss almost every subject known to man. Where should we start? Do you want to talk about politics, religion, sports, or drinking and sex? I know, let's start with religion. "What religion were you brought up in Kelsey?"
"My parents were Catholic but me personally; I guess you could say I believe in a God but that God doesn't interfere in the affairs of man. Pretty simple. And of course I believe in the Bible passage that says, "The more you give, the more you receive. What most religious people don't understand is that it also infers that the more you take, the more you lose."
Sam smiled.

"I have a little trouble even believing in God, because if you do then the next question is who is God's God?" remarked Kelsey.

"I sure never have heard anyone explain their religious beliefs like that. Very interesting," said Sam.

Kelsey continues, "I never did like going to Mass, and the priests and Nuns scared me. The Nuns with their long black robes just seem to mysteriously float along the floor. And some of the priests were just a bit too friendly sometimes. Besides, if there is a God and he is all powerful, why are there so many different religions? Couldn't a most powerful God just make us all believe the same way? I am sure that my personal religious beliefs were a big disappointment to my parents. I only wish I had kept my religious beliefs to myself. What about you Sam?"

"I too was brought up as a Catholic but am starting to question the beliefs of the church. I can certainly identify with some of the things you said. However, my experiences at school were different from yours. I wasn't afraid of the Nuns, maybe because I had an aunt who became a Nun, and the Priests that were my teachers were very good teachers. Father James taught us some principles that will be with me for the rest of my life. He instilled in us some great truths embraced by the masters. Let me give you some examples. He said things like:

- The harder you work, the luckier you get.
- It is better to set free a guilty man than to condemn an innocent.
- The mark of a great mind is to be able to entertain a thought without necessarily accepting it.
- Stepping stones and stumbling blocks look the same but it is your attitude that makes the difference.

"These were just a few of the sayings that Father James instilled in his students. I will be forever grateful for the wisdom he imparted to us."

"Those are powerful thoughts, Sam. They are excellent principles to live by. I better write them down before I forget. No one ever taught me that in school. You were truly fortunate to acquire such wisdom at such a young age."

19

"But, there are many parts of the catholic doctrine that I question. For instance, is Jesus the man really God, you know, the Trinity concept that says Jesus is the Father, the Son, and the Holy Ghost?"

"No, I don't believe that Jesus is God. Maybe a great teacher, prophet and healer, but not God. What made you question the claim that Jesus is also God?"

"I was at the Dublin library one day and they were throwing out a barrel full of old books. I went back at the end of the day and the barrel was outside, ready to be destroyed. I couldn't help but look into the barrel for some books that I might read. One book was about Roman history and the Council of Nicea in 325 AD. It said that King Constantine kept sending home Bishops who would not vote for the "Trinity" concept. The remaining Bishops finally voted to declare Jesus as God because failure to do so would be the same as having a religion that worships a mere mortal man and that would be idol worship; the same as the Pagans' belief. Jesus came very close to not being God. And it appeared that they could have been talking about the Roman Emperor Titus instead of Jesus. It even sounded like Jesus and the Emperor might be the same person. I could see why this book was being discarded!"

"Sam, did you tell anyone about this?"

"I was afraid to. No one would believe me anyway, and would most likely condemn me as an evil person. If I had lived in the Middle Ages, the Catholic Church would have labeled me as a Heretic and would have had me executed."

"I think you are right. It is best to keep this to yourself. Hey, here comes the Captain."

The Captain approached noting that the two men were engaged in a deep serious conversation.

"What are you two lads talking about? You look awfully serious."

" Oh, we were just saying how beautiful it is here on the deck today. We saw a huge whale about an hour ago."

"Don't get too comfortable. Look off to the Southwest. We may be in for a storm in about 4-5 hours. In the meantime, I would like for both of you to get at least some of the wood on the deck varnished. I have six others already working on it now. Will you both give them a hand?"

"Sure Captain, we're on our way."

Sam and Kelsey grabbed a bucket of varnish and a big brush and got to work with the rest of the crew varnishing the rails.

"I was afraid we would sooner or later be put to work on something a little more tiring than cooking and washing clothes."

"I wouldn't worry about it. I think we only have about two more weeks before arriving in Philadelphia. So far the Captain has only used the steam engine to get us out of the Liverpool port and maybe one or two times yesterday. The wind and ocean currents are doing their job. I overheard some of the crew talking about mending sails tomorrow. That will probably be our next job."

All of a sudden there were bright flashes in the sky and it was definitely not lightning. The passengers were noticeably afraid.

"What do you make of that Sam? It's not lightning. I have never seen anything like that."

"I haven't either but I remember my Uncle Pat telling me about something similar to this that he saw in Alaska when he was working on a whale boat. It seems like he said it was called, *Northern Lights*. Something to do with storms on the sun."

Approaching Storm Front

While everyone is looking up at the aerial display, the strong winds that the Captain had warned about a few hours earlier were blasting away at the ship. All the sails were hurriedly dropped. Passengers were running all over the ship, screaming in panic.

One passenger was screaming, "It's the end of the world! We are all going to die! It's all prophesized in the Bible!"

21

"Sam, Kelsey, give me a hand. Get the passenger below deck to their quarters. Hurry up!" hollered the Captain.

"Calm down Madam. It is not the end of the world but rather a storm on the sun that can't hurt us. Now the earthly storm is another matter. Get below deck immediately and take as many as you can with you."

" Kelsey, see if you can get those two small boys below deck before they get blown overboard!"

"Aye aye Captain. I mean aye aye Sam."

The next morning everything was once again calm on deck.

"That was quite a storm last night. Did you think it was the end of the world Kelsey?"

"No, I don't belief in Bible prophecy. The world has been in existence for thousands of years or more, maybe millions. What are the odds it will end in my short life time of 60-80 years? Some of the passengers were sure scared though that the world was ending."

"What I find interesting is that many people believe so strongly in Bible prophesy that they actually associate a current event with something that was written a couple thousand years ago. Now if the Bible had specifically foretold that on May 3rd, 1858 strange lights would be seen in the sky and high winds would come from the south, striking a ship called the 'Alhambra', then I would be inclined to believe that there was something to Bible prophecy."

"I'm glad no one heard our conversations concerning religion. We would probably have been thrown overboard."

Kelsey's Ship Entertainment

The next few days proved to be really boring, but the anticipation of Kelsey's entertainment performance helped cheer up everyone.

A large crowd of passengers began to gather on deck to see Kelsey perform as he had promised the Captain. Kelsey showed off some of his magic tricks, told a few jokes, sang a couple of Irish Pub songs, and finished with playing Amazing Grace on the Pan Flute.

"What do you think Sam? Did they enjoy the show?"
"If the clapping and shouting was any sign of their approval, you were a huge success."
"It was a lot of fun doing it."

Cape May Ahead

"The Captain said we should be in site of Cape May tomorrow afternoon."
"Where is Cape May? I thought we were going to Philadelphia."
"Cape May is on the American coast, South of New York and about a day's journey to Philadelphia up the Delaware River."
"I can't believe we are almost there! What will we do first?"
"I know what I am going to do."
"What?"
"I'm going to lie on the ground and thank God for our safe trip. I hope we will be able to walk on solid ground after being on board a ship for a little over a month."
"I see it Sam! I can see Cape May!"
"No, that's just a cloud. Wait, you are right! It is Cape May. But don't get too excited. I would guess it will still take us a few hours to reach it. It's really hard to judge distance on the ocean.
The Captain said that instead of docking at Cape May, we will head up the Delaware River to Philadelphia. They will fire up the steam engines and we will be there in no time.

Chapter Three
Sam Ronan's Arrival in Philadelphia
May 25, 1858

Sam knew that many of the Irish immigrants coming to America first landed in New York. Even though it was nearly 200 miles shorter than disembarking at Philadelphia, Sam chose the latter.

Arriving at Cape May, New Jersey, and then traveling up the Delaware River, Sam and Kelsey soon arrived and disembarked in Philadelphia, the city of Sam's dreams. Sam wanted to experience living near where Benjamin Franklin had lived and where the Declaration of Independence had been signed. Being very fortunate that he did not immigrate to the U.S. as an indentured servant, Sam realized more freedom than many when he first arrived in America.

Walking down the gang plank of the "Alhambra" and stepping out on American soil was a very emotional moment for both Sam and his friend Kelsey. Sam was all alone, except for Kelsey, in a foreign country with no friends or relatives to help him adjust to his new life but Kelsey was more fortunate. He had a cousin living in Philadelphia that would help him get established. Sam was filled with ambition, drive, and the dreams of a young man eager to become a success. Although he spoke English, it was not the same dialect that was used in America. Customs were different and the way the Americans dressed was different. Sam could feel everyone watching them. At that moment he felt very un-American and alone.

Samuel was only eighteen when he arrived in Philadelphia, bewildered and almost broke. But he was very excited to finally be in the city that was the birth place of American "Freedom" about which he had read so much.

He kept remembering what his mother and father had taught him as a young boy in the old country. Sam's father used to say to him quite often, "Son the most important virtues in life are honesty, hard work and treating everyone you meet with respect. Every day you must strive to be a better person than you were the day before, and you should attempt to enrich the lives of everyone you meet." This message kept repeating itself over and over in Sam's mind, giving him comfort and the feeling that he wasn't really alone. Everything was going to be fine, he kept assuring himself.

In addition to having good moral character, young Sam was a nice looking young man a full six feet tall and with the look of someone who could take care of himself if needed. Anytime he would approach a group of people, almost everyone, especially the young ladies, would pause and take notice of him. Sam had an aura of respectability and importance about him that was hard to miss.

There was a long line of new arrivals waiting to be processed by the immigration authorities in order to be admitted to the United States. Sam definitely wished to become a citizen of the United States but knew that would have to come later. At this time, entry into the country was relatively simple and with few restrictions. A short time later, new immigration laws changed all that but under the current law Sam and Kelsey were easily admitted to America.

Health Officials carefully inspect Sam and Kelsey

The immigration Health Official looked Sam and Kelsey over very carefully, specifically their eyes, skin color, breathing and the condition, of their mental state. He then asked each their names and nationalities.

"Where do you plan to settle young man?"

"Well sir, Philadelphia for now and later I may move west to try my luck at panning for gold," said Sam.

Kelsey said he would probably just stay in Philadelphia.

"You better think seriously about looking for gold in California. I hear the easy gold has all been found," commented the officer, trying to be helpful.

"I know," replied Sam, "but I hear there has been a new strike in your state of Colorado."

The officer smiled and said, "Good luck men and welcome to America."

"Thank you sir," replied Samuel.

"Well we made it Sam. I sure didn't want to be sent to one of those quarantine camps like the two just ahead of us."

"They looked pretty sick but I doubt they will be there very long. Remember those are the guys who got really drunk last night and are probably just suffering from a hangover."

Americans Dress Funny

"We are finally in America! Look how the Americans are dressed! They probably think we are the strange ones. Can't you feel everyone watching us?"

"No, it's just your imagination."

"I wonder how difficult it will be to become a citizen of the United States."

"I doubt that we will be able to become citizens for quite some time. It seems like I heard that you need to live in America for at least a year and maybe even take some kind of an examination concerning American history and law."

"The law part sounds interesting. Maybe I will become a "Solicitor" or as in America, I believe they are called "Lawyers.""

"What do you think we should do first, Sam?"

"Let's see if we can find an inexpensive room to share in a boarding house."

"I have a cousin living in Philadelphia who wrote me and recommended that I find accommodations at a boarding house that she stayed in when she came to America. It's located at 2614 Elmira Street. What do you say? Do you want to give it a try?"

"Sure. I don't have any better suggestions. But how are we going to find it?"

"She told me to take the 26th Street streetcar after getting off the ship, and tell the driver you want to go to the large Irish section of the city. It is only about three miles from the ship's docking area. Then she said, *Watch for the 26th street stop.*"

"Sounds easy enough. Hey, there's the street car now. If we run, I think we can catch it."

"Let's go."

The street car ride allowed the young men to view some of the historical sites of Philadelphia. They passed Independence Hall and some other interesting landmarks.

"Kelsey, looks there's Independence Hall! Let's get off and take a look."

"Let's do things like that in a couple of days. I would rather just get a room and lie down and rest. I'm exhausted from all that has happened today."

"Of course you're right. We'll get a room first. I think we had better get off the street car. I just saw a sign that said 25th and Elmira. Can you reach the pull rope Kelsey?"

"Sure."

The street car came to a halt and several people got off. Sam and Kelsey proceeded to walk down the street until they found the correct address. They knocked on the door and were met by the landlady.

"You boys looking for a room? It's 5.00 a month, payable in advance, no smoking or cooking in your room, and no women in your room. We serve breakfast in the morning 6AM to 8AM and supper 5PM to 6PM. You provide your own lunch."

"That sounds fine with me. What about you Kelsey?"

"Me too. I am just tired and want to lie down and go to sleep in a bed that doesn't move around all night."

"Your room is upstairs, third room on the right."

"Thank you madam," said Sam as they looked forward to getting a good night's sleep. They inspected their room and began to unpack their meager belongings.

"I'm going down to the parlor to write a letter to my Uncle Pat and Aunt Mary. I promised them I would write as soon as I arrived in Philadelphia."

Letter Home

The parlor was nicely furnished. Sam sat down in the dimly lit boarding house parlor all alone, listening to the constant chirping of a canary in the corner of the room and smelling the strong odor of cigar and pipe smoke. He took a seat at the wicker desk and chair and began to write his Uncle and Aunt in Dublin to notify them that he has arrived safely in America.

Dear Uncle Pat and Aunt Mary,   May 25, 1858
    I take my pen in hand to write and tell you that I have arrived safely in America. What a beautiful country.

    The people here speak a bit odd but I can understand them most of the time. I just rented a small room in a boarding house for $5.00 a month with my friend Kelsey whom I met on the ship.
    Kelsey is also from Dublin and is about 20 years old. On our lengthy voyage to America, we had a long discussion about religion and of course politics; comparing Ireland to America. It was amazing how many of the world's problems we were able to solve on our voyage over here. But right now our main concern is to get settled and to secure jobs. I have $10.00 left of the money I started with.
    I will write again as soon as I get settled and find a job that brings in more money than selling newspapers. Aunt Mary, I sure do wish you were here to make those deep fried battered fish and the thick potato chips which you do so well.
    I miss you both.
    Your Nephew, Samuel

Sam finished his letter and returned to his room.

    "I'm back. The first thing we need to do tomorrow morning is find a job. If I don't earn a little money we will be sleeping in the street. I'm just about out of money. What about you Kelsey?"
    "I have about eight dollars left. I need to get a job pretty soon also."

"I think I will first sell newspapers until I get an idea what it is like here in the big city. We had better get to bed so we can get up early and start looking for work."

"Good night Sam. Sleep tight."

"I told you before, I don't know what that means. What if it means something dirty?"

"I doubt it is dirty. It was in a children's book."

"Maybe they were dirty children," says Sam chuckling.

"Go to sleep Sam. I'll see you in the morning."

First Breakfast in America

Sam and Kelsey awoke to a new day in a new country. Both went downstairs to the dining room for breakfast where they found eight other people already eating.

"Good morning folks. Mind if we join you?"

"Only if you wish to eat says a burley old man at the end of the table."

"Thank you sir. What do we have to eat this morning?"

"Same as yesterday and the day before that. "biscuits and gravy". We may get an egg tomorrow and a piece of stale toast if we are lucky."

"That sounds pretty good to me. My friend and I have been eating ship food for the last five weeks. This couldn't be any worse."

"Where are you boys from?"

"We are both from Dublin, Ireland. What about you?"

"I hale from Liverpool, England. Ever been there?"

"Sure have. That's where our ship set sail for America." It was quite a long and boring trip but now we are here in America and ready to make our fortune." Sam smiles!

"Thanks for breakfast madam. Kelsey and I are setting out to find work this morning. I think I will try the Philadelphia Gazette first. What about you Kelsey?"

"My cousin suggested getting a job working on the Erie Canal."

"Good luck to you both. It was nice meeting you lads," said the grumpy old man.

News Paper Office

"Sam arrived at the paper office and noticed a man waiting for someone near the front entrance.

"Excuse me sir. Do you work here?"

"Why yes, I do. Why do you ask?"

"I'm looking for a job."

"I don't know of any openings but if you want temporary work, go around back and pick up a stack of papers to sell on the street. You will have to pay for them though. Bring back the unsold papers at the end of the day and they will give you credit for the next day's papers."

"Thank you sir. I appreciate that very much."

Sam went to the rear alley behind the building to pick up some newspapers to sell. There were young boys there as young as 10 years old picking up papers and smoking cigarettes. Sam felt a little out of place but thought to himself, this is only temporary. I hope.

Sam looked for a busy street to sell his papers.

"Extra extra, Read all about it! Violent conflict in Minnesota Territory between Dakota and Ojibwe Indians! Violent conflict in Minnesota Territory between Dakota and Ojibwe Indians! Read all about it! Read all about it! Read all about it! Abraham Lincoln announces his candidacy for U.S. Senate from Illinois! Abraham Lincoln announces his candidacy for U.S. Senate from Illinois! Read all about it! Extra, extra!"

The newspaper job was easy to get but difficult to sell many papers due to the large number of newsboys competing. Sam was quickly running out of money and was nearly broke. Sam returned to the rooming house to discuss the job situation with Kelsey.

"I can't stand selling papers anymore. There is just not enough money to be made. Plus, you should see my competition. There were young boys as young as 10 years old who were worse off than me trying to sell newspapers. I felt guilty competing with them. I didn't even make enough money today to buy anything for lunch."

" Don't worry about it. Things will improve. I can lend you a few dollars until you find something better."

"Thanks Kelsey. You are a true friend. I really appreciate it but give me a couple more days to see what I can find. Do you think I could get a job down the street at the "Jefferson Emporium?"

"It's worth a try. He will probably remember you. Doesn't he normally buy a paper from you each morning?"

"Yes he does. I think I will talk to him about a job tomorrow morning. He seems like a really nice man."

Jefferson Emporium

Sam rose early to seek employment with Mr. Jefferson, the owner of *Jefferson's Emporium.*

"Good Morning Mr. Jefferson. How are you doing this morning?"

"I'm pretty good but I have been better. Say where is my paper?"

"I quit the paper job. You sound distressed. Is there anything seriously wrong?"

"Well, my son was hurt the other day. A horse kicked him in the leg and the doctor said he shouldn't use that leg for at least a couple of weeks. He helped us a lot here stocking the shelves, making deliveries and general store chores. I really miss him."

"Maybe I could help. I am looking for work."

"I would like to hire you son, but times are tough now. Things are pretty slow. I don't have enough money to pay a salaried employee. My son basically worked for his keep."

"I tell you what Mr. Jefferson, if you would allow me to work for you today and at the end of the day, if you feel I have earned it, instead of paying me in cash you may just give me a loaf of bread and maybe a small sack of beans or potatoes."

"All right son, I will give you a try. Can you start this morning?"

"Sure can! Thank you very much Mr. Jefferson. What do you

want me to do first?"

"I need for you to restock the shelves and generally sweep and clean up the store."

"I'll get right on it sir."

Sam worked extremely hard all day. At the end of the day Mr. Jefferson was truly impressed with how hard Sam had worked. He made four deliveries in the neighborhood and when he was not busy restocking the shelves and tidying up the fruits and vegetable displays, he did some cleaning. Mr. Jefferson was especially impressed when he saw Sam had even laid down fresh sawdust on the meat department floor without being told.

"Sam, I am impressed. You did an excellent job. Pick out a quarter pound of the meat of your choice, a loaf of bread and a sack of beans and four or five potatoes. Sam, you truly earned it. Also I have noticed that my customers seemed to like you helping them. You have a kind demeanor and an honest air about you."

"Thank you Mr. Jefferson."

Mr. Jefferson, after giving Sam a sack full of groceries, stroked his beard, thinking.

"Sam, how would you like to work here next week? My son is still having problems with his bum leg."

"I sure would. Thank you Mr. Jefferson."

"You know, things have been looking up a bit the last few days so maybe I can start paying you a little cash."

"I sure appreciate that Mr. Jefferson. See you tomorrow morning."

Sam could hardly wait to get back to the boarding house to tell Kelsey the good news.

"You must have gotten the job at the Emporium looking at the sack of groceries you brought back. What did he do, pay you in trade and no money?"

"That's right, but only for the first day. He said he would pay in cash tomorrow. I will probably only have a job for a couple of weeks until his son's leg heals enough for him to return to work."

"What are we going to do with the groceries? Remember, we can't cook anything in our room."

"I'm planning on giving them to the land lady and will ask her to give us a few days credit on our room and board."

"Do you think she will agree to do that?"

" Sure, why wouldn't she."

"You are the clever one."

"My job at the Emporium will only last about two weeks until Mr. Jefferson's son has healed enough to get back to work. At least this job will get me through the immediate crisis."

"Kelsey, do you remember me telling you about the Telegraph office that I delivered papers to?"

"I remember you telling me what an interesting place it was and that you might like to work there someday."

"Well, as soon as my Emporium job ends, I think I'll visit the telegraph office to see if they need any help."

Sam's temporary job at the Jefferson Emporium had worked out for both Sam and Mr. Jefferson. Mr. Jefferson bid Sam a hearty goodbye and wished him luck, knowing full well that Sam was going to make his mark in America. He had witnessed Sam as a hard worker, intelligent and having had strong social skills.

Opportunity at the Telegraph Office

Three weeks later, Sam visited the telegraph Office to inquire about a job.

"Excuse me sir, who would I see to inquire about a job?"

"That would be me. I am Mr. Higgins. Are you a telegrapher?"

"Oh no. I am just looking for a job maybe delivering telegrams around Philadelphia. And I could even keep your office clean and tidy. You wouldn't have to pay me much, and hopefully, you could teach me how to become a telegrapher."

"I don't know about teaching you to be a telegraph operator. That takes a great deal of time and skill. Say, you sure look familiar. Have we met before?"

"I delivered papers here a few weeks ago."

"Oh, now I remember you. You are the young man who just recently emigrated from Ireland who is going to become rich and famous in your new adopted country."

"That's right. That's me." Sam smiled from ear to ear.

"We could use someone to deliver the telegraph messages to the various offices around town and the government buildings, and maybe do some cleaning when time permitted. I guess we could arrange for you to learn how to use the key during your time off if one of our existing telegraphers has the time to show you the ropes. Keep in mind though that not everyone can learn to be a telegrapher. It depends on the individual's personal skills. Would this job interest you?"

"You bet. When can I start?"

"How about Monday?"

"That would be fine. I will have finished my part time job at Jefferson's Emporium by then. You know, having been born in 1840, I was not old enough to have shared in the initial excitement of Samuel Morse's invention of the telegraph in 1837."

"Me neither. But at least we can appreciate what it has done to the world of communications. It is much faster than writing letters to be delivered by horseback, trains or ships."

"It's fascinating witnessing messages being sent to distant cities by converting letters of the alphabet to short and long electrical impulses, and then transmitting them over wires."

"Yes Sam, and it does it in a matter of just a few minutes unless it needs to be relayed through more than one Telegraph Company. Even then we can send messages, in a matter of a few hours, across the vast area of the United States and before long it will even cross the ocean. Did you happen to read the ridiculous article in The New York Times about the "Benefits and Evils" of the transatlantic telegraph? If you would like to read it, I posted it on the cork board. Would you like to read it?"

"I sure would."

Sam walked over to read the article posted on the wall.

NY Times Modernized

Superficial, sudden, scattered, too fast for the truth, must be all telegraphic intelligence. Does it not render the popular mind too fast for the truth? Ten days bring us the mails from Europe. What need is there for the scraps of news in ten minutes? How trivial and nearly worthless is the telegraphic news column?

"Pretty funny, don't you think? Makes one question the true agenda of the New York Times," exclaimed Mr. Higgins.

"Some people just can't accept anything new, even when it's better and more efficient."

"Well, I have got to get back to work, Sam. I'll see you Monday morning 8 o'clock sharp."

"Thanks Mr Higgins. I'll be here on the dot."

Sam's long-term dream was to become a lawyer or possibly a statesman. He wanted to be like those great Americans, Benjamin Franklin and Thomas Jefferson, whom he had read so much about and greatly admired. Of course he realized that he would need to become an American citizen first if he hoped to hold any positions of importance. At the present he could not afford to buy any law books to begin studying in earnest but as soon as he had earned enough from his new telegraph job, he was going to purchase, 'Blackstone's Commentaries on the Law of England.' He had heard that this was the same book that was used by Abraham Lincoln to begin his career in law. "If it was good enough for Mr. Lincoln then it is good enough for me," thought Sam.

"I can't wait to tell Kelsey about my new job," thought Sam.

Sam hurriedly returned to the boarding house to tell Kelsey the good news and to see how Kelsey had done, finding work.

"Kelsey, I got a job today at the telegraph office. A real full time job!"

"I didn't know you knew how to work one of those contraptions."

"No, No, I wasn't hired as a telegrapher. Just a telegram delivery person. They said I might be able to learn though, if the telegraphers have time to teach me after normal work hours. Isn't that exciting! What about you? Did you find anything?"

"That sounds great Sam. And yes, I also have some good news. I leave next week to work on the Erie Canal construction. It will be much better than the little amount of money I get from entertaining part time. Hopefully in a year or two I can save enough money to buy a small piece of land and become a farmer. You know that's always been my dream."

"That's wonderful Kelsey. I think we are both on our way to realizing our dreams here in America. We could never have had this same opportunity in Ireland, especially in such a short period of time. Isn't it wonderful! You are on the way to having your own farm, and I am going to have many opportunities working in a telegraph office to meet influential people who can possibly assist me in my dream."

"It was a real stroke of luck when I met you in Liverpool. I guess you might say, *It was the Luck of the Irish.* I hope we can keep in touch with each other."

"Will you promise to write me and let me know how you are progressing? You can always get in touch with me by sending me a telegram to the telegraph office. Please keep in touch and write me often to tell me how you are progressing."

"I sure will Sam. You are my closest friend here in America. In fact you are my only true friend."

Sam didn't have to report to the telegraph office Monday morning until 8 o'clock but arrived at 7 o'clock just to be sure he wasn't late. He didn't want to be late and make a bad impression on the first day of his new job.

New Job at the Telegraph Office

"Good morning Sam! Ready to go to work? We received two telegrams last night for the County Clerk at the Court House and one to Jefferson's Emporium. See how fast you can deliver them.

It's nice weather this morning so you won't need to take the buggy. Just take the gray mare in the barn."

"I am not sure where the Court House is but I will find it. Jefferson's Emporium is where I worked recently. It is just a few blocks from here."

"When you get back, I have some cleaning I want you to attend to."

"That's fine Mr. Higgins. That will help me learn more about the office and how all of this equipment works. I don't really know much about electricity but I sure would like to learn."

Sam made his deliveries while also enjoying seeing the sights of Philadelphia.

"How did your deliveries go?"

"I had a little problem finding the Court House but a nice lady at the *Emporium* showed me where it was."

"Alright. First, I would like for you to clean out the store room and then begin cleaning the equipment. It's very important to keep the sounders and battery terminals clean so that the apparatus will operate correctly."

After completing his cleaning and delivery duties, Sam would hang around the telegraph office and eventually became very good friends with several of the young telegraphers who taught him how to send and receive Morse code. Of course his first job was to memorize the dots and dashes that stood for each letter and number. Being extremely intelligent and a quick learner, Sam soon mastered the art of sending Morse code so well that he could read the short incoming messages without even writing then down. Four months later Sam got his big break. It seemed he was going to be able to move up to become a part time telegrapher.

Sam Promoted to part time Telegrapher

"Sam, while you were on you break this morning, I couldn't help but notice that you were copying the messages being received almost as fast as our seasoned telegraphers. How did you learn that so quickly? You have only worked here for about four months."

"Ah shucks Mr. Higgins, it was nothing. George is a good teacher. He has a unique way of teaching. He first taught me the letters E-I-S-H and T-M-O because they are so similar. And then the numbers 1-10 and some letters that are just the opposite of each other. About all that I have left to learn is the punctuation. Punctuation seems to be a little more difficult to learn but George suggested I just learn the word "STOP" for now. It wasn't nothing."

"Sam. It took me almost six months to be able to perform as well as you are doing in only four months. You have a natural talent for this. I am impressed. In addition to your other duties of delivering and cleaning, I could use you to fill in as a part time relief telegrapher when someone is sick or when we have an unexpected increase in traffic."

"I appreciate that Mr. Higgins! Will I be paid the same as now?"

"Of course not. I just received approval from our home office to raise your pay by four dollars a week. How does that sound?"

"That sounds great!"

Sam was filling in more and more as a telegrapher and finally was working full time and seldom was asked to clean or hand deliver any messages.

Solar Storms Damage Telegraph Equipment

A week later, Sam was stunned to see what had happened at the telegraph office the night before.

"What happened Mr. Higgins! The office is a mess. Smells like something caught fire here last night."

"That's exactly what happened. We lost almost half of our equipment. The magnetic coils are toasted and some of our wiring has been destroyed. What is really strange is that some of our receivers continued to work even when the batteries were disconnected."

"What in the world would cause that?"

"The New York Times said that it was due to 'Solar Storms.' They almost seemed pleased that it happened."

"I did notice that around mid-night last night, the sky was lit up with strange swirling lights. I saw the same type of light display on my ocean trip to America. Many of the passengers believed it was the end of the world."

" It wasn't the end of the world but it sure is going to put us out of business for a few days."

Job Offer out West

After about a year of being a full time telegrapher, Mr. Higgins approached Sam with a job offer out West.

"Sam, I have something here that might interest you. How would you like to go out west to a wild and out of the way place to be a telegrapher?"

"Do you mean California?"

"No, not that far west. Breckenridge, Missouri. Let me explain. Last year the Hannibal and St. Joseph rail line completed a 206 mile line from Hannibal, Missouri on the Mississippi River to St. Joseph on the Missouri River. Breckenridge is a relatively new community and they have been unable to hire a relief telegrapher for the new railroad depot there. I think it would be a good opportunity for you. What do you think Sam? I would hate to lose you but it would be, in my opinion, a good move for you."

"Whoa! What about Richard or William? They have been here longer than I have. I wouldn't want to take this opportunity away from them."

"You wouldn't be hurting them at all. Richard feels like he needs to stay with his mother. She just isn't up to making the long trip, especially not knowing if she would be able to find a good doctor in such a remote area. And William, you know, has three small children. He is not willing to move to such a remote place. Not that Missouri is all that remote. I think it might be just the thing for an unmarried lad like you."

"Can I think it over? I will tell you of my decision tomorrow if that's all right. Let me sleep with it."

"Don't you mean, let me sleep on it?"

"Oh sure, Let me sleep on it. I'm still learning how to speak American."

"If you agree to go, the railroad will pay all of your travel expenses plus give you $50.00 to get settled."

Roughnecks and wild Indians

Sam could hardly sleep that night imagining the possibilities. He had heard that it was indeed a wild and woolly area full of roughnecks and wild Indians. It would be   exciting moving to a town only 60 miles from St. Joseph and seeing the Pony Express riders arriving from California, and maybe even meeting people like the actor John Wilkes Booth or Abraham Lincoln who had been known to stay at the famous Patee House Hotel in St. Joe..

With St. Joseph being only 60 miles west of Breckenridge, one could witness the awesome site of hundreds of travelers in their covered wagons banding together in St. Joseph for their long trip across the plains and the Rocky Mountains to California. And to top it off, the railroad would pay all of his travel expenses.

"This is just too great of an opportunity to pass up," thought Sam. "I will do it!"

When do I leave?

The next day Sam arrived at work early and went directly to Mr. Higgins's office. "Mr. Higgins, I will do it. I certainly appreciate your confidence in me, and I thank you for this wonderful opportunity. When do I leave?"

"I think you have made a wise decision. Best of luck to you. I will accompany you to the stage office next Monday to pay for your trip and to get your itinerary planned."

"Could I take the train the entire way?" asked Sam.

"I suppose you could take the Pennsylvania Railroad to Pittsburg but the route on to Indianapolis is still under construction and difficult to make arrangements on the various other small connecting lines. Besides, it will be cheaper for you to travel by stagecoach until you get to the Mississippi River. From there you can then board the Hannibal and St. Joseph Railroad," explained Mr. Higgins.

"Take the rest of the day off, Sam, so you can pack and get your affairs in order. We should be at the stage terminal by at least 7 o'clock Monday morning." He smiled and said, "Sleep tight Sam. See you in the morning."

Sam replied, "What do you mean 'sleep tight'? My friend Kelsey keeps using that phrase. I'm not sure what it means."

Mr. Higgins explained that it was merely an expression about getting a good night's sleep by keeping the crisscrossed ropes tight on your rope bed platform because over time the ropes would sag and need to be retightened.

Sam just shook his head and thought, "Boy, I sure have a lot to learn."

Pleasant Dreams

"I wonder what the interior of the United States will be like," thought Sam as he tried to go to sleep. "Will everyone carry a rifle or have a pistol strapped to their waist as shown in the 'Dime Novels'? Is it such an out of the way place that there will be little law, resulting in public lynchings for such crimes as horse stealing? Will Indians attack in broad daylight or just at night, or hopefully not at all?"

Sam finally drifted off to sleep, dreaming about his next great adventure traveling west to his new home. Soon all these questions would be answered.

Dear Uncle Pat and Aunt Mary   *July 10, 1860*

I decided to not try and get rich looking for gold. The kind of gold reported recently in Colorado is not the kind that can be panned, it must be mined. I am glad I found out before I went all the way to Colorado. Now I am getting ready to leave Philadelphia and head out west where I have a job waiting for me at the railroad telegraph office in the small town of Breckenridge,

Missouri. I think it will be at least a three week trip by stagecoach.

I was recently promoted to a full time telegrapher in Philadelphia and then a few months later they found a job for me in Missouri. Can you believe it? Breckenridge, Missouri is much too small to have much of a chance of becoming an apprentice to a good lawyer, which is what I really want to do, so I just might eventually move on to St. Joseph, Missouri which is about sixty miles west of Breckenridge.

It will be quite a long trip, first by stage coach from Philadelphia to Indianapolis, Indiana and then another stage line to Hannibal, Missouri where I will board the Hannibal to St. Joseph railroad. I am afraid that there could be a few miles of walking also.

My boss at the telegraph office is taking me to the stage office Monday morning and the railroad has agreed to pay all of my travel expenses to Breckenridge. It should be an exciting trip. I can hardly wait. I was so excited I couldn't sleep much at all last night. I think it will be about a 1100 mile trip to the interior of the country (Philadelphia to Breckenridge, Missouri).

Hopefully my new telegrapher job will allow me enough time to study for my law career and to get my Naturalization papers. They tell me that I will need to go to the Buchanan County Court House in St. Joseph, Missouri to apply. I will write to you again when I get to Breckenridge. The trip will take nearly the same amount of time it took to sail all the way from Dublin to America. Wish I could send you a telegram across the ocean to keep you informed of my adventures here in America; but of course that is not possible. Maybe someday.

Affectionately, Sam

Chapter Four
Westward Ho!

Philadelphia Pennsylvania to Breckenridge, Missouri
July 12, 1860

Sam had planned on going west to seek his fortune in gold prospecting before contemplating becoming a lawyer. Fortunately for Sam, he discovered just in time that the latest news about the new gold rush in Colorado had not included all of the facts. It had been reported or at least assumed that it was alluvial gold but turned out to be lode gold which required a large mining operation.

The only people who could make it a profitable undertaking were those who could finance a large mining company operation. Sam decided to cancel his plans to make it rich in gold prospecting and instead decided to plan his career in law by first settling in Breckenridge, Missouri as a telegrapher.

Upon arriving at the Philadelphia stage office Mr. Higgins introduced Sam to his old friend, Nicholas, the ticket agent.

"Good morning Tom," said the agent. "How may I help you?"
"Nicholas, I wish to purchase a stage ticket to Hannibal, Missouri for my employee here, Samuel Ronan, who is traveling all the way to Breckenridge, Missouri."
The ticket agent stared at young Samuel and then said, "That's quite a long trip. Our stage line only goes to Indianapolis, Indiana;

so you will need to transfer to another stage line to get to Hannibal. From Hannibal you can board the Hannibal to St. Joseph Railroad that will take you on in to Breckenridge."

"Sir should I take a stage line all the way to Hannibal Missouri or go to Cincinnati Ohio and take a steamer down the Ohio River to the Mississippi River?"

"You could do that sir, but it would be a much longer trip. You would then need to go back up the Mississippi River to Hannibal or the Missouri river to St. Joseph and this would add considerably to your travel expense and to your travel time. Besides, the river boats can be a little dangerous. I have heard of river boats' steam engines exploding and even killing passengers. I don't ever recall a stage blowing up," smiled the clerk. "Have you ever ridden on a stage coach before?" inquired the clerk.

"No I haven't," replied Sam."

"Let me give you a list of the rules you will need to follow."

Coach Travel Rules
American Overland
Stage Lines
Philadelphia to Indianapolis

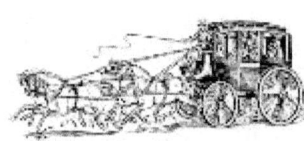

- **Abstinence from liquor is suggested, but if you must drink, share the bottle with your fellow passengers. Otherwise you will appear selfish and un-neighborly.**

- **If ladies are present, gentlemen are urged to not smoke cigars or pipes as the odor may be objectionable to the gentler sex. Chewing tobacco is permitted, but spit with the wind, not against it. The offender may be made to ride with the driver.**

- **Don't snore loudly while sleeping or use your fellow passenger's shoulder as a pillow. He or she may not understand and friction may result.**

- **Firearms may be kept on your person for use in emergencies. Don't fire them for pleasure or shoot at wild animals as the sound riles the horses.**

- **In the event of runaway horses remain calm. Leaping from the coach in panic will leave you injured, at the mercy of the elements, hostile Indians, and hungry coyotes.**

- **Forbidden topics of conversation are: stagecoach robberies, and Indian uprisings.**

- **Gents guilty of un-chivalrous behavior toward lady passengers will be put off the stage. It's a long walk back. A word to the wise is sufficient.**

"I believe I can follow these rules without any trouble. I do have a question though. Couldn't I travel by the railroad all the way to the Mississippi River?" inquired Sam.

"Most of those "Iron Horses" are a series of short, intercity connecting lines and may not be very reliable. Also they will cost more than by travelling by stage. You would be constantly changing rail lines," explained the clerk.

"Okay, thank you sir for all your help, and I will consider your advice, especially on traveling by steam boats. I guess travelling by stagecoach will be quite an adventure."

Sam boarded the stage with a tear in his eye and with a quiver in his voice at leaving the city in which he had made many friends and had come to love.

"Mr. Higgins, thank you for helping me make my dreams come true. You are a true friend and I will be forever grateful. I never told you this, but I was afraid you wouldn't hire me because I was Irish."

"What do you mean?"

"When I first arrived in Philadelphia, I kept seeing signs in front of businesses that said, "Help Wanted-No Irish Need Apply.""

"I too have seen a few of those but I don't believe there are very many Americans who are prejudice against the Irish. It seems to me it is more about different Irish groups prejudiced against other Irish groups. It is prejudice that has been imported from Ireland by the Irish themselves."

"Good luck, Sam. Be sure and write, I mean send me a telegram and let me know how you are doing," laughed Mr. Higgins.

"I sure will. Goodbye and thanks for everything."

Long Stage Ride Begins

As the stage left in a fog of dust and Philadelphia got further and further away, Sam wondered if he would ever make it back to Philadelphia and see his friends again. He couldn't stop thinking about his friend Kelsey and kept wondering how long it would take him to save enough money to buy his farm near the Erie Canal. All Sam could think of was what his new life would be like out west.

Sam was thinking, "The stage was not as uncomfortable as he had expected but perhaps they had crammed too many people into the small coach."

But Sam started wondering if maybe he should have investigated a little further to see the possibility of traveling by train instead of the stagecoach, at least a portion of the way. "Oh never mind, this will be fine," he thought.

There were six adults and one child about the age of seven occupying the space where only four would have been comfortable. It wouldn't have been so bad in colder weather when an extra body or two would have kept everyone a bit warmer but it was hot this time of year.

"Good morning. Has everyone met each other except me? It looks like I was the last person to board. My name is Sam Ronan and I am traveling to Breckenridge, Missouri."

"Good morning Mr. Ronan. My name is Molly and this is my daughter Charlotte. We are going to Indianapolis to visit my parents."

"Nice to meet you Molly and Charlotte."

Sam noticed two men were playing poker with a small board stretched across their knees. They just grunted a faint hello. They didn't talk much except to each other about their card playing. One nicely dressed gentleman finally spoke up.

"How do you do Mr. Ronan? I'm Bartholomew Bernstein but just call me Bart. I'm a Philadelphia attorney and right now I am working for a client of mine who lives in Indianapolis. Where are you from, Sam?"

"I'm originally from Dublin Ireland but came to America last year and first settled in Philadelphia. I was fortunate to become a telegrapher in Philadelphia and they are now transferring me out west to a new job as a relief railroad telegrapher for the Hannibal and St. Joseph railroad in Breckenridge, Missouri."

"Where the hell is Breckenridge?" Inquired the gentleman.

"It's a new railroad town about sixty miles east of St. Joseph, Missouri. You have heard of St. Joseph, Missouri haven't you?" inquired Sam.

"Oh sure. That's where the Pony Express starts. And isn't that one of the staging areas for the wagon trains going to California? Do you have any idea how primitive of an area that is? Not only will you encounter hostile Indians but Missouri is divided on whether or not to join the southern states in seceding from the Union. Be extremely careful to whom you speak and don't let anyone know which side you support. There are vigilante groups out there and *Bushwhackers* that will kill you if you support the wrong side."

Sam thought about what Bart had said. "How long do you think it will take us to get to Indianapolis? Isn't Indianapolis about 650 miles from Philadelphia?" asked Sam.

"I think that's about right Let me see now, the stage travels about ten miles per hour but stops every fifteen or twenty miles to change horses at the relay stations. At ten miles per hour it would take sixty five hours, and then add in the relay stops. Forty three stops averaging about 30 minutes each would be twenty two hours. Sixty five hours plus twenty two hours is eighty seven hours or roughly three or four days. But remember, even though the stage runs 24 hours a day in good weather, it stops for eating, repairs, and personal breaks. It could take even six to seven days to get to Indianapolis, depending on the weather."

"That's impressive calculations Bart. Let's ask the stage relay clerk at the next stop. He probably knows from past experience."

"Before I was an attorney, I worked a few years in the bookkeeping department of a large wholesale dry goods company in New York. We shipped a lot of goods to St. Joseph to outfit the thousands of people moving west to California."

"I find it interesting that we can travel at night. I guess with such big eyes, the horses can see better at night than we humans."

"That's right Sam, but it will still be slow going and a little dangerous."

"I can see that this is going to get pretty tiring when we try to sleep at night in a traveling coach."

"What a great opportunity," thought Sam. "I am going to get to talk to a lawyer for the next few days and maybe learn something about being a lawyer's apprentice."

Conflict between Northern and Southern States

Besides talking about law, Sam also wanted to talk to Mr. Bernstein about the conflict brewing between the Southern states and the Northern states but thought it might not be a good idea to discuss it around the other passengers. Sam felt sympathy for the South. He also felt that they had a constitutional right to secede if that's what they decided to do. Sam thought it was best to keep his thoughts to himself until at least he and Mr. Bernstein could speak in private.

Suddenly as the coach was going up a steep hill, a small flat rock with wire handles slid out from under the seat hitting Sam's foot.

"Wow, what in the world was that?" asked Sam.

One of the poker players remarked, "Looks like you don't travel on the stage much. They must have forgotten to take out the foot warmers when it was used last winter. The ladies put these in the fire at the relay station to get them hot and then put the hot rock on the stagecoach floor to keep their feet warm. We sure won't need to use it today."

Stage Stop for Rest and Repairs

At the next relay station, the stage coach driver noticed that the left rear wheel of the coach had somehow broken a wooden spoke. He advised the passengers that it would take about two hours to make the necessary repairs and change horses. The wheel would need to be removed from the coach, a new spoke inserted and the metal rim reheated and then cooled to shrink back around the spokes and hub to hold the wheel together.

"Welcome folks. Today we are having cold joint, calves' head, and carrots. For desert we are having stewed fruit. There is hot coffee and tea on the table by the stove. Oh, by the way, the cost of your meal is not included in the cost of your stage ticket. The meals here are 60 cents per person, but I think you'll find it well worth the money" explained the station masters wife.

"Sam, don't think that this is a standard meal for a relay station. It isn't. We got lucky this time. Most of the stations will serve something like lard sandwiches made with stale bread, hot tea and cold coffee and some kind of mystery soup. Don't worry though; some of our stops will be next to an Inn or tavern that serves good food. The relay stations located in the towns we pass through will have better accommodations."

"At least, this meal looks mighty good, plus for me, the Hannibal & St. Joseph Railroad is paying for it."

"Can't beat that Sam. Let's dig in. As soon as we are finished eating, we can go outside and sit in the shade of the big oak tree I spotted when we came in. Maybe even take a nap since we will be here for a couple hours or more."

After Sam and Mr. Bernstein had finished their meal at the relay station, Sam asked, "Would you like to step outside and get some fresh air?" Then in a very soft voice, Sam quietly asked, "I would like you to explain to me if you think the southern states are justified in seceding from the Union."

"Sure." replied Bart.

They found a somewhat comfortable place outside with a huge rock for a chair under a shade tree.

"Why are you so interested in the southern states seceding?"

Sam replied, "Well, I wouldn't want to be forced to fight for either side in a war that I feel is unnecessary. And besides, I don't want it to interfere with my studies to become a lawyer."

"Why do you wish to become a lawyer, Sam?"

"I have read quite a bit about some famous American lawyers like Abraham Lincoln and Benjamin Franklin and would like to follow in their footsteps, so to speak."

"Both of these men are considered great Americans but I don't believe Franklin was ever a lawyer," explained Bart.

"That's fine. Still, Benjamin Franklin is someone I greatly admire. Also Thomas Jefferson is one of your American statesmen that I admire. Didn't he say, "I'm a great believer in luck, and I find the harder I work the more I have of it?"

"Looks like you have been studying your American history Sam. However, I wouldn't worry about a war between the states. First of all they haven't seceded yet and even if they do and can't get enough volunteers to fight, my guess is that teachers, clergy members, doctors and probably even telegraphers would be exempted from joining the army."

"Do you think a state has the right to secede from the Union?" asked Sam.

"Well the Constitution may not say that they have a right to secede directly, but it is implied. Let me explain my reasoning. The *Articles of Confederation*, America's first constitution says something like '...we 13 Colonies come together to form a "Perpetual Union'.... Perpetual to me means that they can't secede. But when it came time to ratify the Constitution, some of the Colonies refused to sign it because the word "Perpetual" was once again included that implied that a Colony could not secede. So that word was then left out to get them to sign. In fact some

50

congressmen were so worried about this exclusion of the word "Perpetual" that they unsuccessfully tried to pass a constitutional amendment specifically stating that a state once joined could never secede. Since it never passed, doesn't that mean a state *does* have the right to secede?"

"It is the opinion of the majority of the people, legislators and newspaper owners that states have a right to secede. The Declaration of Independence states that the Federal Government derives its power to govern from the consent of the governed. It follows then that if the southern states no longer consent, then they have a right to secede. Also, the states voluntarily joined the Union and therefore have the right to un-join if they no longer consent. This right is part of the so called 'Checks and Balances' built into the Constitution. It keeps the federal government from acquiring too much power at the expense of states' rights. I am sure Abraham Lincoln, if elected President, understands this and will not involve the states in an unnecessary war.'"

Rectify Injustices of Taxes and Tariff Laws

"Besides, all Lincoln needs to do to keep the southern states from seceding is to have Congress rectify the injustices in the current tariffs and tax laws that treat the south unfairly. Currently the agricultural south pays a higher proportion of taxes and tariffs than the Industrial north. That's why they're considering secession. It's a 'states' rights issue."

"I sure hope you're right, Mr. Bernstein but what about the slavery issue?"

"If Abraham Lincoln got elected President, I doubt very much that there will be any war, especially if it concerns the slavery issue."

"Why would you say that?"

"Well, Slavery is an issue Sam but only a sub issue of 'states' rights. I had the opportunity to attend one of the Lincoln-Douglas debates two years ago when Mr. Lincoln was campaigning for the US Senate. I learned there that he has little sympathy for the Negroes, I can assure you of that."

"I read in the 'New York Times" that these debates were truly a historical event. How did you get the opportunity to hear Mr. Lincoln speak in person?"

"I was pretty fortunate. A judge who is a friend of mine in Springfield made all the arrangements. The debates drew huge crowds. The spectators came from all over Illinois and nearby states by train, by canal-boat, by wagon, by buggy, and on horseback."

"What were the main beliefs of both Douglas and Lincoln?"

"Douglas advocated popular sovereignty, which maintained the right of the citizens of a territory to permit or prohibit slavery, but Lincoln pointed out that Douglas' position directly challenged the Dred Scott decision, which decreed that the citizens of a territory had no such power."

"What did Lincoln actually say about slavery and the rights of the Negro?"

"Here is a copy of his exact speech that appeared in the Springfield Gazette."

LADIES AND GENTLEMEN: It will be very difficult for an audience so large as this to hear distinctly what a speaker says, and consequently it is important that as profound silence be preserved as possible.

While I was at the hotel today, an elderly gentleman called upon me to know whether I was really in favor of producing a perfect equality between the negroes and white people. [Great Laughter.] While I had not proposed to myself on this occasion to say much on that subject, yet as the question was asked me I thought I would occupy perhaps five minutes in saying something in regard to it.

I will say then that I am not, nor ever have been, in favor of bringing about in any way the social and political equality of the white and black races, [applause]-that I am not nor ever have been in favor of making voters or jurors of negroes, nor of qualifying them to hold office, nor to intermarry with white people; and I will say in addition to this that there is a physical difference between the white and black races which I believe will forever forbid the two races living together on terms of social and political equality.

And inasmuch as they cannot so live, while they do remain together there must be the position of superior and inferior, and I as much as any other man am in favor of having the superior position assigned to the white race. I say upon this occasion I do not perceive that because the white man is to have the superior position the Negro should be denied everything.

I do not understand that because I do not want a Negro woman for a slave I must necessarily want her for a wife. [Cheers and laughter.] My understanding is that I can just let her alone. I am now in my fiftieth year, and I certainly never have had a black woman for either a slave or a wife. So it seems to me quite possible for us to get along without making either slaves or wives of Negroes.

I will add to this that I have never seen, to my knowledge, a man, woman or child who was in favor of producing a perfect equality, social and political, between Negroes and white men. I recollect of but one distinguished instance that I ever heard of so frequently as to be entirely satisfied of its correctness-and that is the case of Judge Douglas's old friend Col. Richard M. Johnson. [Laughter.] I will also add to the remarks I have made (for I am not going to enter at large upon this subject,) that I have never had the least apprehension that I or my friends would marry Negroes if there was no law to keep them from it, [laughter] but as Judge Douglas and his friends seem to be in great apprehension that they might, if there were no law to keep them from it, [roars of laughter]

I give him the most solemn pledge that I will to the very last stand by the law of this State, which forbids the marrying of white people with Negroes. [Continued laughter and applause.]

I will add one further word, which is this: that I do not understand that there is any place where an alteration of the social and political relations of the negro and the white man can be made except in the State Legislature-not in the Congress of the United States-and as I do not really apprehend the approach of any such thing myself, and as Judge Douglas seems to be in constant horror that some such danger is rapidly approaching, I propose as the best means to prevent it that the Judge be kept at home and placed in the State Legislature to fight the measure. [Uproarious laughter and applause.]

I do not propose dwelling longer at this time on this subject.

"Gee thanks Bart. May I borrow this paper for a day or two? I would like to read it and contemplate its full meaning. From the way Lincoln talked about how inferior the Negroes are, it would seem very unlikely that he would go to war over the slavery issue.

"I agree Sam but you and I know that politicians don't always do what they say or keep the promises they make. Take your time reading the paper. I thought you would find this very informative."

Wagon Wheel Repaired- Back on the Road

"Looks like the wheel is repaired and it's time to get back on the stage coach," said Sam, who thoroughly enjoyed his private conversation with Bart about states' rights and secession, but was happy to once again be on the coach headed to his final destination.

Delay- Bridge Washed Out

Everything went pretty smoothly for the next 5 days, when the coach came to a sudden stop. The driver climbed down to the ground and opened the coach door to inform the passengers that a bridge had washed out ahead and the water was too deep to ford the river safely. They needed help to get across the river and the next relay station was several miles away.

"Got a small problem. The bridge ahead is washed out. River's swollen with rain, can't get the coach across safely. Or the passengers, for that matter. Looks like we will be here a few hours until either the next stage comes along or the next relay station sends someone out to check on us when we fail to arrive on time. Just try to relax folks. We will have to wait for help.

Sam thought a minute and then said, "I just remembered that I brought my personal telegraph key and sounder with me from Philadelphia to use on my new job in Breckenridge. I can climb that telegraph pole on the side of the road and tap out a message requesting some help."

Everyone on the stage gave a sigh of relief except one of the poker players who said, "Anyone want to make a bet that it won't work? What will you use for a battery?"

The stage coach driver said, "That won't be a problem. As luck would have it, I have a box of six batteries on board that are being shipped to the Indianapolis telegraph office. I am sure they won't mind if we borrow one for an emergency."

Sure enough, Sam was able to climb the pole and attach his equipment to the line. One of the younger passengers climbed partially up the pole and held the battery while Sam tapped out his message. The relay station only took about three minutes to send back the following reply:

"Try using the old ferry that was used before bridge was constructed stop It should still be moored in a small cove about 300 yards north of the washed out bridge Stop If that doesn't work, advise and will send help stop"

The old ferry was exactly where the telegraph message had stated and although it was pretty dirty and covered with small branches that needed to be cleared in order to load the coach, it was still serviceable. The coach driver unhooked the horses from the stage coach and led them across the water. After attaching a rope to the team he swam back across the river and attached the rope to the ferry. The passengers pushed the empty coach onto the ferry and then climbed back into the coach. The team of horses on the opposite side of the river easily pulled the ferry and coach to the other side. Only about two hours were lost, thanks to Sam and his telegraph key and sounder. In a short time they were back on the road heading for Indianapolis. Sam had made quite an impression with everyone on the coach, especially the negative poker player who, by the way, lost his five dollar bet with his card playing friend!

The next relay station was a welcomed site. The station manager apologized for the washed out bridge.

"Sorry about the bridge being out. Must have been washed away with the storm that passed through here early this morning."

The coach driver explained, "If we hadn't had a telegrapher with us, we would most likely still be there waiting for you to come and help. We had no idea the old ferry was still there, covered up with weeds."

"You folks are welcome to come into the station. We already served supper a couple of hours ago but I have some dried smoked buffalo jerky that is mighty good. Only 20 cents a strip. Maybe you folks would like to take some with you."

"I'll take two. One for me and one for my daughter" said Molly.

"I guess I'll take two strips," said Bart.

"Give me three strips," said Sam.

"Thank you folks. You all have a good trip. You should be in Indianapolis sometime tomorrow afternoon if you don't encounter any more washed out bridges."

Once again the stage coach was back on the road.

"I think I can sleep tonight. Even in the coach. Haven't slept much at all the last two nights," said Bart.

Indians- Friends or Foe

Early the next morning , the stage came to a sudden stop between two large rocks.

"Why are we stopping?" shouted Sam to the coach driver.

"Looks like trouble. There are two Indians with a log blocking the road."

"What do they want?

" Just remain calm and don't do anything foolish. I have read that the Miami Indians around here are pretty peaceful. Most left in 1848 but a few remained. I have a pistol concealed in my waist band, if I need it."

"Don't panic anyone. I have dealt with the Miami Indians before while traveling on this road. They are what we call *Beggar Indians*. They more than likely want to beg some food or trade something with us," explained the coach driver.

Indian speaks in broken English.

"Me trade pretty feathered eagle claws for food."
"Anyone have any of that buffalo jerky left?"
"I have a piece," said Molly.
"I have a piece left," said Sam.
Bart said, "Give them to me."
"Indian, I trade feathers for meat."
"Molly added nervously, "Here, take this compact and mirror."

Both Indians took the buffalo jerky and mirror and slowly rode off and appeared to be satisfied with their trade.

"You folks handled that very well. It is a shame that these poor souls have to live in such poverty. I am not sure who is better off. The ones who left or the few who stayed."

"If I'd had a pistol, I would have shot them both," whispered one of the poker players.

"It's a good thing you didn't. You don't want to rile up these beggar Indians. Then the next stage coming through here may not be so lucky," explained the angry and disgusted stage driver.

Indianapolis- Next Stop

After two weeks of rough travel on the highways and trails, Indianapolis was a welcomed sight. The passengers were getting weary from all the jostling about from the deep ruts in the trails. Everyone was looking forward to staying overnight in a nice hotel instead of a relay station in the middle of nowhere. At last they would be able to get a good meal and a hot bath if they so desired. All of the passengers took advantage of this rare opportunity- except one of the poker players who obviously had not had a bath since last spring. Luckily for Sam and the other passengers, neither of the poker players were going any further west than Indianapolis.

"I can hardly wait to stay overnight in a comfortable hotel in Indianapolis."

"Me too Sam. It was with great pleasure I got to meet you. I want to wish you luck in your new job in Breckenridge and if you ever need any references, please have them write to me in Philadelphia."

"Thanks Bart. Looks like we are finally stopping at a relay station across the street from a nice hotel."

Half Way to Breckenridge Missouri

Sam went to bed that night thinking, "Well thank God, I am over half way to Breckenridge. The rest of the trip should be a piece of cake, or was it a piece of pie? He still had a lot to learn concerning the various idiomatic expressions the Americans used. He kept wondering what it would be like to live in such a remote village in the interior of the country.

After a refreshing night of sleep, Sam went to the new stage depot to get a ticket to Hannibal, Missouri.

"I would like to purchase a ticket to Hannibal, Missouri."
"That would be $12.00 Sir."
"What time does the stage leave?"
"In one hour and thirty minutes. 9:30. You may wait here or if you need to purchase anything for your trip, there is a general store one block west on this side of the street."

"Thank you sir, I just might do that."   Sam walked down the street to the general store greeting, "Good Morning" to passersbys.

"May I help you sir?

"Why yes. I need some tooth powder, a brush, and do you have a copy of the *Harper's Weekly* newspaper?"

"Here is the tooth powder and brush, and the latest copy of Harpers. It's about two weeks old. Hope that's all right. The stage drops them off every other Friday. You know, they have to come all the way from New York."

"That's fine. Would you look at this article? Some English

Naturalist named Darwin claims man may have monkeys as ancestors. That sure insults the monkeys, don't you think?" (Chuckling)

"I guess so. That would be 10 cents for the paper and 5 cents for the tooth brush and powder. 15 cents total. Anything else sir?

"No thanks. That's all I need."

Sam boarded a different coach and fortunately this time there were only four passengers and of course sacks of mail in the boot. Sam wasn't sure but thought he saw a strong box up by the driver's feet and noticed that this coach included a large burley man sitting next to the coach driver sporting a double barrel shotgun. He thought, "I hope those bandits I have heard about don't try to rob the stage while I am on it. There's probably gold in the strong box or payroll for some company. Maybe this leg of my trip won't be as easy as I had thought." Sam's thoughts again turned to Breckenridge.

How much different would it be from Philadelphia? Would there be actual stores to buy goods or just trading posts to trade furs, and purchase scarce manufactured items brought in from the wagon trains and steamboats?

Eight days later Sam found himself approaching a small community on the east bank of the Mississippi River and a larger town, probably Hannibal, on the west bank.

Sam hadn't imagined that the Mississippi River would be so large. To get to Hannibal on the other side, he would need to board a ferry boat.

It took a wait of over an hour to finally cross the river.

The first horse drawn buggy had to cross, and there was a covered wagon that had to remove all four wheels, and due to the wind, had to remove its canvas top. Finally after about one hour Sam and three others were able to cross. Sam silently said to himself, "I hope the rope doesn't break. I don't want to end up in St. Louis."

Missouri at Last

Sam was thankful that he had had a safe and, for the most part, uneventful trip from Indianapolis to Hannibal, Missouri. Apparently no bandits knew about the gold being transported to Hannibal. Even Sam didn't find out until he heard the coach driver talking to the sheriff at the Hannibal train depot. It was now clear why an extra guard had been riding on the coach.

Chapter Five
Breckenridge- Missouri
A New beginning
August 1st, 1860

Boarding the Hannibal to St. Joseph Railroad in Hannibal was a completely new experience. Sam had never ridden on a train before. He felt like he was in another world. This was surely the most luxurious means of travel he had ever seen. There was a heating stove at each end of the passenger cars, fancy brass oil lamps to use at night and a beautiful ornamental brass luggage rack above the seats. There was even a privy at the back of the car. He noticed that a railroad employee kept the privy door locked when the train was in a town loading or unloading passengers. He soon figured out why. It wouldn't have been very sanitary for someone to empty the toilet onto the railroad tracks that close to the depot.

"Tickets please, Tickets please" said the conductor as he walked down the aisle.

"I'm sorry, I don't have a ticket. The ticket booth was closed by the time I boarded the train."

"That's OK. Where you headed young man?"

"Breckenridge, Missouri," Sir.

"That will be $2.00."

Sam quickly discovered that you could raise the train window and stick your head out for a spectacular view and feel the wind blow through your hair. The train traveled at an unbelievable speed of almost twenty five miles per hour; fifteen miles per hour faster than the stagecoach. There was one problem though. As long as the train was going straight ahead, everything was fine. But as soon as the train made a sharp turn, the wood ash soot from the engine's boiler blew directly into your face if you were sticking your head out the window.

Sam noticed that at every small town where the train stopped to load or unload passengers or to take on water, there was an easily seen sign from the passenger cars showing the location of the local saloon. At each stop there was usually at least one passenger who would make a mad dash for the saloon to buy a bottle of whiskey. When the train whistled that it was about to embark, those same passengers could be seen hurriedly running back to the train.

"Excuse me sir. What is our next stop?"

"That would be Macon."

"Thanks. Will we stop long enough to eat and drink?'

"We will be there about one hour loading water and fuel.
There is a tavern about a block from the depot that serves pretty good food."

Sam was impressed with the Tavern.   The menu board had quite a variety to choose from.

MENU BOARD

Breakfast:

Corn bread, cold bread, stew, boiled eggs

50 cents

Dinner:

Soup, cold joint, calves' head, vegetables, Puddings

85 cents

Tea, Milk or Coffee... 5 cents

"May I help you sir?"

"I think I will take the dinner menu for 85 cents and add a glass of milk."

"Thank you sir. Coming right up."

Sam finished his meal and rushed back to the train.

"Did you get something to eat?" inquired the conductor.

"Yes I did and you were right. That was a good place to eat even though it was a tavern. What is our next stop?"

"Well, let's see, no one is getting off at Brookfield, so if there are no passengers there, our next stop will be Chillicothe and then Breckenridge."

Sam arrived in Breckenridge Missouri August 1st, 1860. The small town of Breckenridge was named after John C. Breckenridge who was a leading Democrat of Kentucky at one time and later became the Vice President of the United States under President James Buchanan. The construction of the Hannibal and St. Joseph Railroad in 1858 had been influential in the increased immigration into this area. Numerous small towns along its route were established.

As Sam stepped off the train, the 'conductor' placed a small metal step stool on the ground to aid passengers in disembarking from the train. As soon as Sam had placed his feet on the brick paved platform at the railroad station, he notice a middle aged man approaching him wearing a small cap with the words "RR Telegrapher" stitched on the front of this hat. Just as the man was about to speak, there was a loud hissing noise coming from the train engine. "What did you say sir?"

He shouted, cupping his hands around his mouth, "Welcome to Breckenridge Missouri. Are you the new relief telegrapher that is to replace me? My name is Josh Bennett."

"Glad to meet you Josh. Yes and my name is Samuel Ronan from Philadelphia."

"That was quite a long trip for you. Over a thousand miles I would guess. Did you get attacked by any Indians or have your stage coach robbed by bandits?"

"No bandits but we did have an encounter with a couple of Indians. Nothing serious. I'll tell you about it later. I must say that the most pleasant part of my trip was the ride on the train from Hannibal to Breckenridge. I now wish I had traveled more on the trains and less on the stagecoach. Anyway, overall the trip was fine and quite a good experience."

"The railroad people were beginning to get a little worried that they would not be able to find a telegrapher willing to locate in such an out of the way place. I hope this works out for you and the railroad. Do you have a place to stay here in Breckenridge?" asked Josh.

"No, not yet. Maybe you could help me with that, Josh."

"Before your arrival, I checked at the hotel and the rooming house across from the town square and both had no vacancies. With the coming of the railroad, Breckenridge has had trouble keeping up with accommodations for newcomers. However, I most recently decided to explore a job offer at the telegraph office in Denver and will be leaving as of tomorrow. You would be most welcome to stay in my cabin while I'm gone. Of course this would be temporary but it would give you a place to stay until something becomes available at the rooming house or the hotel."

"That's mighty nice of you Josh. I certainly appreciate it."

Sam's New Home North of Town

Josh rented a horse and buggy at the livery stable at the east end of town and both Josh and Sam went out to see his new home.

"Normally I walk to my cabin but didn't think it would be polite to have you walk on your first day in Breckenridge," explained Josh with a grin on his face.

"That's mighty kind of you Josh. However after riding all this way, a walk would probably do me good."

"Don't worry about that, Sam. You will have lots of chances to walk. Without a farm you will find it quite expensive to feed and board a horse and to purchase your own buggy."

"**What** do you do in the winter when there is a lot of snow?"

"If the snow is more than a couple of inches or so, I just hunker down at the telegraph office. We have a nice wood stove and lots of coffee on hand. I can usually get to "Wolsey's Cafe" on the town square if I need something to eat."

The cabin was only a short distant north of town just south of the Trosper Cemetery. It wasn't fancy but certainly served Sam's immediate needs and financial circumstances. Josh's cabin was pretty rustic and nowhere near as nice as the boarding house where

Sam's new home north of Breckenridge, Missouri

he had rented a room in Philadelphia. Josh explained that the cabin only had two small glass window panes. It was expensive to have more because a tax was levied on the number of glass windows in a home. The floor of the cabin consisted of logs hewed flat on one side with the rounded part facing down. It wasn't perfect but still better than having a dirt floor. His 'privy was about a hundred feet from the house and presented a problem at night in cold weather.

Sam then asked, "Josh is there somewhere I can buy some supplies? The first thing I want to do is buy a slop jar to slide under the bed. I know it will be a chore to empty every morning but it is still better than getting up in the dark to go outside to the privy carrying a lantern and trying to stay on the board sidewalk without slipping off into the mud."

Josh, laughing, said, "Are you kidding, Breckenridge is a thriving metropolis now that the railroad has come here. You saw our nice new livery stable at the east end of Broadway and we have a feed store, a bank, post office, four saloons, sheriff's office, blacksmith and a general store that sells almost everything. The general store sells food, as well as manufactured items like tools, boots, glass and pottery, kitchen items, medicines, and coal oil. Just a few weeks ago they started selling embalmed meat and if you don't have cash, they will even trade items you grow or make for items in the store."

"What is embalmed meat?" asked Sam.

"You haven't heard of embalmed meat? It's the latest thing. They now have a way to keep meat fresh in a tin can without it spoiling," Josh explained.

Sam just frowned and said, "That's great but I think I will stick to fresh meat or smoked meat."

"No problem. Feel free to use the smoke house behind my cabin. It's great for stocking up with smoked turkey and beef for the winter months when it's a nuisance to butcher fresh meat. I think you will find Breckenridge a fine place to live and the people very hospitable. The game is plentiful here making it reasonable to feed a family with little cost. In fact, when you are ready to eat, you can just step outside your cabin and shoot a wild turkey. Or you'll find a large supply of wild pigeons to eat, wild honey in bee trees and big bottom hickory nuts. You won't have enough room or for that matter the time to raise hogs but I am sure some of your neighbors will sell you some pork. Many people around here call them *Hazel Splitters*. I sure wouldn't wander far into the woods without a gun though because there are mountain lions and occasionally you will still see a bear in this area."

"What about the Indians, Josh?"

"What Indians are you talking about? Most of the Indians that lived in this area left to go further west after the Platte Purchase in 1836. They were paid for their land and given cattle, tools, etc., and most moved. There's a few that didn't go but they for the most part have become pretty docile. Many people refer to them as "Beggar Indians" because they are quite poor and are usually found asking for handouts. The original Sac, Fox, Sioux, Omaha, Iowa, Oto and other tribes were fairly friendly here because of the good relationship they had with Joseph Robidoux. He's a famous

French fur trader in St. Joseph who established the Blacksnake Hills trading post in 1826. In fact, Joseph Robidoux founded St. Joseph in 1843," explained Josh.

"Thanks for that information. I was a little worried about Indians out here. You should hear the stories they tell back east about the Indians."

"Well, I've got to get to bed. We can talk some more tomorrow. I'm anxious to see the telegraph office and the rest of the town. By the way Josh, how come you have two beds?

"Uh... Uh... sometimes I have company spend the night.

"Oh, I'm sorry, that's really none of my business.

"Don't worry about it. She moved out West two months ago. Sleep tight."

"I keep hearing that expression, "Sleep Tight."

"Oh, that just means to tighten the ropes under your mattress so the bed don't sag."

"My friend Kelsey back in Philadelphia used that phrase ever so often. You Americans have a peculiar way of speaking. See you in the morning."

Laying in Supplies from the General Store

The next morning, Josh and Sam returned the horse and buggy to the Livery stable.

"Let's drop off the buggy first at the livery stable and walk over to the general store."

There was lots of activity early in the morning around the square. Soldiers coming into town to shop and farmers picking up feed bags and filling up barrels of water at the public well in the city park.

"Good morning gentlemen. I'm Isaac Weldon the proprietor here. You two are up awfully early."

"As we say in Ireland, 'Lose an hour in the morning and you will be looking for it all day."

"That's a true statement if I ever heard one."

"Mr. Weldon, I would like to introduce you to my replacement at the depot telegraph office. This is Sam Ronan who came all the way from Philadelphia to work in Breckenridge as a Telegrapher."

"Nice to meet you Mr. Weldon."

"Just call me Isaac. Mr. Weldon was my father. *Smiling* We are not very formal here. Can I help you with anything?

"As a matter of fact you can. Let's see, let me look at my list. I need a dozen eggs, 2 pounds of coffee, two jars of canned peaches, a jar of currant jelly, 5 pounds of potatoes, 5 pounds of flour, a pound of baking soda, a gallon of coal oil for my lamp, a razor, shaving mug and brush, a box of matches, and three sticks of licorice. I almost forgot. Do you have any fresh bread?"

"I get bread in from a local lady who bakes twice each week. She just brought some in yesterday, so it is still fresh. I will have everything ready for you in about an hour."

"Josh said you live just a little ways past his cabin that I am staying in. Do you think you could drop my things off on your way home this evening? If I'm not there yet, just put my purchases inside the cabin. I don't want the critters to get it."

"Why sure Sam. Let me add up your bill. Let me see, that would be four dollars and fifty cents."

Sam still had about $30.00 left from what the Railroad had given him to relocate.

"Here you are Isaac. I sure appreciate you making the delivery. I may not be able to afford a horse and wagon for a while."

"That's quite all right Sam. I appreciate your business and look forward to seeing you again."

Telegraph Office

Josh and Sam walked the four blocks to the Depot.

"Let me show you around Sam. Here is your desk and equipment and that small room in back is a store room and a place to bunk down in bad weather. It is also your job to keep the fire going in cold weather and collect money for the tickets if the station master is not here. You are supposed to make a deposit each night when you lock up."

"I brought my own key and sounder but it looks like I can just use the one here. On my way here, I used it to get help when a river bridge had been washed away. It really came in handy."

"How did you get it to work without a battery?"

"I just borrowed a battery that was being delivered by the stagecoach company to the telegraph office in Indianapolis."

"That was sure a stroke of luck!"

"Sam, I would like for you to meet our station master, Elijah Baker. Elijah is probably one of the fastest telegraph operators west of the Mississippi."

"Glad to meet you Elijah."

"Nice to meet you Sam. We will take turns manning the telegraph station during the day so one of us can get a bite to eat or take a personal break. On the rare occasions that we are required to work nights, we will take turns."

"Good luck Sam," said Josh. Elijah, don't work Sam too hard. I see my train is arriving. In a month or so, I ought to be able to decide if I'm going to stay in Denver. I will send you a telegraph message when I make my decision. If I decide to stay Sam, do you think you could sell my cabin for me?"

"Sure Josh. Just let me know what you want me to do.

Time to Study

It wasn't long until Sam got settled in his new job and had saved enough money to purchase his law books but found it a little disconcerting when he discovered that he couldn't read well enough at night using the oil lamp he had just purchased at the general store. It just didn't put out enough light to read by after it got really dark outside. However, having adequate light by which to study at night didn't present too much of a problem because Sam found he could study some in the daytime at the depot. There were slack times at his telegraph desk when there were no messages coming in. The job at the telegraph office was working out perfectly for Sam.

Note: The incandescent light bulb was introduced December 31, 1879 by Thomas Edison. However, it was some years later before everyone had electric lights; especially in rural areas. In the Breckenridge rural areas in the 1940's, many people didn't have electricity until the Federal government established the NREC (National Rural Electric Cooperative).

When Edison introduced the incandescent light bulb in 1879, he made the comment, "We will make electricity so cheap that only the rich will burn candles."

It was beginning to get a little cooler as winter approached and Sam was not too thrilled about the coming of winter and the expected snow and the long walk to his cabin each day. But then just before he planned to take the train to St. Joseph, the owner of the rooming house visited him at the depot. She informed him that she now had a vacancy and Sam was welcome to move in anytime next week. "What great news," thought Sam.

Track Repairs at Hamilton

Suddenly Sam heard the clickety clack of the telegraph, Click, Click, Click, Clack- Click, Click, Click, Clack... It was a message from St. Joseph advising that the tracks were being repaired at Hamilton and that the next train from Hannibal should be told to wait in Breckenridge until notice that the repairs had been completed.

Two hours later the train arrived in Breckenridge from Hannibal. Sam explained to the twenty or so passengers that the tracks were being repaired and that there would be a few hours delay. Most of the passengers decided they would walk the short distance to town and either do some shopping or maybe even have a beer at the Trosper Saloon or get a bite to eat at the Railroad Café. The city park was only about two blocks south of the depot so several of the passengers decided to take a short nap under the nice shade trees.

"A little warning to you folks who aren't from around here. It's advisable to not talk about the controversy brewing between the states; especially if you are a southern sympathizer. Now, when you hear three short blasts of the train whistle; you will have 20 minutes to board," explained Sam.

Some of the passengers decided to get a bite to eat at the Railroad Café in Breckenridge while they waited for the tracks to be repaired.

All the passengers left the depot except two well-dressed men, one about twenty five years old and the other about thirty five. The two looked like they must be brothers or cousins.

"Aren't you gentlemen going into town with the others?"

The older gentleman replied, "No I will just wait in the depot and get caught up with some paperwork for my new job in Nevada. My brother here is right in the middle of reading a good book and will most likely try to finish it in the time we wait. Oh I'm sorry. My name is Orion Clemens and this is my brother Samuel. We are both from Hannibal, Missouri."

"Glad to make your acquaintance gentlemen. My name is Samuel also and I am originally from Dublin, Ireland. I settled in Philadelphia last year and became a telegrapher, and have recently moved to Breckenridge to be a telegrapher for the Hannibal and St. Joseph railroad here in Breckenridge. What line of work are you two in?"

"Well, I have taken a job to be the secretary to James W. Nye, the governor of Nevada Territory and my younger brother Samuel here is thinking about doing some mining in Silver City, Nevada. In fact, we're on our way there now. It will be quite a long trip. Once we get to St. Joseph, we will take a ferry across the Missouri River and then a stagecoach across the Great Plains and the Rocky Mountains to Nevada territory. It should be quite an experience travelling that far by stagecoach," explained Mr. Clemens.

"I bet it will gentlemen. I had the experience of riding in a stagecoach all the way from Philadelphia to Hannibal and our coach was never attacked by any Indians or robbed by bandits like portrayed in those dime novels. I'm sure it does happen but not nearly as often as you are led to believe."

"Following Mr. Lincoln's election as president in 1860, I was appointed secretary to the new government of the Territory of Nevada.

"That's quite an honor sir. Weren't you somewhat surprised to see the seven southern states secede from the Union, apparently because they feared President Lincoln would end slavery?"

"That's not the only reason they seceded. The agricultural southern states are upset because they are paying higher tariffs and taxes than the industrial North. From what Mr. Lincoln said in his inaugural speech and in the Lincoln Douglas Debates about Negroes, Lincoln sure doesn't believe that Negroes are superior or even equal to Whites. I don't understand what the southern states feared."

Sam noticed that the younger brother hadn't spoken at all, but that was probably because he was so engrossed in what he was reading. Finally the younger brother looked up at Sam and became a bit friendlier as he began to speak.

"I can remember when Hannibal was about the size of Breckenridge. It is amazing the effect that the railroads have on the growth of your community. In a few years you probably won't be able to recognize Breckenridge."

"You're probably right about that. What kind of work do you do Mr. Clemens? Are you also involved in politics like your brother Orion?"

"Oh no, I'm not interested in politics even though politics is interested in me whether I like it or not (Chuckling). I was a journeyman printer with the Hannibal Gazette and then I became an itinerate printer traveling to St. Louis, New York, and Philadelphia. Then I became a river boat cub-pilot, apprentice, for Horace Bixby and even considered a lifelong career as a steamboat pilot. But what I enjoy most is writing. I plan on writing a children's book or two but now I want to experience as much life as possible on our trip west," explained the younger brother.

Religious Beliefs

"I can see you sure have a lot of ambition and drive. I too want to experience life to the fullest, and to leave the world a better place than I found it. I am still undecided about my religious beliefs, however. What about you Mr. Clemens? Do you mind telling me how you feel about religion?"

Samuel Clemens paused a moment and said, "Well, that may take a while. My biggest concern about Christianity is not about its core teachings but the failure of its followers to practice what they preach. They appear to be good Christians one day a week and then leave the church to become sinners the rest of the week. It seems pretty hypocritical to me. Also too many people use religion to justify violence for personal gain, and to mistreat people of other faiths. You know, if Christ were here today, I doubt he would be a Christian. He would probably say, 'you people weren't listening to me.'"

Sam listened intently enjoying his wry humor, as Mr. Clemens espoused his thoughts on religion. Samuel Clemens continued, "And it seems odd to me that God has the power to eliminate human suffering but chooses not to do so. And why did God design man and animals to eat each other. If I were God, I don't think I would have done that. That really bothers me. Finally I am very skeptical of the Bible's contents, especially the Old Testament. If the Old Testament were written as a dime novel it wouldn't be suitable for a youngster to read. You know all the sadistic violence and sexual descriptions with Lot and his daughters, etc. Thomas Paine even said that any system of religion that has anything in it that shocks the mind of a child cannot be true."

"I sure understand what you're saying Mr. Clemens. I had a long discussion about religion with my friend Kelsey on our way to America on board the Alhambra. Kelsey thinks a lot like you Mr. Clemens. He believes that Jesus, if he existed at all, was not God but merely a mortal man who was a great prophet, teacher and healer and that the Bible is not really divinely inspired, especially the Old Testament. You know where it says homosexuals should be executed and if you find your bride is not a virgin on your wedding night, you are supposed to kill her and put her body on her father's doorstep, or you are supposed to kill your children if they talk back to you. Somehow that doesn't sound like divinely inspired scripture to me. I am beginning to believe that Kelsey just might be right."

"I find it very strange and suspicious that someone as important as the Biblical Jesus is mentioned only in the Bible and not in any of the numerous old books on Roman history. If a man 2,000 years ago could walk on water, change water into wine, bring people back from the dead, feed thousands of people from one loaf of bread and one fish, make the blind see, etc., surely he would be written about in the history of Rome, have coins with his likeness on them, paintings of himself, and numerous writings attributed to him. His picture might even be carved on the pyramids in Egypt!"

Samuel Clemens Views on Jesus.

Sam Clemens replied, "Well, some people say that a contemporary historian named Josephus did write about Jesus, but I have read that account and when Josephus writes about Jesus, it is obvious that it is not Josephus writing because the prose style changed. Notable scholars also agree that it is a fake. But, could it be possible that Josephus changed his writing style so he could hide the fact that he was creating a so called fake Biblical history? They even had a term for fake religious writings in those days and referred to them as *Pious Fraud.* Josephus was supposedly working for the Roman Emperor Titus. Some scholars believe that Josephus was writing a fictitious story portraying Emperor

Titus as the personage of Jesus. I'm not sure that we will ever know for sure. "

Mr. Clemens continued. "It sounds like your friend Kelsey is well versed. I can see you have given this a great deal of thought. A bit of warning though. Be careful with whom you discuss this."

"I understand what you are saying about discussing religion with other people. You can never win a religious argument arguing on faith and quoting only one scripture. The only one that appears to win is the one who knows Bible scripture better than his opponent. You can quote the Bible where it says children who talk back to their parents should be killed but your opponent then can quote the Bible where it says, 'Thou shalt Not Kill.'"

"Excellent analogy Sam. But remember, if you do win a religious argument with your superior knowledge of scriptures, you risk losing a friend. It might not be worth winning the argument."

"Aha! Good point. Any other words of wisdom you would like to share Mr. Clemens? The tracks should be repaired shortly."

"Well Sam. the secret of getting ahead is getting started. The secret of getting started is breaking your complex overwhelming tasks into small manageable tasks, and then starting on the first one. Does that make any sense?"

"It sure does Mr. Clemens. Thanks so much for sharing your insight."

Track has been Repaired in Hamilton

The telegraph started sending the message that the track had been repaired and the train could now depart Breckenridge and head toward St. Joseph. Sam advised the train engineer and he blew the train whistle three short blasts. In a few minutes the train was ready to leave. Sam shook hands with the Clemens brothers, Samuel and Orion, and told them how much he enjoyed talking to them the last four hours. They all bid farewell and waved as the train pulled away from the depot.

Sam was really impressed with the Clemens brothers, especially Samuel. He thought to himself, 'Someday that young man will be a very famous and successful person with all his wit and charm and knowledge of people and world affairs.'

Sam Applies for Naturalization Papers

Sam began to make plans in earnest to visit St. Joseph to apply for his naturalization papers in order to become a citizen of the United States. He felt that tomorrow would be the time to go. Since he had to work an extra shift for a sick relief telegrapher, he decided to stay at the depot instead of going home that evening. The evening train that was going to St. Joe was due at 10PM. Sam thought to himself, 'I wonder if I should even be going to St. Joe at this time, hearing that there had been a great deal of violence between the Union soldiers and the Southern sympathizers. But I will go directly to the hotel and then the court house early the next morning. Everything should be fine.'

On September 3rd, 1861, as Sam was waiting for the evening train to St. Joseph, he spotted a newspaper that a passenger had left in the depot. With nothing else to do he started reading the news even though it was a few months old. The newspaper had printed a copy of a telegram from Simon Cameron, Secretary of War, Washington D.C. to the Governor of Missouri C.F. Jackson and the governor's reply.

Telegram

From: Simon Cameron, Secretary of War, Washington, D.C.

To: C.F. Jackson, Governor of Missouri

Fort Sumter was fired upon April 12, 1861. On April 15th, President Lincoln issued a proclamation, calling for 75,000 men, from the militia of the several States to suppress combinations in the Southern States therein named. Simultaneously

76

therewith, the Secretary of War, sent a telegram to all the governors of the States, excepting those mentioned in the proclamation, requesting them to detail a certain number of militia to serve for three months, Missouri's quota being four regiments.

****

In response to this telegram, Gov. Jackson sent the following answer April 17, 1861

To: Simon Cameron, Secretary of War, Washington, D.C.
From: C.F. Jackson, Governor of Missouri, Executive Department of Missouri Jefferson City, April 17, 1861

Sir: Your dispatch of the 15th inst., making a call on Missouri for four regiments of men for immediate service, has been received. There can be, I apprehend, no doubt but these men are intended to form a part of the President's army to make war upon the people of the seceded States. Our requisition, in my judgment, is illegal, unconstitutional, and cannot be complied with. Not one man will the State of Missouri furnish to carry on such an unholy war.

Upon reading the governor's reply to the president, Sam thought to himself, 'Governor Jackson is sure an honorable man, standing firm with the Constitution even when the President of the United States orders the opposite action.'

On April 21, 1861, U.S. Arsenal at Liberty was seized by order of Governor Jackson. Things were really getting out of control and getting worse every day. Sam found it unbelievable that President Lincoln had completely ignored the U.S. Constitution and had become Dictator Lincoln instead of President Lincoln by declaring war against his own people.

Up until this time it was the general consensus of the electorate, the newspapers and legislators that the states had a constitutional right to secede. It was part of the checks and balances built into the Constitution to protect states' rights. Something had gone terribly wrong.

Little did Sam realize that his life could be in jeopardy as he traveled to St. Joseph. Up until now, the *War Between the States* had seemed so far away from Breckenridge even though there were Union troops usually stationed there. There were sporadic periods where the Union troops would hunt down southern sympathizers and imprison them and sometimes even kill them in the process of their capture.

As Sam soon found out, the war was now closer than ever.

Chapter Six
Confederates Sabotage the Platte River Railroad Bridge
September 3ʳᵈ, 1861

Sam was now traveling to St. Joseph to declare his intentions of becoming a U. S. citizen. Even though he probably could have made an application at the court house in Kingston, Missouri, which would have been a shorter trip, Sam felt like it would be more interesting to go on to the Buchanan County Court House in the bustling city of St. Joseph. He had heard a lot about St. Joseph being the starting place for the pioneers making their long journey westward. What a sight that would be.

Sam had already discovered that he would have to prove that he had lived in the U.S for five years and that he had been a resident of Missouri for two years before becoming eligible to apply for citizenship. Since Sam had only just arrived in the United States on October 17, 1859, he could not become a U.S. citizen until October 17, 1864. Sam wanted to at least complete step one of the process as quickly as possible. The three part naturalization process in becoming a citizen was; (1) Aliens must declare their intentions to become a citizen, (2) observe a residency period, and (3) then petition an authorized court for admission to citizenship.

Sam planned to explore St. Joseph a bit after picking up his paper work at the court house. It was exciting to think that while in St. Joseph, there was a small chance that he might get to meet a notable person like President Abraham Lincoln whom he heard had traveled through St. Joseph in the past. And it would be quite exciting to see the Pony Express riders arrive with the mail and the latest news from California. The St. Joseph Gazette was the first newspaper sent on the Pony Express to California. A recent article in the paper read:

"Through the politeness of the Express Company, we are permitted to forward by the first Pony Express, the first and only newspaper which goes out, and which will be the first paper ever transmitted from the Missouri to California in eight days. The nature of the conveyance necessarily precludes our making up an edition of any considerable weight. It, however, contains a summary of the latest news..."

As exciting as the Pony Express operation was, Sam couldn't help but wonder how long the Pony Express would last now that the pacific Telegraph line to California was completed.

Working for the Hannibal and St. Joseph Railroad telegraph office in Breckenridge afforded Sam the opportunity to ride the train from Breckenridge to St. Joe at a reduced rate and sometimes at no charge at all if his trip was related to his job as a telegrapher. This was a great benefit for Sam since he was still not making much money and hadn't had time to save much.

Little did Sam know that his sixty mile train ride to St. Joseph would nearly cost him his life! At this same time, Confederate partisans, also called bushwhackers or guerillas, were disrupting service on the Hannibal and St. Joseph Railroad. Just months previously, the "War Between The States" had begun. The South had been tricked by Lincoln into firing on Fort Sumter in April 1861. Lincoln needed support of the northern citizens so he tricked the South into firing the first shot. Lincoln had promised to honor the armistice of not sending supplies and more soldiers to Fort Sumter which was now in the newly declared Confederate States of America. But Lincoln secretly sent his ships there in the middle of the night. This provocation on southern soil caused the South to fire the first shot. The North then stated that the South was the instigator of an armed rebellion, but the South stated that they were merely defending themselves against the invaders. *To force the South back into the Union, Lincoln's armies, over the course of four years, ended up tragically killing about 300,000 southern Americans--one out of every four males aged 20 to 40 years old.*

Platte River Bridge Burned

Just hours before Samuel's trip to St. Joseph the Confederates had secretly set fire to the lower support timbers of the 160 foot railroad bridge over the Platte River near St. Joseph. The top of the bridge had remained intact, cleverly concealing the damage below. As Sam's train approached the bridge about midnight, the passengers were totally unaware of the impending disaster. The weight of the train caused the bridge to collapse as soon as it started to cross. At least seventeen people lost their lives and over 100 were injured.

The citizens of the town of St. Joseph rushed to the crash site to tend to the injured. Luckily for Sam, he had stepped outside at the rear of the passenger car to get some fresh air just as the bridge collapsed and he was thrown clear of the wreckage onto the river bank, hitting his head so hard on the sandy ground that it knocked him unconscious.

Sam awoke almost an hour later to find a beautiful young lady bending over him holding his head.

Sam, slowly and in a dazed state of mind, said, "Where am I?..... Who are you?..... What's going on?..... Where's the train?"

The young lady, quietly and noticeably caring said, "My name is Maggie Delaney and you were thrown from the train. The trained crashed as it crossed the bridge over the Platte River. The bridge is on fire. Oh, it's terrible! You are very fortunate to be alive. Is anything broken? Let me see you wiggle your toes. Can you move your legs and arms? Do you think you can walk?"

Sam stunned and in a great deal of pain, replied, "I don't know. I'm a little dizzy and bewildered." Sam slowly and carefully rose to his feet and Maggie helped him walk a short distance to a small boat that would take them to the west side of the Platte River. There were wagons and carriages everywhere waiting to take the injured and deceased to St. Joseph only a few miles west of the river. Some of the rescue crew had built huge bon fires on both sides of the river. The light from the bon fires and the train burning made the crash scene as bright as day. Arriving at a rescue wagon and with the help of another rescue volunteer, they lifted Sam up into the wagon which was full of straw and blankets to cushion the injured for the trip into the city. Sam was going in and out of consciousness and as they neared the Patee House Hotel in St. Joseph, he awoke and said, "Is that a hospital you are taking me to? It is quite large."

Maggie replied, "No it is not a hospital; but rather one of the finest hotels in the United States."

Union Soldiers to Occupy the Patee House

The Patee House Hotel in St. Joseph, which had just recently been completed, was made available to the injured passengers only temporarily because the Union soldiers were occupying almost the entire hotel. Maggie said that they were setting up a temporary recovery room for a few of the injured at the United Brethren Church on Lafayette Street. The church parish was vacant since the pastor had just left to serve as a pastor for another church and they had still not found a replacement.

The next day Maggie, with the help of two other volunteers, transported Samuel and three young men from the Patee House to the nearby church.

"Maggie," enquired Sam, "Can you go to the telegraph office at 2nd and Jules Street or the train depot and send a telegram to the telegrapher in Breckenridge and explain what happened and that I will return as soon as possible?"

"I have already done that Sam. They of course had already received a telegraph message about the wreck but were especially concerned about your wellbeing. I told them that you had survived with only minor sprains and bruises and should be able to travel in a few days," replied Maggie.

"Thanks so much Maggie. You must surely be an angel in disguise."

It was nearly a week before Sam was able to walk without a cane and to feel like he would not topple over. I know my fellow telegrapher in Breckenridge must be tired of working a twenty four hour shift and sleeping in the train depot but please Maggie, can you please help me to get to the court house to file my "Declaration of Intention" to become a U. S. citizen?"

Maggie cheerfully agreed to help him board a buggy and get to the court house that was only about a twenty minute ride.

Are You Married Maggie?

After Sam's business at the Buchanan County Court House was completed, he and Maggie returned to his temporary home at the church on Lafayette Street.

Sam had become extremely fond of Maggie but just knew that she must already be married.   Finally he got up enough nerve to ask her.

Very slowly and cautiously Sam asked, "Maggie, You're a beautiful lady with a beautiful spirit and uh..uh you must be married?"

She slowly lifted her head and replied, "No, I am a widow. My husband was killed just two months ago fighting in a small battle just south of St. Joseph.   Actually it wasn't even a battle; more of an ambush. I was told he and his friends were attacked by 'Bushwhackers', but I suspect they were actually Union soldiers. I am sure they knew he was a Confederate sympathizer."

"I am so sorry," said Sam.

"This Civil War between the southern and northern states is just awful and so unnecessary," declared Maggie.

Civil War or War Between the States

"You shouldn't call it a 'Civil War' Maggie. It's not a Civil War at all! All the southern states want to do is secede from the Union. They are not trying to take over the United States government which is typical of what takes place in a Civil War."

"Many people are calling it a Civil War but you are right, it should not be called that. I hear that many Southerners are calling it the *War of Northern Aggression*. I guess it depends on your perspective."

Sam continued, "Besides, the Declaration of Independence says that the Federal Government derives its power to govern from the consent of the governed. Due to the unfair taxes and tariffs, the agrarian South is paying a disproportionate share of taxes to support the industrial North. The South no longer consented to be governed by the Federal U.S. government because of the unfair taxation. All Congress would have to do to avert a war with the South would have been to rectify the unfair taxes imposed on the Southern states. It's unbelievable to me that the President and Congress do not do this."

"We can't even talk about this in the company of strangers. Talk like this is probably what got my husband killed. It is a terrible thing and causing so much unnecessary death and destruction. You just never know who among you supports the South or North. Did you know Missouri was added to the Union as a 'Slave State' and Maine as a 'Free State in 1821 as part of the Missouri Compromise? There are people living in Missouri supporting both sides of the issue. My Uncle Weldon living near Breckenridge was dragged out of his cabin a month ago by Union troops and murdered because one of his neighbors reported him to be a southern sympathizer. I have even heard that President Lincoln has suspended Habeas Corpus and has begun imprisoning citizens without a trial, simply because they publically stated that they didn't support the war. He even imprisoned most of the Maryland legislators. To save the Union, he has become a dictator, ignoring our country's Constitution. The states voluntarily joined the Union, not through conquest, so should be able to unjoin voluntarily!" cried Maggie with indignation.

"I certainly agree with you Maggie. I think I will write President Lincoln and tell him that all he needs to do to end this unholy war is to have Congress fix the tax and tariff problems that unfairly tax the Southern states."

"Oh please don't do that Sam!"

"Why not, Maggie?"

"President Lincoln will have you arrested and put in prison!"

" I hadn't thought of that, Maggie, you are probably right."

Time to Return to Breckenridge

Sam could not stop thinking that the southern states that wanted to secede had the right to do so. After all, the right of secession was merely a part of the "checks and balances" where a state could rectify a situation when the Federal government over stepped its power over the sovereign states. Even Bart, the lawyer he had met on the stage to Indianapolis, had agreed with him.

After visiting the court house, Sam was ready to return to Breckenridge but since the railroad bridge was still out over the Platte River, and there were long delays over the wagon bridge, Sam decided to take an alternate route by horse and buggy. Maggie explained that he could also cross the Platte River southeast of St. Joseph at a place called Agency Ford. Hopefully it wouldn't be too congested with wagons heading for California. She stated that it was a safe place to cross even though there wasn't a bridge because a large area in the river bed was solid rock and shouldn't be very deep this time of year.

Maggie looked at Sam, smiled and said "I hope to see you again Sam. I want to see if my nursing skills were successful." Sam replied, "I am so thankful for what you have done for me in my time of need. I too would certainly like to see you again after I get to feeling a little bit better. Maybe in a few weeks."

Then Sam left for the scenic fifteen mile drive to Agency Ford. As Sam approached Agency, he couldn't believe what he saw. There were oxen and horse drawn covered wagons as far as one could see. 'What was it like ten years ago?' wondered Sam.

"Maybe I should have tried the wagon bridge over the Platte River near St. Joe even though there were reported long delays because of the Union soldiers checking everyone crossing in both directions;" thought Sam.

Fortunately three wagons stopped long enough for him to get his horse and buggy across the Agency Ford. It was quite an experience hearing hundreds of cow bells clanging and listening to the sounds of four times that of hooves going in and out of the mud. It was a hard trip for Sam but Maggie had packed food, water, 2 blankets, and a small oil treated tarp in case of rain. Sam wasn't too fond of sleeping on the ground but thought that one night wouldn't be too bad. He arrived home in the middle afternoon the next day.

After arriving back in Breckenridge, Sam took his horse and buggy to the local livery stable just east of town. The company that owned the Breckenridge stable also owned the stable in St. Joe, so he was able to leave the horse and buggy with them.

Sam was constantly thinking about Maggie. They kept in touch by writing letters back and forth at least once a week. Sam sensed that Maggie felt the same about him as he did about her but was probably still grieving for her late husband who had been killed by the *Bushwhackers* or as Maggie had suspected, the Union Troops. Maybe in time they could become closer.

Kelsey Joins the Union Army

One afternoon as Sam was sitting at his desk, he began to wonder how his friend Kelsey was doing, working on the Erie Canal, and if he had yet saved enough money to buy his farm.

"I would like to write Kelsey but have no idea what address to use. I'll send a telegram to the Erie Canal people and maybe they would be able to give him my telegram," thought Sam. Working as a telegrapher did have its advantages.

A few weeks later Sam received a telegram from the Erie Canal management who advised that Kelsey had quit his job to buy a small farm and had moved to Woodbury, New Jersey, just south of Philadelphia.

Sam was elated! Now all he had to do was send a telegram to Woodbury, New Jersey and as small as that community probably was, someone at the telegraph office would surely know Kelsey, especially if he had just recently purchased property.

Four days later he received a telegram from his friend Kelsey advising him that he had purchased a small tract of land but didn't have time to improve it because he had joined the army to help save the Union from the newly formed Southern states. Kelsey said he would send a letter in a few days explaining what had happened.

Sam was delighted to hear that Kelsey had purchased some land but saddened to think he had gotten involved in what he felt was an unjust cause. Sam thought it best to not put in writing how he really felt about the war for fear of being arrested and imprisoned.

On September 20th, 1862, Sam received a letter from Kelsey informing him that he had joined the 12th Regiment, New Jersey Volunteer Infantry, Company D.

To My Good friend Sam Ronan   *September 23, 1862*

It was so nice to receive your telegram just before I left Woodbury, New Jersey. It sounds like the telegraph job suits you fine. Do you have enough time to study your law? The area you are in is growing so fast that there will probably be many opportunities for you.

I am well at present and on guard today; I hate it though for we are going to have a big dinner today, and I won't be there. I cannot help it. We take our turn when we are on duty. Hopefully I can become an assistant to Charley Gamble, our regiment's cook. That job would be less dangerous and of course the food would be better.

Yesterday after we had been on our parade in the afternoon, a friend of mine, Dave Smith, had a hard fit, as hard a one as ever I saw and when he came to he did not know where he was and he asked Charley and me to take him home. Charley got him up and led him around a while and he found out where he was; when he found out where he was he asked me for something to drink and I had some and I gave him some whiskey. This morning he is all right except he is sorry. A soldier's life is hard to adjust to.

It is pretty near time for me to go on duty, and I shall have to bring my letter to a close. Good-bye. Your friend, Kelsey

Sam felt so sad about Kelsey needing to delay his dream of having a farm but knew that he was doing what he thought was right. Almost everyone thought it was important to keep the

Union united but there were disagreements on how that should be done. Sam kept thinking to himself, 'Was a war really necessary to keep the Union together?' Sometimes there were brothers fighting against brothers, military leaders fighting and killing each other who had been close friends at West Point before the war, and there was death and destruction that was unimaginable.

Moral Issue of Slavery Brought Into the War

Now the issue of slavery was being brought into the war. Was it a war to free the slaves or just a political ploy to get more recruits like Kelsey because of the added moral issue? The Emancipation Proclamation was to free slaves in states that had seceded from the United States and where Lincoln had no jurisdiction. Sam thought, 'Why doesn't the government simply buy the slaves from the owners and then free them? There must be more to this war than is evident,' thought Sam.

Authors Note: Many people believe Abraham Lincoln's Emancipation Proclamation of 1863 was a law which freed all the slaves. But the proclamation was actually only "a war measure" as Lincoln put it. (To punish the South) The war had been going on for over a year and a half at this point. Emancipation would take place only in rebel states and not those under Union control.

The London Spectator recognized it as a brilliant propaganda tactic. In the edition of October 11, 1862 it was written:

"The principle of the proclamation is not that a human being cannot justly own another, but that he cannot own him unless he is loyal to the United States."

Authors note: The slaves were not actually freed by federal law, in both the North and South, until after the War Between the States in 1865 when the 13ᵗʰ Amendment was passed If it were such a moral issue to do what was right for the Negroes, why would it be another 100 years before the Negroes would get their "Civil Rights" guaranteed and why did Ulysses S .Grant and others want to send them all to Liberia or the Caribbean Islands?

Chapter Seven
Lawyers Assistant
September 1862

Maggie knew that Sam's dream was to become a lawyer so she was always on the lookout for a local lawyer who might assist Sam in that regard. One afternoon while visiting the Buchanan County Court House to obtain a copy of her husband's death certificate, she met a lawyer named Abe Abercrombie in the County Clerk's Office. Mr. Abercrombie was trying to hold a large armful of documents without much success. All of a sudden most of them dropped to the floor.

Maggie said, "Here let me help you sir," as she stooped over to assist.

"Thank you very much Madam," said Mr. Abercrombie.

"Oh that's quite all right, glad to be of service." That's when Maggie noticed one of the documents said something about Breckenridge, Missouri and Caldwell County.

"It looks like you have business in Breckenridge," said Maggie.

"I do Miss. In fact more than I can take care of now that the Hannibal and St. Joseph Railroad has been built. I am an attorney and that area is growing so fast that I can hardly keep up with the increase in clients. I have many cases involving the train hitting and killing farmers' cows, and many property boundary disputes and of course estate settlement cases."

"Do you have an office in Breckenridge?"

"No, but I would like to," said Mr. Abercrombie.

Maggie immediately offered her information, saying, "I have a good friend in Breckenridge who might be available to become your agent there. He presently works as a telegrapher for the railroad but has been studying to become a lawyer."

"As soon as the Platte River Bridge is repaired, I plan to visit Breckenridge to attend to some legal matters involving a property dispute. What is your friend's name? Maybe I will have time to look him up."

"His name is Samuel Ronan and you can normally find him at the railroad telegraph office or at the rooming house just west of the town square."

"Thank you Madam. What did you say your name is?"

"Maggie Delaney," she beamed.

"Maggie, I will call on your friend, Mr. Ronan in a few days."

A few weeks later the Platte River Railroad Bridge had been re-opened by building a temporary pontoon bridge and Union troops had been stationed nearby to protect it from any further sabotaging.

Abe Abercrombie did indeed contact Sam in Breckenridge a short time later. Abe located Sam one evening as he was leaving the depot to go home.

"Mr. Ronan, I am Abe Abercrombie, a lawyer, from St. Joseph. Maggie Delaney, a friend of yours, said you were interested in becoming a lawyer."

"That's quite true but the only thing I have been able to study so far is "Blackstone's Commentaries on the Law of England.""

"That's good Mr. Ronan. That's certainly a wise place to start. However, have you read Bastiat's most famous work, 'The Law' originally published as a pamphlet in 1850? It simply and eloquently defines the development of a just system of laws and then demonstrates how such law facilitates a free society.

Bastiat believed that the sole purpose of government was to protect the right of an individual to life, liberty, and property. He concluded that the law cannot defend life, liberty, and property if it promotes socialist policies. He explains that, if the privileged classes use the government for "legalized plunder" (Forced taxation and income distribution), this will encourage the lower classes to revolt.

"No sir, I haven't read that, but it sure sounds like I should. His philosophy is identical to mine." replied Sam.

"Would you like me to mail you a copy of his work?"

"Would I! Of course, that would be very kind of you sir."

"Do you have any formal schooling, Sam?"

"No sir, not after primary in Ireland. I'm just pretty much self-taught. I do a lot of reading on my own."

"Well, for some time now, I had planned on opening up a law office in Breckenridge but did not have anyone to oversee it. Would you be interested in pursuing a position with my firm?"

"I certainly would, but I wonder how the pay would measure up to my job as a telegrapher?"

"I am sure you would think it satisfactory but first I have some other literature for you to read and I need some time to talk to you and find out how well you know the law and what special abilities you possess. Of course you would start out doing mainly research on my cases but if you have the ability to speak authoritatively and knowledgably about the law, you might eventually be able to pass the state bar exam and become a full-fledged lawyer," said Abe.

"Sir, I hope to get a little experience in a court room in just a few days. I have been summoned by the Caldwell County Court in Kingston to serve as a juror next Thursday. If chosen, I will be serving on a trial that is trying an alleged horse thief. I've heard that they sometimes hang horse thieves here in Missouri. A dear friend of mine told me that the defendant is an honorable man that does not deserve to be hung. I think he can be found innocent, if necessary, by using the concept of Jury Nullification," explained Sam.

"I am quite impressed that you know about *Jury Nullification*. However, you must not allow the judge to know that you understand how jury nullification works. As you apparently know, jurors have the right to judge the law in a case as well at the facts, but the judge will more than likely not inform you of this," said Abe.

"Yes sir. I understand what you're saying. I will explain it to the other jurors after we are sent into the deliberation room to discuss the case," said Sam

"Wait a minute Sam. There may be a problem. Are you a citizen of the United States?"

"No, not yet," said Sam. "But I've applied for my papers."

"I'm afraid you won't be allowed to serve as a juror until you become a U.S. citizen. Maybe I can help though. I will see to it that at least one person chosen for the jury knows about jury nullification and their constitutional rights. I will be back in Breckenridge next month to see how you are doing and discuss what you know and don't know about the law," said Abe.

Sam Asks Maggie to Mary Him

Sam was so excited and couldn't wait to write Maggie and thank her for telling Abe about his desire to become a lawyer. 'Hopefully the railroad won't have any trouble replacing me as a telegrapher,' thought Sam. Then, his thoughts turned back to Maggie. It was becoming all too obvious how Sam felt about Maggie. As soon as he was sure that he was to work as an apprentice to Abe's law firm, Sam planned to ask Maggie to marry him.

Just as Mr. Abe Abercrombie had promised, he returned to Breckenridge to talk to Sam about managing a law office there. Have you had time to read 'The Law' by Bastiat?" inquired Mr. Abercrombie..

"I sure did. It was very informative. I thank you very much for sharing it with me. It looks like President Lincoln has not read Bastiat's book."

"You are very perceptive Sam. Have you read the U.S. Constitution?"

"Oh yes sir. That is one of the first things I studied when I came to America. Your constitution is what makes America special and a beacon of light for the whole world to follow. I only wish Abraham Lincoln had followed the Constitution. I fear he has set precedence by not allowing the southern states to secede that will haunt this country for years to come. I'm afraid future presidents will assume that they can do whatever they wish regarding states' rights because it has been proven, so they will reason, that the states *don't* have a right to secede."

"Sam, I am afraid you may be right. You are beginning to sound like a constitutional lawyer already. I am impressed."

"Well, thanks. By the way, have you heard about how the horse thief trial went in Kingston?" asked Sam.

"Thankfully one of the jurors already knew about 'Jury Nullification' and after explaining to the other jurors that they had the constitutional right to judge the law itself as well as the facts in the case, they could not get a unanimous guilty verdict. You see, the defendant admitted that he did take the horse but did not actually steal it. He could not get permission from the owner because the owner was passed out drunk in his home. The defendant was desperate to get his wife to the doctor that lived five miles away. The other jurors finally admitted privately that they could see, especially in this case that the law should not apply here. They all agreed that yes, the defendant did in fact break the law, but the law did not apply because of the special circumstances. I was very happy to see that our constitutional rights were observed here in Missouri. That was a good lesson for you to learn, Sam"

After conferring with Sam for over two hours, Mr. Abercrombie said with all seriousness, "I am very pleased to offer you the job of managing my law office here in Breckenridge. I feel you will be a great asset to the firm and I look forward to the day that you can pass the Missouri Bar and become a full-fledged lawyer."

"Thank you very much Mr. Abercrombie! I appreciate the confidence you have placed in me and look forward to a long and prosperous relationship with your law firm."

Sam continued, "I just received a telegram yesterday from Josh telling me that his job in Denver didn't work out and that he was hoping he could get his old telegraph job back in Breckenridge. This will work out just fine since I will now be the manager of your local law office and Josh can have his old job back. I'll send him a telegram tomorrow telling him of the great news."

Sam Becomes Lawyers Assistance

"The president of the 'Farmers and Exchange Bank' is a friend of mine and has agreed to rent us a small office in one corner of the bank," explained Abe enthusiastically.

"I will come back in a few days to help set up your office and will have a desk, files, office supplies, etc. shipped on the railroad by the end of next week," said Abe.

"Fantastic!" I'll see you next week and thanks very much for putting your trust in me," said Sam with enthusiasm and excitement noticeably showing as his face beamed with pride.

Sam could hardly wait to write Maggie and tell her of his new job as an assistant to Abe, the highly successful lawyer from St. Joseph, and to thank her for telling him about his desire to become a lawyer.

Sam wasn't sure what the requirements were to becoming a lawyer in Missouri but he knew that in some states, if you had a college degree you had to be an apprentice to a lawyer for two years, and if you did not have a college degree you had to be an apprentice for four years.

"Surely with the experience I get working for Abe and researching his cases, in four years, I will be able to pass the Missouri Bar Exam," reasoned Sam.

"Maybe this is a good time to ask Maggie for her hand in marriage," thought Sam. "I can't ask her in a letter. I will invite her to visit me here in Breckenridge," decided Sam.

Chapter Eight
June Wedding Bells and Secret Society Intrigue
June 10. 1863

Maggie could feel that something special was happening as she stepped off the train in Breckenridge and saw Sam beaming from ear to ear.

"Maggie, will you marry me?" Sam blurted out, almost before she got off the train.

Maggie had suspected that this might be what Sam had in mind since he had been so secretive about the reason he had asked her to come for a visit.

"I am much honored, Sam that you have asked for my hand in marriage, but I think you should know a little more about me first. Can we go over to the park in the city square and have a private talk?"

As they walked the short distance to the park, Sam wondered what Maggie was alluding to. The only person in the park was a farmer loading up his tank wagon with water at the community water well. There was no one else in the park so they had their choice of picnic tables to sit on. There was one nicely nestled in the trees and in the shade next to the band stand.

Maggie's Secret

"Alright, what big secret do you have to tell me?" asked Sam.

"Well, I hardly know where to begin. After you hear what I have to say, you may never speak to me again. But here goes. Have you ever heard of the *Knights of the Golden Circle*?

"No, I don't believe I have. Who are they and what do they believe? Is it some kind of secret society like the Masons?" asked Sam.

"I don't know much about them but I believe my husband may have been a secret member and might have been killed because of it. Remember I hinted at that a few weeks back when I said I suspected Union soldiers were responsible for killing my husband, thinking he was a Confederate sympathizer? Some people believe that the Knights of the Golden Circle's main agenda is to prepare the way for the annexation of a golden circle of territories in Mexico, Central America and the Caribbean for inclusion in the United States as slave states. I can't keep from thinking that they were involved somehow in burning the railroad bridge over the Platte River that almost got you killed. Some of them apparently believe that this *Civil War*, I'm sorry, I mean *The War Between The States*, is a mistake and that the increasing power of the Federal government was leading to tyranny, and I think others were simply just supporters of slavery. You know I am a southern sympathizer but would never do anything violent for the southern cause and I believe that slavery should be abolished," said Maggie.

"I know that, Maggie. I'm not worried about your secret. With my new job we can live here together in Breckenridge and raise a family like I have always dreamed of. I love you so much Maggie and you don't need to be concerned about the Knights of the Golden Circle because it doesn't concern you anymore."

"I'm not so sure about that. There is one more thing. I found a note in my husband's dresser drawer after he was killed that said, *'Take care of the supplies and guard them with your life as you have sworn to do.'* Rather than a signature, there was a symbol that looked like an anchor. The more I looked at it, I could see that it could possibly be two J's back to back that made it look like an anchor. I remember my husband had met Jesse James on several occasion and therefore concluded the anchor could have been a secret signature for Jesse James. You know it was rumored that the James gang, in conjunction with the KGC, had money, guns and supplies hidden in mine shafts and caves around the eastern part of Kansas and the Northwest part of the United States to help finance the southern cause for independence. Also the coroner gave me a note that was found in my husband's pocket that had a picture drawn on it of a medieval rock castle. It is a very strange drawing. I believe that there may be some type of hidden message encoded in the drawing," said Maggie with some bit of anguish.

"Did you bring it with you?"

"I did. Here, take a look at it," Maggie cried as she pulled it from her pocket. Sam carefully scanned the paper, and then a small smile appeared on his face.

Secret Code

"This is incredible! Look how the stones are arranged in the wall. The slight variation in the stone pattern appears to hide a Morse code message. Let me see if the message makes any sense." Sam studied the drawing for several moments and then exclaimed, "I think I can read it." After a few seconds, "I can read it! It is Morse code just like we use in the telegraph office. It says, *Bank of Montreal 2348.* It could be a bank account number. Do you or did your husband have a bank account in a Canadian bank?" inquired Sam.

"I certainly don't know anything about it, if he did," replied Maggie.

"Do you want me to send a telegram to the bank tomorrow and find out whose name is on the account and how much money is there?" asked Sam.

"I guess so. Will they give you that information?"

"Probably, but only if I can prove you are the wife of the man's name on the account. We will just have to wait and see," said Sam.

The next morning Sam received a reply from the bank in Montreal stating that they were unable to release any information on this account unless he could provide them with an identification number in addition to the bank account number. Now what was he to do? Sam hurried over to the hotel to see if Maggie would once again show him the encrypted picture. A second look did indeed reveal that there were additional numbers encoded in the artwork showing in the water in the moat flowing in front of the castle. That must be it. There was definitely the numbers 762 in code within the artwork of the water.

After sending the identification numbers to the bank, they advised him, John Delaney, Maggie's deceased husband, did have on deposit $5,000, and if she wanted to withdraw it she would need to send them a death certificate and proof that she was the widow. Then the Bank of Montreal will transfer the money to the First National Bank in St. Louis who will in turn send it to the Farmers and Exchange Bank in Breckenridge.

What a surprise! This could help Sam and Maggie get established in Breckenridge. Maggie was still a little concerned, all the while hoping that her good fortune was not 'blood money.' Sam assured Maggie that there could not be any connection with her to the **Knights of the Golden Circle**. Her husband had never confided in her that he was involved in any secret organization. He must have known that it would have been too dangerous to have his wife know of his active assistance to the Confederacy. But was that really true? Did anyone else know about this account besides Maggie and Sam? Hopefully not!

Sam suggested that they get married in the Lick Fork Church which was northwest of Breckenridge. Sam had hunted deer in this area several times and knew that it would be a beautiful setting for a marriage ceremony. It is a very beautiful area and that in June the flowers would be beginning to bloom and the temperature should be suitable

Wedding date set for June 10, 1863

Sam taking Maggie out to Lick Fork near Breckenridge to show her what a beautiful place they will have for their wedding.

June 10th would give Sam time to get established in his new job and they would have time to have a house built or at least to get a good start on it. Sam and Maggie didn't particularly want to be farmers. However with the money from the secret account in Montreal, plus the help the railroad was providing, giving them a loan for ten years at five percent interest, they had enough money to build a nice home. The Hannibal and St. Joseph railroad had received a grant from Congress for over 600,000 acres of choice farmland and woodlands within fifteen miles on each side of the railroad tracks. Sam thought that he might want to raise a few horses to sell to the army and chickens for fresh eggs, but decided they would buy most of their meat and other food items at the general store or from the local farmers.

"A June 10th wedding sounds fine with me. Looks like Breckenridge will become my home too. However, I will need time to make the big move, packing and closing up a lifetime in St. Joe. I have a lot of shopping to do before moving. I can see that shopping is rather limited in Breckenridge except for horses and farm equipment. I love you so much Sam."

The day was as beautiful as Sam had promised. It was only a short buggy ride to the Lick Fork Church. The church had just recently purchased a new pump organ with the help of Sam's donation.

"I hope you haven't forgotten anything, honey. How many invitations did you send out?"
"I can't believe it Sam. I mailed almost 50 invitations. I had no idea that I even knew that many people. I'm a little nervous that I may have forgotten something."
"Don't worry about it. Didn't you say that your sister was handling the refreshments and decorations?"
"Oh yes. She is dependable and I know she did a good job."
"Just look at the huge crowd and all the horses and buggies."
"I think I am supposed to go into the church and proceed down the aisle as the music starts," giggled Maggie.
"Next time we meet, you will be Mrs. Samuel Ronan."

The organ began to play, "Here comes the bride..." and the preacher turned to face Maggie.

"Please repeat after me. I, Maggie Delaney take Samuel Ronan to be my husband, to have and to hold from this day forward; for better, for worse, for richer, for poorer, in sickness and in health, to love and to cherish, till death us do part, according to God's holy law. In the presence of God I make this vow."

After repeating her vows, "I do."

Preacher turns facing Samuel.

"Please repeat after me. I, Samuel Ronan take Maggie Delaney to be my lawful wife, to have and to hold from this day forward; for better, for worse, for richer, for poorer, in sickness and in health, to love and to cherish, till death us do part, according to God's holy law. In the presence of God I make this vow."

After repeating his vows, "I do."

"I now pronounce you husband and wife. You may now kiss the bride."

As the couple exited the church, everyone threw rice at the newlyweds and congratulated them.

"Have you decided where you will go on your honeymoon?" asks Maggie's sister.

"We had planned on taking the train to Hannibal and then the riverboat to St. Louis to see a play. But the Provost Marshall said it was too dangerous and wouldn't give us a pass. Sam didn't even want to go to St. Joe even though the Platte River Bridge had been rebuilt and guarded by the Union soldiers. I suppose we will just delay our honeymoon until the war is over. Actually, the Breckenridge Hotel Weldon is mighty inviting. All we care about is finally being together."

That night after the wedding, Sam said, "Maggie, please forgive me but I need 30 minutes to write my Aunt Mary and

Uncle Pat. I must tell them what a wonderful day we have had, what a beautiful wedding, and what a beautiful bride you are. If it wasn't for them I would not be standing here this moment, living this perfect life with my beautiful bride."

"Of course Sam. In fact, I need a few minutes myself to unwind."

Sam and Maggie decided the next day to honeymoon close to home and take in a play in St. Joseph at the Pioneer Opera House. The play, 'The Indian Prince,' by James Nelson Barker would be playing there all week. It was an old musical comedy dealing with the relations between Native Americans and the first European settlers in America.

"Maggie said with a loving look, "Sam, anything at all with my new husband would be absolutely wonderful."

'The play in St. Joseph should be almost as exciting as going to St. Louis,'' thought Maggie.

Starting out his marriage with a beautiful wife, a job as a lawyer's assistant and the prospect of moving into a brand new comfortable home was most assuredly a dream come true. Sam knew he was on his way to realizing all his goals and ambitions in his adopted country.

"As soon as the war is over, we can take a second honey-moon to St. Louis.. That will give us a lovely outing to look forward to."

"Sam, you received a letter from your friend Kelsey

Camp near Warrenton Junction, Virginia
July 29th, 1863.

Dear Sam and Maggie
It was nice hearing from you and finding that you were planning on getting married in June. Congratulations to you both. I received your letter and it found me in good health and I hope that this letter may find you all the same. We have been here two days and I hope that we will stay here a week so that we may get

rested as we have been on the march for 43 days and a hard march; and you must judge that we want some rest by this time. They say that it is the hardest march that was ever done in this country by any army. I hope that the hardest part of our Campaign is over for the summer. I think that we have had some of the hottest days here that I ever did experience in my life. Although it rains here very nearly every other day and night.

We are now where we can get plenty of rations again but we have been scant of them for some time and we could not have got along without starving if we had not went on foraging expeditions. Our boys would go out and fetch in fresh pork, mutton and veal; chickens, potatoes and green beans and we made out very well. Charley and I have not done any foraging yet but we had someone to do it for us; for we have not got a heart large enough to go to so many houses and kill hogs and sheep and take chickens from the women. It is so depressing to see the death and destruction of the farmer's homes, crops and livestock knowing that many will probably either starve to death or die from the elements because of what we took from them. But we have enough that like to do such work and it is no hardship for them to do it.

Sam, I have to get back for duty so will continue my letter when possible. Your friend always, Kelsey

Sam and Maggie have a Baby Boy

Exactly one year later, Sam and Maggie were blessed with the birth of a healthy baby boy they named Jefferson after Sam's American hero, Thomas Jefferson. According to neighbors and friends, Jefferson was the most beautiful and sharp little boy they'd ever seen. Maggie and Sam were quick to agree. Sam was on top of the world with his little family.

As little Jeff began to grow up he was a great help on their small farm and was always eager to do his share of the chores; gathering the eggs, pulling weeds and even weeding the garden. He followed his Poppy around like a little puppy. By the time he entered grammar school he could write his name and read a few passages from his Poppy's books.

U.S. Citizen

A most important event in the life of Samuel Ronan occurred on October 17, 1864. That was when he became a United States citizen. Now everything was in place. Sam could finally become a lawyer and actually serve legally in a court of law for his employer, Abe Abercrombie. With the experience and knowledge Sam now had of the law, Abe decided to have the state of Missouri recognize him as a full-fledged lawyer. Abe's standing in the community and his influence in Missouri law and politics was a great aid in the process. Sam was confident that he would soon pass the bar exam. All of his hard work and studying would finally pay off.

In March of 1865 Sam and Maggie received a letter from Kelsey stating that the awful war was finally ending.

Camp near Stevensburg, Virginia
March 4, 1865

Dear Sam and Maggie

It looks like this awful war is almost over. It appears that the Confederate soldiers have just about run out of everything; food, ammunition, and will power to fight. It is so sad that our president made us go through this even though I feel he thought he was doing the right thing.

It would have been so much easier and humane to simply equalize the tax obligation between the north and south and have the federal government free the slaves by buying them from the slave owners.

It is surprising what large numbers of northerners there are who did not support the war effort. President Lincoln should be very careful when he is in public because I fear someone will attempt to take his life. I am sure that those that he put in prison for not supporting the war effort would not lose any sleep if Lincoln was made to pay for his actions.

I am looking so forward to building up my farm. Once I get established, I will try to get on the train and come to Breckenridge for a visit. I will write again when I get back to Woodbury.

Your friend, Kelsey

Authors note: *The end of the War Between the States only appeared to be over. It wasn't over for everyone. For several years after, the James boys and the Younger brothers would continue their bank and train robbing for what some believed was to gather arms and money to resurrect the war again. A common saying heard from some Southerners was, "The South shall rise again!"*

Jesse James was killed in St. Joseph on April 3, 1882 by Robert Ford. Others of the so called outlaws (Confederates) were either killed, pardoned or released from prison for time served.

Cole and Jim Younger, the surviving Younger brothers, were paroled in 1901 within the confines of Minnesota after serving 25 years in prison. Jim Younger killed himself on October 19, 1902 in St. Paul Minnesota apparently because he was depressed that he was not permitted to return home to Missouri.

The war officially ended in 1865 but the horrific wounds to the South were slow to heal, lasting for many many years. Countless Americans still feel that Abraham Lincoln was wrong for not allowing the Southern states to secede. They point out that the Constitution says nothing about preventing secession. In fact this so worried some of our early leaders that they attempted to add a constitutional amendment preventing secession but could not gather the support necessary to amend the Constitution.

The threat of Secession is just one of many checks and balances built into the Constitution to protect the rights of the states and the people.

Chapter Nine
Reconstruction

Gen. Robert E. Lee's surrender
Appomattox Courthouse
April 9, 1865

Now that the war was over, Sam had hopes that things would return to normal and that ***Reconstruction*** efforts would not punish too harshly those Southerners who had fought for the Confederacy or those in the North who were Southern sympathizers.

Sam reflected on this awful saga of American history which had just ended. The "War Between The States" of 1861-1865 was unbelievably horrific and deadly for American citizens. Six hundred twenty thousand soldiers and an unknown number of civilians were tragically killed. One quarter of the country's male population was destroyed. Death and destruction was everywhere. Was it worth the sacrifice? Could there have been a better way to save the Union?

Both the North and the South felt they were fighting for a just cause. But was this horrible war really necessary? Perhaps this costly tragic war could have been averted if President Abraham Lincoln and Congress would have rectified the legitimate grievances of the South. They could have made the system of taxes and tariffs fairer for the southern states. And Lincoln could have honored "States Rights" as provided for in the Constitution.

Lincoln's noble and tremendous desire to keep the Union intact is understandable but his flagrant violations of the Constitution led to so much unnecessary misery and death and paved the way, as the Ronan family will see, for future presidents to systematically erode the sovereignty of the states and an individual's freedom.

Many people were left with the impression that the South rebelled mainly so they could keep the inhumane institution of slavery intact; that the North had to "preserve the Union" and that President Lincoln demanded the freeing of all the slaves." But the most common rallying call in the north was "Preserve the Union", not "Free the Slaves". In fact, Lincoln stated that if he could preserve the Union without freeing a single slave he would do that. His only concern was to keep the federation of states intact.

Yes, slavery was wrong, but that wasn't the reason Lincoln fought the Confederate States. The real reason the business and political leaders in the north were so intent on keeping the southern states in the union was a monetary concern. If they allowed the South to secede, they would not have enough money to fund government expenditures because the source--tariffs on imports to the southern ports--would not be available. In addition, tariffs raised the price of imported goods to a level where the less efficient manufacturers in the northeast could be competitive. The former Vice President John C. Calhoun aptly stated:

"The North had adopted a system of revenue and disbursements in which an undue proportion of the burden of taxation has been imposed upon the South, and an undue proportion of its proceeds appropriated to the North...the South, as the great exporting portion of the Union, has in reality paid vastly more than her due proportion of the revenue."

Lincoln's unfair bias for the North was obvious. He supported the more than tripling of the tariff percentage on goods coming into the southern ports which unfairly hurt the South. And he also was a proponent of "corporate welfare" for favored northern companies.

Abraham Lincoln- The Benevolent Dictator

In order to support his agenda, during the War, Abraham Lincoln effectively became a dictator, illegally ignoring the Constitution. He declared martial law and suspended the writ of Habeas Corpus. He imprisoned, without a trial, thousands of northern antiwar protesters even including the arrests of the mayor of Baltimore, its chief of police, a Maryland congressman and 31 state legislators. He shut down over 300 newspapers that disagreed with his war policy. He blockaded southern ports and invaded the South with troops *without* the consent of Congress as required by the Constitution. Lincoln also introduced taxation on income, which is a mild form of slavery because you are forced to work a portion of each workday without getting paid.

Yes, Abraham Lincoln saved the Union but unfortunately the result was a giant blow to Liberty and effectively the death of "States Rights". The Federal Government was now much more powerful and tyrannical. The precedent had been set. Our great Constitution was now eroding away with greater centralized government power and a growing "police state" to protect that power. Sam worried about the future of America.

Maggie and Sam's son Jefferson, who was born at the end of the war, was an extremely bright and industrious child; so much in the image of his mother and father. They were so thankful that Jeff would not have to fight in this awful war between the states.

After the ***War Between the States***, Sam began to seriously study to pass the Missour Bar exam. Abe was a great help plus the experience Sam had gotten working in the law office helped immensely.

"Maggie, now that the war has ended, and I am an American citizen, it's time for me to take the Missouri Bar Exam. Abe agrees and has made arrangements for me to go to Jefferson City to take the exam the first of the month."

"That's great Sam. Just don't buy anymore horses when you get to Jeff City. Our little forty acres can't support anymore."

"Don't worry honey. I plan to sell most of what I now have after I get them broke. But it is so enjoyable for me to raise and train the horses. Everyone has to have a hobby, you know."

Sam Passed the Bar Exam

Sam passed his bar Exam with flying colors on February 7, 1867.

"Maggie, I could open up my own law practice now but don't feel that it would be fair to Abe. Especially after all the effort he put in for me to get my law license."

"Why don't you try and buy his law practice here in Breckenridge?"

"Maybe someday, but for now, I will just continue with Abe. He will probably make me a partner in a few months anyway. That would be almost as good as owning the practice. Besides we are doing pretty well with the law office and me raising and training horses. As long as we have loyal employees at the feed company we bought last year, we will do just fine."

Of course Sam wished for his son to get a good education and attend only the best schools and maybe even become a lawyer.

The Ronan home library was quite extensive and Sam and Maggie encouraged their son to read everything possible including the U.S. Constitution.

On Jeff's twelfth birthday, 1876, Sam bought him the popular book, *The Adventures of Tom Sawyer*.

"Maggie, come and look at this. The author of the book I purchased for Jeff is Mark Twain but his real name is Samuel Clemens! I met Mr. Clemens and his brother when I first came to Breckenridge in 1861! We had a long conversation in the Breckenridge train depot while they were waiting for the tracks to be repaired near Hamilton. You know at the time I remarked that this man would someday become famous. I guess I was right. I think I will read the book as soon as Jeff finishes with it," exclaimed Sam.

Fishing On the Grand River

Sam and Jeff spent many hours fishing on the Grand River and as Jeff grew older they had long talks about politics, banking, philosophy and religion. Sam was raised as a Christian, but over time he had expanded his views on religion and came to be less of a strict Bible believer and more of a Deist like his hero, Thomas Jefferson. Sam and Maggie did not go to church regularly but did want their son to explore all religious doctrines and make up his own mind as to which he would associate with, if any. Sam and Maggie thought of themselves as *spiritual* rather than *religious*. They believed in a *Creator*, the *Ten Commandments* and the *Golden Rule* but that was about it. They believed that much of organized religion was merely based on mythology designed to keep the masses of the people ignorant and controlled and to keep the church powerful. Jeff learned a lot from his parents and had wisdom beyond his years.

Jeff Accepted at Harvard
1882

Sam was so thankful to have had the opportunity to immigrate to America and become so successful; including raising a fine son. With the help of Abe and his influence, Sam was able to get Jeff accepted at Harvard. His parents would surely miss him, and due to the long distance between Harvard and Breckenridge, Jeff would be able to return to Breckenridge for visits only seldom.

"This is indeed a great country even though Lincoln nearly destroyed it by engaging in an unnecessay war." reasoned Sam.

"We are very fortunate to be able to send Jeff to Harvard. I want him to get the formal education I didn't have," said Sam.

"Don't be silly Sam, you have a good education. You are self taught."

"That's true but his education from Harvard should make it much easier for him to succeed. A formal education doesn't guarantee success but it will at least open a few doors in the beginning to get him started."

Jeff and his friend helping Sam train some horses that will be sold to the United States Army

Sam and Maggie's new home in Breckenridge, Missouri
July 4th Celebration with family and friends

Notable Quotes and Notes:

"The powers of financial capitalism had (a) far-reaching aim, nothing less than to create a world system of financial control in private hands able to dominate the political system of each country and the economy of the world as a whole. This system was to be controlled in a feudalist fashion by the central banks of the world acting in concert, by secret agreements arrived at in frequent meetings and conferences. The apex of the systems was to be the Bank for International Settlements in Basel, Switzerland, a private bank owned and controlled by the world's central banks which were themselves private corporations. Each central bank...sought to dominate its government by its ability to control treasury loans, to manipulate foreign exchanges, to influence the level of economic activity in the country, and to influence cooperative politicians by subsequent economic rewards in the business world." **Carroll Quigley**

Part II
Jefferson Ronan
1864-1948
Personal aid
To President Wilson

Chapter Ten
Jefferson Ronan Graduates from Harvard
Magna cum Laude

Dear Mom and Poppy   *May 10, 1886*

Hope everything is going well in Breckenridge and you are both in good health. I have been burning the midnight oil as they say, getting ready for my final exams.

Dad, I never realized how important your talks were with me about our country's banking system. I remember the long talks we had about how evil and unfair our banking system was while we were out fishing on the Grand River. In all my law and economic and government classes scarcely anything was said negatively about our country's monetary system. If I even brought it up or questioned the legitimacy of our monetary system or how it works for the benefit of the bankers and to the detriment of the people, the professor would quickly cut me off and change the subject. It sure makes one not trust the academics.

If I ever hope to help revise our system of government, I will need to become a Congressman and move to Washington D.C. It is a little frightening though because I feel that if I let people know how I really want to change our monetary system, I could never get elected. The powerful banking interests would do everything in their power to keep me from getting elected and the public at large doesn't even understand the issues involved in banking.

I feel that the best course of action is to just be low key and only confide with my closest friends how I really feel until such time that a majority of the most influential legislators are ready to act in mass.

I hope you won't be disappointed but I am not sure I want to be a lawyer. I know it has been an excellent profession for you but I feel that I can do more if I can eventually get elected to the

federal legislature. Hopefully I can get a job in Washington as an
assistant to a legislator until I am ready to run for office.

*Do you believe you and Mom can come to **Cambridge** in time*
for graduation ceremonies?

Love, Jeff

Sam and Maggie enjoyed hearing from their son and promptly
sent a reply letter.

Dear Jeff   *May 20, 1886*

Glad to hear you are doing well and are prepared for your
final exams. Having a degree from Harvard will surely help you a
great deal in obtaining employment in Washington. If you need a
letter of recommendation, Abe Abercrombie said he would be
happy to oblige.

Yes, Mom and I plan to attend your graduation. It is so nice
now that we can take the train the entire way. I am getting too old
to travel by stagecoach anymore.

I got a letter yesterday from my old friend Kelsey. He is doing
very well now. He said he bought another 340 acres which now
gives him a whole section. He has 200 head of cattle, 50 hogs and
so many chickens he can't count them. We plan to visit him in
Woodbury, New Jersey after your graduation since we will
already be in the area.

Some time back you had mentioned that you had attended a
lecture at Harvard presented by a man named Albert Pike. You
failed to say much about what he talked about or if you were
inspired by his message.

I have followed Mr. Pike's career, mostly as portrayed in
'Harpers Weekly.' Did he tell you he was a Brigadier General in
the Confederate States army and quite active in the Masonic
organization? He was the "Sovereign Grand Commander of the
Scottish Rite's Southern Jurisdiction in 1859' and in 1871 wrote a
very popular book for the Masons called "Morals and Dogma of
the Ancient and Accepted Scottish Rite of Freemasonry".

Many of our founding fathers were Free Masons and their
secret organization was probably of great assistance to them in
forming a constitutional government; free from King George III of

113

England. I personally know of some fine patriotic citizens here in Breckenridge and in St. Joseph who are Masons but don't feel that it would be in your best interest to be a member of a "Secret Society" while being a representative of the people. There have been claims made that Albert Pike was a high ranking member of the Ku Klux Klan but, I have been unable to substantiate this and I personally have my doubts. In any event, I would not join any secret organization.

We hope to arrive, for your graduation, three days early so that you can give us a tour of the Harvard campus and the historic town of Cambridge. Your mom and I are so proud of you and are looking forward to participating in your graduation ceremonies.

Love, Mom and Poppy

The train from Breckenridge arrived two hours late on Sunday morning which added somewhat to Jeff's anxiety. But it was a beautiful spring morning with the birds chirping and a nice cool breeze. There was the hustle and bustle of people disembarking the train, and freight wagons loaded with boxes and suitcases that were being loaded and unloaded from the train. Jeff's fiancée, Catherine Garman was anxious to meet Jeff's parents whom she had heard so much about. Jeff could hardly wait to introduce Cathy to his parents. Cathy was a beautiful 24 year old young lady with long flowing blond hair with lots of spunk and energy.

Train Arrives from Breckenridge

"There they are Cathy!"

"I'm so nervous, "said Cathy, Jumping up and down with excitement. "Do you think they will approve of me?"

"Of course honey."

"Mom, Poppy, I'm so happy to see you! How was your trip?"

"Well, let me tell you. It was certainly better than taking a stagecoach. We even got to sleep in one of these fancy Pullman cars and not only that, this train had a dining car. It was a very comfortable trip except the train traveled a little too fast for me.

"Yes Sam, it was faster than a stage coach or the Hannibal and St. Joseph railroad, but I found it very exciting. A couple of times I was afraid we might hit a farm wagon waiting to cross the

114

tracks."

"Let me introduce my friend, Cathy Garman. She is also graduating Wednesday."

"How do you do Cathy? I've heard so much about you. Glad to make your acquaintance."

"Cathy You are even prettier than Jeff described in his letters," giving her a big hug.

"I have heard so much about you both. It is a real pleasure to finally meet both of you."

"Let me get your luggage off the railway express wagon and loaded into the buggy and then we will get you checked into the Parkside hotel. Then, if you are up to it, we will take a tour of the city," said Jeff.

"Which would you like to see first, Henry Wadsworth Longfellow's home or maybe the home of Oliver Wendell Holmes? Tomorrow you will be on your own because I have some last minute business to attend to concerning the graduation ceremonies. I think I will show you the two authors' homes first and then we will ride by the New England Glass Company, if that's acceptable to you all," said Jeff.

"That's fine with me. Whatever you suggest," said Sam.

"We have been a little worried that the glass company may be sold to a man named *Libby* and he might move it to Toledo, Ohio, but it is only a rumor. We would sure hate to lose such a huge employer," explained Jeff.

"How far do you think it is to Woodbury, New Jersey?" asked Sam.

"I would guess it is a little over three hundred miles. Don't you remember Dad? It is just a few miles south of Philadelphia."

"Oh, that's right. I remember now. I hadn't even heard of Woodbury until Kelsey told me that is where he bought his farm land."

"Say, Jeff, Are you going to show us where the Boston Tea Party took place?"

"Sure, that's only a couple of miles from here. Not really much to see though. We will go there after I show you the glass works."

115

Everyone had a great time riding around Cambridge, and Sam and Maggie got to know Jeff's friend Cathy better. Both Mom and Dad could sense that Jeff and Cathy were pretty serious and would most likely get married. Cathy, they learned, came from a well-to-do plantation owner from Kentucky. Her family had been quite fortunate during the war to have their property spared because it just so happened to be away from where most all the battles had been fought.

Harvard Graduation Ceremonies

The graduation ceremonies were spectacular and the Ronans were so happy that they had made the long trip to honor their son's achievement and to meet Cathy.

There was a huge crowd near Austin Hall. The Commencement Speaker made a one hour boring speech but everyone endured out of respect for the occasion. As the dean read off the names of Cathy Garman and Jeff Ronan, both Jeff and Cathy's parents beamed with pride.

Shortly after the ceremony, the three Ronans and Cathy boarded the train. Jeff and Cathy were going to Washington D.C. to check out the area since they might seriously consider moving there, and Sam and Maggie were going to Woodbury, New Jersey to visit Sam's longtime friend, Kelsey.

Sam thought, "This should give me a little more time to get acquainted with Cathy and find out more about her family and back ground. She certainly appears to be a very fine young lady."

"Cathy, please tell us about your family." .

"My family has owned a plantation in Kentucky since colonial days. I am an only child. My father is quite interested in politics. One of his favorite statements to people who brag about not being interested in politics is, 'You may not be interested in politics but politics is interested in you.' Each election cycle he seeks out the most qualified candidates and gives them substantial monetary support. He won't sponsor anyone who does not agree to abide by his oath to support the Constitution. He is a strict *Constitutionalist*.

116

"I certainly support his views on the Constitution. I only had a short time to talk to him at the graduation ceremonies but could tell he was very well informed in how our government operates and the dangers involved in electing the wrong people. I'm sure that much of his philosophy has rubbed off on you Cathy."

"Oh, I'm sure it has. Maybe that's why Jeff and I are so compatible. We think a lot alike. You know, just like you and Jeff," smiling.

Sam and Maggie got off the train at Woodbury, New Jersey and Jeff and Cathy continued on to Washington, DC.

"Sorry to have to leave you two.

"Maggie and I have sure enjoyed our visit and the opportunity to share in the joy of you two graduating from Law School. Whatever you do in life, I wish you much success. Our generation is counting on your generation to protect us from those unscrupulous people that only want power and money for themselves at the expense of others."

"We love you both. Maybe you can visit us soon in Breckenridge."

"Write us as soon as you get home and let us know how your trip went."

Kelsey's Farm- Woodbury New Jersey

Sam and Maggie had sent a telegram to their friend Kelsey advising him of their visit. As the train pulled into the Woodbury, New Jersey train depot, Sam could see a rather elaborate buggy with a bright colored fringed top.

"That must be him Maggie!"
As they got closer Sam said, "That's Kelsey. He looks a little older, but that's definitely him."

Kelsey extended his hand shaking Sam's hand so hard that Sam was wondering when he would let go.

"Maggie, let me introduce you to my good friend Kelsey."
"Kelsey, this is my wife Maggie."

117

"It's with great pleasure that I have finally gotten to meet you. You are just as pretty as Sam described you."

"Thank you Kelsey. Sam has told me how you met in Liverpool and the good times you had sailing on the Alhambra to America. Are you still doing some entertaining?"

"I still sing a little and play the pan flute. For the last several months, I have been learning to folk dance. Its lots of fun. Hey let me take you out to my farm. It's only three miles west of here."

"Where is your wife, Kelsey?"

"Sorry but she isn't here. I didn't get your telegram until two days after she left to visit her sick mother in Philadelphia."

"That's too bad Kelsey. I hope her mother gets better."

The three mile buggy ride gave Sam and Kelsey time to talk over old times. It was obvious that Kelsey didn't want to talk about his experience in the war. Sam knew that Kelsey was devastated when his good friend Civil War buddy, Charley Gamble had died. Also he felt bad for the great hardships that the Union troops made for the innocent southern farm families by taking their food and livestock knowing that they would most likely die when winter set in.

The Ronans were quite impressed with Kelsey's farm. He was farming several hundred acres and had four hired farm hands to help.

"Have you ever thought about going back to Dublin for a visit?" said Kelsey.

"No, I think it would be too emotional for me. My Aunt and Uncle passed away a few years ago and I don't have any other close relatives to visit."

"That's pretty much the same story with me. My parents also died before they could come to America. What's really sad is that now, I could afford to pay their passage."

Everyone had a good visit but it was now time to get back on the train and make the long journey back to Missouri.

118

Chapter Eleven
Jeff and Cathy's Home In Washington D.C
June 10, 1886

Living in Washington D.C. was quite an experience for Jeff and Cathy. It was a city like no other, established by the Constitution of the United States to serve as the nation's capital. This indeed was a place of many different personalities; members of Congress from every state, thousands of government workers, foreign emissaries, petitioners and of course protestors. Yes, a perfect place for Jeff Ronan to start his political career.

Finding a House

With the help of Cathy's well-to-do father, Jeff and Cathy were able to afford a nice house near the Capitol. They chose the LeDroit Park area which is a neighborhood immediately southeast of Howard University. LeDroit Park was one of the first suburbs of Washington. Cathy was a little hesitant to live so close to the University because it was primarily attended by the Negroes.

"Cathy, I have never been plagued by prejudices against the Negroes, thanks to my mother. Once we were traveling to St. Joe from Breckenridge on the train to do some shopping. Our rail car was so full; several people had to stand up. My mother spotted an elderly Negro lady and had me get up and give her my seat. It is something I will never forget; the looks of disgust from the other white passengers are still fresh in my mind. The point is that my mother, through this one small act of kindness, gave me a gift that will last me a lifetime. Unlike many people, I am not burdened with prejudice and the mistaken feeling that I am better than people of other colors and races. We all have the same God."

No Race Prejudice for Me

Jeff assured Cathy that living in this neighborhood would be fine and if he were to be involved in politics, he couldn't afford to be recognized as someone to harbor prejudices against Negroes,

Indians or even the Jews. Jeff's father Samuel had a debt of gratitude to his Jewish benefactor Abe Abercrombie, who had assisted him greatly in becoming a lawyer and even made him a partner in his law firm in Breckenridge. Jeff further explained that as a child growing up, he had both a black playmate and an Indian playmate who were still his close friends. One of these friends was a Negro boy, William Ballew, who was two years older than Jeff and lived in Chillicothe, Missouri. Billy's grandfather, Charlie Ballew, had been a slave belonging to John Conway Ballew but was freed when his master died. Billy's father worked for the railroad and visited Breckenridge about three times a year on the work crews, repairing and installing new track in the area between Breckenridge, Utica and Chillicothe. The whole family would stay a couple of months in Josh's vacant log cabin north of town. The hotel refused to rent them a room which the Ronan's found disgusting. Jeff truly believed that the only difference between the races was their skin color. The Negroes and Indians only appeared to be different because they had not had the same opportunities that the white man had.

Of course Jeff and Cathy could not move into their new house until they were married. What would their friends and neighbors think? The wedding date was set for August 5, 1886. Jeff was able to find a small apartment and Cathy decided to live alone in their new house with the maid until she and Jeff were married.

"I sure hope Mom and Dad are up to another trip. It is a long way from Breckenridge to Washington D.C.," thought Jeff. But of course their wedding was an important event that he knew his parents wouldn't want to miss.

Dear Mom and Poppy,   *July 5, 1886*

As you probably expected, Cathy and I are getting married. We sure hope you can come to Washington. I know you don't mind travelling so much when you can travel by train.
Cathy's father gave us a nice house for a wedding present. Cathy is living there by herself now and I will join her after the wedding. It is a beautiful house with three bed rooms, a nice large

parlor, a library and even has indoor toilet facilities. I know Dad, you had often said you wouldn't want a toilet inside the house close to where you ate, but this is really nice. I think you will approve when you see it. It is even hooked to a sewer and is very clean looking.

Our property is too small for a horse and barn so we won't have our own buggy but that is no problem because Washington has street cars running throughout the entire city. I can walk one and a half blocks and catch a street car to go anywhere in the city.

I have applied for a job as an assistant to Senator Cole from Ohio and I am scheduled to go back for a second interview next Monday.

How does this year's corn look in Breckenridge? The weather has been pretty dry here so not sure how it will affect their yield.

Hope to see you soon.

Love, Jeff and Cathy

Sam wrote Jeff immediately.

"Son, Congratulations! Your mother and I send loving wishes for your wedding. However, we do not feel we can make another trip so soon after our trip east for your graduation. My body is fighting me now, probably from my injuries of several years ago when I was involved in the train wreck. I'm sure I'll feel better soon but don't think another trip so soon would be wise. Your mother is fine and sends you both her love as do I. Lovingly, your Poppy.

"It's too bad your folks can't come to our wedding."

"Maybe we can go visit them next summer in Breckenridge."

Wedding

Jeff and Cathy's wedding was a glorious affair held near Cathy's home town of Lexington, Kentucky.

"Looks like the whole town was there!" Remarked Jeff.

"Everyone except Mom and Poppy, sadly to say. But hopefully we can take a trip back to see them soon in

121

Breckenridge. It's been a wonderful day Cathy. Now I'm looking forward to a long and happy life for us and for all our little ones in Washington, DC."

"Did I tell you that I am meeting Senator Coles' staff tomorrow about a job? Your father must have put in a good word for me. If hired, I will only be acting as a glorified intern but I should be able to advance from there. At least I will have the camel's nose under the tent!"

"That sounds great Honey!"

Jeff caught the trolley the following morning.

"Excuse me Driver. Will this trolley take me to the Capitol Building?"

"Yes Sir. We should be there in about 30 minutes, depending on traffic."

Congressman Cole's Office

"May I help you Sir?"

"Yes, I'm looking for Congressman Coles' office."

"I believe he is in the Committee Room right now on the second floor. Please follow me."

Jeff and the clerk climbed the stairs and passed several rooms before finding the committee room.

"Are you Jefferson Ronan?" asked Senator Cole's secretary.

"Why yes, I am Jefferson Ronan."

"We were expecting you. Follow me Sir."

The secretary led Jeff through a maze of desks and commotion of loud noise and smoke filled spaces of other senators sharing the small space in the Committee Room.

"You must be Mr. Garman's son in law. He has highly recommended you to be an intern for me. Sorry for such a small crowded office. We do have plans in the works to build a bigger House and Senate Chamber."

"Don't worry about it Senator. I'm just happy to be considered for this job."

"I assume you have political beliefs similar to your father-in-law?"

"Yes Sir. I'm a strong constitutionalist and an isolationist when it comes to international affairs. I support the Monroe Doctrine 100%. My great American heroes are Thomas Jefferson, Benjamin Franklin, Andrew Jackson, and James Monroe."

The *Monroe Doctrine* was a U.S. Foreign policy regarding domination of the American Continent in 1823. It stated that further efforts by European nations to colonize land or interfere with states in North or South America would be viewed as acts of aggression, requiring U.S. Intervention. Also the doctrine noted that the United States would neither interfere with existing European colonies nor meddle in the internal concerns of European countries.

"Looks like we will get along just fine. You've got the job if you still want it. Our views are pretty much the same. Will you be able to start next Monday? Your first task will be for you to write a speech for me to address a group of women pushing for a constitutional amendment allowing women to vote. How do you feel about women voting?"

"Sooner or later the U.S. will have to address this issue. Women are beginning to get their voting rights in countries all over the world. It's only natural to believe that the U.S. will follow suit."

"That's true, Jeff, but I'm not sure that my colleagues are ready to pass a constitutional amendment for women's voting rights. Keep that in mind when you write the speech. We want to make it appear that we support both sides." (Laughing)

"I will be here Monday morning Senator. Eight o'clock sharp."

This was Jeff's first job and he so much wanted to succeed that he decided to keep most of his ideas about banking to himself; at least for the time being. Cathy cheerfully accepted her role as homemaker and was looking forward to having children.

Washington Hospital- September 10, 1893

The doctor entered the waiting room to tell Jeff he was the father of an adorable 8 pound baby girl.

"Is everything alright? How is my wife doing?"

"Everything is fine. Have you chosen a name for your daughter?"

"If it had been a boy we would have called him Caleb. But since it is a girl, we will call her Amanda Suzanne."

"Why don't you go into the recovery room now. I believe your wife wants to introduce you to that little girl Amanda Suzanne."

"Well what do you think about our adorable little girl? Isn't she beautiful? She looks just like your mother. I just wish she could talk to us now."

"What do you mean; you wish she could talk now? You know that's impossible."

"Of course, silly, but if she could talk now she might be able to tell us where she came from and maybe even why she is here. But by the time she learns to talk she will have forgotten all of that. Especially with all the new thoughts and experiences interfering with her past thoughts."

"You didn't tell the doctor that you wished our baby could talk now, did you?"

"Of course not. You don't think I want the doctor to think I'm crazy!"

"Phew! You had me a little worried for a minute. I thought you must still be under the influence of the anesthetic."

"Jeff, I hope you will understand this, but I don't think I could ever go through this again. One child will be enough, don't you agree? You have no idea what child birth is like."

"Just give it some time honey. You will feel better soon. You may change your mind. Now can I hold our new daughter?"

124

Jeff and Cathy became very well known in Washington; not only professionally but also socially. Working for a senator provided Jeff with many opportunities to meet highly influential people. His assistance to the senator in writing bills and researching information concerning the many committees that the senator was involved in helped prepare Jeff for a job that he hoped to get in the White House. Cathy and Jeff were able to host several parties at their home each year.

Religious Views on Usury

Jeff was interested in learning about all American institutions; law, politics and history, but had a particular interest in learning about money and banking. For some time Jeff had become concerned with the American banking system and the manner in which not only physical money (coins) was created but also paper money with its associated interest payments. Jeff was also familiar with the religious views expounded in the Bible on money and the evilness of 'Usury' (Interest).

"The love of money is the root of all evil." (1 Tim. 6:10)
"If thou lend money to any of my people that is poor by thee, thou shalt not be to him as a usurer, neither shalt thou lay upon him usury." **Exodus 22:25**
Jeff had read in the King James Bible- *Unto a stranger thou mayest lend upon usury; but unto thy brother thou shalt not lend upon usury....*Jeff thought to himself, ' Is the Bible saying that it is acceptable for a Jew to charge interest to a Gentile but not a fellow Jew?' **Deuteronomy 23:20**

"It seems like banks would have to charge some interest for risking their own money knowing that a certain percentage of the loans will not ever be paid back," said Cathy..
"Alright, I agree that they should be allowed to charge a fair interest rate but only if it is their own money."
"I don't understand. Why wouldn't it be their own money that they would be loaning?"
"Have you ever heard of the 'Goldsmiths?'"

125

Goldsmiths

"What's a Goldsmith?"

"In the Middle Ages and probably even earlier, a goldsmith was a metalworker who specialized in working with gold and other precious metals. In Europe, goldsmiths performed many of the functions we now regard as part of banking; storage and lending but usually restrained from lending at interest, which was regarded as usury. One important issue is how the goldsmiths sometimes cheated their customers. Let's say a man brought in 20 ounces of gold for the goldsmith to keep in safe-storage. The goldsmith would give his customer a paper receipt so the customer could redeem his gold sometime in the future. The customer might be several miles from town, buying cattle, and use this receipt as a form of money. Rather than going all the way back to town to get the gold, he would just give the receipt to the man selling the cattle who could redeem the gold next time he was in town or he could pass the receipt along to someone else that he owed money to."

"I don't see anything wrong with that."

"The problem arises when the Goldsmith prints more gold receipts than he has on deposit in his vaults. This creates great wealth for the Goldsmith but if everyone tries to withdraw their gold at the same time, the goldsmith (bank) is in big trouble. This is exactly the kind of thing I fear will happen when private banks are in charge of our country's banking system."

"A lot of what I just told you was what my dad taught me while I was growing up in Breckenridge. He said Mayer Amschel Rothschild, the Jewish patriarch of the powerful Rothschild banking dynasty who lived in the mid-1700s had once said, "Give me control of a nation's money and I care not who makes its laws." This is a really scary thought. We must be very vigilant because I fear that the bankers will try to establish another Central Bank in America for their benefit at the expense of the common man."

Jeff knew that from 1776 through the present, there had been an ongoing battle between the politicians like Alexander Hamilton who supported a privately owned central bank being in control of our country's monetary system versus having the federal government in control as provided for in the Constitution. The Constitution specifically gives the Federal government the power to coin money; not a private bank, especially one controlled by European bankers. Jeff kept thinking, 'The U.S. won the wars with England, both in 1776 and in 1812, but lost the battle to maintain its sovereignty when Alexander Hamilton and the Federalists set up a central bank controlled by the European bankers instead of by the people.'

Jeff came to the realization that a nation can be conquered by economic conquest much more efficiently than by war. It might not be conquered by an invading army but rather stealthily by international bankers. It takes place *without* the use of visible force or coercion, so that the victims do not realize they have been conquered. A privately owned Central Bank controlled by international banking cartels and authorized by the government collects not only unnecessay interest from the people but also benefits immensely from being allowed to make use of *Fractional Reserve Banking*. Fractional Reserve Banking creates Credit, not actual paper money which still increases inflation which erodes the purchasing power of the citizens' existing dollars.

Jeff realized that this was a serious matter and also knew that there were powerful forces constantly trying to use the banking system as a means to obtain not only wealth but also power. It would be almost impossible to change and it could be dangerous.These powerful bankers would do almost anything, including assassinations, to protect their interests. They even have the power to intentionally cause a wide spread depression by limiting the money supply. President Andrew Jackson apparantly experienced the wrath of the bankers when an attempt was made on his life-most likely for not renewing the charter of the private Central bank. Jackson, survived the assassenation attempt, and later when he died, inscribed on his tombstone was what he felt was his greatest accomplishment: *I killed the Bank.*

Jeff was aware that his father had briefly discussed the country's banking system with his boss Abe but got the impression that Abe disagreed with him. Jeff knew that his father had been such a great friend of Abe that he did not want to pursue the subject any furthur. His father didn't want to believe that Abe's position on banking had anything to do with the fact he was Jewish.

This really bothered Jeff because he understood this awesome power led to corruption and the confiscation of the citizens' wealth. He also knew that from the 1820's through the 1830's, the Rothschild's became involved in the financial affairs of the United States. Through their agent, Nicholas Biddle, they attempted to defeat Andrew Jackson's move to abolish the control of the international bankers. Jackson struck back by vetoing the move to renew the charter of the "Bank of the United States" which was a central bank controlled by the international bankers. Jackson won in 1836 and the bank went out of business. The Rothschild's had lost the first round. Many people didn't believe it was a coincidence that there was an assassination attempt on Andrew Jackson's life after the Bank Charter was not renewed.

Hospital waiting room 1908

Jeff paced back and forth. The doctor came out to announce that Jeff was the father of a second baby girl. Jeff went in and kissed Cathy and proceeded to hold baby Sarah Jane, rocking her back and forth, in his arms.

Cathy and Jeff couldn't be more pleased with their new baby daughter as was Amanda with her new baby sister. "I feel that our family is now complete," sighed Cathy in ecstasy. "It's the four of us now, the perfect family." Of course Jeff wholeheartedly agreed.

However, It wasn't long before the happy family of four had to regroup as they added child number three to their perfect group. Matthew Charles Ronan was born on September 12, 1908. "OK, now we are a perfect family of five! Nothing in the world could be better," exclaimed Jeff enthusiastically.

Chapter Twelve
Woodrow Wilson Elected President

President Woodrow Wilson was elected President of the United States in 1912 and took office in March of 1913. Jeff wondered if his new president was a 'Nationalist' or 'Internationalist.' Time would tell.

Again, Jeff's father-in-law had put in a good word about Jeff with his old college friend Woodrow Wilson, the new president. Both had gone to Princeton together, and even though they had not always agreed politically, had become good friends.

Jeff nervously walked up the steps of the White House to meet with the newly elected president. He wasn't sure that President Wilson was the right man to be president but was willing to hold off passing judgment. It was unclear to him as to how the new president felt about the country's banking system. There were rumors that Wilson was following orders from his advisor, Colonel House, who was a known globalist and against American sovereignty.

Jeff Meets With President Wilson

"Good morning. You must be the person that was recommended to be one of my aids," said President Wilson."

"Yes Mr. President. My name is Jefferson Ronan. My father in law sent you a letter of introduction a few weeks ago. I have a copy here if you would like to read it."

"No that's fine. I have already read it. It is quite impressive except that you went to Harvard instead of Princeton." The President laughed and said, "I won't hold that against you though. Harvard is almost as good as Princeton," smiled the President. "I see you had a four point grade average while at Harvard and then worked for Congressman Cole for several years. Very impressive."

"Thank you Mr. President. I am honored to be considered for this position."

"Are you a Democrat or a Republican?"

"I was afraid you would ask that. Actually I usually vote Republican but I try to vote for the man and his platform rather than the party," explained Jeff.

"That's a good honest answer. I like that. I understand from your father-in-law that you are quite opinionated on the banking issue."

"I assure you that I won't let my banking ideology interfere with our relationship."

"No. No. That's quite all right. I want all the information I can get, as long as it is respectful information (smiling). As it just so happens, I am currently involved with a committee on our country's monetary system. Particularly how we can avert another 1907 banking collapse."

"I did quite a bit of research in this area for Senator Cole."

"Just because we may not always agree, please feel comfortable to discuss any issue with me. I want to hear both sides of all issues, not just the side the lobbyists are pushing. Do some more research on the banking issues because we will be discussing how to avert another banking collapse next week."

"Does that mean I have the job Mr. President?"

"If you still want it."

"Of course. When do I start?"

"Monday morning 9 o'clock."

"That suits me. I'll be here."

Jeff left the office of the President and returned home to share the exciting news with his family.

"How was your appointment with President Wilson?"

"I can hardly believe it. I was accepted as an aid and advisor to the President."

"There is only one problem though, I mean issue," said Jeff.

"My first assignment involves the banking issue and you all know how opinionated I am on that."

"Just remember honey. Don't bring up the Bible quotes denouncing "Usury". That would surely be an insult to the Jewish bankers and politicians present."

"Oh, I won't do that. But it looks like there is a move to

130

completely revise our country's monetary system with another private Central Bank, like the ones we got rid of in the past. It's almost as if Alexander Hamilton has been reborn. Hopefully, I can exert some influence in stopping this absurd, unconstitutional banking movement that enriches the elite at the expense of the people."

"I'm sure it will all work out for the best. Don't you think the President will listen to you?"

" I'm not so sure honey. I think he listens too much to his advisor, Colonel House. We are having another meeting next week. Time will tell."

Colonel Edward Mandell House

As time went on, Jeff could see that he was at times at odds with not only the president but most of his advisers; especially Colonel Edward Mandell House. It was sometimes hard to know how far he could go and not jeopardize the position he had worked so hard to attain. He would need to learn how to express his opinions in such a way as to possibly influence those in attendance and at the same time to not bring undo attention to himself.

He Who Asks the Questions Controls the Conversation

Jeff had learned a technique while working for Senator Cole that had served him quite well. Instead of trying to do all the talking and putting his foot in his mouth, he learned to ask questions and then use the answers to tailor his further remarks. Once someone asked Jeff what his religious persuasion was. Instead of saying he was an agnostic, he replied, "Why do you ask?"

Their answer was, "Well I am a Christian and I was hoping we had the same values." So instead of saying he was an agnostic he replied that he was a *Deist* and believed the basic teachings of Jesus were good to follow. By asking the question first before replying gave him the additional advantage of tailoring his answer in a more positive and less combative way. Sam had discovered an important concept. *Those who ask the questions control the conversation.*

President Wilson, being a Democrat, was able to persuade the Democrat Congress to pass major progressive reforms. One of the goals of the progressive movement was to try to eliminate corruption from the *political machines* and bosses. Many of them supported *prohibition* of alcohol so they could destroy the political power of local bosses. Others attempted to achieve efficiency by identifying old ways that needed modernizing and replacing them with modern scientific solutions. They adopted numerous policies of change, some good and some bad, but the one having the greatest negative impact on the citizens of the United States was the passage of the Federal Reserve Act in 1913 and the 16th amendment allowing an income tax to be collected on a person's wages.

Jeff was convinced that both the Federal Reserve Act and the 16th Amendment were a big mistake. It was more about the bankers taking complete control of America for their personal profit than it was for solving the *boom and bust* business cycle and establishing sound money policies. Jeff could see that this was the biggest scam in the history of the United States but could not influence Colonel House or the President enough to block the passage of what he thought were unconstitutional acts.

Monetary Suicide

The United States government was embarking on a course of monetary suicide. Jeff had always reasoned that the government expenses should be paid for by *transparent taxes* and not from hidden *debt financing* that was to be available with the Federal Reserve System and ultimately would cause inflation of enormous proportions. Worse yet, the controllers of the government, *Banksters* as he privately referred to them, could finance their profitable wars at the expense of the people without them even knowing what was happening until it was too late. All the bankers had to do was print up the money and collect interest which then eroded away the value of the citizens' existing money.

Jeff thought, 'This is so depressing; but what can I do?' Somewhat later, Jeff discovered that Colonel House and some of House's college classmates had become members of the Cecil Rhodes Round Table group. The Round Table Group, a secret society, had four pet projects; (1) a graduated income tax, (2) a private central bank, (3) creation of a Central Intelligence Agency, and (4) a world governing body. Unfortunately for most of the committee members, they did not know that Colonel House had written anonymously, in 1912, a novel entitled *Philip Dru: Administrator.* It was a fictional story set in 1920-1935 involving an American diplomat, politician and presidential foreign policy advisor who leads the democratic western U.S. in a civil war against the plutocratic East, and becomes the dictator of America. Dru, acting as dictator, enacts a series of reforms that resemble the Bull Moose platform of 1912 and then vanishes. The question was, was this just a fictitious novel or an actual plan for the future overthrow of the U.S. government led by Colonel House and orchestrated by the Vatican? Both Jeff and President Wilson's wife shared their suspicions of Colonel House as to what his true agenda entailed. It appeared that Colonel House had complete control over the President, possibly because of secret information about the President that he didn't want exposed. There were rumors that President Wilson was being blackmailed.

Jeff did find some support for his banking ideas with Congressman Louis Thomas McFadden. Congressman McFadden had been elected as a Republican Representative to the Sixty Fourth Congress and to the nine succeeding Congresses. He had worked for the First National Bank in Canton, Pennsylvania in 1892 and in 1899 was made a cashier and was to become President of the bank in 1916.

In 1927 he managed to get passed, the *McFadden Act of 1927* which limited the Federal Branch Banks to the city in which the main branch operated. This gave state chartered banks competitive equality, but his greatest accomplishment was his exposure of the Federal Reserve's true agenda.

Congressman McFadden claimed that the Federal Reserve which was created in 1913 was run by European banking interests who conspired to economically control the United States. He claimed that the Wall Street Bankers funded the Russian Bolshevik Revolution in 1917 through the United States Federal Reserve system and the European Central Banks.

President Wilson, Jeff Ronan and ten committee members met to discuss the new banking proposals. President Wilson began:

1907 Banking Panic

"You all know why we are here today. The Banking Panic of 1907 was a United States financial crisis. Starting in mid-October of that year, the New York Stock Exchange fell almost 50% resulting in panic. Remember the country was already in an economic recession. There were numerous runs on the banks throughout the nation. Many banks and businesses were forced to declare bankruptcy.

The Knickerbocker Trust Company of New York City collapsed causing vast numbers of people to withdraw deposits from their regional banks.

Gentlemen, with the support of our Democrat controlled Congress; this administration can ensure that a banking crisis will not happen again. Banking reform must be our top priority."

"Remember Mr. President that the panic could have been worse if not for the intervention of banking financier J. P. Morgan who pledged large sums of his own money, and convinced other New York bankers to do the same, to shore up the banking system. I propose that we once again establish a private Central Bank to insure that these panics don't keep occurring," explained one of the Committeemen.

"I certainly don't agree with that. A private Central Bank that controls our nation's monetary system is extremely profitable for the International Bankers but a disaster for the American public. Remember, President Andrew Jackson in 1834 refused to renew the Central Banks charter. Didn't he refer to the Bankers as a Den of Vipers? In fact, I have heard that he had inscribed on his tombstone, "I killed the Bank." There was a failed assassination attempt on Jackson, probably by the banker's agents. Doesn't that expose their true evilness? I certainly don't want to go down that road again," claimed another committeeman.

"Could I interject something here Mr. President?"

"Gladly Mr. Ronan. What do you think?"

The Federal Government, not a Private Bank, has the Power and Authority to Coin Money

"The Constitution says that the Federal Government, not a private bank, has the power and authority to coin money. Article 1 Section 8. Can't that be interpreted as requiring our money to be gold or silver or paper money backed by gold and silver? Do we really want to ignore the Constitution and allow a private bank to be in control of our monetary system?"

"Mr. Ronan, we are not talking about allowing a private bank to issue paper money that is not redeemable in gold or silver."

"That may be true now but what about in the future? If we disallow a central bank to control our money supply now, we will not need to address this issue in the future. Let's not create unnecessary problems. This whole issue is more about the bankers taking complete control of America's monetary system for their personal profit than it is for solving the boom and bust business cycle and establishing sound money policies. In my opinion, this would be the biggest fraud perpetrated against the American people in the history of our country."

"Mr. Ronan, you have made some good points, but are you all aware that there is a push to establish a central bank that will be called The Federal Reserve? Some of Mr. Ronan's concerns may be diminished somewhat because, it requires that the president appoint the board members and that any profits the bank realizes, after expenses, will be returned to the tax payers."

"I'm sorry Mr. President but I, like President Jackson, don't trust these bankers nor those pushing for the adoption of a Central Bank. In my opinion they are a bunch of scamps."

"Mr. Ronan, just what is a scamp?. I'm assuming it's not

good," laughing.

"A scamp is a highway robber or swindler."

"OK Gentlemen. That's enough for today. Thank you all for sharing your views. Let's meet again next week at this same time after we have had time to let some of this digest."

A little disappointed that he didn't seem to have much influence on the banking issue, Jeff returned home to discuss this troubling day with his wife Cathy.

They Favor Allowing a Private Central Bank to Control our Nation's Money Supply

"How was your committee meeting dear? Was it all about banking as you suspected?"

"Yes, I'm afraid it was. I don't know why we even had a meeting to discuss it. It seems as if the President and the majority of the committee members are in favor of allowing a private Central Bank to control our nation's money supply. To heck with the constitution or what's in the best interest of the people!"

"I'm sorry honey. I know you were hoping to give enough reasons not to allow this to happen. It sounds like they didn't even listen."

"No, they listened with respect but it was as if their minds were already made up to once again establish a private central bank. It made me wonder if maybe the President was being black mailed in some manner to get him to approve of this crazy unconstitutional banking reform. I think the other cabinet members are influenced by the large donations that were given them to get elected. It must be something like this because they must know it is wrong to give a private bank the authority to control our nation's monetary system. It's very depressing."

"Well, at least you presented your case. Let's have supper. We can talk more about this later. I cooked your favorite meal; catfish stew."

"Thanks honey. Maybe I should have a glass of wine or maybe several glasses of wine. I need to relax some."

" Let's talk about it some more tomorrow after you get a good night's rest. Things will probably look different tomorrow."

"I've got an idea. I'm going to call on my good friend Frank Templeton that I worked with in Congressman Cole's office and get his take on all this. It all seems pretty sinister."

Jeff got dressed early in the morning in anticipation of meeting with Frank Templeton at Congressman Cole's Office.

"Cathy, did they get our telephone repaired yesterday? I would like to call Frank from home. Maybe he can meet with me today."

"Oh yes, I forgot to tell you. The wire was broken where a tree limb fell on it. Also they said we needed a new battery. It's working now."

"Hello, Central. I would like to place a call to a Mr. Frank Templeton on Jefferson Street here in Washington DC."

"Hello, Frank. This is Jeff Ronan. Sorry to bother you so early in the morning but I was wondering if I could set up a meeting with you this morning at your office. I would greatly appreciate this."

"I have a meeting at ten so could you make it about 8:30?"

"That would be fine," replied Jeff.

" What's this all about?"

"I'd rather not talk on the telephone."

"All right then. I'll see you at 8:30."

Jeff finished getting ready and left the house to catch an early morning trolley.

"I sure appreciate your meeting with me on such short notice Frank."

"Glad to do it. Say, how is your job working out with the President?"

"The job is great but it is somewhat depressing to be so close to the President and have such little influence on what happens."

"Just remember, you are an advisor and not the President of the United States," chuckling.

" Of course, I know that, but the President is about to vote for something called the Federal Reserve Act which is nothing more than another attempt to allow privately owned central banks to control our nations monetary system. Are you aware of this?"

"I'm afraid I am."

"Well, what do you think of it? Is there any part of it that will be good for our country? I feel like there is something very sinister going on here. The President listened to my objections but it seemed like he and the rest had already decided to adopt this private bank they call the Federal Reserve."

"I agree with you that it will harm our country; maybe not so much now but surely in the future; as this Federal Reserve monster expands its slimy tentacles. And you are absolutely correct, it's sinister."

"Why do you agree it is sinister?"

"I hesitate to go into any detail. You know these bankers are powerful people and may harm anyone who gets in their way. I will tell you what I know about this but please don't divulge what I am about to tell you or mention my name in any connection to the banking reform going on right now."

"Of course Frank, you can count on that. I'm just curious as to what is really happening here."

Bankers Secret Meeting on Jekyll Island in 1910

"The banking bill they are considering today has been under development now for quite some time. In November of 1910, the international bankers secretly met on Jekyll Island off the coast of Georgia. This secret meeting was attended by investment banker Paul Warburg, Treasury official Abram Piatt Andrew, Senator Nelson Aldrich, and others."

"I'm not familiar with Paul Warburg."

"Paul Warburg was born in Hamburg, Germany, to the Warburg family, a Jewish banking dynasty with origins in Venice. He has a great deal of influence in this country; probably even more than President Wilson! This secret meeting was organized by financiers and bankers whose main goal was to once again install a private Central Bank in America to enrich themselves at the public's expense. You know, like the one whose charter President

Jackson refused to renew. These banking shysters had pretty well succeeded in installing their Central Banking system in the rest of the world. They didn't think the public would accept a plan created by the bankers, so they took extraordinary efforts to keep the meeting, set up by J. P. Morgan, a secret. They supposedly met in the middle of the night at the train station posing as Duck Hunters. They even went to the trouble to bring their shotguns. They were instructed to use only first names or aliases and tell others that they were on a duck hunting trip."

"I can see why they wanted to keep their meeting a secret. So the Federal Reserve Act they will try to pass will appear to be developed by the Senate but actually the Bankers are the ones who actually wrote the bill to their liking. This is very upsetting!"

"I would suggest that you not let on that you know about this secret meeting and just stay out of the limelight. As you know, the Aldridge Bill didn't pass but they then cleverly introduced the Owen-Glass Federal Reserve Act. It was basically the same as the Aldridge Bill but with minor additions and deletions and by moving the paragraphs around a bit no one seemed to notice. Then the bankers had two Democrats sponsor the bill and then the group set out to say they were against the Bill which made the ignorant public to believe, 'If the Bankers are against it, the Bill must be good.' Jeff, this bill will most likely pass and anyone opposing it could have their political career put in jeopardy or even worse..." (Grimacing)

The Sinking of the Titanic or was it the Sister Ship Olympia

"Don't worry Frank. I won't repeat what you have told me.

"One more thing Jeff. Do you recall that there were three wealthy men that purportedly were against another Central Bank and they died with the sinking of the Titanic last year? They were Benjamin Guggenheim, Isa Strauss and Jacob Astor IV. Some of the wealthiest men in the world. Did you know that JP Morgan funded the building of the Titanic and was booked on the voyage but canceled at the last minute?"

139

"Never mind. I shouldn't have even mentioned that. I've got another meeting to attend. It was nice seeing you again Jeff. Be careful."

"Wait just a minute Frank! Are you insinuating that J. P. Morgan sunk the Titanic on purpose killing nearly 1500 people to get rid of these three men who might have been against the adoption of a privately owned Federal Reserve Bank?"

"Not exactly. It is a little more complicated than that. You see the sister ship to the Titanic, the Olympia, which by the way looked almost identical to the Titanic had been involved in two collisions that did such extensive damage that it couldn't be economically repaired. Plus the insurance company would not cover the cost of repairs because the English government had claimed that it was the Olympic ship that was at fault and not the British war ship that had struck her."

"I realize that a lot of people didn't like J.P Morgan and saw him as a ruthless banker, but I can't believe that he intentionally killed all these people so he could collect the insurance on the Olympic masquerading as the Titanic."

"Well, some believe that the killing of 1500 people had not been part of the original plan. Another ship, the Carpathia, was supposed to arrive in time to rescue the people on the Titanic. To make it even more suspicious, the Carpathia didn't have any passengers or cargo except for life boats, blankets and other rescue supplies. For some reason the Carpathia didn't get to the sinking Titanic in time to save everyone. If I remember correctly, only 200 were rescued and about 1500 died."

"I'm still having a difficult time believing that even someone like J. P. Morgan could have done such a deplorable thing. Thanks Frank. You have been very helpful. Ring me up sometime and bring your wife over for supper. My wife and I would love to have you visit us."

" I'll sure do that Jeff. Good luck."

Jeff didn't have much to say the remainder of the day. Fortunately there weren't any meetings scheduled so he had time to digest what Frank had told him about J. P. Morgan and Jekyll Island. Just how much of this should he share with Cathy?

"How did your meeting go with Frank dear?"

"It was fine."

"You sure don't sound very optimistic! What's wrong?"

"You wouldn't believe all that he told me. It looks like it's all over with. The United States government is to once again have its third privately owned Central Bank and it will control our nation's monetary system. Even though it is unconstitutional, they will be permitted to print our country's paper money and loan it to the government charging interest. I feel like such a failure. I can't do anything about it. I can't even express my own opinions on this issue without jeopardizing my political career or maybe even something worse."

"What do you mean something worse? You seem worried honey."

We are Becoming Slaves

"I'm sorry I don't even want to talk about it. Oh, one more thing. The bankers want to pass a Constitutional amendment to allow the Federal Government to collect a tax on the common man's income. You know, someone must pay for the banker's interest that they will be charging. This will make slaves out of the American people!"

"Why would this make us slaves? I don't understand your reasoning. It's just a tax."

"Well, the working man will need to work a certain number of hours each day just to pay this additional tax. In other words he will be working for free to pay the tax. Isn't that one definition of slavery? Working without being paid? But everything will be fine they say because this tax will be extremely small and will apply to only the wealthy. Right, but the camel's nose will already be under the tent. They will figure out some way to gradually increase the tax and make it apply to everyone."

"You did your best honey. At least you have exposed the evils of our country's monetary system. Others in the future will most likely correct it, just like President Andrew Jackson did."

"I sure hope you are right Cathy."

141

𝕮𝖍𝖊 𝖂𝖆𝖘𝖍𝖎𝖓𝖌𝖙𝖔𝖓 𝕲𝖑𝖔𝖇𝖊

December 23, 1913

PRESIDENT'S SIGNATURE ENACTS CURRENCY LAW

Wilson declares it the first of series of constructive acts to aid business.

Makes Speech to a group of Democratic Leaders.

Conference Report Adopted in Senate by a vote of 43 to 25.

Banks all over the country hasten to enter Federal System.

Gov. Elect Walsh calls passage of Bill A Fine Christmas Present.

WILSON SEES DAWN OF NEW ERA IN BUSINESS

Wilson's New Freedom Underwood Tariff Con't on page 7 Sect. E

Substantially reduced Import Fees and graduated Income Tax adopted.

President Harding Dies- Replaced by Calvin Coolidge

Jeff continued to do his job as WWI came to a close and he continued working in the White House as Harding replaced Wilson as President. Harding died in office in 1923 and was replaced by Calvin Coolidge.

1916
Matthew Ronan and father Jefferson.

Samuel Ronan Died
1923

Jeff arrived home from work a cold and dreary day late in December to be confronted with the sad news that his father, Samuel Ronan, in Breckenridge, Missouri had passed away. Cathy greeted Jeff at the door with tears in her eyes.

"What's the matter dear?"

"I just got off the phone with your mother. She said your father died last night in his sleep. They believe it was a heart attack."

(Sniffling holding back his tears) "You know, I have been expecting this but didn't want to think it would ever happen. I know he has had health problems ever since he nearly died in the train wreck."

"Your mom said the funeral will be Friday, four days from now. Do you think we can get train tickets and get to Breckenridge by Friday?"

" I'm sure we can. I'll get them first thing in the morning. You know no matter how old you are, until your parents die, you are still your parents little boy or girl. This is a big transition in my life. I am now the adult member of our family. It's a very strange feeling."

Jeff and Cathy and their three children boarded the train to Breckenridge, Missouri to attend the funeral and help Maggie get her affairs in order. It was extremely cold and a light snow was falling as the train left Washington. It was a sad trip for Jeff and he barely talked to Cathy and the children the entire trip. The clicking sound of the train wheels and the cold snowy view out the train window seemed to hypnotize the whole Ronan family as they traveled west to Breckenridge, Missouri.

"Cathy, I was just thinking how great my father was coming to this country from Ireland, all alone in 1858, with only $10.00 in his pocket. He was able to become a successful telegrapher for the railroad and then a highly respected lawyer in Caldwell and Daviess county."

"I too, admired him so much. I see so much of his goodness in you Jeff. He encouraged you to respect everyone you met, even when you might not agree with their political or religious views. He greatly respected the U.S. Constitution and the principles of state sovereignty and individual liberty. Sad to say, these attributes are sorely missing in our government today."

"I had many long conversations about politics when we visited grandpa and Grandma in Breckenridge a few years back. He told me how proud he was of you Dad, for getting a law degree from Harvard."

"I can see the Breckenridge Depot ahead," said young Matthew. "They didn't get as much snow as we did. Oh, I see grandma. She looks so sad," as Matthew begins to cry.

"How was your trip everyone?" Maggie hugs Jeff, Cathy, Matt, Amanda and Sarah Jane.

"It was fine. How are you Mom?"

"I still can't believe he is gone. Every time I see his boots or cloths I start to cry. It seems like he should be sitting across from me at the dining table. I'll be all right. Just give me some time."

Several Model T'S and horse and buggies were parked around the Trosper cemetery on this cold December morning. The preacher began:

"We gather here today to honor the life of Samuel Ronan who was born on April 16, 1840 in Dublin, Ireland and came to this countries in 1858 at which time both of his parents were deceased. Sam and his family experienced many hardships during the Irish Potato Famine but against all odds Sam became a well-respected lawyer in Daviess and Caldwell Counties.

Sam was a longtime resident of Breckenridge. He passed away Thursday, December 20, 1923 at the age of 83.

Mr. Ronan emigrated from Ireland arriving in Philadelphia in 1858. A year later he traveled by stage coach from Philadelphia to Hannibal and then by the railroad to Breckenridge to become a relief telegrapher for the Hannibal and St. Joseph Railroad.

After becoming a U.S. citizen, he became the office assistant for the Law Office of Abe Abercrombie. After passing the Missouri bar exam, Sam was made a full partner in the Law Firm.

In addition to being a fine lawyer and respected member of the community, Mr. Ronan was well known throughout northwest Missouri as a horse breeder of note. He had raised many fine saddle horses and mules which he sold to the United States Army.

On June 10, 1863 Sam Ronan was married to Maggie Delaney, resident of St. Joseph. To this Union a son, Jefferson Ronan was born on June 2, 1864 who resides in Washington D C with his wife Cathy and son Matt. Two daughters, Amanda and Sarah Jane reside in Fairfax County, Virginia."

145

Samuel Ronan
1840-1923

Breckenridge, Mo. - Samuel Ronan, longtime resident of Breckenridge passed away Thursday, December 20, 1923 at the age of 83.

Mr. Ronan emigrated from Ireland arriving in Philadelphia in 1859. A year later he traveled by stage coach from Philadelphia to Breckenridge to become a relief telegrapher for the Hannibal and St. Joseph Railroad.

After becoming a U.S. citizen he became the office assistant for the Law Office of Abe Abercrombie. After passing the Missouri bar exam, Sam was made a full partner in the Law Firm.

In addition to being a fine lawyer and respected member of the community, Mr. Ronan was well known throughout NW Missouri as a horse breeder of note. He had raised many fine saddle horses and mules which he sold to the United States Army.

On June 10, 1863 Sam Ronan was married to Maggie Delaney, resident of St. Joseph. To this Union a son, Jefferson Ronan was born on June 2, 1864.

Mr. Ronan is survived by his wife Maggie of the home and son Jeff and his wife Catherine and their three children Matthew, Amanda and Sarah Jane.

Services will be at the Weldon Funeral Home in Breckenridge
10 am Thur. Dec. 2 7

Interment will be at the Trosper cemetery north of Breckenridge.

"Thanks Grandma for everything. Let us know if you need anything. We've got to get back to DC...."

The long train ride back to Washington was a very sad time for the Ronan Family. Things would never really be the same now that grandpa had passed away.

Movie Night- 1924

"Hey, would anyone like to go with me to the grand opening of the Chevy Chase Theater? It's a brand new movie theater in Northwest DC."

"I might Matthew. What's playing?" inquired Amanda.

"I'm not sure but I have heard that the Detroit News Reels are worth the price of the ticket."

"All right. I'll go if you pay for my ticket. Are you going Sarah Jane?"

"Sure if Matt pays for my ticket." (Smiles)

Matt even agreed to pay for his sisters' trolley fairs.

"I sure hope we can get a good seat. From the looks of the ticket line, it looks like the theater will be packed."

Matt and the two girls bought tickets and entered the theater. It is so crowded; they had to sit on the front row.

"Matt, this is awful. I can hardly see the screen unless I slouch way down in my seat," complained Sarah Jane.

"Oh quit complaining Sarah Jane. You didn't even have to pay for your ticket."

"Both of you be quiet, the show is about to start. I believe they will show three or four newsreels first."

Matt was almost right. However *Coming Attractions* was shown first and then the *News Reels*; First Detroit News Reel: *Cities United by Air Line* and *First Detroit-Cleveland passenger air service- 1923* and the second was a *1923 Pathe News Reel.* The feature movie was the 1923 American silent epic film, *The Ten Commandments* produced and directed by Cecil B. DeMille.

147

This was quite an event for the girls as this was their first experience in viewing a movie. The movie plus the news reels lasted a little over one hour.

"Well, what did you two ladies think of the movie?"

"I knew how the **Ten Commandments** was going to end, so I wasn't impressed much. I have read the book, you know," said Amanda sarcastically.

"I thought the movie was all right but it would have been better if we could have heard them talking instead of just seeing their conversations printed on the screen," complained Sarah Jane.

"I have read that in three or four years the film studios will be able to add sound to their movies and not have to have an organist play music and sound effects. That's really going to be exciting. You know, just like the radio. Actually, I enjoyed the News Reels almost as much as the feature movie," said Matt.

"All right Matt. Don't ask me to go to the movies with you again until they add sound. (Laughing) But, I still appreciate you paying for the tickets and trolley fair."

The kids returned home to find Jeff and Cathy eagerly waiting for the reports from the movie experience.

"Well kids, how was the movie?

"Sarah Jane didn't like it because there was no sound, and Amanda didn't care for it because she already knew how the 'Ten Commandments' ended. I thought the best part was seeing the news reels. It's much more exciting than reading about the news in a newspaper even if there is no sound," said Matt.

"At least it was a fun experience."

Author's Summary:

The International banker's victory of 1913

In 1913 President Wilson signed into law the unconstitutional Federal Reserve Banking Act and supported having the states ratify the 16th Amendment which allowed income tax to be

148

collected on a person's labor. The 16th Amendment <u>was not</u> properly ratified by the states.

*The American people only thought they had gotten rid of slavery after the **War Between the States**, with the adoption of the 13th Amendment in 1865. In 1913 both blacks and whites effectively became slaves, working a portion of each day, without pay, to pay the unconstitutional income tax on their labor. The tax started out being very small, but later would creep up to become a large burdensome amount.*

*As they say, **"The camel had gotten his nose under the tent."** Over the next few years, the personal income tax on a person's labor would be gradually increased and most people would accept it without question. It is like the parable of boiling frogs; they don't jump out as the heat is gradually raised, and then it is too late. The citizens are like live frogs boiling in a pot on the stove and fail to jump out in time. Those that didn't agree with the income tax on their labor would be unfairly deemed unpatriotic and even as possible terrorists by the Missouri Fusion reports in February, 2009.*

The Sixteenth Amendment:

The Congress shall have power to lay and collect taxes on incomes, from whatever source derived, without apportionment among the several States, and without regard to any census or enumeration.

Following is a statement allegedly made by President Wilson. Some claim that he never actually said this and others believe that it may just be someone's recollection of something he said in private:

"I am a most unhappy man. I have unwittingly ruined my country. A great industrial nation is controlled by its system of credit. Our system of credit is concentrated. The growth of the nation, therefore, and all our activities are in the hands of a few men. We have come to be one of the worst ruled, one of the most completely controlled and dominated Governments in the civilized

149

world no longer a Government by free opinion, no longer a Government by conviction and the vote of the majority, but a Government by the opinion and duress of a small group of dominant men." -Woodrow Wilson, after signing the Federal Reserve into existence.

Only a few of our legislators have been brave enough to stand up and protest against our country's unconstitutional monetary system; mainly Republican Congressman Ron Paul from Texas, Democratic Congressman Denis Kucinich from Ohio and Gary Johnson, former Governor of New Mexico and Libertarian Candidate for President in 2012.

On June 10, 1932, McFadden made a speech before the House where he accused the Federal Reserve of deliberately causing the depression. McFadden tried to impeach President Herbert Hoover in 1932 and introduced a resolution to bring conspiracy charges against the Fed's Board of Governors. The impeachment resolution failed to pass by a vote of 361 to 8. House resolution No. 158 was introduced by McFadden in 1936 to impeach the Secretary of the Treasury, two assistant Secretaries of the Treasury, the Board of Governors of the Federal Reserve and the officers and directors of the 12 regional banks. Congressman McFadden was definitely a thorn in the side of the banksters. McFadden died suddenly in 1936 on a visit to New York City. Some said he died from food poisoning and others simply chalked it up as "Natural Causes." With all of his enemies, it is unlikely his death was the result of natural causes. Following is an example of one of McFadden's most powerful speeches that shows that secretive foreign entities took over our country's banking system.

Congressional Record January 8, 1934

Congressman McFadden: *"The Congress of the United States must immediately throw the searchlight of investigation into this dark corner, or we are going to be swamped with political*

150

influences that are manufactured in foreign countries and that will lead us to the surrender of our heritage of living, just has been done on former occasions."

"I stand here and say to you that I have studied these records, and not only did we adopt this monetary policy without debate, not only did we adopt it without consideration but we adopted it without even knowledge of what we were doing! It was a piece of legislative trickery; it was a piece of work in the committee that was silent and secretive. Even members of the committee did not know what was being done, according to their own declarations. The President and members of the House did not know they were acting on such a measure. But, as I have said before, the shadow of the hand of England rests over this enactment.

Quotes by Benjamin Franklin

Light houses are more helpful than churches.

Half a truth is often a great lie.

The way to see by Faith is to shut the Eye of Reason.

To follow by faith alone is to follow blindly.

If men are so wicked with religion, what would they be if without it.

Notes concerning Benjamin Franklin

In 1729, Benjamin Franklin bought a newspaper, the Pennsylvania Gazette and he often contributed articles to his own paper under aliases. His paper soon became very successful in the colonies and was one of the first papers to include political cartoons which were written by him.

In 1733 he began publishing Poor Richard's Almanac. It included such things as weather reports, recipes, predictions and homilies. Many of the famous phrases associated with Franklin, such as, "A penny saved is a penny earned" come from Poor Richard's Almanac.

In the 1720's and 1730's Franklin organized the "Junto" a group dedicated to self-improvement and civic improvement. He also joined the Masons about this same period.

By 1749 he had retired from business and started concentrating on science, experiments, and inventions. He invented an efficient heating stove, called the Franklin Stove, swim fins, the glass armonica (a musical instrument) and bifocals.

"World events do not occur by accident. They are made to happen, whether it is to do with national issues or commerce; most of them are staged and managed by those who hold the purse strings."
Denis Healey, former British Secretary of Defense

Chapter Thirteen
Matthew Ronan-University of Missouri
1926

"Mom, Dad, I've decided to go to college at Northwest Missouri University in Maryville, Missouri, majoring in Political Science and minoring in Agriculture. Also I will be able to spend some time with grandma in Breckenridge. Maryville is only about 90 miles from Breckenridge."

"I was sort of hoping you would become a lawyer. Like me and grandpa."

"I don't believe that I want to be a lawyer, but a farmer can always run for a political office. Can't he?"

"Sure Matt. Whatever you decide to do will be fine with Mom and me."

"Why didn't you consider Howard University here in DC? Your mother took some history courses there and really liked it."

"Howard University might be all right but I believe that the Northwest Missouri University would be better since I want to major in agriculture. I'm thinking about being a farmer, Dad. I know you wanted me to become a lawyer like you but even a farmer can get involved in politics. You don't have to be a lawyer to become a congressman, do you? You know, I just may decide to run for Congress someday."

"No, of course not. But it has worked out well for your grandpa and me. Isn't Northwest Missouri University fairly small?"

"Probably only about 700-800 students. Besides, Poppa, I really fell in love with the Northwest Missouri area the many times I visited Grandpa in Breckenridge. I can see many opportunities in farming with the rich soil and thousands of acres of rich farm land in the Missouri River and the Grand River bottoms."

Washington DC Train Depot

On August 15th, 1926, the entire Ronan family gathered at the Washington DC train depot to bid Matthew a fond farewell.

Matt waved good-by to Mom and Poppa and his two sisters as the train left for Maryville, Missouri. The conductor came down the aisle collecting the tickets.

"Tickets please. Tickets please. Where to son?"
"Maryville, Missouri."
"You are in for quite a long trip. At least 1,000 miles or more. Are you going to school there?"
"Yes I will be enrolled as a freshman."
"You will need to transfer at Kansas City and then go on to St. Joseph. Then Maryville is about 40 miles further north."
" Thank you sir for all the information."

Matt dozed off to sleep every few minutes as he listened to the constant clicking of the wheels against the tracks and noticed the names of the towns outside the train windows indicating he was getting closer to Kansas City.

The Kansas City train Depot was almost as busy as the Washington DC depot. Lots of noise echoing through the huge tall ceiling of the luxurious depot.

"Now Boarding passengers to St. Joseph on track seven....,Now Boarding passengers to St. Joseph on track seven..." Although smaller than Kansas City's depot, St. Joseph's too was quite remarkable. After arriving in St. Joseph Matt had only one more hour of travelling.

The Maryville train depot was quite small compared to Washington DC and Kansas City. Arriving two days early gave Matt ample time to get enrolled and to tour the campus. Matt got settled in, assigned a dorm and purchased all his books and lab equipment. He felt a little apprehensive being so far away from home and his friends but was looking forward to visiting his grandmother in Breckenridge.

154

Matthew and his college buddies touring Northwest Missouri
(Matthew on the left)

Matt Calls Home

"Hello Poppa. I thought I had better telephone you and Mom today and let you know that I am all right. You may have read in the papers that there was an explosion in the chemistry lab here. It caused about $10,000 worth of damage."

"No, I hadn't heard that. Were you near the lab when it exploded?"

"Luckily no. I wasn't feeling well, probably just a cold, and had skipped the lab class. Outside of that, everything is fine here. Oh except for one more thing. The University ran out of coal last week and had to close down for two days. I would guess we will need to attend two extra days at the end of the school year or they may cut spring break two days."

"Well, it is good to hear from you."

"How are you and Mom doing? How are Amanda and Sarah Jane and their families?"

"We're all fine. Just getting older and set in our ways. (Chuckles). Amanda just bought a larger house in Fairfax and Sarah Jane is still with her and is learning to drive an automobile. When do you think you will be able to come home for a visit?"

"I'm planning on coming home for Christmas. It would be pretty lonely here in Maryville with the school shutdown and nearly everyone out of the dorm."

"Good, Matt. Thanks for calling. We'll be looking forward to your visit at Christmas time."

Dale Carnegie Lecture

Three months before graduation, 1930, Matt attended a University lecture presented by the popular motivational speaker, *Dale Carnegie*. Almost every seat in the auditorium was filled. It was obvious that his was going to be an enlightening experience. You could feel the excitement in the air. Dale Carnegie begins:

Thanks for coming today. My sincere hope is that I can impart some basis knowledge to you that will help you succeed as you are about to enter the business world for the first time. By the way, as some of you may already know, I was born here in Maryville in 1888. I was a poor farmer's boy, the second son of James Carnagey and Amanda Elizabeth Harbison. In 1911, I pursued a lifelong dream of mine becoming a Chautauqua lecturer and taught public speaking. From this 1912 debut, I evolved to develop the Dale Carnegie courses. I tapped into the average American's desire to have more self-confidence. I don't wish to sound like I'm bragging, but by 1914, I was earning $500 every week. By 1916, I was able to rent Carnegie Hall itself for a lecture. Maybe it was because I changed the spelling of my name to be the same as Carnegie Hall. (Chuckling) Being a poor farmer's boy need not keep you from succeeding!

The title of my presentation today is based on my recent book, How to Develop Self-confidence and Influence People by Public Speaking. I would like to pass on some personal experiences that I discovered over the years.

A successful speaker hinges only on two things; your native ability and the depth and strength of your desires. If you wish to be rich, you will be rich. If you wish to be learned, you will be learned. If you wish to be good, you will be good, and if you want to be a confident public speaker, you will be a confident public speaker. But you must really wish it. Speaking in front of people can be terrifying to some people. Some would argue that it is even more intimidating to speak in front of a smaller audience. To overcome this fear, you must practice your speech multiple times, be absorbed in your subject, have something to say, expect success and assume control over your audience.

It's really that simple! But remember, to make it happen, you must really wish it to happen.

To be successful in any business, you must learn how to make people like you. I have discovered that there are six ways to make this happen.
- *First, become genuinely interested in other people.*
- *Secondly, smile.*
- *Thirdly, remember that a person's name is to that person the sweetest and most important sound.*
- *Fourthly, be a good listener and encourage others to talk about themselves.*
- *Fifthly, talk in terms of the other person's interests.*
- *Sixthly, make the other person feel important and do it sincerely.*

You may not have ever thought of this before, but you never really win an argument. You can't because if you lose it, you lose it; and if you win it, you lose it. Why? Well, suppose you triumph over the other man and shoot his argument full of holes and prove that he is not of sound mind. Then what? You will feel fine. But what about him? You have made him feel inferior. You have hurt his pride. He will resent your triumph.

As wise old Ben Franklin used to say, "If you argue and rankle and contradict, you may achieve a victory sometimes; but it will be an empty victory because you will never get your opponent's good will. So figure it out for yourself. Which would you rather have, an academic, theatrical victory or a person's good will? You can seldom have both.

Mr. Carnegie continued for another hour...

Thanks again for coming today. If you have any questions or comments I will be available for about thirty minutes before I have to leave to make another presentation in St. Joe. Also I have several copies of my books for sale at the back of the auditorium.

If any of you or your friends would like to take one of my courses, my assistant will give you a list of which cities are offering them.

Dale Carnegie's speech lasted a little over one hour but was well worth it. The crowd applauded vigorously indicating that they were highly impressed with Dale Carnegie's presentation and could certainly see that his advice would help them succeed.

Matt could hardly wait to call home and tell his parents what an inspiring presentation he had just witnessed.

Matt Called Home

"Hello, Dad. How is everybody in DC?"

"We are all fine except your sister Amanda ran her new Model A car into the ditch. Fortunately she wasn't seriously hurt. Just shook up a bit."

"Glad she wasn't hurt. Actually I called for three reasons. Remember that 160 acre farm north of St. Joseph I was telling you about? The owner has lowered the price by $2,000. I was hoping that you and Mom would help finance its purchase. You would have little risk because I know I can make a go of it. Also, will you be coming up for my graduation?"

"Yes we're all planning on going to your graduation, even your sisters! Maybe we can take a look at the farm while we're there."

"That would be great Dad. One more thing. Have you ever heard of a man named Dale Carnegie? "

"No, I don't believe I have. Why?"

"I will tell you more about him and the presentation he gave this morning at the University when you come up for graduation. He is an excellent motivational speaker and teaches people how to be successful. I left the auditorium feeling like I could conquer the world. I've got to go now. I am looking forward to you all coming to Maryville. Bye. Love you Dad. Give my love to Mom."

"Bye son, we love you."

President Hoover is a Fine Man...but
1930

Jeff arrived home after an exhausting day from working in the capitol. His tie was undone and he was carrying his suit coat.

"Looks like you had a rough day dear!"

"I sure did. You know President Hoover is a fine man. I've heard that he donates all of his paychecks to charity. He has honorably attempted to combat the Depression with government public works projects such as the Hoover Dam and the record tariffs imbedded in the Smoot-Hawley Tariff, and aggressive increases in the top tax bracket from 25% to 63%, is projected to yield a "balanced budget." It is fantastic that we will have a balanced budget."

"So, what's the problem Jeff (chuckling)? It sounds to me like he is a fine President doing the right things."

"All of these things sound great Cathy, but the economy has plummeted and unemployment rates have risen to afflict one in four American workers. He seems to be doing all of right things all right but it isn't working. It's just very frustrating! Let's eat. I'm hungry."

"I guess you don't feel too badly. You still have an appetite, laughing."

"I got a call from Matt this afternoon at the office and he wants to know if we will be coming to Maryville for his graduation. I told him that yes, we would be going and that Amanda and Sarah Jane would be going also."

"It's hard to believe that he is ready to graduate."

"He asked me again if we were going to help him buy that 160 acre farm north of St. Joseph that he told us about two months ago. He said it was still for sale and that the owner has dropped the price."

"What did you tell him?"

"I told him we would take a look at it when we came up for his graduation, if it is still for sale. Will you buy the train tickets in the next day or two? We only have two weeks until the big day. Matt has been asked by the president of the university to give the commencement speech."

"That's quite an honor! Sounds like he may have bought that Dale Carnegie's book about public speaking. He always seemed so shy while he was in high school. I'll pick up the train tickets tomorrow on the way home."

Washington DC to Maryville Missouri

Jeff's friend, Frank Templeton took Jeff, Cathy, Amanda and Sarah Jane to the D.C. train depot.

"Call me when you get back from Maryville. I will pick you up," said Frank.

"Thanks Frank for the ride to the depot. I believe we will be back next Friday, but I'll give you a call as to the exact time."

"Have a good trip."

The long train ride from Washington DC to Maryville gave Jeff and Cathy time to decide if helping Matt buy a farm was the right thing to do. Both parents could see why their son Matt had fallen in love with the area. Northwest Missouri was a beautiful area. The only problem was that it was too far from Washington DC. Jeff and Cathy realized that they would only be able to see their son once or twice a year.

The University auditorium was packed with graduating students, friends and relatives to witness this auspicious occasion. The President of the University rose to speak.

"I would like to welcome the class of 1930 graduates, the parents, and members of the faculty. Let me introduce now our commencement speaker Matthew Ronan."

160

Matt's Commencement Speech

There was much applause and loud clapping. Jeff, Cathy, Amanda, and Sarah Jane were noticeably proud.

I want to thank the University for this great honor of being the Commencement speaker. Northwest Missouri State University has been a phenomenal experience for me. Not just from what I learned in the courses I was enrolled in but I used to sit in on lots of classes I hadn't even signed up for. (Chuckling) Dorm life was terrific. There were always lots of people in my dorm room late at night discussing everything from successful farming techniques, politics, and religion and of course girls, not necessarily discussed in that order, chuckles."

One of my biggest memories here at the University was when I attended the lecture by Dale Carnegie that the university sponsored. It was like a summary of all that I had learned here at the University and then was that final push out of the nest, so to speak, to enter the business world and become a successful Entrepreneur. What I remember above all about the University was being in the midst of so much energy and intelligence. It was exhilarating, intimidating, sometimes even discouraging but always challenging. It was an amazing privilege for me. I was transformed by my years at Maryville, the friendships I made and the ideas we all acquired to help us succeed in life.

I only hope I can stand up to my Grandfather's ideals and my Father and Mother's expectations to carry on the family tradition to serve my fellow countrymen.

My grandfather, Samuel Ronan, came to America from Dublin, Ireland in 1859 with just a few dollars left in his pocket, settling first in Philadelphia and then in Breckenridge, Missouri. He first worked for the Hannibal and St. Joseph Railroad as a telegrapher and later became a well-known and well liked attorney in this area. I am sure many of you have heard of him. Both my grandpa and parents stressed getting involved in our country's political system to ensure that we had a government that abided by the constitution, developed sound monetary policies, honored the Monroe doctrine by not interfering in other countries' afairs, and

161

respected state sovereignty and an individual's liberty.

Our parents' generation is counting on our generation to (1) solve the problems that caused this deplorable depression that lingers in our midst and (2) to honor the constitution that our fore fathers fought and died for. I hope and pray that we are all up to the challenge. Thank you.

Matt exited the auditorium with the crowd and met his parents outside. He hugged Mom and vigorously shook his Dad's hand.

"That was a great commencement speech Matt. We are so proud of you."
"Is that farm you want to buy near here?"
"It's only about 30 miles south of here. I called the owner yesterday and told him that my parents and I might stop by today to look things over."
"Are you still driving that old 1925 Model T son?"
"Yep! I know it isn't as nice as your LaSalle but it will get us where we're going."

All five climb into the car and headed for the farm tour, Matt, Jeff, Cathy, Sarah Jane and Amanda. There was much talking as the car traveled through the back roads of the beautiful northwest section of Missouri.

"I sure hope you like this farm. It's really a great deal. I think I told you on the phone the other day that he has reduced the price by $2,000. The owner has had some financial problems these last few years especially with the depression lagging on. You know, low prices for farm products and ever increasing high prices for farm equipment. He wants to retire and move to St. Joe to be closer to his children."

"You know son, this depression isn't over yet. Things are still pretty much a mess; at least for the farmer. I know congress is attempting to come up with a program to raise farm prices but they can't seem to come up with anything that is constitutional."

"Since when does congress have to pass a bill that is constitutional? (Chuckles) I plan to run my farm as a business and not just be a poor farmer trying to squeeze out a meager living. I have plans to eventually expand my farming to a couple thousand acres."

"I will say this son; you sure have a lot of enthusiasm! I admire that. I guess you get that from both the Ronans' and the Garmans'. Just look how successful your grandpa and I were. (Chuckling) At least grandpa. I also realize that you have received a good education and you have much more common sense than many of the politicians I work with."

"We're getting close to the farm. See that white farm house up on the hill and the red barn just to the east of the house? That's it!"

Let's Meet the Owner of the Farm

The car stopped at the driveway entrance to the house while they all admired the view. There were beautiful rolling hills and a nicely maintained fence line. The car started up again and drove up to the house to meet the owner of the farm.

"I see you came back son. Looks like you brought the whole family."

"Let me introduce everyone. This is my father, Jefferson Ronan, my mother Cathy, and my sisters Amanda and Sarah Jane. They all live in Washington DC and came up to Maryville to attend my graduation today and to look at your farm."

"Glad to meet you folks. Come on up to the house first and then I will show you the barn and out buildings, and then we can drive around the fields. You know, I have 160 acres here but about 20% is in timber. The way the trees face and the slope of the ground gives me good frost protection from the northwest. It gives me a superior growing climate."

"Thanks for pointing that out to me about the trees. I would have missed that."

"My house isn't really big but I think you will find it comfortable and efficient. Even though we don't have electricity yet, it should be here soon. I hear the Federal Government is working on a program called REA, or something like that, that will hook nearly every farm in America to the electric power lines. I do have a Wincharger generator on my windmill that keeps the storage batteries charged that provides power for my At-Water Kent Radio and house lights. When the batteries are low, because of little wind, you can always light up your oil lamps."

"Hopefully the REA, which stands for Rural Electrification Act, will be passed by congress soon. It will help provide electricity to almost every farm in America. As it now stands, only about 10% of American farms have electricity."

"Dad, maybe you can help hurry that along a bit, smiling. How do you heat the house?"

"Well, as you can see the Fireplace here heats the front room and the cook stove in the kitchen heats the kitchen as well as cooking food."

"How do you heat the two bed rooms?"

"Oh, we have a portable kerosene heater that can be carried from room to room. Let me show you the kitchen. Here is a nice cook stove, which by the way, goes with the house. Notice the dry sink and pitcher pump over the sink. I built the house right over the well so I wouldn't need to go outside to fetch water. You can't see it but there is a hose going from both the sink and icebox to the outside for draining. I put a lot of thought in making my place comfortable and efficient. Don't you think?"

"Very nice." said Amanda slightly frowning.

"Yes, very nice." said Sara Jane smiling.

164

Both of Matt's sisters were almost laughing out loud. Thankfully, the farmer didn't seem to notice.

"Let's go outside now. You can see that I put the chicken yard and chicken coup between the house and outhouse. That makes it handy to gather eggs and keeps the outhouse a safe distance from the house. Don't worry about the mud between the house and outhouse. I laid down boards to walk on through the chicken yard to keep your feet clean when it rains. Also the outhouse is a two holer so you can take the kids with you when needed. As you can see, I have arranged everything to make it extremely efficient."

The ladies could barely keep from laughing. This wasn't quite what they were used to in Washington DC.

"That small building on your right is the smoke house and then next to it is the small barn for the cows and garden tools. Most of the larger farming equipment is kept in the larger barn in the center of the field; so that whenever I need to get to it, I only have to walk halfway across the farm."

"What crops do you mainly plant?"

"For the first 20 years, I mainly planted corn and some soybeans and alfalfa. For some reason the corn stopped producing as much as it once did. We had a small vegetable garden to the south of the house, mainly just for the family and a little trading at the city market in St. Joe. Well, that's about all I can tell you. Any questions?"

"No, I think you've about covered everything. Let my dad and me go out to the car to talk for a minute. We'll be right back."

Matt and his dad go to the car to talk privately about buying the farm.

"What do you think Dad? Should I buy it? It's just what I've been looking for."

"The price is all right but are you sure you want to live like this? You know it's quite different from what you were used to in DC."

"I know Dad, but I won't have to live like this forever. I plan on building a new house and a larger barn, a potting shed, a large vegetable garden and eventually buy some cattle and pigs. Did you notice he said that over the years his corn yield became less and less? That's because he didn't rotate his crops. Proper crop rotation will enrich the soil and increase the yield to make more profit. Planting soy beans when corn isn't in season increases the nitrogen content in the soil. Then you alternate by planting clover and alfalfa instead of wheat and corn. These crops return nutrients to the soil. It sounds like he didn't do any crop rotation, unless it was accidental."

"Sounds like you know what you are talking about son. What about the drought? It is not as bad here as it is in other areas but it's still not ideal. Guess you can pump some water from the creek with a windmill until the rains get back like a few years ago."

"Does this mean you'll finance the farm for me?"

"Alright. Go back and tell him you will buy his farm."

Matt returned to the house and shook hands with the farmer and returned to the car with the biggest smile on his face!

"Before dropping you off at the train depot, let's stop by the Missouri Valley Trust in St. Joe and have them draw up a contract and show you how to wire the money to the St. Joe Bank."

Missouri Valley Trust
The Ronan's Bank in St. Joseph

166

Matt and Jeff entered the bank and conducted their business. A short time later they exited the bank to go to the Train Depot in St. Joe. Everyone waved good-by as the train left the station to head back to DC. The country had still not recovered from the depression. There was the doubling of unemployment to 16.3%, and the 1929 stock market crash was still having far reaching effects. Nature even conspired to make things worse by causing a serious drought in the Midwest which in turn made food more expensive and turned some areas into dust bowls. Matt's father was a bit concerned but had confidence in Matt that he could make a success of his farm.

Industrial Hemp

Although Matthew did quite well growing beans, corn, and wheat, there was one crop that he really wanted to plant; industrial hemp or sometimes referred to as "agricultural hemp. Matthew was aware that even people like George Washington grew hemp. However, there was a stigma attached to its cultivation because its physical appearance was similar to marijuana. The majority of the public and even the politicians did not understand that agricultural hemp, with only 1% THC, was *not marijuana*. There were attempts to halt its cultivation by the politicians, influenced by the cotton lobbyists, and most active in curtailing its cultivation was William Randolph Hurst. He had a tremendous investment in timber to manufacture paper for his newspaper empire. Hurst tried to keep it a secret that almost anything that could be made from cotton could also be made from hemp and at a greatly reduced cost. The issue was that there was not much of a market for hemp because of the ignorance of the public and the resistance from the politicians. There were a number of other powerful interests that would not allow the cultivation of hemp to flourish, (1) the timber industry that provides wood pulp for the manufacture of paper, (2) the chemical industry represented by DuPont that had patent rights to the sulfuric acid wood pulp paper process and nylon rope made from synthetic petrochemicals, (3) cotton growers, and (4) pharmaceutical companies that feared drugs would be produced from hemp that would compete with their existing drugs.

"Hopefully, someday there will be a market for hemp that will allow the American farmer the chance to become successful growing hemp even on a small farm of 80 to 160 acres," thought Matthew.

It would be a tremendous boon to the economy if farmers could add *energy production* through hemp cultivation to their already important and profitable food production. Hemp, with its varied uses and the fact that it needs little fertilizer or weed control to produce, would greatly improve the farmer's chance of success and at the same time would help to keep the small farming communities throughout the United States profitable.

After Matt had achieved success from his hard work, planting and harvesting his crops the first few years, he felt it was time to start working on the nicer and larger house he had planned. With the help of contractors the new house soon took shape. It was a gorgeous two story house with a wraparound porch, indoor plumbing and the expectation of soon to be electricity. He figured the original house could be used by his farm helpers.

Frog Hop Ball Room

One Saturday evening Matt decided to go to the popular night spot in St. Joe, *The Frog Hop* on Pickett Road. Matt parked his 1939 Pierce Arrow and entered the Ball Room.   Matthew was about to meet Barbara Calvin who had come to the Frog Hop with her friends, Jack Spratt and Evelyn Nelson, alone because she had just recently broken up with her boyfriend, Richard Winfrey. Matthew noticed Barbara, wearing a nice red dress, sitting alone at the table while her friends were dancing, so assumed she might be available. She was a very attractive young lady with a figure that displayed her elegant dress in a most attractive way.   He approached her table and asked for a dance.

"How are you, beautiful? My name is Matthew Ronan. Would you like to dance?"

"I don't think so. I prefer to just sit here and listen to the band. But thanks for asking. I'm sorry but I am recovering right now."

"You mean you're sick?"

"Oh no, nothing like that. I just broke up with my boyfriend that I had gone with for the last two years. He found another girl he liked better!" she bitterly stated.

"I am so sorry; can I get you a beer or a soda?"

"I don't drink beer, but I would like a bottle of pop. You see, my father was an alcoholic before he died and I don't want to have anything to do with alcoholic drinks."

"Fine, I will get us both a bottle of pop and a bag of popcorn."

After Matthew returned with the sodas and popcorn, the other couple returned to the table.

"Aren't you going to introduce us to your friend, Barbara?"

"Oh, I am sorry, this is----what did you say your name was?

"I'm Matthew Ronan."

"Matthew, this is my friend Evelyn Nelson and her date Jack Spratt."

"Nice to meet you Evelyn and Jack. This sure is a nice place to hear good music and to dance. Don't you think?"

"It sure is Matthew. Jack and I come here often, depending on which orchestra is playing. I can't wait to see Jimmy Dorsey next month. His whole group will be here in St. Joe!"

"Barbara, will you go to the powder room with me?" Both girls hurry to the ladies room. (Evelyn is noticeably excited)

"Barbara, do you know who you just introduced me to?"

"Sure, his name is Matthew Ronan."

"No, No. I don't mean that. Haven't you ever heard of Ronan Farms? His name is in the paper almost every other week. He owns a huge farm north of St. Joe and serves on several important committees appointed by the governor. And I read a few months ago that the President has appointed him to a position with the U.S Agricultural Department. I think you should be really nice to him."

"Don't be silly, Evelyn. He is pretty nice looking though."

After the ladies got back to the table, Matthew again asked Barbara if she wanted to dance. This time she accepted. After three dances, Matt had to apologize for leaving early.

"I must excuse myself. Could I call you when I get back next week? I have to leave early tomorrow morning to go to Washington D.C. for a committee meeting. My train leaves at 6:00 AM."

"I suppose that would be all right. Here, let me write my telephone number on this napkin."

"It was sure nice meeting all of you. I promise, I'll call you, Barbara, as soon as I return from Washington. Bye now."

Matthew left the Frog Hop Ball Room to find his car in the huge parking lot. As Barbara, and her friends Evelyn and Jack were leaving, they all saw Matt leaving in his Pierce Arrow.

"Look, that's your friend driving away in the Pierce Arrow convertible. That's a beautiful and quite expensive automobile. A little nicer than our Model A Sedan."

Off to Washington DC September 1, 1939

September 1, 1939, Matthew left the St. Joseph Depot to go to Washington D.C. A loud echoing voice was heard from the train dispatcher. "All aboard for Washington DC, now loading on track four. All aboard for Washington DC, now loading on track four." Steam could be seen coming from one of the engines with a loud hissing noise. Matthew climbed aboard carrying his suitcase and a brief case. He placed his suitcase, brief case, and hat on the brass storage rack above his seat and sat down to read the New York Times.

The headline read *Nazi Germany Invades Poland. Chancellor Hitler proclaims action as one of self-defense.*

Matt was noticeably concerned and couldn't help but worry that the United States was going to be sucked into a second world war.

Hopefully, President Roosevelt would honor his promise;
"I have said this before, but I shall say it again and again and again: Your boys are not going to be sent into any foreign wars."

Matt had the feeling that his work in Washington was coming to a close. He reasoned that if true, It was a good thing. Now he would be able to give more attention to his farming interests.

The first thing Matt did after arriving back in St. Joseph was to call Barbara.

Date with Barbara

"Barbara, this is Matt Ronan. I met you three weeks ago at the Frog Hop. Do you remember me?"

"I do remember you. How was your trip to Washington?"

"It was fine except that the new administration doesn't seem to need me, or maybe they just want to replace me with their friends to whom they owe political favors. Actually I'm glad that my term is up because now I will have more time to devote to farming. I have a good farm crew but things don't run as smoothly as when I am here. I thought I would ask you to go to the Country Club Friday night for a dinner sponsored by the Buchanan County Republican Club. What do you think?"

"I guess that would be acceptable except I doubt I will know anyone there and I don't know anything about politics."

"Don't worry about that. I will teach you everything you need to know. For example, do you know the difference between a Republican and a Democrat?"

"Not really."

"Well, the Democrats represent the poor people and the Republicans represent the rich people."

"Yes, I know that. That's what I have always heard."

"Well, that's not true. I was only kidding. That's what many people believe though. That's not a good way to explain their differences. It is a little more truthful to classify them as conservatives and liberals, but even that has some problems; it really depends on the issue. Actually, I have found that there is about as much difference between the two parties as there is between a violin and a fiddle. There are slight differences but not much. One wants to raise taxes a lot and the other wants to do the same thing but a little less."

171

"I'll go but I don't want to embarrass you in front of your friends because of my ignorance."

"I'm not worried about it. I just want to see you. I will pick you up about 7:30, all right?"

"Do you know where I live?"

"I guess it would be a good idea for you to give me your address."

(Laughing) "I live at 2614 Duncan Street. Do you know where that is?"

"Sure, it is one block east of Hall Elementary School. Right?"

"How did you know that?"

"I'll tell you later. See you Friday night at 7:30."

"Fine. I'm looking forward to it. Good-by."

Off to the St. Joseph Country Club

Matthew rang the doorbell and fidgeted some as the porch light came on and Barbara opened the door. He couldn't believe how beautiful she was. He had noticed how attractive she was at the Frog Hop but tonight she looked even more spectacular.

"Barbara, you look stunning. Here let me pin this corsage on you."

"Oh, that is so pretty Matthew, thank you."

"All right, let's go. I'm going to be the envy of all the men at the club tonight."

"Thanks Matthew, but I suspect that there will be many prettier than I."

Matthew held the door open and Barbara sat in the luxurious Pierce Arrow, rubbing her hands on the rolled leather seats and looking at the fancy dash and convertible top.

"Thank you for not putting the top down."

"I'll do that later. I wouldn't want to mess up your beautiful hair."

"Oh Matt, you are so thoughtful."

172

Matt parked the car at the Country Club and the two of them entered the front door of the club. There were many guests already there and *Moonlight Serenade* by Glenn Miller could be heard in the background.

"Hey, Matt how are you doing? Who is this beautiful lady you are with?"

"Barbara, I would like you to meet John Graham. He is the president of the Republican club. John this is my good friend, Barbara Calvin."

"I'm honored to meet you Barbara. I'll save a place for you two at my table."

"Thanks John. There is Senator Roy McKittrick Barbara! I want you to meet the senator. Senator McKittrick, I would like to introduce you to my date this evening, Barbara Calvin."

"Glad to make your acquaintance Barbara. How did you ever meet this guy and how did he ever talk you into coming to a dance with so many politicians in one place?"

"Come on now senator, I can't divulge all of my secrets," laughing.

Both Matt and Barbara had a great time at the Country Club and it was obvious that the other men were quite envious of Matt's new friend. Barbara seemed to fit in with everyone and didn't have any trouble at all carrying on an intelligent conversation with Matt's friends. As the party wore on and people were loosening up a bit telling jokes and unbelievable stories, Barbara came up with a joke of her own.

"Hey everyone, I have a joke. Matt went into the Haberdashery last week and asked the sales clerk if he could try that suit on in the window. The clerk said, *Sure, if you want to, but we have a dressing room in the back.*"

Everyone laughed including Matt. Matt took Barbara home about 1:00 AM and told her what an enjoyable time he had and hoped he could see her again.

"It wasn't so bad now, was it Barbara? Didn't you have a good time?"

"I really did Matt. All of your friends were really nice except that one that kept wanting to dance with me."

"Oh that was Bob Mitchell, our city attorney. He's harmless. At least when he's inebriated," laughing.

"I had a nice time. You have some really nice friends. I couldn't stop laughing at the jokes that Senator Kemper was telling. I think he may have had a little too much to drink."

"I think you're right. Say, would you like to take a tour of my farm sometime?"

"That would be nice, but I will be busy all next week. I have company coming from out of town. But the following week is open."

"How about next Saturday, since you don't have to work at the insurance company on Saturdays?"

"How did you know that? Have you been spying on me?"

"Oh no. I met your friend Evelyn at the bank last week and she told me that you worked for the Prudential Insurance Company. I had another friend that had worked there a few years back and I knew that the office was closed on Saturdays."

"I do have to work occasionally on Saturday but this coming Saturday, I will be free. Sure, I think it would be fun touring your farm. What time Saturday?"

"Why don't I pick you up about eleven in the morning so we can have lunch and then spend the rest of the day at the farm, and then I will have Fu Le, my housekeeper, prepare a meal for us in the evening."

"You mean you are even going to feed me supper?"

"No, I'm going to feed you dinner."

"We call it supper where I'm from."

"You may call it whatever you like. Well, I got you home safe and sound."

Matt jumped out of the car and ran around to the passenger side to help Barbara out of the car and escorted her to the house. At the porch, Matt gave Barbara a quick kiss on the lips.

"Good night Barbara. I really had a good time this evening."

"Me too Matt. I'm looking forward to Saturday. Good night."

Matt drove away out into the night, whistling.

Barbara was looking forward to her date with Matt. The more she found out about him, the more impressed she became. He appeared to be a very successful businessman, a person well known and well liked in the community and seemed to be on a path to success in politics. Besides that he was nice looking and so far had been very respectful to her.

Hoof and Horn Restaurant

Matt really liked the **Apex Buffalo Saloon** downtown but thought it more appropriate to take Barbara to the **Hoof and Horn**. The famous **Hoof and Horn Restaurant** in South St. Joe was only a short drive from Barbara's house on Duncan Street.

"Where are you taking me to eat, **Honey**? Oops, I didn't mean to say that. That just kind of slipped out, embarrassed."

That's all right Honey. Oops, I **did mean to say that**. It shows how I really feel, smiling." I'm taking you to a restaurant in south St. Joe. It is one of St. Joe's finest old restaurants, having been around since 1898. After lunch we will take the beautiful boulevard up to Savannah road and then on up to my farm."

"That sounds like it will be a nice day's outing."

The interior of the restaurant was western style with wagon wheel lights, a rustic bar with a large mirror behind the bar. The chairs were the old curved back type strengthened with wire bracing the spindles under the seat. The glasses on the table were thick barrel glasses. There was much noise with farmers in overalls and some men in suits waiting to be served. The waiter with a white apron approached their table.

"How are you doing Matt? Who is this beautiful lady you have with you?'

"Hi Joe. This is my friend Barbara Calvin."

"Barbara, this is Joseph Mollus, the owner of the Hoof and Horn."

"Glad to make your acquaintance Barbara. What can I get for you folks?"

"I don't know what to order Matt. Why don't you order for both of us?"

"Do you like steaks?"

"Sure steak is fine. But aren't they a bit expensive?"

"Don't worry about that, Honey."

"All right, we will take two 10 ounce steaks, baked potatoes and corn on the cob. Or as I used to say when I was a youngster, *corn on the bone*. Oh, may we have two salads?"

"Would you like something to drink?"

"I would like a glass of tea," said Barbara.

"I believe I will have a Goetz Country Club Beer."

"We are busier today than usual. There is some kind of celebration over at the stock yards today. Oh, how do you want your steaks cooked?"

"Is medium all right with you Matt?"

"That's fine, but Joe, make mine medium well."

"Thank you Matt and Barbara. Your meal will be out in about 20 minutes."

"You were right Matt. This seems like a great place to eat. Look how busy they are."

"Do you keep up with the news?"

"Sometimes but recently it has been pretty depressing. I just read where Hitler attacked Great Britain. I thought they were allies or something. What happened?"

"Adolf Hitler only undertook the bombing of British civilian targets after the Royal Air Force had started bombing German civilian targets. This whole thing is a real mess. The sad part is that the Treaty of Versailles, signed in 1919 at the end of the World War actually set the stage for WWII. Germany was forced to pay reparations way beyond their ability plus much of Germany was carved up leaving many German speaking people living in other countries. It would only be natural for Germany to make an attempt to regain their old boundaries."

"This is depressing. Let's not talk about it. Let's just enjoy this beautiful day together. How is your steak?"

"Very good and it is cooked just like I like it. How's yours?"

"My steak is good but my company is fantastic!"

"Thanks Matt. You are very kind. I enjoy being with you also. I'm looking forward to seeing your farm. Are you ready to go?"

Hoof and Horn Restaurant
1940's photo

Farm Tour and Diner

This time, Matt lowered the top on his Pierce Arrow convertible. They drove around for several hours taking in all the sights including Barbara's grade school, South Park, the mansions on Hall Street, the Patee House, Jesse James House, and Barbara showed Matt where she lived before moving to Duncan street. Then they drove onto the beautiful St. Joseph boulevard and then on up the old Savannah road to the farm.

"Is that your house in the valley with the spruce trees bordering both sides of the long driveway to the house?"

The entire scene looked like one of the pictures featured on a seed company's calendar. What a beautiful view, thought Barbara. Matt drove around the circle drive to the front of the house and escorted Barbara to the front door.

"I hope we made it in time for dinner...I mean supper." Matt smiled. "My cook Fu Le gets agitated when I'm late for a meal."
"Let me introduce you to my foreman. Jack, this is my friend Barbara Calvin. Barbara, this is my foreman Jack Townsend."
"Nice to make your acquaintance Barbara."
"FU Le, will you come in here and meet our special guest?"
"Yes boss. Right away."

Fu Le is a Chinaman that had served as Matt's cook and housekeeper for the last 7 years. He was short, middle aged wearing a white smock and white pants. He also prided himself as being an accomplished magician.

"Fu Le this is my good friend Barbara Calvin."
" The honor is all yours. I mean all mine. I hear much about you from boss man. He like you very much."
"Thank you Fu Le. It is an honor to meet you. Matt has told me so much about you and what a good cook you are."

"Okee Dokee. All sit now. I bring out food."
"The three of them, Matt, Barbara and Jack sat down at the elegant twelve chair mahogany ball and claw foot Chippendale dining table. There was a huge crystal chandelier over the center of the table and sterling silver trays and tableware that Barbara had never seen before.

Strange Things Adorn the Dining Table

"Matt, there are things on this table that I have never seen before. Would I appear stupid, if I asked you to explain what they are?

"Of course not Barbara. That big round object is a dinner plate and the three metal objects are a knife, fork and spoon."

"No no, I don't mean those, silly. What is that glass barbell thing and the small curved plate?"

"I'm sorry, Barbara. I was just trying to be funny at your expense. Please accept my apologies."

"Don't worry about it Matt. It was pretty funny."

"Those small glass 'bar bell things' next to each plate are to hold your knife blade so it won't get the tablecloth dirty, and the small curved dish is to deposit your discarded bones. The sterling silver figural piece next to each plate is a napkin ring holder. You notice each one is different. You wouldn't want to return to the table and use someone else's napkin."

"You must do a lot of entertaining."

"He sure does Barbara. I think Matt likes to talk and by doing a lot of entertaining, he gets a captive audience. You know almost no one will turn down an invitation for a free meal."

"Now Jack, don't give away all of my secrets. Some of my most important business decisions were made right here at this table. I remember my father telling me years ago, to be successful, take a rich and well versed man to dinner, and then shut up and listen. I have never forgotten that. And then to top off dinner, we sometimes have a little musical entertainment. Jack here plays the guitar and Fu Le performs his magic tricks. On really special occasions I hire professional musicians to entertain us. Good food, good friends and good music. What could be better than that?"

Fu Le brought out the desert.

"Amen to that Matt. As long as I'm invited. No desert for me Fu Le. It looks delicious but I'm trying to lose a few pounds. Sorry to leave you folks but I have some chores to attend to before dark. Nice meeting you Barbara. I hope to see you again."

179

"Hope to see you again too Jack.

"Most of the farm hands that live here on the farm join me for dinner every Friday night for a business meeting and we also celebrate most holidays here with the hired hands. The help have their own bunk house and kitchen area but eat here on special occasions. We're really just one big family."

Magic Show

"You like me show Miss Barbara magic tricks boss?

"That's up to Barbara. What do you think Barbara?"

"Oh please do. That would be fun Fu Le. Go ahead."

Fu Le did the standard metal ring trick, linking and unlinking rings, and the disappearing cage with a stuffed bird inside.

"That was really good Fu Le. How do you do those tricks?"

"Can you keep secret Miss Barbara?"

"Sure!"

"So can I. (Smiling) I taught by famous Chinese magician. His name "Foo Ling Yu.""

"You mean like F*ooling you*! Very good Fu Le. You are very good."

"Barbara, let's go out on the porch and sit for a spell."

Love is in the Air

Matt and Barbara sat in a small two seated swing. The sky was full of stars with a full moon and you could hear the locusts chirping and the dripping water in the fountain. A train whistle could be heard in the distance.

"I would guess that all of your employees would get along well together just by meeting your foreman, Jack. I noticed that you had a colored man working for you. Does that present any problems? You know, does he sleep in the same bunk house and eat with the rest of them here in the dining room?"

"It better not be a problem. If it is, someone is going to get fired and it won't be Cotton. Cotton is one of my best hands. In fact I made him the **Assistant Foreman** a few years ago. He only had an eighth grade education but is much smarter than many others that finished high school. He is not worldly but has lots of common sense."

"I am glad that you do not possess any racial prejudices. That tells a lot about a person's character."

"I have always believed that we all have the same God, so we should respect everyone based on their character rather than their race or religion," explained Matt.

"Barbara, why don't you tell me more about yourself?"

"No, you go first."

"Well, my grandfather immigrated to this country in 1859 from Dublin Ireland and stayed in Philadelphia for only a few months and then moved to Breckenridge, Missouri to be a telegrapher for the Hannibal and St. Joseph Railroad. He traveled by stagecoach all the way from Philadelphia to Hannibal, Missouri and then took the train to Breckenridge. He had a son, Jefferson who is my father, who graduated from Harvard and moved to Washington D. C. to be the personal secretary to President Woodrow Wilson. I'm the third child of Jefferson and Cathy Garman Ronan. I have two older sisters, Amanda and Sarah Jane who are both married and have presented me with two wonderful nephews and a niece, the smartest three kids ever."

"I was born in 1908 and after graduating from high school in Washington, decided to enroll at Northwest Missouri State University in Maryville, Missouri. I graduated in 1930 and now I am a farmer.

"Oh, and I am a Republican and a 'Deist'. Now it's your turn," smiling.

"Have you ever been married?"

"Oh yes, I forgot about that. I was married right out of college but it only lasted two years because she had an affair with one of my farm hands. I fired the farm hand and divorced my wife. Fortunately we didn't have any children. I would rather not talk about it."

"I'm sorry Matt, I didn't mean to pry. Ok, where do I begin?

"My grandfather, Joshua Calvin immigrated to this country from Baden Baden Germany in 1830, landing in New York. He was an indentured servant but when he got to New York his sponsor was nowhere to be found. Being nearly broke and no one to help get him started, he decided to go to Cincinnati, Ohio, Hamilton County, where he had some relatives living. With little money, he had to walk most of the six hundred miles. It took him over two months to make the trip. He became an itinerate preacher, preaching mainly to the German immigrants that belonged to the United Brethren Church. The story often told by my father was that he carried a Bible on one side of his saddle and a whisky bottle on the other. His son, Robert Calvin, my father, was born in 1864 and later moved to Vevay, Indiana and later to St. Joseph, where I was born in 1910. I had two older sisters and a brother who died in infancy. My folks were older when I was born, and have both passed on. That's it. Never been married before but hope to someday meet the right man, get married and have a family."

"Me too. How do you remember all of those details about your family?"

"My mother was an avid genealogist. She had all the family bibles back four generations with the family information. One more question for you.

Deism

What is a Deist? Aren't you a Christian?"

"Deism is a religious philosophy that does not need an organized religion to explain the natural world. I believe in a Creator but don't believe that Creator normally intervenes in human affairs except through maybe serious prayer. I don't believe in prophecy or miracles. In my opinion, there are no such things as miracles, and not even Nostradamus could predict the future. Miracles are only natural laws which man has yet to understand."

"I'm going to need a little time to digest that! It's very interesting."

"The reasons why I am not a Christian as described in the Bible are: (1) I do not believe in the virgin birth of Jesus, (2) I do not believe that Jesus rose from the dead, (3) I don't believe in the

Trinity, and (4), I don't believe that Jesus performed any miracles. In fact, I have read of several other religions having a leader born of a virgin, and that virgin even being named **Mary**. There were so many religious false writings during the origin of Christianity that they even had a term for them. They were called *pious fraud*. My beliefs should in no way diminish the importance of the Jesus stories nor the Christ Consciousness that resides in all of us. The positive message that has been attributed to Jesus has helped millions of people cope with their problems. That's a good thing for them but something I don't need. I'm not even sure that Jesus was a real person or just someone made up to resemble Rome's Emperor Titus. He could have been possibly made up of more than one person. I really believe that the Biblical Jesus is most likely a myth. I cannot explain it in any more detail and don't believe anyone else can either. How do you prove something based on faith? Now I bet you wish you hadn't asked," frowning.

"No, that's fine. I appreciate your honesty and I can tell you have given this a great deal of study and thought. Do you believe in prayer?"

Prayer is a Natural law

"Certainly but probably not like you. Prayer is a natural law like gravity. If you drop something, it falls to the ground whether you believe in gravity or not. Gravity doesn't care if you believe in it. So it follows that prayer is a natural law that works for Christians and non-Christians alike; even atheists. Would you believe that all my prayers have been answered?"

"No Matt. I do have a difficult time believing that. But what do you mean?"

"First let me explain the steps I take to pray. There are three different parts to us humans; the spiritual, physical and mental. The real you is the spiritual you that lives forever. The mental you is your brain, and the physical you is the body in which the mental and spiritual resides. When I pray, I find it most effective to be as close to the spiritual self as possible. To get into this mental state, I plan a fifteen minute prayer session sitting in a chair in my parlor early in the morning with my feet together and my hands in my lap facing upward in a receiving position. Then I protect myself by stating that I won't accept anything into my being that is not Christ like or God like, and I picture myself in the center of a bright glowing light surrounded by darkness. I make an affirmation to God, the Creator, as to what I am praying for, and then I shut up and listen. I guess some would say that this is meditating. After that I try to *not think* in words because that would transport me back to the physical state."

"A prayer consists of three parts, first you talk to God, then you must listen, and finally you must take some form of action. You know like searching for a capable doctor, changing your diet or lifestyle."

"And finally the reason my prayers are always answered is that I state that if in the overall cosmic realm there is a lesson I must learn, making it impossible for my prayer to be answered, then please assist me in understanding this and help me cope with that decision."

Matt leaned over to gently kiss Barbara and she immediately hugged him passionately. It certainly appeared that they were soul mates and meant for each other.

Chapter Fourteen
Marriage Proposal
1939

Matthew Ronan proposed to Barbara shortly after a dinner date at Matt's farm to celebrate Barbara's birthday.

"Barbara, sweetheart, will you marry me? I love you so much. Ever since that first night we met at the Frog Hop, I knew that you were a very special lady and I wanted you to be a part of my life."

"Oh Matt, I love you. Yes, yes, I will marry you. I have never felt this way about anyone before. I feel like I am exploding inside with happiness. When do you think we should get married?"

"I think that June would be best. I would like to have the wedding here on the farm. The weather should be suitable then. How do you feel about that? Can you be ready by then?"

"Do you think your house is big enough?"

"No but the yard is. I can rent a large tent and we will have an outdoor barbecue and lots of entertainment. There's a really good band in St. Joe that entertains at events like this. I'll give them a call tomorrow. I think Jack would be willing to build us a white trellis for us to stand next to while the preacher takes our wedding vows. Isn't it a law you have to stand next to a white trellis with roses on it to be officially married?"

"I think you are right Matthew," laughing with excitement.

The next few months kept Barbara busy. Barbara rushed from store to store buying a wedding gown, shoes, purse, and an arm load of packages containing everything that she thought would be needed for a wedding. Next on their list was to talk to a stationary printer for the invitations. Matt was soon helping Jack build a trellis. With that finished he contacted a company in Kansas City for renting a large tent. After a busy eight months of preparations Matt's able farm hands got the barbecue ready and began setting up the bar. Each table was gorgeous with loads of tiny flowers trailing down the centers after Barbara's friend Evelyn had worked her magic. She also had prepared a table for the wedding gifts.

Another crew brought and set up tables and chairs. Excitement was in the air!

"Oh Evelyn, how can I ever thank you for helping me with all this? You know the wedding is one o'clock tomorrow. Do you think we will be ready?"

"Of course, don't you worry. Just look at this crew setting up everything. Looks like they have had experience doing this sort of thing before."

"I think you are right. Matt does a lot of entertaining. I think we both will be surprised at all the important people who will be here tomorrow. I believe Matt knows almost everyone in Northwest Missouri."

"About all that's left to do is for you and Matt to get a good night's sleep. Then tomorrow I'll help dress you. And then the big occasion!"

Ready for the Wedding

Finally everything was ready for the big wedding. The exhausted workers sat down to rest.

"We did it Barbara. It looks like we are ready. Now let's just hope that it doesn't rain."

A long line of fancy cars could be seen coming down the road trying to find a place to park in the field next to the house. One of the farm hands was smartly dressed for the occasion and was parking cars. There was a mix of dress styles; formal, casual and western attire.

"Well Evelyn. Are you ready to greet the guests since Barbara is hiding? It seems like a strange tradition to make the bride hide on the wedding day until the ceremony begins."

"But Matt, I don't know any of these people."

"Don't worry, I'll help you. There may be a few that I don't recognize. Oh, here comes Charles Palmer and Henry Bradley from the Gazette and News Press. How are you doing Charley and

Henry. Glad you both could make it."

"Wouldn't have missed it for the world Matt. You sure have a nice looking place here."

"How many acres do you farm here Matt," asked Charley.

"We farm about 4,000 acres total with 3,000 owned by Ronan Farms and then we lease another thousand acres from the neighbors' farms. It takes quite a crew to keep it all running properly."

"I'll bet it does Matt. Say, are you still thinking about running for Congress? If you do, we will support you as much as we can at the Gazette."

"I certainly appreciate that Charley. Don't tell Barbara though. I haven't told her that I was thinking about being a politician and a farmer. She might not have agreed to marry me if she knew that. Go on over there and get a cool drink, I'll see you both after the wedding ceremony."

"How do you do Mr. Mayor? Thanks for coming. This young lady assisting me here is one of our greeters, Evelyn Nelson, a good friend of Barbara's."

"How do you do Evelyn? Thanks for inviting me Matt. It's a splendid day for a wedding."

"Go on over to the bar in the tent. I'm sure you will find something to your liking, smiles. Here come some people I don't know but they look like they belong. I'll turn the greeting over to you now Evelyn."

"Don't leave me Matt. I don't know any of these people."

"Don't worry about it Evelyn. Just smile and welcome them. Be polite and ask them their name and then introduce yourself as a family friend."

"All right, I'll do the best I can," frowning.

More and more guests arrived until the yard was full of several hundred people. Music could be heard in the background from the band. The official wedding finally started with the band playing the wedding march. Both Matt and Barbara approached the preacher near the white trellis.

"Welcome one and all to this beautiful home of Matthew Ronan and soon to be wife, Barbara Calvin. What a beautiful day God has made for us! Let us bow our heads and thank God for all his heavenly gifts... Amen. We are gathered here today to join together Barbara Ellen Calvin and Matthew Louis Ronan in holy matrimony."

"Who gives this woman in marriage to this man?"

Barbara's favorite uncle, Raymond Calvin, stepped forward.

"If it is your intention to take each other as husband and wife, please unite your hands and step forward."

"Do you, Barbara Ellen Calvin, take this man, whose hand you hold, to be your husband, and do you solemnly promise, before God and these witnesses, that you will love and honor him according to the instructions of God's Holy Word, and that forsaking all others for Matthew alone, that you will be faithful to him, so long as you both shall live?"

"I Do."

"Do you, Matthew Louis Ronan, take this woman, whose hand you hold, to be your wife, and do you solemnly promise, before God and these witnesses, that you will love and honor her according to the instructions of God's Holy Word, and that forsaking all others for Barbara alone, that you will be faithful to her, so long as you both shall live?"

"I do."

"May I have the rings, please?"

"As a token that you will faithfully perform these vows, you will now exchange rings. The ring is an endless circle: a symbol of the covenant you are making here today."

"Barbara as you place the ring on Matthew's finger, repeat after me: 'As I place this ring on your finger, I pledge myself to you. I am yours."

"As I place this ring on your finger Matthew, I pledge myself to you. I am yours."

"And now Matthew as you place the ring on Barbara's finger,

188

repeat after me: 'As I place this ring on your finger, I pledge myself to you. I am yours.'"

"As I place this ring on your finger, Barbara, I pledge myself to you. I am yours."

"Now that you, Barbara Ellen Calvin and Matthew Louis Ronan, have agreed together to enter the holy state of marriage, before God, and these witnesses of your vows, I therefore, by virtue of the authority vested in me as a minister of the gospel, pronounce you husband and wife."

Matthew kissed Barbara, to claps and cheers as the music began to play. Matthew spoke:

"Ok everyone. We have plenty to eat and drink so line up over at the tent and Fu Le and his helpers will fill your plates with barbecued buffalo, beans and potato salad. And stay as long as you like. I believe they are clearing the patio for dancing. Thanks again everyone for coming. I am truly the happiest and luckiest man alive to have such a beautiful wife and so many loving friends."

The crowd ate and had a wonderful time. As the sun was setting the crowd began to get smaller and smaller. By seven only Matt and Barbara and a few workers on the farm were left cleaning up the debris.

"We did it Matthew. Here we are now, husband and wife. I love you so much Matthew."
"And I love you too Barbara. Now don't you think we need to get started on that big family we both planned?" Both smile.

Barbara soon resigned from her job at the insurance company to help Matt manage the farm. She couldn't believe the amount of book work it took to keep track of all the employees' expenses and crop records. She thoroughly enjoyed this work as it enabled her to use more of her accounting skills than had been possible as merely a clerk at the insurance office.

Chapter Fifteen
Matthew's Political Career
1944

After a few years Barbara and Matt began to wonder what had happened to their expected bundle of joy. They wondered if he or she was really to be. But then their prayers were answered with the arrival of a healthy baby boy they named Paul Matthew Ronan. Paul was born April 16, 1944. They called him their miracle child. He was a very inquisitive lad, thoughtful and kind. Being the only child in the family he was very close to his father. Both Barbara and Matthew were wise and caring and had a positive influence on their son, suspecting that he just might be destined for a special place in history. Of course if people were to hear them say such they would follow with, "Oh sure!"

"Honey, why did you insist on naming our son Paul? Was it because Paul is a biblical name?"

"No No, I read once that a person with the name Paul has a deep inner desire for order and physical creativity, and wants to be involved in many things. That just seemed to relate to me. I sure hope you agree."

"Anything you say boss. Do I sound like Fu Le?"

In 1947 Matthew was 41 years old and young Paul was three. Matthew decided to run for the U.S. House of Representatives from the Missouri sixth district.

"Honey, I think I will try to run for the U.S. Congress."

"Why would you want to do that? You have plenty of work to do here on the farm."

"I know dear but there are things happening in Washington that are just not right. Maybe I can help fix some of them."

"Like what?"

"Well, for starters, all of these price supports for farmers are just making things worse. Plus, they are unconstitutional."

Monetary System Needs to be Revised

Matt was both impressed and proud of his father's accomplishments of working as an assistant to President Woodrow Wilson and his patriotic stand on trying to revise the country's monetary system. However he was disappointed in the fact that his father had not been able to influence the President in 1913 to not sign the Federal Reserve Act. Also disconcerting was the fact that President Wilson had supported the 16th Amendment authorizing an income tax on a person's wages, and the 17th Amendment making Senators elected by popular vote instead of each being appointed by the state's governor and legislators. The original Constitution had been written so that Senators were *appointed* rather than by being elected thus freeing them from undue influence so that they could truly represents the states' interests. The idea was to have the Senate represent the *states' interests* and the House to represents the *people's interests*. "With the passage of the 17th Amendment, we may as well have 530 Congressmen instead of 96 Senators and 434 House members," reasoned Matt.

Matthew thought to himself, 'What can I do to abolish the insidious and unconstitutional Federal Reserve? Probably nothing,' he thought, but I won't give up.

Enacting a constitutional amendment is a very difficult process, as it should be. There must be an educational process first so the people will understand what an important issue this is and then support it. Its time will come, thought Matt.

Matthew had been very active in the local Northwest Missouri Farmers Coop and was well known and liked. It seemed natural for him to run for Congress since he had already been appointed to several high profile advisory positions by the Governor of Missouri and even had one appointment by the President to the Department of Agriculture.

With a great deal of support from Matthew's parents, who were still living in Washington D.C., and his political connections, he was easily elected as a Republican Congressman in 1948.

Twin Engine Piper Apache

To make it easy to travel back and forth from Washington to St. Joseph, Matthew purchased a twin engine Piper Apache airplane in 1954. He had always wanted to learn to fly, and this gave him an excuse to justify the expense of owning and operating such an expensive air plane. Matthew was an extremely cautious person and would only fly in good weather and in the daylight hours. The plane was equipped to fly at night under IFR (Instrument Flight Regulations) and though he was rated with an IFR certificate, Matt preferred to fly only in daylight hours and good weather.

There were two extremely important things about flying that his instructor, Bill Cummings had taught him. Number one-Anytime you lose power to the airplane on takeoff, do not attempt to make a 180 degree turn to return to the runway. When you bank the plane, without adequate flying speed, the plane will "stall" and drop like a rock. At a low altitude of a few hundred feet or less, this would be fatal. You should always fly straight ahead and make a controlled emergency landing.

Number two-If you are a business executive or Congressman, do not fly your own airplane. Because you will invariably make the wrong decision to fly in dangerous bad weather conditions in order to make that 8 AM meeting. Number two was good advice but Matthew thought he was intelligent enough to not make that mistake. He knew he could always drive to Washington or take the train when necessary.

Industrial Hemp

Matthew was a successful congressman for over 30 years. He was well respected but occasionally was a thorn in the sides of the powers-that-be. In the 1970's, Congressman Ronan would state on the floor of Congress, *"It is time that we use reason based on facts instead of emotions based on myths and make industrial hemp a viable crop once again. Hemp can be used to make almost anything that is made from cotton, timber or petroleum. It has been claimed that farming 6% of the continental U. S. acreage with biomass crops could provide all of America's energy needs. Not only did Henry Ford design his first Model T to run on hemp gasoline, later models of Fords were designed to be constructed from hemp plastic panels whose impact strength was 10 times stronger than steel. If today's automobiles were required to run on gasoline, diesel and biomass fuel from hemp, we would be well on our way to energy independence."*

Congressman Ronan, being a farmer himself, realized what a benefit it would be to both the Missouri farmer and the entire country's economy to have another cash crop to add to the well-being of the farmer. The growing of agricultural hemp would allow the farmer to engage in the production of energy as well as food crops. Making alcohol for a gasoline additive from hemp made more sense than making it from a food crop like corn about which many people in the energy business were contemplating.

"If that were done," Matthew thought, "I'd hate to think what it would do to the price of food."

Abolish the Privately Owned Federal Reserve

Not being successful in getting any bills passed to legalize the growing of industrial hemp, Congressman Ronan turned his attention to the abolishment of the privately owned Federal Reserve. Also failing to make any headway with this issue he encouraged his son Paul to take up the fight. He hoped that Paul would enter politics, as he was intelligent, knew the issues and seemed to want to help people. Congressman Ronan used to think that the TV and print media would educate the public to the seriousness of these issues. After a few years in office, he decided that this is "Just Not Going to Happen." The corporate news media has the power to make positive changes for the people but instead was geared towards entertainment and ratings and benefits for the controllers of our country; bankers, military industrial complex companies, lobbyists, etc.

Matt was ready to pass the torch to his son Paul, hoping that he could accomplish what he himself had not. He had instilled in Paul the importance of the Federal Government adhering to the

Constitution and to developing sound monetary policies while at the same time respecting the sovereignty of the states and individual freedom. He also believed that the U.S should not try to be the policeman of the world. Not only was it unconstitutional but also immoral for a civilized country like the U.S. to attempt to impose its values on other countries; especially since the real purpose was to take control of their banking system and natural resources. It was an insult to civilized humanity.

Matt soon realized that his son wanted to become a medical doctor, but he secretly hoped that at some point in his career Paul would become more involved in politics.

Chapter Sixteen
Early Life of Paul Ronan

Paul Ronan, the great grandson of Samuel Ronan, grandson of Jefferson Ronan, and whose father was Congressman Matthew Ronan, grew up on his family's farm north of St. Joseph, Missouri in the 1940's and 1950's. Paul was well liked and respected at St. Joseph's Central High School becoming class president in his senior year. He was also active in basketball and track, getting a letter in each. Paul was interested in so many things that his friends didn't see how he had time to fit all his hobbies and interests into his busy schedule, but he certainly did fit them in. He used to explain to his friends that, "You must be organized," and then he would laugh.

Amateur Radio License

Paul was among the first people in the St. Joe area to have a color television set. He even built it himself by purchasing parts from the 'Acme Radio and Supply, a local electronic supply store. His understanding of electronics helped him get his Amateur Radio Novice License in 1957 when he was only 13 years old by passing a test administered by the Federal Communication Commission (FCC) in Kansas City, Missouri. This encouraged him to learn even more about electronics, and made it possible for him to communicate with other 'ham' radio operators throughout the world. He was especially fond of 'CW,' the use of communicating by Morse code rather than voice communications with a microphone. He discovered early on that it was much easier to make worldwide contacts using CW than it was with voice. Because of the constant static on some stations, it was easier to copy code (dots and dashes) than it was to distinguish the human voice, plus he was following in the footsteps of his great grandfather, Samuel Ronan, who had been a telegrapher for the Hannibal and St. Joseph railroad in Breckenridge, Missouri during the 'War Between the States.'

In his senior year at Central, the teacher of the business class he was taking obtained a job for Paul as "Floor Director" at the local TV station, KFEQ TV Channel 2. Paul's main job was to set up scenery and props for the various live shows and to 'que' the announcers as to how much time was left to the end of a program. One finger held close to the camera lens, where the announcer could easily see it, meant one minute remaining and a bent finger meant 30 seconds and a shaking fist signaled it was time to end the program.

Paul had been the floor director for only two months when he was given the chance to direct the news program and the local children's program, and in addition, he even did some sports broadcasting himself on KFEQ radio whose radio studio was in the same building as the TV station. Occasionally he would clown around on the radio by saying things such as, "The sun will rise tomorrow morning and set tomorrow evening, this is KFEQ St. Joseph, Missouri," leaving off the exact times. Once he said on the air, "We are running a little short on time so here is a quick rundown on the sports scores; 7 to 3, 8 to 2, and 50 to nothing." Most of his clowning around was done late at night when there were few people listening.

Fun at KFEQ TV

As floor director, one of his favorite things to do was to develop special effects for the children's show. Since Paul was also interested in magic, thanks to Fu Li, his family's cook, he thought it would be fun if he could make Don Berlie, the MC of the children's show, disappear while he was standing in front of the cartoon set. Before the show went on the air, Paul took a Polaroid picture of the *empty* set and placed it on an easel that could be accessed by camera one. Then he had camera 2 focus on the live set. Both cameras were then turned on at the same time so that the pictures could be lined up exactly. When they went live on the air and Don said he would disappear on the count of three, the director merely transferred the picture from the live set (camera two) to the Polaroid picture (camera one) that had been previously taken with no one in the picture. When you were looking at the studio monitor or your home TV and Don said "Three," sure enough it looked as if he had really disappeared. In fact some of the office personnel came running down to the

196

viewing room to see how Paul had made Don disappear! They could see that he was actually still there but the TV monitor showed he had disappeared. On another one of the children's cartoon shows, Paul laid on his back on a desk covered with a black cloth with a black curtain behind the desk. When the camera man electronically turned the camera upside down and Paul moved his hands and feet, it looked like he was swimming in midair.

His job at the TV station demonstrated what imagination and talent he had. Paul would remark later in life, "that working at the TV station was one of the most fun jobs he ever had."

Aeronca Champ
Paul Ronan's first airplane
for flying lessons

Another one of Paul's hobbies was that of flying. Flying was an expensive hobby even if you rented a plane; especially for a high school student. Fortunately Paul's father, Congressman Matthew Ronan, agreed to pay for his flying lessons and bought him an Aeronca Chief two seater airplane for $1200.00 after he soloed. His father did have his own plane to fly back and forth to Washington, but it was way too complicated for Paul to begin learning; it was a twin engine Piper Apache. Paul decided to learn to fly in a more economical and simpler air craft. Those included the Aeronca Champ, J-3 Cub, and the Cessna 120 and 140. The small planes didn't even have an electric starter! The instructor/pilot pushed on the brakes while the student turned the propeller by hand until it started, which was kind of like starting your lawnmower by turning it upside down and turning the blade with your hands.

Where Am I

One afternoon Paul ran into a bit of trouble. It was only his second solo flight when he became disorientated and couldn't locate the Rosecrans airport. At 2,000 feet up, the runway would appear about the size of a postage stamp. He wasn't even sure in which direction to look. Paul had studied navigation but had normally relied on his Omni Directional Radio which he soon discovered was not working; so he quickly went to plan "B". As he would often remark, "One must always be ready in an emergency and have **plan B** ready." He opened up his notebook binder with all of his flight manuals and calculators and pulled out a roadmap of Missouri. He then flew down low by a water tower and observed the town's name printed on the side. The tower said 'Platte City'. It was then a simple matter to follow the railroad tracks and highway 71 north out of Platte City toward St. Joseph and Rosecrans field. Plan "B" worked, but Paul vowed to make sure the radio was working the next time before he took off.

Baylor University-Texas

As many young people do, Paul decided to move away from home to be on his own. He was pretty sure he didn't want to be a farmer or politician like his father. He decided to enroll at Baylor University in Texas; later to be named the Baylor College of Medicine. Paul was influenced by the college's rise in prominence beginning in the 1950's when Dr. DeBakey's innovative surgical techniques received international attention. Baylor was known for its excellence in education, research and patient care, plus it had a Christian atmosphere which appealed to Paul. Paul enjoyed college life, was an excellent student and pursued a career in medicine. Paul had obtained his Master's Degree and was well on his way in the field of medicine when the advent of the Vietnam War placed a block in his studies.

While being from a very patriotic family, Paul, wanted to serve his country so decided to join the Navy. He knew he could always go back to further his studies in medicine after doing his part in the war. He considered himself to be a patriot and wished to do his part in protecting the U. S. from outside aggressors but didn't feel comfortable participating in the Viet Nam war, a war that he thought was more about *America's* aggression than a foreign country's threat to our security. He didn't understand why the North Vietnamese were considered a threat to America's security.

Paul reasoned that it was the same hidden agenda all over again; a means to make huge profits for the international bankers and the military industrial complex companies. He felt that the American people had been lied to about Russian Communism by exaggerating the threat. Was North Vietnam really a threat to the U.S.? Was Vietnamese Communism the same as Russian Communism? A few years later he would discover that the cold war with Russia was largely a hoax and that the Gulf of Tonkin attack in 1964 by the North Vietnamese never happened.

He kept asking himself, "What did we really accomplish in Vietnam except the sacrificing of so many lives of both the Vietnamese and Americans? If I am to serve, Paul reasoned, life on a ship would be preferable to sleeping in a fox hole and marching through the swamps in Vietnam."

Paul's opinions on this issue were greatly influence by reading General Smedley Butler's book, *War is a Racket,* first published in 1935." General Butler honestly discussed how business interests for profiteering were the main reasons for war.

Chapter Seventeen
Paul Joins the Navy
1966

Paul's first assignment in the Navy was on the USS Liberty, a United States Navy technical research ship. Paul Ronan served as a medic and as an auxiliary member of the radio communication team because of his experience in communications and electronics.

USS Liberty Ship photo courtesy of James Ennes, author of: "Assault on the Liberty: The True Story of the Attack by Israel on an American Intelligence ship."

"Good morning Captain McGonagall," said Paul as he boarded the USS Liberty.

"Good morning, welcome aboard. I guess this is your first tour of duty in the Navy."

"Yes sir. Although I'm not technically a doctor quite yet, I have quite a bit of training as a medic. I hope to complete my medical training and become a Doctor of medicine after my tour of duty in the Navy. I plan on returning to Baylor University in Texas. "Wise choice Ronan. It's good to have another Medic on board. You realize of course our mission of reconnaissance can still be fraught with danger because we are many times close to the actual battles, obtaining highly classified information to report back to Washington."

"That's fine. I will do my job and serve my country as best I can," replied Paul.

Paul is Deployed Off the Sinai Peninsula Near Egypt

Paul spent the first three weeks getting accustomed to his new home aboard the ship and learning how to cope with seasickness. His first deployment was in the international waters off the Sinai Peninsula near Egypt. Shortly before Israel's Six Day War with Egypt had begun, the USS Liberty was ordered to proceed to the eastern Mediterranean to perform an electronic intelligence operation mission. Since there was a war going on between Israel, Egypt, and several Arab states, the captain had requested Vice Admiral William I. Martin of the U.S. 6th Fleet to send a destroyer to accompany the Liberty to serve as an armed escort and as a secondary communication center. The following reply was received:

"Request denied. *Liberty is a clearly marked United States ship in international waters, not a participant in the conflict and not a reasonable subject for attack by any nation."*

It further stated that if they were attacked, he could assist them with jet fighters from the 6th Fleet in ten minutes.

USS Liberty Purposely Attacked by Israel

Everything was fairly routine until the morning of June 8, 1967. Paul thought he could hear approaching aircraft and when he looked up he saw aircraft flying over and around the USS Liberty. Paul hollered to the captain, "Who are they? They sure don't appear to be American."

The captain replied, "They look like they're Israeli to me. There is a *flying boxcar* and what looks like *Mirage III jet fighters*. That's strange. I can't see any markings on the planes. They're surely Israeli and will recognize us as American and an ally. Once they see the American flag flying on our vessel they will know we pose no threat to them. Look, one of the pilots is waving to us. Its ok, they can see we are an American ship. They probably just wanted to get close enough to our vessel so they could verify who we were," explained the captain.

"I sure hope you're right, Captain. There's a lot of fire power up there," said Paul.

But after all their discussion and contemplation, terror suddenly began relentlessly to rain down on the USS Liberty. A little after 2:00 PM, the Mirages began attacking the USS Liberty with cannons, rockets and bombs. No one on the Liberty could believe what was happening. There was chaos everywhere. Crew members were being shot and blown completely off the deck. Paul could see that the radio officer had been wounded, so he rushed to the radio room to see if he could help but the strafing from the jets had destroyed the antennas and some of the radio equipment. Paul hurriedly took an emergency dipole antenna and strung it up between the ships two remaining antenna masts before the jets returned. The makeshift antenna was not very high but just high enough that the signal could reach the 6th Fleet. Or so he hoped. Paul proceeded to send out a CW (Morse code) signal "SOS…SOS…SOS Under attack by unidentified jet aircraft, possibly Israeli, require immediate assistance!"

Paul ran out of the radio room to attend to the injured and saw two aircrafts that looked like *Dassault Mysteres* armed with napalm bombs. They dropped their payloads over the Liberty and strafed it with their cannons. The entire superstructure of the ship was on fire.

During the interval between attacks, some of the Liberty's crew hoisted another large American flag so the attackers could not miss that they were an American ship in international waters. But would they be able to see it with the dense cloud of smoke obscuring its view?

6th Fleet Fails to Aid USS Liberty

The 6th Fleet had received the Liberty's distress call and the aircraft carrier USS America dispatched eight aircraft. It was later discovered that Vice Admiral William I. Martin had recalled the aircraft minutes later with the excuse that he feared the attackers of the USS Liberty were Soviet and did not want to risk starting a nuclear war, *(At least that was the excuse used).*

Next the attackers, which now clearly appeared to be the Israeli's, launched five torpedoes at the Liberty; one hit her on the starboard side forward of the superstructure killing 25 servicemen and wounding dozens of others. It was sheer luck that the other four torpedoes missed the ship. The Israeli's were obviously trying to sink the ship and kill everyone on board. Then torpedo boats closed in and fired at those seamen preparing to enter the lifeboats. Paul briefly wondered, why. Why are they doing this?" But he had no time to think about it. He heroically put himself in harms way to attend to his wounded shipmates. Then suddenly it appeared that finally, Israel had discovered their mistake and halted the attack. But had it really been just a mistake?

Although the *USS Liberty* was severely damaged, her crew kept it afloat and it was able to leave the area under its own power. The destroyers, the *USS Davis and the* USS *Massey*, and the cruiser *USS Little Rock finally* came to assist. Medical personnel were transferred to the *Liberty* to assist Paul Ronan who was included in the wounded. The ship was then escorted to Malta.

Ronan later learned that the Israeli bombers had used unmarked planes and vessels to launch the attack against the *Liberty* that was clearly flying the American flag. Thirty four American servicemen were murdered and at least 171 were wounded. An inquiry was made but both Israel and the American authorities agreed, "It was all a mistake," and Israel apologized.

Warning- Do Not Discuss Attack

The American sailors were threatened to not discuss the matter with anyone. They feared that their pensions would be suspended and that they might even be killed if they discussed what really happened. Some believed it was Israel's intention to leave the impression that the U.S. had been attacked by Egypt so the U.S. would then retaliate by attacking Egypt. This would have made it much easier for Israel to win the Arab Six Days War with Egypt, Jordan and Syria. Others believed that the U.S. had intercepted radio transmissions showing that the Israeli's were systematically executing captured Egyptian soldiers and wanted to keep it a secret.

If a Russian ship had not passed nearby it is believed that Israel would have killed all aboard and sunk the *USS Liberty* ship. There would have been no witnesses and the U.S. would have most likely blamed Egypt and no one would have known about the alleged massacre perpetrated by Israel. Sometime later US Secretary of State Dean Rusk, purportedly stated, "I was never satisfied with the Israeli explanation... Through diplomatic channels we refused to accept their explanation. I didn't believe them then, and I don't believe them to this day. The attack was outrageous." (It was rumored that even President Johnson, referring to the USS Liberty had said, "I want that God D--- ship sunk.")

Lieutenant Paul Ronan spent the next year recuperating and then spent the rest of his tour of duty in a military intelligence group. The experience of Israel's attack on the USS Liberty and how both Israel and American officials lied about what had happened troubled him immensely. He felt he was in great danger if he even talked about it. He had been threatened with demotion, imprisonment and even a hint that his life or a member of his family could be in danger if he even talked about the attack.

Chapter Eighteen
Medical Career or Politician
1971

After his honorable discharge from the Navy, Paul continued with his medical career. After receiving his doctorate he eventually relocated to Katy, Texas to start his own medical practice. However, because of his experience on the USS Liberty, he seriously contemplated running for Congress. Maybe as a Congressman he could convince Congress to initiate an inquiry as to what really went on concerning Israel's attack on the *USS Liberty,* and even more importantly, why? That and other issues regarding how the US was rapidly becoming a nation that had lost its way kept gnawing away at him. However, he decided to put off a risky political career and make use of his education.

Katy, Texas was a growing community just a few miles west of Houston, Texas that had tremendous growth potential because of its proximity to Houston and the booming oil business. Katy will be a wonderful town to settle in, and to start my medical practice. Most of his friends said they had never heard of Katy, Texas until he reminded them of watching trains pass at railroad crossings all across the United States with *Katy Railroad* printed on them.

"Oh yes," they would remark. "I have heard of Katy, Texas."

Early on it dawned on Paul that he had been educated to be a doctor of medicine and not a business man. He had taken one accounting course but could not picture himself as a doctor and an accountant too.

The first thing to do in setting up my practice is to put an ad in the paper to hire an office manager, thought Dr. Ronan.

A few days later he began to get some applicants. He had each one fill out an application with references and told them he would be in touch. The one that impressed him most had just graduated from college with a business management major and a minor in accounting. He had hoped to find someone with some medical experience but none of the applicants had ever worked for a doctor or even in the medical field.

Paul reviewed the four applications he had received and called the one that looked the most promising, Ms. Carol Blakely, to come in for an interview. He nervously dialed the number on the application and said, "Carol Blakely, this is Doctor Ronan. You left an application here last week for employment as an office manager and I was wondering if you could come in tomorrow about 2:30 for a personal interview?"

"Yes I can, Doctor Ronan. Thank you very much. I will see you tomorrow afternoon."

Carol Blakely Interviewed for Office Manager

Carol arrived at the office about thirty minutes early which impressed Dr. Ronan. She had a pleasant demeanor and was also quite attractive. He didn't mean to stare but the first thing he was looking for was a person who would make a good impression with his patients. As they were talking he tried to determine if she smoked. She didn't smell like she had been smoking and she seemed very calm and sure of herself.

"Do you want to tell me a little about yourself, Carol?"

"Of course, Dr. Ronan. I most recently graduated from college and though I don't have actual experience working in the human medical field, I worked all through college for my father in his veterinarian hospital in Houston. I know accounting fairly well, I'm not a CPA, but I can handle a complete set of double entry accounting records plus payroll accounting."

"Hmm, that sounds good. I don't know an asset from a liability," laughed Paul. "I've heard that if your liabilities are more than your assets, your assets in jail."

"That's funny Doctor but I have heard that one before. Let me explain the difference between an asset and a liability. An Asset is

206

what is owned and a Liability is who owns it. All you really need to understand is the accounting equation which is *Assets equals Liabilities.* Your assets are what you own, like cash in the bank, real-estate, office furniture and equipment, etc., and your liabilities are who owns them like the bank carrying the mortgage on your property, your credit card balance, etc. When you subtract the liabilities from the assets the equation is out of balance. The difference to make the equation balance is called your net worth or in other words, how much of the business is owned by you," explained Carol.

"You make it sound so simple, Carol."

"One other thing that I sort of invented myself is what I call *Comparative Analysis Records.* I post the monthly accounting records for the *Income and Expense statement* on one large analysis pad showing the entire year at a glance, plus at the far right there is a monthly budget and yearly budget and variances. This makes it a simple manner to compare individual expense and income amounts, month by month."

"That sounds good, Carol, but I don't think we need to be concerned with budgeting."

"Most people think, in error, that budgeting's only function is to make sure that you don't spend more money than you take in. But that's only part of the reason you do a budget. Let me give you an example. Say you budget an expense item at $500.00 per month and in April your accounting records show you spent $1,000.00. A quick glance at March and April shows the 500 dollar amount in the March column and the 1,000 dollar amount in the April column. Additionally the budget variance would be out by $500.00 (far right column) which would draw your attention to it and demand an explanation. Upon checking you find that you paid the same bill twice. It is better for *you* to discover this error rather than rely on the payee to inform you."

"I see what you mean, Carol. That's quite impressive. What do you know about hiring people?"

"When I worked for my father and we needed help, I would call a temporary agency. If they sent someone who did a good job, I would ask them to come back the next day. If they did a poor job, I simply thanked them and waited a couple of days and requested another temp. If that person did a good job after a week or two, I would offer them a full time job."

"That's pretty clever, Carol. I would never have even thought of that. Is that legal?"

"I don't see why not. It is good for both the prospective employee and the employer because it gives both of them a trial period and if it doesn't work out for either one , no one is hurt."

"Carol, I would like to make you an offer to work for me as my office manager. It would be Monday through Friday 8:00 to 5:00. After the first year you will get one week paid vacation and after two years you will get two weeks paid vacation."

"Good. I think I'd like to do that. I can start immediately if you'd like," said Carol.

"Fantastic, the first thing I'd like you to do is set up an accounting system for us, and then hire a medical assistant. I will have you interview all perspective employees first and then I will make the final choice," said Paul.

"Carol, I think we're going to make a great team."

Six Months Later

It took about six months for Dr. Ronan to get enough patients to begin covering most of his expenses. After spending so much money on equipment, it would take another two years for him to make a decent profit. Dr. Ronan felt very good about hiring Carol. She had been a real lifesaver in setting up his practice initially. There were several times each month when the books had to be closed that both Dr. Ronan and Carol had to work late. Usually when they finished about 9:00 in the evening Dr. Ronan would take Carol out for dinner as a way to say *thank you* for all her hard work.

Tennis Elbow Cure

Carol was quite an employee. She would on occasion read medical journals about new treatments and diets that could be very beneficial to a patient's wellbeing. Dr. Ronan had been treating one of his patients for tennis elbow without having much success. He had injected cortisone into the elbow to relieve the man's pain but it only lasted a few weeks and then the patient was back complaining that he couldn't even pick up a bucket of water without experiencing a shooting pain in his elbow.

While typing up the results of the office visit and the corresponding treatment, she remembered reading about tennis elbow in one of the journals. After the office was closed for the day, she went into the doctor's office.

"I read in one of your journals how to cure most patients' tennis elbow."

"Ok, Carol. How would you do it?" inquired Paul, a little sarcastically.

"First you would have the patient hold a 3 pound bar bell using the affected arm. Then have him exercise the arm moving the elbow. If it hurts, have him slightly change the angle until there is no pain. Then advise him to do this twice a day for 10 minutes each time, for two weeks, and make an appointment to come back. In most cases the pain will be gone," explained Carol.

"And just how would you explain this miraculous cure, *Doctor* Carol?"

"It's no miracle. You know the painful tightness you feel in your arm when you paint for several hours? Well when you exercise the arm in the position that doesn't hurt it builds up the muscles surrounding the torn elbow muscles allowing them to heal."

"Carol, you are amazing. I think that could work. Please don't tell anybody that it was your idea. Remember, I am the doctor," laughed Paul.

Doctor Ronan and Carol are Smitten

As time went on, Carol and Paul became closer and closer until they both realized they were in love. They quietly got married and Carol continued to work in the office but most of the patients didn't realize that Dr. Ronan was Carol's husband.

Dr. Ronan Considers Running for Office

In 1989 Paul again began to think seriously about running for Congress. He had become quite active in the local Republican groups and was beginning to become well known from the speeches he had made and the letters and articles he had published in the local papers and professional medical journals. Much of his political knowledge was derived from his father, Matthew Ronan, who had spent 30 plus years as a congressman from Missouri. The Houston Chronicle had interviewed him several times concerning his take on the country's economy and the part the bankers played. Also Dr. Ronan was asked to speak regularly at political events in his area and was so well known politically that many of the political candidates would regularly seek his endorsement.

"Carol. I have been asked to give a speech next month to the Republican Central Committee about Patriotism. Since you have heard me talk about this numerous times in our own conversations, do you think you would have the time to write a short discourse that I could expand on to make a thirty minute speech?"

"Of course. When is your speech to be delivered?"

"It is the second Thursday next month but I would like to have it ready next week so I will have time to expand it and make changes if necessary."

"Ok, but when I'm through with it, you won't need to change it one bit!" (Smiling)

Carol- the Speech Writer

Carol turned out to be an excellent speech writer and it proved to Paul that she really did listen to him when he was talking politics. Some of Paul's friends had heard his same stories so many times that he felt they weren't always paying attention. He understood that, but was still sometimes aggravated when they wouldn't show the same concern as he on the really important issues like abolishing the privately owned Federal Reserve and the fact that the Federal Government didn't always respect states' rights by completely ignoring the Tenth Amendment.

Right on time Carol had completed a synopsis of his patriot speech.

"Paul, read this and let me know what you think."

Who are the Real Patriots?

It is an honor to be speaking to you this evening. Your chairman, Bob Strickland, has asked me to speak to you on one of my favorite subjects, **Who are the real patriots?**

It is ironic but one country's patriot is often times another country's enemy or even a terrorist. I don't suppose that King George the Third considered George Washington and Thomas Jefferson as patriots. However the founding fathers of America are considered patriots today because they risked their lives and fortunes in signing the Declaration of Independence and by adding their names to the United States Constitution.

Until recently the Constitution served as a positive example to the world and gave hope to millions of immigrants like my great grandfather who came to this country from Ireland in 1848. He came to this country so he could be free to pursue his dreams without interference from the government. Our elected representatives, for the most part, represented the people and honored their oath to abide by the Constitution. However, today, many of our legislators have been ignoring the Constitution and they instead represent foreign interests and vote in a manner that is more beneficial to the international bankers and special interest lobbyists than to the American people. Those legislators are certainly *not* patriots. The fact that they wear a flag lapel pin and salute the flag does not make them a patriot. There are a higher percentage of true patriots involved in the Libertarian Party, and even the John Birch Society than there are in our country's status quo Republican and Democrat leaders. Please note, I said *leaders* and not *Representatives!*

A true patriot believes that the Federal government (1) must abide by the Constitution including the Bill of Rights (2) adopt sound monetary policies by abolishing the private Federal Reserve Banking cartel and Fractional Reserve Banking except for those banks owned by the state (Taxpayers) (3) stop acting as the policeman of the world and (4) respect the sovereignty of the states and an individual's liberty...

The non-patriots don't offer solutions; they only criticize the true patriots. Why shouldn't a patriot question events like the *Kennedy Assassination* and the *1967 Israeli attack* on an American ship that killed 34 American sailors? It's not like we have been told the truth in the past-i.e. the *Gulf of Tonkin incident, weapons of mass destruction* in Iraq *Operation Northwoods,* and the exaggerated *Russian cold war threat hoax...*

By today's standards of the controlling elite and the dumbed down electorate, George Washington, Thomas Jefferson and Benjamin Franklin would be labeled as unpatriotic and suspected terrorists by the news media...

Be wary of those labeling the true patriots as *Anti-Semitic, conspiracy nuts, paranoid, right wingers, birthers etc.* Those doing the labeling are the real threat and are the most unpatriotic because of their attempt to unfairly marginalize the true patriots...

"That was excellent Carol! A few additions and minute changes will make it perfect. You are so helpful. Thank you, thank you, thank you!"

212

Besides wanting to abolish the privately owned Federal Reserve Bank that charges the taxpayers interest for loaning them their own money, Paul wanted the judges to begin advising prospective jurors about 'Jury Nullification;' the idea that the jurors can judge the law itself as well as the facts in a case. It has been recognized, beginning with our founding fathers, that the law does not always apply to a particular defendant under certain circumstances. Following are three Guest Columnist pieces Dr. Ronan wrote:

Secret Power of the Juror
By Guest Columnist Dr. Paul Ronan

Most people have no idea that when they serve as a juror, that they have more power than the President of the United States. Even though they are seldom told, the juror can find the defendant innocent for any reason, even if he broke the law.

The Sixth Amendment of our Constitution guarantees the defendant to a trial by a jury of one's peers (not the defendant's peers *and* a judge) as a final 'check and balance' for protection from a possibly tyrannical governmental law that may not apply in all cases, or protection from a biased judge.

For instance, it used to be a felony to help a slave escape. However, there were cases where the jury found the defendant innocent because all he was doing was saving the life of a drowning slave who was attempting to escape. In other words, the law should not apply in this case.

I have questioned several judges to find out their opinion on this issue and discovered that most preferred not to comment. One politely disagreed, explaining that if the jurors exercised this right, it would be extremely difficult to ever convict anyone. I explained that that was the idea because if a mistake were to be made, it would be preferable to being made by a jury of the defendant's peers than from a possible biased judge or an unfair law.

Another judge was not so kind. He said, "What law school did you graduate from?" I wanted to ask him how he became a Judge if he had flunked his constitutional law course. Don't ever let a judge or the prosecuting attorney know that you understand your rights as a juror (Jury Nullification). You could be held in contempt of court and will most certainly not be chosen as a juror during the selection process.

This letter caused quite a ruckus from local judges. One even wrote a rebuttal letter claiming that Dr. Ronan didn't know what he was talking about. This even further caused Dr. Ronan to run for office to see if he could get elected and make the necessary changes to save our country from ruin.

The Ultimate Solution
By: Dr. Paul Ronan- Guest Columnist

Let's face it. Our country is in a financial crisis and few of our Representatives know what to do. Those few who do know are unfairly marginalized by being labeled far right extremists. However, they only appear to be far right because there are so many that are so far left.

Not only is our country headed for bankruptcy, it is broken in so many other ways:

- A large majority of our politicians do not honor their oath to uphold the Constitution

- Our Presidents continue to abuse executive orders to go to war without approval from Congress which has done nothing but create more terrorists and huge profits for the bankers and military industrial complex companies

- State sovereignty is completely ignored when the Federal Government continues to ignore the Tenth Amendment which states, "The powers not delegated to the United States by the Constitution , nor prohibited by it to the States, are reserved to the States respectively, or to the people

214

- The Commerce clause in our Constitution is used by Washington to justify almost any action they claim is in the best interest of the people and

- Starting in 1993, there has been a huge increase in questionable 'Over the Counter' (OTC) derivatives, which has been estimated to be over a hundred trillion dollars annually. These investments were virtually ignored by the regulators which allowed companies to be exempt from regulation in the trading of derivatives. The economic losses to investors have been astronomical.

Abolish the Privately Owned Federal reserve

One immediate solution to our country's economic problems is to abolish the private *Federal Reserve System* that charges the taxpayers interest for loaning them their own money. The U.S. Treasury Department can print our money 'Interest Free' and it is Constitutional, as long as it is backed by gold or silver. However, it should be noted that currently the Federal Reserve notes have no precious metal backing.

The Federal Reserve Act has failed miserably in eliminating the boom and bust business cycles caused by inflation and poor financial management. Abolishing the private Federal Reserve is one the most important issues you will ever consider, followed closely by drastically curtailing our governments out of control spending. We must finance our country's expenses through transparent taxes instead of the hidden inflation tax caused by debt financing.

Every one of us needs to diligently study these issues so we can intelligently vote for those legislators who will make the necessary changes to return our country to that which was envisioned by our founding fathers.

Our National Debt is the Biggest Threat to Our Country
By: Dr. Paul Ronan- Guest Columnist

Neither the Democrats nor the Republicans have any intention of paying off the national debt. It is politically more beneficial for the politicians to finance their excessive spending through hidden *debt financing* rather than through *transparent taxes.* Financing our government through transparent taxes, would immediately inform the taxpayer of the folly of the politicians' excessive spending because of extremely higher personal income tax. This would most definitely assure the politicians of being elected for only one term.

Even if our government's leaders wanted to pay off the country's debt, it is not possible under our current banking system. Our economy (money supply) is always short the amount of interest that *was not* created through fractional reserve banking. When the bank approves your loan, they create the principal out of thin air but the interest is not created at all. The Federal Government will, at some future date, have to create this money by borrowing it from the privately owned Federal Reserve Bank which charges the taxpayers interest. The interest, not created by the Federal Reserve's loan, forces our government to borrow even more money. It is a never ending cycle; the federal debt can never be paid off.

The only solution is to:

- Abolish the *unconstitutional Federal Reserve* and allow the U.S. Treasury Department to issue our money supply interest free, as provided for in the Constitution. This would not be inflationary as long as they don't issue more than the difference between the total GDP less the money already in circulation. In other words, there is not enough money in circulation to conduct commerce in a way as to consume the excess production. In order for the people to consume this excess production, they could purchase it by charging it to their credit cards, which is done now, or the Federal Government could give all Americans a stimulus check instead of allowing the banks to profit for something they had nothing to do with. This concept is referred to as *Credit as a Public Utility*. Even if you think this is an unrealistic idea, and is unlikely to be adopted, it still helps to explain our flawed and unconstitutional banking system.

- Allow *fractional reserve banking* for only those banks owned by the state. North Dakota is currently the only state with a state-owned bank. Instead of private banks profiting from fractional reserve banking, the taxpayers would profit. This profit could then pay for many of the state's public works projects, *interest free.*

- The Federal Government should declare bankruptcy and write off the trillions owed to the privately owned Federal Reserve Bank. Don't feel sorry for them. They have stolen much more than that from the American people since 1913. (Write off just the amount owed to the Fed and any other banks in the world that are affiliated with them; not individual bond holders.)

- The next step is to finance the operation of our government only through *transparent taxes* instead of through *non-transparent* debt financing. Debt financing should only be used in extreme emergencies, like when another country invades the U.S., or a meteor hits the U.S. and destroys huge areas of the country. Everything else must be paid for through taxation. Debt financing taxes the people twice; a hidden inflation tax plus the normal income tax.

A side benefit to my proposal, besides paying off the national debt, would be that it would almost eliminate all wars or *Regime change*, as some refer to it. Just imagine the President appearing on the six o'clock news and saying, "My fellow Americans, the United Nations, not Congress, has advised me that the U.S. must nuke Iceland because they won't allow us to steal their oil or allow the international bankers to take over their banking system. Since we can no longer resort to hidden *debt financing to* finance this operation, we are going to double your income tax for the next five years.

What do you think would happen? We definitely would not go to war and the President would probably be impeached; it surely would be the end of his political career.

We continuously vote every four years for both Republican and Democrat leaders that represent the **Banksters** instead of the people. Nothing much will change, until the public understands that our current banking system is unconstitutional and that the Federal Reserve Bank is privately owned, created for the sole purpose of making huge profits for themselves at the expense of the American people.

"Maybe the time has come that I should consider ruining for U.S. Congress," thought Paul.

Chapter Nineteen
Congressional Candidate
1990

The failure of the Federal government to abide by the Constitution and to respect the sovereignty of the states and an individual's liberty was more than Dr. Ronan could bear. And the Federal Reserve banking scam against the American people really bothered him.

"I simply have to do something," thought Paul. "There must be something I can do to remedy the situation. If I could just get elected to Congress perhaps I could have an influence on our country's problems. But what do I know about getting elected, the ins and outs, the what ifs? Oh well, maybe I can do it."

Paul spent many hours discussing this with his father , former congressman Matthew Ronan.

These thoughts went through his mind endlessly, for months, until he finally came to the decision to run for Congress. I hate to turn my practice over to my partner, but I feel I can do so much more that is needed by serving in congress. Dr. Ronan hired Jack Wilson to be his campaign manager. Jack had had some experience, not at the Federal level, but at the state level where he successfully helped get a State Representative, Albert Black, elected. Paul's father, Congressman Matthew Ronan from Missouri was well known, so he should be able to take advantage of *name recognition*. Paul's father, Matt, was elated when Paul told him he had decided to run for the U.S. Congress.

"Jack, before I launch a serious campaign, we need to develop a platform that explains to the public what changes need to take place to save our country from destruction," said Paul, emphatically.
"That's true Paul, but we need to develop **two** political agendas, one public and one private."
"Why on earth would we do that?" asked Paul.

"Let me explain. Instead of coming right out and saying you want to abolish the private Federal Reserve banking cartel, you want to relegate that goal to the private agenda. If that were revealed publically, you would immediately have the powerful international bankers alerted to your agenda and they would take whatever measures necessary to insure your failure."

"I see what you mean but how can I convince the voters to vote for me if I don't specifically state that I want to abolish the Federal Reserve? You know there are literally millions of people who would agree with me."

"You are right, Paul, but instead we will simply say that you wish to adopt 'Sound Monetary Policies', and after you are elected, you can pursue your true agenda when you are sure you have enough support in both the House and Senate to pass a banking bill. This is such a huge change to our system you might want to wait until you become President to pursue abolishing the Federal Reserve," said Jack with a smile on his face.

"You are correct, and as President, instead of attempting to pass a banking bill to abolish the Fed, which by the way would be next to impossible, I could do what President Kennedy did three months before his assassination. Remember, Kennedy had the U.S. Treasury Department simply print, by executive order, several billion dollars of *interest free* treasury notes instead of *interest bearing* Federal Reserve notes. This bypassed the unnecessary private bankers. Kennedy most likely reasoned that if this procedure could be continued, in a few years the old paper Federal Reserve notes would naturally deteriorate and cease to exist. The Federal Reserve's function would then have been primarily just a clearing house. That would be much easier than getting a bill passed or a constitutional amendment to abolish the Fed."

"Yes but there is one serious problem to consider, Paul. Remember, Kennedy was assassinated shortly after he did that. The banking interests were poised to lose billions, maybe trillions if the Federal Reserve were to be abolished."

"I know, Jack, but just look at what it would do for the American public. Their living standard would most likely increase by at least 30 to 35% because they would no longer be required to pay an income tax on their salaries to pay the Fed's unnecessary interest. Did you know that our citizens' income tax collected on salaries does not go to pay for government services but rather pays mainly for the interest the Fed charges us for loaning us our own money?"

"Paul, how would we pay for our schools and highways if people didn't pay an income tax?"

Paul explained, "Jack, Jack Jack. We'd remind them that schools are funded primarily from local county property taxes, and highways are funded by State and Federal motor fuel taxes or tolls. Don't tell me you didn't know that. I didn't say, they wouldn't pay *any* income tax; just not on their wages. Small business and corporate profits and commercial real estate profits would still be taxable. Also, keep in mind that an income tax on a person's wages is in reality a form of slavery since an employee must work several hours a day just to pay the tax and does not derive personal benefit from it."

"You are exactly right Paul, and yes, I did know that, but that's the type of questions that will be asked by the uninformed electorate."

"Jack, you also know that I don't believe that the United States can continue to be the *policeman of the world*. We have hundreds of military bases around the world costing billions of dollars to maintain, and our unwanted presence in many of these countries is simply creating more terrorists. This has got to stop. Not only can we not afford it, it's un-American. A civilized nation should not be doing this! I advocate bringing the majority of our troop's home immediately. Let's return our country to the era where we have a *strong defensive military* instead of an *imperialistic offensive military.*"

"Again, I agree with you Paul, but let's be careful how we state your opinion on this matter. We don't want to bring down the wrath of the bankers **and** the military industrial complex companies that make billions in profits from war. Remember, there is more profit to be made for them in war time than in peace time."

"You know that one of my views is that our legislators and president must abide by the Constitution. I believe that three fourths of Congress could be impeached because they did not uphold their oath to obey the Constitution. They continually vote for Acts that are not allowed because of the Tenth Amendment. The Tenth Amendment states, 'Powers *not delegated* to the United States by the Constitution, nor prohibited by the states, are reserved to the states respectively or to the people."

"I don't think we should get into that either, right now, Paul- Just leave it to me. We will write your platform in such a way that it will appeal to both liberals and conservatives. We need to state the facts in such an ambiguous way that it can be interpreted in two different ways. That's what politicians do."

"I don't like that Jack."

"I know, I don't like it either, but that is the way it must be done if you are to ever get elected to Congress."

"Jack, I just thought of something we haven't discussed."

"And what might that be?"

"We haven't talked about "Fractional Reserve Banking. The abolishment of the Fed applies mainly to the Federal government but the states have their own unique banking issues," explained Paul.

Fractional Reserve Banking

"Paul, I have no idea what Fractional Reserve Banking is and I doubt very much that the American people do either."

"Let me try and explain. First you need to understand that about 90% of our money supply is in the form of *Book Credit* and 10% is actual paper money. When you deposit One thousand dollars of your money into a local bank, that bank is required to keep 10% as a reserve but can create a loan of 90% or nine hundred dollars. In other words, they are licensed to counterfeit money. They don't actually print paper dollars but simply created credit of $900. The private bank makes a profit by creating money out of thin air and loaning that money out at interest. But it gets worse. The bank created the $900 principal but did not create the interest. Right away there is a shortage of money in the market place to cover the interest. Someone in the chain of events in paying off a loan will need to default because there is not enough money to complete the transaction. And it's even worse- that $900 created out of thin air eventually gets deposited and 90% of this $900 can be created out of thin air. This eventually results in the creation of 9 times the original money. (900 + 810 + 729... I propose that Fractional Reserve Banking be permitted by only those banks that are owned by the state. In this way the state (taxpayers) would benefit from this 'license to create money out of 'thin air' instead of the private Federal Reserve bank.

Banking as a Public Utility

"Just think, if a state, county, or city owned the bank, they could finance many of their municipal projects, interest free, by using the profits generated by the taxpayer owned bank. In other words, the people would benefit from the profit generated instead of the private banks. This concept is called *Banking as a Public Utility.*"

"Paul that is unbelievable. How did you every discover this?"

"My grandfather and his father studied our banking system for several years and concluded that the current banking system does not serve the needs of the people but makes tremendous profits for the bankers at the expense of the people. I think the time has come for a real change in our monetary system."

"I wouldn't even mention how you feel about Fractional Reserve banking to anyone. I wouldn't even write it down. Once the media knows that you intend to allow only Fractional Reserve Banking for taxpayer owned banks, your political career will be over. I am not sure that the public is ready for this. First they somehow need to be educated. Maybe you could encourage others to write blogs, newspaper articles, etc., and gradually educate the public, but don't ever let anyone know you are behind it."

"I understand, Jack. America is now bankrupt: financially, economically, politically, and morally. What a mess we are in. Can we change the system alone? No. We must get the support of the state legislators and governors and other political groups in electing both conservative Republicans and Libera Democrats who

will revise our monetary system and adopt fiscal responsibility."
It's going to take both sides of the aisle to make monetary reform
a reality.

Ways to make Change

"There are three other ways to make changes, Paul. (1) You
can have a **Revolution** but the danger in that is that we may wind
up worse than before with someone gaining power like Fidel
Castro. (2) States could *secede* but the majority of the American
people, wrongly, believe that Abraham Lincoln already solved that
issue even though the eleven southern states had a right to secede.
and (3) the state governments can nullify unconstitutional Federal
laws. You know like what has already been done by states passing
legislation to disregard Federal laws about immigration, about
prayer in schools, legalization of marijuana etc. Of course these
are challenged by the Federal courts but if enough of the states act
in concert, things can change at the Federal level."

"Well, let's hope and pray we can make the necessary changes
through the use of the 'Soap Box' and 'Ballot Box' instead of the
'Cartridge Box', said Paul.

"Paul, I just thought of another way. No...on second thought
it would still be under the category of a Revolution. Never mind."

"Go ahead Jack. We are in a private unrecorded conversation;
explain what you mean by that remark."

Let's Drain the Swamp

"Ok, understand that I am not advocating this method but it
would be an interesting scenario for a novel. The President, not
you Paul, could invite the top 50 or so CIA, NSA and FBI
directors and managers to a special meeting at Camp David and
then have them arrested and held until their replacements could be
appointed. You know they have been corrupted and are controlled
by unelected bureaucrats. Remember when Jack Kennedy tried to
clean house in the CIA and FBI and then he was assassinated?
The Presidents have even been denied access to classified
information on UFO's, aliens and advanced technology systems.
This should indicate we have a huge problem in this country. The

public is not informed of new scientific discoveries for at least 20-25 years after a discovery, letting the elitists have more control over the people. Of course they would argue this is because military advantages would be lost to our enemies. For the most part that is a pile of crap. At the same time, the President could arrest approximately two thirds of the House of Representatives and Senate and prepare impeachment proceedings because they did not honor their oath of office when they voted for unconstitutional acts. Then finally, abolish the privately owned Federal Reserve and write off the trillions owed them and make Fractional Reserve Banking legal for only those banks owned by the taxpayers."

"Jack that was very interesting and might be the basis for a good novel, but please don't discuss that with me or anyone else, ever. OK?" pleaded Paul.

"I understand. Sorry. And I agree with you and your ideas one hundred percent. We have a big job ahead of us, perhaps bigger than either of us can imagine. But if we can accomplish all we are talking about, just think of the rewards, not only for us but for the people, the people of this great United States of America!"

"Jack there is one more issue that we must address. I just remembered that once I published a commentary in the paper concerning my views on banking that pretty well outlined my true feelings about banking and our interference in the affairs of other countries. Someone will probably try and use that against me."

"Let's hope that no one will find that old article about banking. Let's just not add any more fuel to the fire and simply say you wish to adopt *sound monetary policies.*"

Doctor Paul Ronan Elected to Congress

With perseverance and hard work campaigning, and Jack's professional help, Dr. Ronan was elected to the Congress of the United States. Through the years, Congressman Ronan very slowly educated the public and other Congressmen as to the true nature of our country's problems and what to do about them. But the slow pace of progress was a bit disappointing to the longtime congressman.

225

Twenty Years a Congressman
Time to Run for POTUS
2015

After serving twenty five years as a member of Congress and not being very successful in getting his fellow legislators to upset the status quo, Dr. Ronan decided that he would run for president and if elected he might have to make use of *presidential executive orders*-like his predecessors-to make the necessary changes to save our country from almost certain ruin. This seemed like the only way, even though it was repugnant to Dr. Ronan to operate our government in this most unconstitutional manner; bypassing Congress.

President Kennedy, three months before his assassination, used a *presidential executive order* to bypass the privately owned Federal Reserve that printed *interest bearing* Federal Reserve notes and had the U.S. Treasury issue *interest free* Treasury Notes. It wasn't clear whether it was Kennedy's intention to destroy the Federal Reserve or if he was merely abiding by the Constitution to issue a certain percentage of treasury notes backed by silver. Whatever his true intentions, the *banksters* clearly saw this as a threat to their money making scheme, and as many believe, *took care of the situation* in Dallas three months later. After Kennedy's death, President Lyndon Johnson suspiciously ordered all of Kennedy's *interest free* Treasury notes recalled. The Federal Reserve was back in business.

The current president, Barack Hussein Obama, was completely destroying the country by supporting and signing unconstitutional bills such as *mandated federally controlled health care* and the *National Defense Authorization Act (NDAA)* which was signed into law December 31, 2011.

President Obama described the NDAA as addressing national security programs, Department of Defense healthcare costs, counter-terrorism within the U.S. and abroad and military modernization. The most controversial provisions, that the general public failed to understand, was contained in Title X, Subtitle D, entitled *Counter-Terrorism* (particularly sub-sections 1021 and

226

1022) This section deals with detention of persons the government suspects of involvement in terrorism. Mostly the concern is with the potential for abuse from Presidential authority. The detention portion of this act is of great concern to the ACLU in that U.S. citizens, whether actually guilty or not could be arrested on American soil by members of the Armed Forces and detained indefinitely with no trial. The NDAA completely destroys the Bill of Rights when the President has the power to decide which American citizens are terrorists and without a court order or any legal representation are arrested, incarcerated and even executed.

Destroyed from Within

Actually the destruction of our country was being systematically destroyed from within for some time. It didn't seem to matter whether the President was a Democrat or Republican; we continued to fight undeclared wars and spend way beyond our means, accumulating a 16 trillion dollar debt. But the fact is, if all Americans were required to pay a *100% income tax* there would still not be enough taxes collected to pay off the national debt. The true conservative Republicans like Senator Rand Paul kept saying, "We don't have an income problem, we have a spending problem," but the Democrats didn't seem to understand. Or, maybe they understood but were merely following orders from their unelected controllers instead of the people whom they were supposed to represent.

Dr. Paul Ronan thought to himself, '**Liberalism** is definitely a sickness. Maybe we need to hire Jerry Lewis to start a telethon to raise money to discover a treatment and cure for *Liberalism*.'

Paul again agreed with Jack, his campaign manager, that this type of sarcastic remark best be kept to himself.

Paul realized that even if he were elected president, it would be imperative to have like-minded people elected to congress so as to have a majority in both the House and Senate to get things done. Of course there was always the possibility of the President declaring Martial Law to make the necessary changes but Paul wanted to avoid that if at all possible.

Chapter Twenty
Presidential Candidate 2016

PAUL RONAN
PRESIDENT 2016

Jack had done a superb job in getting Paul elected to Congress so it was only natural for Paul to ask him to act as his presidential campaign manager.

"Jack I have decided to run for President of the United States. I want you to head up my campaign. What do you think?"

"Paul, I'm honored, but this will be a long drawn out fight. There are powerful interests who will do all in their power to keep you from being elected. And as you know, the voting process is getting more crooked with every election. It is almost like it was designed that way so the election results could be altered to fit the agenda of whoever is currently running the show-Democrat or Republican. Even the election of delegates is suspect. Most of the caucuses do things that are highly suspect and unfair."

"I know, but something must be done now to save our country and I would like to be a part of it. Our government is being assaulted by secretive and powerful international globalists from without and by corporofascist traitors from within. This elite group of arrogant, greedy men and women have attacked and jeopardized the freedoms of our once prosperous nation in their quest to establish a One World Government, a feudal state in which they will rule and we will serve! Have you not noticed a deliberate and systematic loss of our freedoms and how our leaders, both Democrats and Republicans, continue to destroy the Constitution and Bill of Rights; our sovereign rights given to us by our Creator? This incremental process has come about so slowly that few realize that we have lost the liberties and rights we once had. Remember, once we relinquish our freedoms, they are difficult to restore, if not impossible. Sorry for the long speech Jack, but that's how I feel."

"That's OK Paul, I feel the same way."

Paul continued, "People seem to have forgotten what made the United States of America so great. More than 200 years ago our wise founding fathers set up a unique form of government, a Constitutional Republic of the people, by the people, and for the people. Three branches of government-the Executive, Legislative, and Judicial-were created with built-in checks and balances to prevent any one of them from acquiring too much power. The people had recently been under the tyrannical rule of King George the III of England and did not want that type of government here. The Constitution required the Federal Government to be small, with certain well-defined duties, and with most of the powers and responsibilities to be delegated to the states or to the people."

"That's right. What is really scary is that very few people are even aware of what has happened. It has happened slowly over a period of years. You know, it's like cooking a frog so slowly that he doesn't jump out of the water to save his own life."

Federal Government has Grown to Such a Monstrous size

"That's an excellent analogy Jack. Today the Federal Government has grown to such a monstrous size that it no longer operates efficiently, economically and beneficially for **the people** but provides lifetime benefits for those who **once** promised to serve and protect this sovereign nation and its borders. Examples include the ineffective *War on Drugs, No Child Left Behind, border security, the irresponsible response to Hurricane Katrina and the excessive influence of corporate lobbyists.* Most disturbing is that these past few years have seen the Executive branch ominously grab an enormous amount of power. 9-11 and the War on Terror was George W. Bush's regime's excuse to assault our liberties and to trash our Constitution. George W. Bush, when sworn in as President, promised with a solemn oath, to preserve, protect, and defend the Constitution of the United States of America. But incredibly, in November of 2005, he actually said, **'Stop throwing the Constitution in my face. It's just a God damned piece of paper'** (*Ref: Capitol Hill Blue web site*). And

President Barack Obama has continued the assault on our Constitution.

Unconstitutional NDAA
National Defense Authorization Act

Obama even made sure that included in the National Defense Authorization Act, was the power for himself to lock up American citizens with no court proceeding, and no lawyer, and that he could even kill a person if he himself says they are a *Terrorist*. It's unbelievable that the American people are not up in arms over this bill. I swear that won't happen if I am elected President!"

"I know that and I think the people of Texas know that from your track record of being elected over and over from your congressional district. You know, it was George W. Bush who signed **Presidential Directive 51** and other **Executive Orders** giving him sole authority to impose martial law and suspend Habeas Corpus. This gives the office of the President dictatorial powers over the people without any checks and balances," said Jack, in agreement.

"You mean like what President Abraham Lincoln did to get us into the *War Between the States?*" asked Paul.

"Exactly. The misnamed Patriot Act was hurriedly passed by Congress only **one month** after the 9-11 attack. Apparently it was written several months or maybe even years before 9-11. It appears that the authors of the bill either had advanced knowledge of the attack or were just waiting to take advantage of it. The 9-11 attack against the United States was just what was needed to alter public opinion and encourage Congress to approve of attacking Afghanistan and Iraq; an event that had been planned for some time. Some members later admitted that they didn't have time to read the entire bill. This abusive act permits:

- **Secret** FBI searches of your home
- **Secret** government wiretaps on your phone and internet
- **Secret** investigations of your financial records
- **Secret** searches of your library activities, medical, travel and business records

- The freezing of funds and assets without prior notice or appeal
- The creation of **secret** watch lists for airline travel, and more!

"And then the Military Commissions Act of 2006 was passed which gave the President the power to call any U.S. citizen an 'enemy combatant', with the President defining what 'enemy combatant' means. A citizen's simple criticism and dissent of our government's actions could be cast as 'treason' resulting in their arrest, property seizure and incarceration for life without a trial or lawyer. The Bush regime even justified the use of torture to coerce 'confessions'. Then the Obama administration passed the *National Defense Authorization Act* in 2011 that even further strengthens the grip on the citizens and completely abolishes the *Bill of Rights*."

Posse Comitatus Act Violated

"Paul. Don't forget that the Bush administration also violated the *Posse Comitatus Act* with the passing of the John Warner Defense Authorization Act of 2007. This act authorizes the President to declare an 'emergency' and to **send Federal troops to a state**, even if that state's Governor and citizens object. After Hurricane Katrina in New Orleans, the police and National Guard also violated the Second Amendment of our Constitution by confiscating law abiding citizens' guns which were needed by them for protection. The propaganda arm of the Bush regime, the media corporations, attempted to program and indoctrinate us to trust 'Dictator' Bush and surrender our constitutionally protected liberties so that he and Vice President Dick Cheney could protect us from the evil terrorists. This means our liberties are predicated only upon the grace of the Chief Executive—the President of the United States. And President Obama has continued these outrageous actions."

"Jack, I like to quote one of our wise founding fathers, Benjamin Franklin. In the 1750's Franklin printed a timeless and insightful quote, *Those who would give up essential Liberty, to purchase a little temporary Safety, deserve neither Liberty nor Safety.* That pretty well sums up what has happened in this country."

"Yes and the Federal Government is rapidly diminishing every patriotic American's freedoms. The coming National ID cards with RFID (Radio Frequency Identification) chips embedded in them are not about fighting terrorism but all about controlling American citizens. In fact, tiny hidden spy chips are being planned for use in virtually every item on the planet for total 'Big Brother' surveillance and control."

Detention Centers or Prison Camps

"Did you know that Halliburton was given hundreds of millions of dollars for the construction of camps in the United States, capable of holding a million people? The New York Times on February 4th, 2006 ran an article by Rachel L. Swarns entitled, *Halliburton Subsidiary Gets Contract to Add Temporary Immigration Detention Centers.* The article states KBR would build the centers for the Homeland Security Department for an unexpected influx of immigrants, or to house people in the event of a natural disaster *or for new programs that require additional detention space.*"

Paul continued, "In possible conjunction with this construction program, the President could declare **Martial Law** against the American people and detain them in the event of an insurrection, as stated in the Military Commission Act of 2006. Here, let me read to you what this massive act in Section 333 states, *"The President may employ the armed forces, including the National Guard in Federal service, to restore public order and enforce the laws of the United States when, as a result of a natural disaster, epidemic, or other serious public health emergency, terrorist attack or incident, or other condition in any State or possession of the United States, the President determines that domestic violence has occurred to such an extent that the constituted authorities of the State or possession are incapable of ("refuse" or "fail" in) maintaining public order, "in order to suppress, in any State, any insurrection, domestic violence, unlawful combination, or conspiracy.*

Our Government is Afraid of the Power of the People

"Jack, it should be obvious to everyone, the government is afraid of the power of the people and appears to have very sinister plans for their total control. The framework is all in place for this President or a future President to declare and implement total martial law and dictatorship. All that is needed is an 'emergency' event to occur, whether by happenstance or created. Whenever there is a terrorist act perpetrated against us, ask yourself, 'Was this a true terrorist attack from outside or was it a *State Sponsored* terrorist Attack from within, planned to tightened the control of the people?

"Read the following excerpt that I wrote some time ago to include in a book I have been planning to write. I would appreciate it if you would give me your opinion on it:

Our founders gave us plenty of sound advice to protect our form of government. They warned us to obey the U.S. Constitution with its checks and balances, because power corrupts.

They wanted to keep our nation sovereign and independent. Yet the 'globalist elites' are destroying the United States with 'free trade' agreements like NAFTA and with the Security and Prosperity Partnership with Mexico and Canada. They are creating a North American Union with the ultimate goal of a One World Government. They are currently destroying the value of our dollar in order to bring about the new currency they call the Amero.

"David Rockefeller, member of the Council on Foreign Relations and the Bilderberg Group admitted what the arrogant 'globalist' plan for the world is in the following quote from his book, '**Memoirs**', page 405-published by Random House, October 15, 2002.

Rockefeller: *"Some even believe we are part of a secret cabal working against the best interest of the United States, characterizing my family and me as 'internationalists' and of conspiring with others around the world to build a more integrated global political and economic structure-one world government, if you will. If that is the charge, I stand guilty, and I am proud of it."*

Our founders warned us about the dangers of foreign entanglements. A strong national defense is important but our **pre-emptive** offensive wars are damaging our nation. People around the world can see the unjustifiable aggression of the United States with the resulting millions of casualties. These wars are also crippling us economically by saddling our citizens and grandchildren with a growing National debt, currently at nineteen trillion dollars and rising.

Our founders warned us of the dangers of allowing a private Central Bank (the Federal Reserve) to be in charge of our money, especially if it isn't backed by gold or silver. We have allowed these private bankers to print money out of thin air, loan it to us and charge us interest. And the creation of more and more money causes the devaluation of our dollar through inflation. Our government allows this fraud to continue because they can spend more money than they take in from taxes. The public has been fooled about the reality and origin of this *hidden inflation tax.*

Our founders warned us of the importance of an honest, independent and unbiased press. Yet there is a small elite group of interlocking families and financial interests who rule America through their control of all the major newspapers, magazines, and broadcasting networks. Most of the public is not aware that they choose our politicians for us through their attention and promotion of some candidates and by ignoring and destroying other candidates. The 'Global elite' with the help of the media, control both parties, Democrat and Republican, to fool the public into believing they have a choice. Crises are continually being introduced or hyped to keep us in fear, to give up our rights for protection and for us to accept the 'New World Order'. Examples include gun crime, AIDS, SARS, Bird Flu, Communism, 'Islamic-Fascist' terrorism, and global warming. We need to recognize that we are being manipulated for the benefit of the 'Global Elite' who wish to rule us as slaves. David Rockefeller once said, 'We are on the verge of a global transformation. All we need is the right major crisis and the nations will accept the New World Order.

Our founders warned us that the price of liberty is eternal vigilance. Yet the ignorance and apathy of many citizens is obvious. We must remember that obeying the Constitution and the Bill of Rights is what makes America great. We must recognize that our rights and liberties are being destroyed. We need to remember that this government was created for **us** and we need not be afraid to restore it back to the great Constitutional Republic as originally founded. Thomas Jefferson perhaps said it best when he said, 'When the people fear the government, there is tyranny. When the government fears the people, there is liberty.

In 1787 at the close of the Constitutional convention in Philadelphia, a woman asked Benjamin Franklin what kind of government had just been set up. He replied, 'A Republic if you can keep it.'

"We must elect politicians who will follow the wishes of the people and not special interest groups that have no regard for what is best for our country. We must act quickly and decisively to return our great nation to the one our founding fathers intended."

"Very well said, Paul. Now I know why I have given you my support now for over twenty years. You are one of a handful of politicians, or should I say *Statesmen*, that truly understands what is happening and brave enough to make an honest attempt to change the corrupt status quo."

"Let's do it!"

Chapter Twenty One
Conspiracy Theories

(After 2000)   (Before 2000)

"Paul, look at these two Republican logos. Notice that the stars on the logo after the year 2000 are shown pointing down and the one before 2000 are shown pointing up. What does that mean to you? I mean, how would you explain that?" asked Jack.

"Well, someone in the art department probably made an honest mistake. Does it really matter which direction the stars point?"

"Well, some people believe that when the star points down it represents the *Goat of Mendes* satanic symbol and that it signifies demonic forces, and that the Republicans are secretly signaling their allegiance to these satanic forces. This alludes to the fact that it is somehow connected to George W. Bush's membership in the secretive group at Yale called the 'Skull and Bones.' Then you have those that believe like you, Paul, that it was probably just an error made in the art department.

"This is exactly the type of subject you want to avoid when being interviewed by the press. They want to destroy you and are able to do it with very subtle remarks implying that you are a *Conspiracy Nut*. The press has already conditioned the gullible public that anyone harboring a conspiracy theory is someone who cannot be trusted and most certainly is not qualified to be a Congressman, or for that matter, the President of the United States."

"That is ridiculous, Jack."

"I agree, but the point is, don't get tricked into saying anything other than it was most likely a mistake or error made by someone

236

laying out the art work for the logo, or just that you hadn't even thought about it.

"Paul, when you are attacked and mislabeled by someone calling you a *Conspiracy Nut* or *Anti-Semitic,* because of your views, you should demand that your accuser define their terms. Once the terms are defined and agreed upon by both parties, there may not be any argument at all. To make my point, I have often used the example about the tree falling in the forest. If there is no one there to hear it fall, is there any sound? It is futile to try to answer this question until you define the word *sound.* If your definition of sound is a vibrating body like a tuning fork, a medium to transfer the vibrations like air or water, and a receiver to pick up the sound, then of course there is no sound by this definition because there is no one there to receive or hear it. But if, in your definition, you exclude the receiver, there is *sound.* It's pretty simple once you agree on the definition of terms. If you cannot nullify the attack by defining the terms then you should openly and forcibly accuse the attacker of attempting to conceal the truth by using this unfair labeling ploy. When being interviewed, you will most likely not have time to get into a philosophical discussion, so I would just avoid getting trapped in the first place," advised Jack.

Anti-Semitic Accusations

"That's good advice, but what about when you are referred to as an *anti-Semite?*" asked Paul.

"Let me explain. I used to think and even strongly argued that I was not *anti-Semitic.* However as the years have passed, I have come to the conclusion that, yes, I could be *anti-Semitic* in some cases but again it must be explained in the context of one's definition of *Anti-Semitism.* I certainly don't deny that the Holocaust happened nor do I believe that all Jews should be killed and wiped off the face of the earth. I do question the claim that six million Jews were systematically gassed by Hitler. It is a little suspicious to me that this was the same number of Jews that was claimed killed in WWI. And at the same time, these statistics need to be kept in perspective. The Jews were not the only people to suffer greatly in those unholy wars. Look at the fire-bombing the

United States did in Dresden, Germany during WWII against non-military targets, or the atomic bombs we unnecessarily dropped on Nagasaki and Hiroshima killing millions of Japanese civilians. The Japanese wanted to surrender but were not allowed to because the United States government wanted to severely punish Japan for their attack on Pearl Harbor, and of course the bomb devastation in Japan would be a symbol to the world of the power the United States had to control the world. Don't forget the millions of Chinese that the Japanese killed and the twenty million or so gentiles that Russian Jewish leaders killed in the 1917 Bolshevik Revolution which was supposedly partially financed by the United States Federal Reserve bankers."

"That's incredible. I hadn't thought of it in that way," said Paul.

"Once I was asked by a Jewish man if I were *anti-Semitic*. I asked him if he was anti-Gentile. He looked at me and didn't know what to say. Then I continued, 'I am only *anti-Semitic*, if you are *anti-Gentile*.' I think he got the message.

You Can't Criticize Israel

"What really bothers me Paul is that when you criticize Israel, they immediately label you as *anti-Semitic*, when in reality you are criticizing the Israeli governmental policies and not necessarily the Israeli people. Besides that, I have read that there has not been one true Israeli Prime Minister that can trace his linage back to the Biblical Abraham. Some scholars believe that the Jewish leaders are all from the lineage of the Khazarian Jews who were Asiatic warriors who joined the Jewish faith in the Caspian Sea area sometime near the Seventh Century. In other words, they are about as much Biblically Jewish as Sammy Davis Junior who merely joined the Jewish faith. To help conceal this fact, I have read that the Zionist Jews of today have mixed the Yiddish language of the Khazarian Jews with the Hebrew language of the true Jews. It is best to not get into this argument because even Jewish scholars today argue who is actually Jewish and can trace his lineage to Abraham. An important point to remember is that not all Jews are *Zionist* Jews supporting the nation of Israel. True religious Jews, not the atheist Jews, follow what their Holy books state; they are supposed to live in peace and harmony within their host country until such time as their Messiah comes and then the country of Israel can be established. Their Messiah hasn't come yet, unlike the Christians, and they don't accept Jesus Christ as their Messiah. In other words, they don't support the idea of a nation of Israel, just yet."

Need to Develop a Political Action Committee

"Jack, we have a lot of planning to do. We need to develop an organization and a web site to help me get elected. You know this entire election process is designed to keep someone like me from getting elected," explained Paul.

"That I know. We will need to just outsmart them. An anonymous Texas oil executive has agreed to donate a building he owns for our office and I have at least three Liberty groups that are supporting you. They agree on the majority of your positions; a government that (1) abides by the constitution (2) adopts sound monetary policies, (3) stops being the policeman of the world, (4) respects the sovereignty of the states and an individual's liberty and (5) either passes a *Balanced Budget Amendment* or easier yet, have the president advise Congress that all unconstitutional and unfunded bills and those not pertaining to the bills title will be vetoed," said Jack.

Legalize Drugs

"What did they not agree with?" queried Paul.

"They have a problem with you legalizing illegal drugs."

"I thought we had kept that relegated to the secret agenda."

"Somehow it got out," said Jack.

"Now that it is out in the open, we will have to explain our position. First I will explain that the *Federal government* has no constitutional authority to regulate what drugs a person takes because of the 10th Amendment. In other words it must be left up to the individual states to regulate if they see fit, and they have the power to do so within the confines of their own state's constitution. We will explain that the war on drugs has failed miserably and has cost billions of dollars to the taxpayer. It costs more to apprehend a drug addict or dealer, prosecute him and incarcerate him than it would cost to send him to Harvard. We must start treating these addicts, who have not harmed anyone except themselves, as sick people instead of making criminals out of them. A side benefit, if legalized or best we say decriminalized, is that the illegal profits would no longer be used by law enforcement groups, both Federal and State, to finance their clandestine operations.

"I also suspect that many aspects of the stock market and gold and silver prices are inappropriately affected by coordinated sales and purchases using these illegal profits. If true, this puts the legitimate investor at a disadvantage." explained Paul.

"That will be a tough sell. Your opponents and even the religious groups will accuse you of advocating the use of drugs. The media and the government propaganda has brainwashed the public for so long, it will be difficult if not almost impossible to convince them otherwise," said Jack.

"I understand that but we can do our best to convince them."

"Paul, we haven't talked about how you feel about the 9-11 attacks on the World Trade Center and the Pentagon."

"That's another touchy subject. I certainly don't want to be classified as a *Conspiracy Nut*. But confidentially, I believe it was similar to what happened when Japan attacked us at Pearl Harbor. "

"What do you mean?"

"President Franklin Roosevelt stated before the 1940 election that he was against getting into the war in Europe but actually he secretly wanted to do so. And then came the attack on Pearl Harbor which swayed public opinion to support the involvement of the United States. Prior to Japan's attack on the United States Naval Base at Pearl Harbor on Sunday morning, December 7, 1941, the American people were not willing to go to war in Europe. After all, WWI had been the 'war to end all wars.' The attack on Pearl Harbor pushed the public's opinion from isolationism to an all-out acceptance of the war. The alleged *surprise attack* completely destroyed 188 aircraft and approximately 2400 American service men lost their lives with

1,178 more being wounded. Two destroyers were damaged beyond repair, two US Naval battleships were a total loss and one mine layer was heavily damaged."

Paul continued. "The next day, December 8, 1941, President Franklin Delano Roosevelt addressed Congress requesting a Declaration of War with Japan. The Senate and House of Representatives approved of the war declaration unanimously with the sole exception of one vote. President Roosevelt made this now famous quote, *A date which will live in infamy.*

"And, there is evidence that shows Roosevelt provoked the Japanese and that he knew of the impending attack and allowed it to happen in order that public opinion would accept the United States going to war with Japan. Sound familiar?

World Trade Center attack on 9-11

"Now let's fast forward to the 9-11, 2001 attack on the World Trade Center in New York City. I kept a diary of this tragic event, just in case I needed to refer to what happened at a later date. Fortunately, I never had it published. I don't want either of us to be labeled *Conspiracy Nuts*. Prior to the 9-11 attack the American people did not approve of us attacking Iraq. However after 9-11 the public was then willing to support our government in invading Iraq even though the supposed hijackers were mostly from Saudi Arabia."

"This made quite an impression on almost everyone, Jack. I am sure everyone old enough to remember that fateful morning recalls the terror and disbelief of what happened. I had gotten up early that morning and had just turned the TV news on when the first plane hit one of the towers. Quickly I called to Carol to get up to see what was happening. We, the same as most people around the world, spent nearly the entire day glued to the TV. We watched as the twin towers *imploded* and collapsed at *free fall* speed."

"A passport from one of the hijackers was even found which had *miraculously* survived the huge fireball explosion. It allegedly came out of his pocket and floated to the ground. As the story unfolded over the next few days, I had more and more questions as to what really happened. Information that was being broadcast by the controlled media didn't seem to adequately answer my questions. The whole incident appeared highly suspicious!"

"As the months and years passed I became even more skeptical of the government's version of what happened and who was involved. How could 19 Arab hijackers have actually taken over these planes using box cutters and done this much damage to our country? If you believe that our government was not involved in any way and believe that those that do believe that our government was involved or had prior knowledge of the attack are *Conspiracy Nuts*, then you have simply not studied the facts enough. If you have never heard of the term, *Thermite* or don't know that Building Seven collapsed, the third building, without being hit by a plane then it is obvious you are not qualified to pass judgment on the so called *Conspiracy Theorists*. View the documentary movies like *Loose Change Final Cut* and *9-11 Ripple Effect*. After viewing these documentaries, you may change your mind as to what really happened."

"Paul, I didn't say that our government wasn't somehow involved, I simply didn't get the same impression as you. I want to make it clear that I don't believe you are a *Conspiracy Nut*," explained Jack.

"I know, I just wanted to make it crystal clear on how I feel about 9-11. There are two basic theories put forth by the *Conspiracy Theorists*; (1) individuals in our government knew of the impending attacks and intentionally failed to act or (2) high level rogue elements in the US government performed *a false flag* operation intending to blame the attacks on Arab terrorists so as to alter public opinion and give us an excuse to attack Afghanistan and Iraq. This would also facilitate increased military spending and allow our government to reduce domestic civil rights. All of this would greatly enhance Israel's position in the Middle East. The Patriot Act was passed only one month after the attack. There are many other excellent theories voiced by the *9-11 Truth Movement.*"

"Jack, allow me to summarize the *Federal Government's conspiracy theory*. Here read my notes:

242

The government's account stated that 19 Arab terrorists hijacked four commercial airplanes by using knives, box cutters, pepper spray, and fake explosives. At 8:46 AM and 9:03 AM flights 11 and 175 crashed into the twin towers of the World Trade Center causing them to collapse soon afterward. Building Seven also collapsed from fires started by debris from the collapse of the North Tower. This is what the National Institution of Science and technology expects us to believe. The NIST explanation is ridiculous! Fire did not cause Building 7 to collapse and the planes hitting the other two towers did not cause them to collapse.

American Airlines Flight 77 crashed at 9:37 AM into the Pentagon and flight 93 crashed in an open field in Pennsylvania at 10:03 AM after the passengers stormed the cockpit. Our government was able to identify all the hijackers with names and photographs the very next day after the attack. Can you really believe that? They were able to link them to the terrorist organization al-Qaeda, headed by Osama Bin Laden who later claimed responsibility for the attacks." *(Note: Experts have said that the video tape of Osama Bin Laden claiming responsibility for the attack is a fake)*

"Paul, I agree that it is difficult to believe the government's account as to what happened on 9-11. Why were known terrorists ordered to be let into the U.S. and then trained at government run bases and could barely fly a small Cessna airplane? Rather, it appears that these Muslims were set up as *patsy's* to take the blame. You know, like Oswald assassinating President Kennedy. Here is a list of some more unanswered questions I would like to see addressed because they have not been adequately explained or covered by the government.

"Sit down for a few minutes, Jack, and read what my thoughts were shortly after the attack. Keep in mind; I promise you, I won't discuss this with the media or in a debate."

Pilots took no evasive action

"One would think that the pilots flying in the four hijacked airliners would have taken some type of evasive actions such as cabin decompression or rolling the planes over when they discovered that the plane had been taken over and passengers were being killed. Weren't there any military passengers, retired police officers, or other able bodied passengers that could have resisted the intruders with a knife or box cutter in their hands? It has been reported that Todd Beamer was the passenger that led the now famous passenger revolt on Flight 93, by uttering the words, Let's Roll. The only problem is that there were several other passengers that would have been more likely to have taken on this job.

Reportedly there was on board Jeremy Glick, a former national judo champion, Mark Bingham, a former champion rugby player, Tom Burnett, a former college football quarterback, Louis Nacke 200 pound weight lifter, Cee Cee Lyles, a former police detective, Richard Guadagno, an enforcement officer who had received training in hand to hand combat, and William Cashman, a former paratrooper with the 101st Airborne. It is unbelievable to me that the Arab hijackers armed with box cutters were just too much for these passengers. If, as we were told, flight 93 (the plane that crashed in Pennsylvania) did have passengers that resisted, why was there no resistance on the other three?

Independent Investigation- Over a Year Later

Why did it take our government almost a year and a half to initiate an independent investigation into the worst case of domestic terrorism ever made against the United States?

With a huge budget of thirty billion dollars a year, why were the CIA, FBI and the other intelligence agencies caught completely unaware of the attack and yet 24 hours later had pictures and files on the alleged 19 hijackers?

On the morning of the terror attacks, the original reports were saying that *five* planes were unaccounted for. Later the Federal authorities revised the number to four planes without giving an adequate explanation.

Prior to the attack, these transcontinental flights were heavily booked. However on 9-11 only 266 passengers were on those flights that would normally carry as many as 1,328 passengers. Why were they only booked at 20% of their capacity?

Why weren't our fighter jets sent to intercept the four hijacked airliners as soon as it was obvious they had been hijacked? Wouldn't it be an extremely odd and unbelievable coincidence that a similar training exercise was going on at the same time with a scenario closely approximating the real attack, as was explained?

Why would the government refuse to release and then keep secret the copies of the recorded transcripts made between the air traffic controllers and the hijacked planes?

The grainy, inaudible video tapes that supposedly proved that Osama bin Laden was linked to the attacks were adamantly dismissed by translators because they disagreed on the Arabic translation. How can our government continue to insist Osama bin Laden was linked to the attacks when he repeatedly denied that he had anything to do with it?

How can the reports of explosions coming from the basement and upper floors of the Twin Towers, witnessed by many people including firemen, be dismissed, especially when the buildings' collapses appeared to be exactly like a controlled demolition?

No Large Building has ever Collapsed when hit by an Airplane

Other planes have hit buildings in other parts of the world resulting in fire but no building collapse. What was the difference in this case to cause the collapses?

Why was debris at the World Trade Center removed before the evidence could be properly examined?

It would be interesting to see a list of employees who did not show up for work that day at the World Trade Center and a list of the people who profited from selling their airline stock just a few days before the attack.

How do you explain that at least 6 of the suicide hijackers have been reported to still be alive?

What connection, if any, is there between the spy network of *Israeli art students* that were operating throughout the U.S. in close proximity to where the hijackers were purported to be living?

What caused the complete collapse of the nearby WTC Building 7 when it wasn't even hit by a plane?

Was key evidence planted to implicate Arabs in the attack? How could Arab flight training manuals and religious material be found at Boston's Logan airport and a passport of one of the alleged hijackers be found in the WTC rubble? The odds are extremely high that this would not have happened. And, how could a paper passport survive the high temperatures and fire at ground zero?

Five Israelis seen cheering when the Twin Towers Collapsed

Why haven't we received a full explanation of the five Israelis seen cheering and photographing the collapse of the Twin Towers? Especially, since later, these Israelis admitted on Israeli television that they were sent to New York to document the event.

Have the investigators looked into the technology that allows the remote control of a military 'Global Hawk' which is the approximate size of a Boeing 737? Since it is a well-known fact that none of the hijackers were accomplished pilots or navigators, this scenario should warrant further investigation.

Why does the U.S. media and government authorities continue to ignore the business relationship between the Bush family and the Bin Laden Group?

U.S. had plans to invade Afghanistan before 9-11

Why did the United States military have war plans to invade Afghanistan several months *before* the 9-11 attack on the World Trade Center and the Pentagon? Did they have advance knowledge of this event?

How do you explain the two huge spikes in the seismic record on 9-11 that were recorded prior to the collapse? Wouldn't this be proof of a huge explosion that could have been instrumental in bringing down the Twin Towers?

Remember the old adage that says to solve a crime, just follow the money? Just ask yourself, 'Who profits'? The Muslim fanatics profited by bragging that they could inflict enormous damage to the United States which in turn gave them a great deal of prestige and the ability to recruit even more terrorists to their cause. But by far, the groups that profited the most were the neo-cons in our government, the Israelis and the American Zionists. This *does not prove* who was responsible but should certainly warrant further investigation into the possibilities of Israel being involved.

"Wow. Those notes pretty well sum up what really happened on 9-11. I understand, Paul why you feel the way you do."

Jack acknowledged, the **government's version** of what happened on 9-11 is the **most farfetched conspiracy theory** of all.

"It is amazing to me that the public actually believes that 19 Arab hijackers controlled by a man in a cave half way across the world, armed only with box cutters and without the skills to fly even a small Cessna type airplane, were able to hijack four commercial airliners, and crash two of them into the World Trade Center and one into the Pentagon."

"I agree with almost everything you said, Jack. It looks like you too have done your homework on the 9-11 attack."

"Yes I have Paul, and what really upsets me is that the corporate controlled media has not exposed these lies. If it hadn't been or the Independent Media, and the internet social media sites, the majority of the American people would still believe the propaganda and lies espoused by the 9-11 Commission. We still need to exercise extreme caution when we discuss this issue."

Janet Evans Volunteers

"To change the subject, I have someone in the outer office who wants to meet you. She is willing to donate her time as one of our coordinators."

"Janet, come on in and let me introduce you to Paul Ronan. Paul, this is Janet Evans from Houston."

"Glad to meet you Janet. Just curious, what made you decide to support my run for President?"

"I have been reading your editorials that have been in the *Houston Chronicle* now for some years and I heard you speak at the Republican Lincoln Day dinner last year. Your ideas on what we need to do to save our country from a total economic collapse really made an impression on me. I would like to be a part of what you are doing," explained Janet.

"Well welcome aboard Janet. There is plenty for all of us to do," said Paul.

Chapter Twenty Two
The Election Process

"Paul, I would guess that many people believe that the *Electors* in the *Electoral College* and the political party *Delegates* are the same. They are not! Furthermore they don't realize that the popular vote does not elect the President and Vice President but rather the *Electoral College* does which consists of only 538 votes; corresponding to the representation of 435 House members, 100 Senate members and 3 to represent Washington D.C. The *Electors* are generally chosen by the candidate's political party, but state laws vary on how the electors are selected. The *Delegates* are also chosen by the political parties; people who are selected to represent their states at their party conventions prior to a presidential election. A Candidate does not become a party's presidential nominee until a vote is taken by party *Delegates* at the Republican, Democrat, or Independent presidential nominating conventions. These *Delegates* normally support the views of the voters who cast ballots during their states' primaries and caucuses. However, each party's rules make it possible for multiple rounds of balloting, horse trading, plus sometimes unorthodox maneuvers.

"In order to get elected President and Vice President of The U.S., the candidates must win a minimum of 270 votes from the states appointed *Electors* in the *Electoral College* and if none do, there will be what is called a brokered convention where the 538 electors previously selected and obligated for a particular candidate will be released from this obligation and can then vote their own personal conscience for the candidate of their choice."

"You are correct Jack; also we need to educate the electorate so people will understand that a candidate can be elected president even if they do not get the majority of the popular vote as long as they receive at least 270 electoral votes. Our strategy will be to keep both the primary votes by the people and the caucus votes run by the local Republican Central Committees honest," explained Paul.

"That's a huge issue. Remember all the problems some states had with the new Diebold voting machines? It has been proven that they are susceptible to hacking and can easily be tampered with to affect the results of an election. I would like to see a system where all ballots are serially numbered and when you vote you receive a receipt that can be verified the next day on a government web site by referencing the serial number."

"Great idea, but I wouldn't get too excited about thinking that serial numbers will be added to the ballots anytime soon. It's almost like both Republicans and Democrats want to be able to rig the elections. We will just have to work with what we have, the best we can," explained Jack. "The honesty of the various state and county caucuses are another matter.

"Remember what happened in your own district where we were attempting to get a share of the 30 delegates that would be supportive of your candidacy? The local Republican committee chairman was *hell bent* on making sure that you and the other two front runners received zero delegates. Their rules committee had made sure that only their delegate slate would be accepted. In other words, the other candidates had zero representation at the caucus. Never mind, that like the popular vote, the selection of delegates should also represent *all* the candidates. There were 220 people attending the caucus; 60% were your supporters and 20% supported candidate B, 10% supported candidate C and 10% supported candidate D. The slate of delegates that were elected, if done honestly and fairly would have resulted in:

Paul Ronan	60% x 30 =	18
Candidate B	20% x 30 =	6
Candidate C	10% x 30 =	3
Candidate D	10% x 30 =	3
Total		30

"The unscrupulous chairman orchestrated the entire meeting to make it impossible for any of the other candidates to be represented. His candidate was allowed to erect over 50 campaign signs on the Court House lawn, have a table outside the caucus meeting room with promotional stickers, etc. for his candidate, and one of his own people was allowed to stand in the front of the caucus so that he was already standing when the chair asked for delegate slates to be submitted. Of course no other candidate's supporters could be recognized by the chairman because his plant was already standing.

"This is why I prefer a *Primary Election* by the people instead of a *Party Caucus* that is easily manipulated by the party chairman. Fortunately, Missouri, at least will hold a *Primary Election* this year instead of a *Caucus.*"

"Jack, can you attend the government auction that was advertised in the paper yesterday and see if you can buy three copiers, desks, file cabinets, etc. for our campaign office?" asked Paul.

"Sure, maybe I should knock off a little early so I can get up bright and early in the morning for the auction. Janet, could you go with me to keep an eye on the things I buy and keep track of what I pay?"

"Of course, do you want to pick me up about 7 in the morning?"

"Sounds good. See you in the morning."

Office Equipment Auction

Fortunately for Paul, the auction was not very well attended and Jack knew that would greatly improve his chances of getting some good deals. As it turned out, Jack was able to buy three copiers, six desks, ten file cabinets and several miscellaneous boxes of office supplies; all for only $1200.00; new price value probably over $12,000. All in all, Jack felt that he had done quite well. The auction finally concluded at 4 o'clock in the afternoon.

"Janet, it's still early, would you be willing to get a bite to eat and then go over to the office and see if the copy machines work? Then we can explore the boxes of supplies to see what all we bought!"

"Sure Jack, let's eat first. Would Mexican food be all right with you? There's a nice Mexican restaurant near the office. I think it's called *Casa Bonita,*" said Janet.

"That's fine with me. That should give the delivery guys time to deliver our things to the office."

251

By the time Jack and Janet had finished eating, everything had been delivered to the office. The first thing Jack wanted to do was confirm that the copy machines worked. He knew they were top of the line digital photocopiers that had originally cost the government several thousands of dollars.

Jack noticed something interesting. "Janet, look, the hard drives are still in the copiers. Surely the drives have been professionally erased so we won't be able to view any classified government documents, you know, like those that might be marked, 'For Your Eyes Only' or *Top Secret*," laughed Jack. A company called Digital Copier Security has developed software called 'INFOSWEEP' that can scrub all the data on hard drives. Surely the government used this or similar technology to erase the hard drives before they were sold. But let's check, just in case. There is a forensic software program available for free on the internet that will allow us to download anything left on the hard drive. Let me see if I can download the program and see if the drives are blank. We want to be sure they are blank when we start up the office next week."

Top Secret Data Left on Copy Machine Hard Drive

After about two hours, Jack confirmed that two of the copiers' hard drives had been erased but the third copier had data still on the drive.

"Jack, do you know how to erase the hard drive?" asked Janet.

"Yes, it's pretty simple, but I am curious to see what is still on the drive. It could be top secret information," laughed Jack.

All of a sudden Jack let out a yell.

"Janet, oh my God! This drive is full of secret information with the words classified on the top of each file and document! Some of the words are blacked out but it looks like over 90% is still readable. I can't believe the government didn't erase the drive before it was sold. Apparently they missed this one."

"Maybe we shouldn't read those files. We could get in a lot of trouble," said Janet.

Secret Bases on the Moon and Mars

"Nobody will know. This must remain our secret. Ok, let's see what we have got here. Oh my God! You're not going to believe this. This first one is talking about alien bases on the Moon and on Mars and it's referring to some kind of treaty made between the U.S. government and the aliens to keep us from interfering with the aliens' work there. It appears that the aliens have agreed to share some of their technology with us so we can travel more efficiently in space. There seems to be two space programs in our country; the public program and a highly secret program utilizing anti-gravity technology for space travel instead of rocket power. I can't understand everything that is discussed and it appears that some of the data is coded further. This is incredible!

Junk DNA is not Junk DNA

"Wow, the next document is talking about DNA and the so called junk DNA. Up until recently we only understood about 5% of the DNA and the remainder was referred to as 'junk DNA'. According to this, the so called junk DNA turns out to be a recording, so to speak, of everything that the particular individual or his ancestors have experienced since their beginning."

"You mean if my ancestors saw a dinosaur thousands of years ago, my DNA would allow me to see and hear that dinosaur?"

"Apparently that's what its saying. Isn't that incredible!

"Here is one that talks about **Edward Leedskalnin and his stone structure of a Coral Castle that was built around 1923 just north of Homestead, Florida.** He was able to mysteriously lift pieces of stone that weighed several thousand pounds. Some of his plans and equipment mysteriously disappeared shortly after his death and apparently ended up in the hands of the government. It refers to the same technology that was used by the Egyptians and Mayans to build the great pyramids. Apparently he used an anti-gravity device that creates a resonant frequency that is 180 degrees out of phase with the object that is to be lifted. This allows an object of several thousand pounds to be lifted effortlessly by one person alone!

Israel Implicated in the 9-11 Attack

"Here is a document that talks about the 9-11 attack that implicates the Israeli Mossad and high levels of our own government. It is talking about new technology using 'nano thermite' to bring down all three World Trade center buildings making it appear that airplanes and the resulting fire was the cause. Also it explains how the 19 Arab hijackers were set up to be the patsies for the attack, and the plan to keep the public from knowing that most of the hijackers were still alive!

"Oh, oh, this is an interesting one. Apparently they have discovered a way to implant data into your brain so you will no longer need to go to school to learn. They started out loading only foreign language data into a person's brain for our ambassadors but have now advanced to loading other data that allows you to reason based on this new data you have acquired. Just think of the consequences this will have on our schools and universities!

"Here is another one about weather modification to be used as a military weapon. It's talking about cloud seeding and heating up the atmosphere with the HAARP (High Frequency Active Auroral Research Program) radio transmitters in Alaska. Here it is even talking about how to create a tsunami like occurred off the coast of Japan with an atomic blast in the ocean making the public believe is was a natural occurrence.

Black Budgets

"Oh, Oh, here is one about the so called "Black Budget." This is exactly what Paul and I were talking about a few weeks ago. Why are so many budget items being kept secret? Paul estimated these secret budget items that are kept from Congress and the President are in excess of $30 billion dollars a year. Now that the cold war with Russia is over it is obvious from declassified Russian documents that the cold war was greatly exaggerated to justify huge expenditures. It would be interesting to see how extravagant a life style these government officials in charge of keeping these items a secret have by living way beyond their reported income. It would seem to invite theft and fraud," exclaimed Jack.

GMO's (Genetically Modified Organisms)

"Here is a letter to a company involved in GMO's (Genetically Modified Organisms) describing a process to add pharmaceuticals (Medicines) into GMO corn. In this particular document they are planning on secretly adding birth control medicine to the corn we eat to reduce population growth.

Disinformation or Fact

"Oh, oh, wait a minute. Here is something about dis-information. Now I am not sure what part of this is true and what part is dis-information. I need to spend more time on this to see what is really the truth and what is disinformation."

Jack looked up at Janet, seeing that she looked half asleep. "It's getting late Janet. Look, its quarter past two. We need to go home and get some sleep. Remember; don't breathe a word of what we have discovered here tonight. I feel that our lives could be in danger if any of this were to leak out."

"I understand Jack. But I won't be in the office until about noon tomorrow rather than in the morning. OK? I have had an exhausting day."

"I am going to take this copier's hard drive home with me so I can continue to read the classified documents more leisurely tomorrow. Remember, keep this quiet. Not a word to anyone," pleaded Jack.

Government Agents barge In

Shortly after arriving at the office the next morning three government cars, all with dark tinted glass windows and several odd looking antennas on them, pulled up in front of the office and six men in black suits rushed into the office.

Looking directly at Jack, one said, "Are you the one who purchased the three copiers at the government auction yesterday afternoon?" as he was frantically checking the serial number on all three copiers. "Where is the hard disk on this one?" he bellowed..

Not wanting to get into any trouble, Jack quickly answered, "I determined that this one *had not* been erased so I had planned on returning it today after seeing that it might have some sensitive data still on it."

It was obvious the government agent didn't believe him but grabbed it and said, "If you ever divulge anything that was on this disk there could be serious consequences for you and your family! Do I make myself clear, mister?"

"Yes sir, no problem, I didn't really have time to read anything but assumed it could have some classified or sensitive documents still on the hard drive," said Jack with a slight quiver in his voice.

Jack couldn't wait until Paul came into the office which was only about an hour later to explain to him what had happened.

"Paul you are not going to believe what happened concerning the copiers I purchased yesterday."

"It must be good news because you got a heck of a deal on the office equipment you bought."

"Well, I have an interesting story to tell you about the copiers, but you cannot reveal anything I tell you because it could cost all of us our lives."

"What in the world are you talking about Jack? This sounds pretty serious."

After Jack explained what had happened, Paul agreed that they must all agree to not talk about this again. "If any of this were to leak out, there would be high government officials ready to do whatever was necessary to insure that our political careers were over and maybe even something worse," explained Paul.

Republican Debate

"Paul, I have some bad news. The mainstream network executives are not going to allow you to debate the other republican presidential candidates on national television."

"They can't do that!"

"I'm afraid they can. But don't worry. I have a plan. Several of the independent internet news sources are going to report, in depth, this story from a press release I sent them last week. *Democracy Now* with Amy Goodman, *RT* (Russia Today), *SRN News, Michael Rivero's 'What Really Happened', Alex Jones of Infowars and several others.* We are going to have a presidential debate on the Internet. Those bastard mainstream TV executives hadn't counted on that! Also I will see that the debate gets a lot of shares on Facebook and Twitter."

"Good job Jack! You are a genius."

Two days later Jack walked into the war room carrying a load of campaign signs. "Paul, Paul, you're not going to believe this! With the independent news stations agreeing to carry the debate, the mainstream people caved! They just couldn't be left out; they decided they would also carry the debate! Can you believe it?"

Republican Debate Participants

"Paul here is a partial list of the candidates who have pledged to take part in our debate". Theodore Crosse, Matt Ruby, Mark Rubistano, Dr. Ken Larson, Jed Basher, and John Casey.

The first Republican presidential Debate was held at the Toyota Center in downtown Houston. A capacity crowd gathered to hear the start of a new era if Dr. Paul Ronan was to become the next president of the United States. The moderators were Michael Terry, a popular Houston radio talk show host and Michael Rover, an alternative news source commentator based in Hawaii.

The days for the debates arrived all too soon. As Jack worried Paul might not be ready, Paul was cool as a cucumber. With his confident demeanor, Paul was able to come in second in the first two debates with 12 candidates participating, and was declared the winner of both the third and fourth debates. It was obvious that the people were gradually coming around to his vision of what was needed to return our government to a "Republic" form of government as created by our founding fathers. More and more of the electorate were being convinced that our so called "Democracy" had become a failure. It was quite an accomplishment to educate the people that a Democracy form of government was bad, i.e., a majority vote disregards the minority vote. In a *Republic* the majority vote counts but the rule of law must also be followed by adhering to the constitution.

"Good evening everyone. Welcome to this very important debate which we hope will help you decide who will next lead our country during these trying times. My name is Michael Terry and my good friend here on my right is Michael Rover the popular internet host of "What's Happening.""

"My first question is for Dr. Ken Larson. Would you abolish the Affordable Care Act?"

"Yes, the Affordable Care Act is awful and cannot be sustained without government subsidies. It is estimated that 18 million people now have health care but the costs are rising so fast that many of the insured can no longer afford it and insurance companies are leaving the system. I have spent a large part of my life in the health field and know that, in its present form, it will fail."

"Mr. Casey, how would you respond to the fact that under Obamacare, Premiums and Deductibles are rising, and for Americans who already had health insurance the cost has gone up 27 percent in the last five years?"

"The Soaring Costs of Health Care under Obamacare are just Glitches. We must work on that. Let me just say, I want very much to get the costs down, and that is going to be my mission."

"Mr. Rubistano, same question. Would you work to abolish the Affordable Care Act if you were elected president?"

"You know Obamacare is really the worst thing that has happened in this nation since slavery. It is similar to slavery because it makes all of us obedient to the government. Besides it was never about health care. It was about control. There are some good points like you can't be turned down for preexisting conditions but there is so much wrong with it. Yes I would work to abolish it and allow the states to develop their own health care laws. It is unconstitutional for the Federal government to even be involved in health care since nowhere in the constitution is it mentioned. The tenth amendment says," The powers not delegated to the United States by the Constitution, nor prohibited by it to the States, are reserved to the States, respectively, or to the people."

"Dr. Paul Ronan. Same question."

"I'm unsure if The Affordable Care Act should be completely repealed. There are some aspects of it which are good but I agree with Mr. Rubistano and Dr. Larson's comments that it is unconstitutional because of the Tenth Amendment. It could be made constitutional with a Health Care Amendment but that is unlikely to happen. I would prefer to have each state set up their own health care System adopting the best parts of the federal system. As a Doctor, I see that the federal record keeping and reporting adds a great more cost to the health care system. Also it should be obvious that the more federal government control and levels of approval for health care, the costs will continue to escalate. I remember hearing someone say, "If you think health care costs are expensive now, just wait until it is free."

As the debate continued it gradually escalated into more and more disparaging comments. It seemed that the entire nation was developing less and less tolerance and respect for other's opinions. The third and fourth debates were no less denigrating.

It was a bitter battle that at times seemed to divide the nation even more than before the debates. However, Dr. Ronan still was able to win the RNC vote for the Republican Presumptive Presidential nomination.

Chapter Twenty Three
Paul Ronan's Acceptance Speech for
Presumptive Presidential Nomination.

Presumptive candidate Dr. Paul Ronan proudly stood behind the podium with thousands cheering and holding signs saying "RONAN FOR LIBERTY." A huge sign could be seen, "Restoration of the Republic." Cheering continued with loud patriotic music.

"Thank you. Thank you. Thank you. Delegates and American Patriots. I accept your nomination for Republican candidate for President of the United States."

The crowd continued shouting. The audience was shouting and clapping with expressions of joy. Paul Ronan continued:

"It's a great honor and responsibility and I am asking you to join me in Celebrating the "NEW AMERICA". We have just begun to destroy the old failed Democracy and will return to our Founding Fathers' vision of a Free Republic that represents us all! Thank you for your confidence and trust!

"For the next few weeks I will be campaigning across America. Let's keep up the momentum and with your help, I will be the next President of the United States who will *represent you instead of the lobbyist, international bankers or the military industrial complex companies.* It will be a new era for America as we make *America Great Once Again!*"

Final Debate

"Paul, are you ready for our final debate with the Democrat nominee Mallory Fenton"?

"I am as ready as I possibly can be. Our staff has done an excellent job in drilling me with the questions that they suspect will be asked. I am a little concerned though. It is rumored that the corporate media has provided Mrs. Fenton copies of the questions that will be asked her. This is very disturbing. It could be a disadvantage for us."

"It will be a bigger disadvantage for her if it can be proven and then leaked to the public."

"I guess the most difficult part will be to keep from getting emotionally involved to the extent, I wouldn't look presidential."

"You will do fine Paul. Don't worry about it."

Mallory Fenton seemed to be leading in the polls as reported by the biased corporate media; CNN, ABC, NBC, CBS, MSNBC. But it was discovered, by the Independent Media, that the polls showing Mallory Fenton was leading Dr. Ronan had been unfairly obtained by polling a larger percentage of democrat and women voters than Republican voters. It was quite obvious that Dr. Ronan was leading simply by witnessing the huge numbers of supporters attending his rallies. Dr. Ronan would have literally 30-40,000 in attendance while Mallory Fenton would attract only 2-3,000 and it was suspected that many of these had been paid to attend. The corporate media was complicit by making sure that the camera angle did not show such a small turnout for Mrs. Fenton.

A barrage of WikiLeaks emails about her using an unauthorized email server kept hammering Fenton to such an extent that her lead over Doctor Ronan was lessening.

Thanks to the Independent Media, Mrs. Fenton and her husband's criminal history was being exposed dating clear back to Mena, Arkansas. Also it had been proven that Mrs. Fenton had used a foreign charity front for world leaders to donate to which would conceal their buying influence and accessibility to the White House if Mrs. Fenton were elected President of the U.S. It was referred to as *Pay for Play*.

Also, there was much speculation about Mrs. Fenton's health because of several stumbling episodes, unusual head shaking, and much coughing; all documented on live television.

Probably the most damning evidence against Mrs. Fenton was the fact that her unauthorized email server exposed "Classified" material to the entire world. All she would say about it was that, *I take full responsibility for that.* As if that would exonerate her.

To makes matters worse, the President himself was guilty of communicating with her using her private server. There were rumors that a new Attorney General might bring espionage charges against both of them. This made it even more important for Mrs. Fenton to be elected president in order to protect the sitting President and other Democrat co-conspirators. Never in the history of the U.S. was a presidential candidate running for office while being threatened with such serious charges being leveled against them. The rest of the world watched in amazement and disbelief!

The consensus was that the only way Mrs. Fenton could be elected president of the U.S. was by participating in a fraudulent voting process. Even before November 8th arrived, there were charges against Mallory Fenton of election scamming and vote tampering. The controlled mainstream media had insisted, without any evidence that if any vote rigging occurred, it would most likely be by either Russia or Dr. Ronan. The leaked Fenton emails made it clear that Mrs. Fenton's staff members' and supporters had been actively manipulating and rigging the presidential election from the beginning.

NEW PRESIDENT

After a grueling election, of course, Dr.Paul Ronan was elected president by both the popular vote and the Electoral College vote. It had been a long, hard, and drawn out battle but Paul Ronan had made it in spite of all the dishonest and questionable tactics used at the polls and at the state caucuses.

There was no doubt that Dr. Ronan was elected President because of the independent news media and the various internet social media sites like Facebook and Twitter. No longer could the controlled main stream media dominate the information that had previously been sold to the unsuspecting victims; the electorate.

Doctor Ronan had been elected President, even without taking advantage of a brokered convention. Fortunately the various Tea Party groups and other Constitutionalists and true patriots helped elect him and enough congressmen to maintain control of both the House and Senate.

Introduction of Paul Ronan- President of the United States

January 20th arrived, a cold, sunny day with all the excitement designated for the occasion. Amid cheering and shouts of joy, the speaker announced, "It is my great pleasure to introduce the 45th President of the United States, President Paul Ronan!"

The crown cheered as the speaker left and the new president took the stand.

"Thank you. Thank you. My fellow citizens. I stand here today, truly humbled, to mark the new birth of our great nation. As I say, "Out with the old tyranny and in with the new liberty."

The crowd continued to cheer!

"Congress is on notice that any bill brought to my desk will be promptly thrown in the trash that is more than 50 pages long and has more than one subject to be considered. A Veterans' Bill cannot include spending one billion dollars in support of the Guatemalan army or 10 million dollars allocated to study the sex life of a turtle!"
"**Furthermore**, no longer will the U.S. be allowed to replace democratically elected leaders of other countries by using our own armed forces or hired mercenaries as was done in Syria."

The crowd cheered in thunderous support. The mood of the people had changed to euphoria as they looked forward to a new and honest government.

Oval Office Meeting

"Well Mr. President, what do we do first?"

"Jack, we have got to go slowly at first and not do anything so radical as to give our adversaries an excuse to destroy us. There are two extremely important issues that we must tackle immediately. First we must actively work on balancing the budget which is now over a trillion dollars, and then we must seriously work on paying off the national debt which is over 16 trillion dollars. To help accomplish this, I plan to first cut every government agency's budget 10% across the board and then as time passes we will cut out additional waste, duplication and inefficiency and even some entire departments. We will completely abolish some of the unnecessary bureaucratic nightmares that have been created. For example, do we really need a Department of Energy, Department of Education and the Food and Drug Administration (FDA)? The states are quite capable of handling these issues. And remember the federal government does not have jurisdiction over these areas because of the Tenth Amendment which basically says the federal government possesses only those powers delegated to it by the United States Constitution. All remaining powers are reserved for the states or the people."

"That's right Paul. And another point to remember is that the Supreme Court cannot lawfully hear court cases that aren't constitutional issues. Nowhere does the constitution talk about drugs, education, healthcare, abortions, etc. To hear these cases an amendment to the constitution would need to be passed."

"Jack would you believe that some liberals in my hometown of St. Joseph, Missouri act like the federal government should be allowed to decide such things as the speed limit on Frederick Avenue! I am exaggerating, of course but you get my point."

"What you are really saying Paul is that Liberals do not support the constitution."

"To prove my point Jack, just review their voting record. Liberals, for the most part score way less in voting for constitutional issues while conservatives, score much higher. Liberals fail to remember that our Founding Fathers had just been freed from the tyrant King George the Third of England and wrote a constitution to protect us from tyranny that would stand the test of time. It could always be amended when necessary to bring it up to date."

Stop Being the World's Policeman

"Alright, next we will adopt the attitude that we cannot continue to act as the world's policeman. It was unconstitutional, evil, and a crime against humanity for the U.S. to invade countries like Afghanistan, Iraq, Yemen. Libya, Syria and Ukraine. Neither can we afford it nor is it ethical for a so called civilized country like the United States to impose its will on others. Our *status quo do nothing legislators* failed to stop the President's unlawful aggression! We will reduce the military budget of our Offensive Military by once again adopting a Defensive Military.

America's Foreign Policy Hijacked in 1991

"I don't know if you know this Jack, but In 1991 America's foreign policy was taken over by a few traitors within our own government. They didn't involve the Congress or the American people. It was all done in secret."

"How do you know this, Paul?"

"Well, In October, 2007, I attended a meeting where General Wesley Clark gave a speech at the Commonwealth Club in San Francisco. He described a secret plan that was instigated to attack and destroy seven countries in five years. They were to start with Iraq, then Lebanon, Libya, Somalia, Sudan and Iran; not necessarily in that order. This, policy coup, as he called it, was engineered by neocons in the wake of 9-11 and was plotted by Dick Cheney, Don Rumsfeld, Paul Wolfowitz and what he called a half dozen other collaborators from the Project for the New American Century (PNAC)."

Planned Destabilization of the Middle East

Paul continues. "Clark said the aim of this plot was this: 'They wanted us to **destabilize the Middle East**, turn it upside down, and bring it under our control.' He then recounted a conversation he had had ten years earlier with Paul Wolfowitz, in 1991. The then number three Pentagon official, after criticizing George Bush Sr. for not toppling Saddam, told Clark, 'But one thing we did learn from the Persian Gulf War is that we can use our military in the region, in the Middle East, and *the Soviets won't stop us*. And we've got about 5 or 10 years to clean up those old Soviet regimes; Syria, Iran, Iraq, before the next great superpower comes on to challenge us. Clark said he was shocked by Wolfowitz's desires because, as Clark put it, Wolfowitz implied *'the purpose of the military is to start wars and change governments, not to deter conflicts.'*

"The General also claimed that, 'Richard Perle and Bill Kristol of The Weekly Standard could hardly wait for us to finish off Iraq so we could move into Syria."

"Jack, this type of so called unconstitutional Regime Change is going to stop under my administration. The bankers and military industrial complex companies will just have to find another means to make money, and Israel will have to fight its own wars without America's help."

Money Creation

"Jack, now to change the subject. I have an ingenious method to use in not only stimulating the economy but it will also create millions of jobs without being inflationary."

"That's a pretty tall order, Mr. President."

"Yes it is, but not impossible. Remember your history Jack, when Hitler in 1933 got Germany out of a depression in only five years by creating money out of thin air which in turn created jobs for his people and enabled them to begin repairs and construction on many worthwhile infrastructure projects. They were able to build the famous German Autobahn, dams, hydroelectric plants, etc. and pay the workers' salaries. The so called money he created to do this was referred to as Work Receipts and the workers could spend the *Work Receipts* just like money; greatly stimulating their economy. In a very ingenious way, Hitler created his money using only the printing press. He had been unable to borrow little money from the banks so he simply printed several billion dollars of his Work Receipts, and they weren't backed by gold or silver.

"Germany had been able to escape from the horrors of the world wide depression and was on its way to recovery while the United States and other countries were still struggling. I feel certain that the bankers would have liked this to remain a secret so no other country would try the same strategy. In other words the bankers don't want us to discover that we can create our own money supply without involving the banks and with no gold or silver backing. I am sure they would prefer to keep this a secret. Secret or no secret, I plan on doing something similar in our country to stimulate the economy and create jobs."

Paul continued, "The American Society of Civil Engineers (ASCE) estimates that it would take $2.2 trillion to solve the problems of our decaying and neglected infrastructure. My solution is for the U.S. government to issue $2.2 trillion dollars of interest free US Treasury Notes that would look almost identical to the interest bearing Federal Reserve Notes and they would be accepted as legal tender. The only cost to the tax payer would be a couple thousand dollars for paper and ink. These notes would be used to finance the infrastructure projects. The governors of each state would submit to the Federal government a list of their state's infrastructure projects that are the most important to the people's safety and well-being. The total of all states requests for assistance that would be approved would be 2.2 trillion dollars. The federal government would reimburse the state governments with the U.S. interest free Treasury notes for labor and material to complete these projects."

"This would not be inflationary because the paper money would be merely traded for labor and materials for each project. In other words, these Treasury notes would be backed by the improvements and safety factors added to the states' infrastructure. An additional benefit would be that there would be zero interest due to the Banksters. There will be those who will claim that this will be inflationary and won't work, but Germany already proved that it would work, and Abraham Lincoln also proved it would work when he created Green Backs, paper money, to finance the Civil War. The Green Backs, like Germany's Work

Receipts, did not have precious metal backing; only the trust of the government."

President Kennedy Issued Interest Free Treasury Notes

"That sounds pretty good Mr. President, but how will we sell that to Congress and the American people?"

"Jack, don't forget that I am now President of the United States and will simply use my authority to invoke an Executive Order to issue $2.2 trillion dollars of interest free U.S. Treasury Notes."

"That may very well work, Paul. But remember what happened to President Kennedy when on June 4, 1963, he used executive order #11110 to bypass the Federal Reserve and ordered the U. S. Treasury Department to print several billion dollars of interest free Treasury notes. That meant that for every ounce of silver in the US Treasury's vault, the government could print new money into circulation because it was physically backed by the silver bullion in storage. More than $4 billion in U. S. two dollar, five dollar, ten dollar, and twenty dollar notes were printed but never put into circulation. Shortly after Kennedy's assassination, the notes were ordered destroyed. Was the assassination a warning to future Presidents to not mess with the private Federal Reserve? We will probably never know for sure. This executive order could have returned to the Federal Government the Constitutional power to create and issue money without using the private Federal Reserve Bank which had been created in 1913. Most of the American people have no idea how important this could have been to honest monetary reform for the country."

"I see a problem Paul with your plan-a big problem."

"I already know what you are going to say. You are going to say that Kennedy's plan was Constitutional because his interest free treasury notes were backed by silver in U.S. vaults and that my notes are backed by nothing, therefore it is unconstitutional. You are exactly right but our existing interest bearing Federal Reserve notes are not backed by anything either, which is unconstitutional. What I am doing is merely trading one unconstitutional act for another unconstitutional act. Eventually we will need to amend the Constitution to make it legal to print paper money without any precious metal backing."

"Also Jack, I am extremely worried about the possibility of an assassination attempt by the *banksters* but we will just have to take that chance and at the same time, be on high alert to keep something like that from happening. An interesting sidelight to this is that once Congress and the people see that this simple idea creates millions of jobs and increases tax revenue without being inflationary, it will be much easier to convince them that the Federal Reserve is not needed and therefore can be abolished. We won't even need a Constitutional amendment. In time there will be no more interest bearing Federal Reserve notes because they will have all been replaced with interest free U.S. Treasury notes as the paper itself deteriorates over time."

War Not to be Financed by the Inflation Tax

"Another benefit is that future presidents will no longer be able to finance unholy and unconstitutional wars or Regime Change as they like to refer to it, by hiding the cost in the inflation tax. Can you imagine a President appearing on the six o'clock news saying, 'My fellow Americans, the United States is going to nuke Iceland next week and since we can no longer hide the financing of war by printing money out of thin air and hiding the costs in the inflation tax, I am announcing that we are doubling your income tax for the next five years. The people would be up in arms and the President would most likely be impeached but he surely would not be elected to another term. We would definitely not go to war now that the people could clearly see how it would affect their tax liability. Don't underestimate the huge positive effect this would have on our society. Of course it would be a disaster for the bankers and military industrial complex companies who would lose trillions of dollars in ill gained profits. Remember, there is more money to be made in time of war then there is in peace time.

They will do everything possible to stop this; including assassination attempts."

Governors- Commander in Chief

"Also I plan to once again, make all governors Commanders In Chief of their states' national guard units; both in times of war and peace. If an unscrupulous President orders the State National Guard activated so we can nuke Iceland for example, the governors can refuse and say, 'I am sorry Mr. President, the state of Missouri believes that Iceland poses no threat to the United States. We don't agree with that decision and will sit this one out."

"We will gradually make changes that will help protect the people from tyranny by once again adopting those laws that will assure a system of checks and balances that were originally built into our Constitution."

Government Finances

"Paul, let me see now if I understand this money issue. First we can finance the operation of our government either by the collection of taxes or through debt financing (borrowing). I know you say that it must be financed through taxes because that is transparent and debt financing is not transparent. Under debt financing, the government can borrow from (1) other countries, or (2) from the American people through the issuing of bonds, or (3) from the private Federal Reserve. When the government borrows by selling bonds to the public, the government receives Federal Reserve notes in return and agrees to pay interest to the bond holder. When the government borrows from other countries it receives either money in the form of Federal Reserve notes or gold or silver and also agrees to pay them interest. However, when the government borrows from the Federal Reserve, the Fed. doesn't give the government money of their own but rather instructs the U.S. Treasury Department to print the money. By the way, this money is the governments and not the Feds. Yet the Fed., still charges the government interest. That's a pretty sweet deal for the private Federal Reserve Bank. They have been screwing the American taxpayer now for over 100 years."

"Exactly Jack, I think you've got it."

Credit as a Public Utility

"One more caveat, Jack. The interest free paper money printed by the U.S. Treasury Department, with no gold or silver backing, must not be used to pay the government's expenses because the money used in this fashion would be highly inflationary. It has absolutely no backing and would cause the value of the existing dollars in circulation to go down. This money can only be used in a way that is referred to as "Credit as a Public Utility."

"Remember when we talked about it earlier, Jack? Let me try to explain and maybe go into more detail. Today, we have pretty sophisticated computer programs that can fairly accurately monitor our GDP, Gross Domestic Product, and the actual dollar value of all money in circulation. Oftentimes our country's GDP is more than the money in circulation which keeps commerce from operating efficiently. In other words, there is not enough money in circulation to consume all the products produced by society. There is a gap between GDP, goods produced and the amount of money in circulation needed to purchase the products represented by the gap. There are two ways to consume this gap; (1) the consumer can borrow from the banks and pay interest to get the money to purchase the products in the gap, or the government could issue a stimulus check to the American people enabling them to purchase the products represented by the gap. Why not allow the American people to participate in this production gap instead of a private bank that had nothing to do with the effort that created the gap in the first place."

"I don't see this as being much different where Alaska allows the people in Alaska to participate in the profits of their oil production. Most of the government entitlements like food stamps, government housing assistance, etc. would no longer be needed since the people would receive a yearly stimulus check for participating in the creation of excess production. A few years ago this stimulus check would have amounted to approximately $10,000 for each American adult."

"Wow, that's quite an interesting concept Paul! If you can pull this one off, you are really a genius!"

"Even if we can't get the idea of Credit as a Public Utility implemented, understanding the concept helps explain to the public how our monetary system works and why the banks are not necessary; except to act as clearing houses for financial transactions and handling of the safe storage of our money. In the beginning, it could be undertaken in small steps each year giving the economy time to adjust."

Fractional Reserve Banking

"I hate to admit it Paul but I still don't understand Fractional Reserve banking. Could you explain it one more time?"

"All right, let me explain it as simply as I can with an example. First let me point out that the banks are allowed to create only credit and not actual paper money. Let's say you go into your bank and deposit $1,000.00. That bank is then allowed to loan out 90% of your money which would be $900.00, and after a person receiving a loan deposits his $900.00, the bank can then loan out 90% or $810.00 and so on until the bank has in effect created ten times the money it started with. Remember, their loans were made from the depositor's money and not from the banks money. There are two issues here. (1) Why should a private bank be allowed to create money (credit and not actual paper money) out of thin air and profit from it, plus (2) they only create the principal of the loan and not the interest. Right away the market place is short the amount of the interest that was not created. Where is that money going to come from when it comes time to repay the loan? My argument all along has been to allow only state, city, and county owned banks (those owned by the taxpayer) to take advantage of Fractional Reserve Banking profits. I would allow private banks to exist but they would only be able to loan out their own money."

"Alright Paul, I think I finally got it."

"Paul, How do you propose to clean up Congress, you know get rid of the almost three fourths of them that have broken the oath they took to abide by the Constitution?"

"Well, since they have not obeyed their oath of office, I will begin impeachment proceedings against those who are the worst offenders. Hopefully only a few will need to be impeached because the others, out of fear, will probably begin voting for only Constitutional laws."

"I hope that works Paul, I mean Mr. President. I'm sorry, I have a hard time remembering you are now President of the United States."

"Jack, you don't need to call me Mr. President except maybe when we are around the press or foreign dignitaries or strangers."

"Of course, that makes sense; I will try to remember that."

"Jack, I recognize that there are many dedicated and patriotic employees in the government but there are also some rogue traitors within the CIA (Central Intelligence Agency), FBI (Federal Bureau of Investigation), DIA (Defense Intelligence Agency), NSA (National Security Agency), DDI (the secret Department of Dis-Information) and the DHS (Department of Homeland Security). All the covert activities and secret assassinations, not only around the world but also here in this country must stop."

State Sponsored Assassinations

"You mean state sponsored assassinations like President Kennedy and his brother Bobby?"

"Well... yes like the Kennedy's and many more. What about *Martin Luther King, Jr.* who was killed in 1968, most likely with the help of rogue elements in our own government? And *John Lennon's* criticism of the Vietnam War resulted in Richard Nixon's administration attempting to have him deported. On December 8, 1980, Lennon was murdered by Mark David Chapman at the entrance to the building where he lived. Many people believe that Chapman was a Manchurian Candidate and was directed by others to murder Lennon. *Sonny Bono*, Mayor of Palm Springs and former husband of Cher, was clubbed to death in

1998 and made to look like it was a skiing accident when he allegedly hit a tree. *Vince Foster*, the White House Deputy Counsel, was murdered on July 20, 1993. His body was found in Fort Marcy Park just outside of Washington D.C. His death was ruled a suicide but almost immediately it was rumored that the story of the suicide was a cover up for something much more sinister. There was so much conflicting evidence that it was nearly impossible to ascertain the truth. It had all the hallmarks of a murder and not a suicide. *Ron Brown*, who had been U.S. Commerce Secretary from 1993-1996, died in a plane crash in 1996 in Dubrovnik, Croatia. It was later reported that there was a hole in his head that looked like a bullet hole or trauma from something hitting him in the head, the likely cause of his death. The cause of the plane wreck and the mysterious body wounds made this highly suspect of foul play. *Pat Tillman* and members of his platoon, while travelling through Afghanistan on April 22, 2004, were engaged in a firefight where mistakes were supposedly made that resulted in Tillman's death. Was it an accident that he was killed by friendly fire or was it something else? The autopsy proved that Tillman was shot at point blank range. The way the investigation was handled would indicate that there was more to the story than just friendly fire and that it was covered up. It was reported that Tillman was about to speak out publically against the war."

Unelected controllers

"Hopefully we can get to those unpatriotic bastards involved in these covert operations before they get to us! These same unelected controllers are those behind the constant wars and assassinations which give them a great deal of power and profit.

"Jack did you know that the Department of Homeland Security (DHS) was created in response to the September 11, 2001 attacks, and has the primary responsibilities of protecting the United States of America from (1) terrorist attacks, (2) man-made accidents, and (3) natural disasters? Sounds great doesn't it? The main problem here is that they are extending their power and corruption into the states in the guise of protecting the states from terrorists. The reality is that the Federal Government is taking over the states' responsibility for local law enforcement which is unconstitutional. This sets the stage for any future President to take over the power of the states."

"There wouldn't be any terrorists if we had a decent foreign policy in the Middle East. The more Muslims we kill with the drone attacks, which usually kill more than just the intended target, the more terrorists we create."

"Also, our continued support of Israel is becoming a liability that we can no longer afford. The Israeli government is not America's friend! I served on the *USS Liberty ship* in 1967 when Israel attacked us and killed 34 of my fellow sailors. I will never forgive them for that.

Weather modification

"Jack, I bet you have never even thought of this. I fear that weather modification is now being used as a weapon of war, and a means to spend our way out of a recession or depression. Our military has been secretly experimenting with weather modification with tragic results. There are some scientists, who want to remain anonymous, who believe rogue criminal elements in our government created and directed the storm of the century (Frankenstorm) on the East coast in November of 2012."

"Surely not, Paul. Why would they do this?"

"Maybe they thought it would help President Obama get re-elected because Obama was to look like a hero in taking charge of a crisis, or maybe this was a better way to stimulate our economy than going to war. You know, look what it will cost to rebuild all the devastation. Lots of money will be spent but also lots of money is to be made by the *banksters*, plus it will get people's minds off our monetary problems. Didn't WWll get America out of the depression? If true, this is just not acceptable."

"Now that's hard to believe. That just sounds like one of those conspiracy theories."

"Well maybe not Jack. There was a United Nations Treaty which was entered into force on October 5, 1978 which prohibits the military from using weather modification to induce damage or destruction. In 2010, I think, there was also some type of ban on some other types of weather modification or geo-engineering.

The treaty was named the Environmental Modification Convention or formally referred to as the Convention on the Prohibition of Military or Any Other Hostile Use of Environmental Modification Techniques. Why would the United Nations even consider such a treaty if weather modification wasn't possible? I think they are privy to secret weather modification techniques that the general public is unaware of."

"Where do you get all this information?"

"Jack, over the years in Congress, I have developed close friendships with people in the Pentagon and some of our top research scientists. These are people I trust and they are true patriots. I was merely waiting for this day, where, if I were elected President, I could make full use of this information."

"Well, I certainly admire and respect you for being so well informed on such a wide variety of subjects.

Weeding out of Traitors in our Own Government

"And now just how are you going to accomplish this weeding out of traitors in our own government without getting assassinated yourself? I'm sure you have this all figured out too."

"We will use the powers that were recently granted the President in the National Defense Authorization Act, (NDAA)."

"I thought you hated the unconstitutional NDAA and was going to take steps to have it repealed."

"You are exactly right, it must be repealed but not until I use their own weapon against them. Remember, this act gives the President the legal right to arrest, incarcerate and even kill anyone that is suspected of being a terrorist; without the benefit of legal counsel. We will simply name those individuals in those departments whom we deem the biggest threat and label them terrorists."

"Then will you kill them?"

"Of course not Jack, that would make us as bad as them. We will hold them under house arrest until a hearing can be conducted by a select group of a special chosen committee to determine who will be released and who will be incarcerated. This will need to be kept top secret and even that is authorized by the NDAA. We can thank President Obama for signing the NDAA and making these clandestine procedures legal.

"We will invite these individuals-I suspect that there are about two hundred-to a meeting at Camp David where they will be promptly arrested and held for a secret trial. None of this needs to be reported to the press under the conditions outlined in the NDAA. As soon as they are incarcerated we will either replace their positions with our own people or in some cases abolish their entire organization. We will immediately review all of their secret correspondence and covert agreements to determine if any further people should be arrested.

"Then anything that does not involve national security will be given to the press; things like suppressed technology and secret energy manipulation and even information involving UFO's and Aliens. Also we will do a full audit of all government gold and silver storage, including the holdings at Fort Knox, to see if any exists at all, and if it does exist, determine to whom it belongs to."

"Wow, you are going to create a lot of enemies! Particularly if you declare Martial Law."

"That may be true, but it will also create millions of supporters," explained the President.

Margaret Sanger Population Growth

"Another thing that I am greatly concerned with is all the covert operations that affect our citizens' health."

"I don't understand what you are referring to. I haven't heard of any secret and sinister plans to destroy our health, Paul."

"They are very clever in hiding their agenda and their modus operandi. This probably all started back in the 1920's when people like Margaret Sanger (1879–1966) started a group to control population growth. At first they seemed to be legitimate and apparently had the best interests in the people's well-being. But as time went on they had to conceal their real agenda because of all the negative publicity due to Sanger's belief in Eugenics. They even changed the name of her group to "Planned Parenthood" to facilitate some degree of acceptance. I have no proof, but I suspect that the Eugenics people have made some sinister changes in our diet to affect our birth rate."

"How in the world could someone, group or corporation, accomplish something like this in secret?" asked Jack.

"Remember they have had almost 100 years to accomplish their dirty deeds. Our own government in the 1960's, had Congress appropriate federal assistance for domestic and foreign population control. Eventually there were billions of dollars available to fund global campaigns for mass abortion and forced sterilization. This resulted in a worldwide human catastrophe. The worst part of this is that many of the methods used were done in secret."

Genetically Modified Organisms (GMO's)

Paul continued, "The introduction of Genetically Modified Organisms (GMO's) by companies like Monsanto was promoted as a means to help alleviate world hunger. Here we are today still experiencing world hunger and find that small family farms worldwide have been destroyed, allegedly by using chemicals that have caused havoc in the fields, and a myriad of GMO's that have been introduced into our agricultural system. Many people, including noted scientists, are fearful that not enough research has been done to assure us that GMO's are safe. California did not pass Prop 37 which if passed would have required all food processors to identify those foods as being GMO. Whether you believe GMO's are harmful or not, this bill would have given you, the consumer, the ability to make an intelligent choice when purchasing food products."

"Paul, I'm not concerned with eating hybrid food where they have combined the best traits of two varieties of say, corn, through grafting, etc. but I do have a problem with eating food that has been artificially created by combining the DNA of plants with the DNA of animals or with the DNA of viruses. For example, I would not want to eat an ear of corn that has had its DNA combined with an elephant's DNA in order to create a larger ear of corn. I doubt that has been done, but you get my point."

"I sure do Jack. There are several countries today who currently have GMO labeling laws and almost no one buys the

GMO food now. I plan to see to it that we have a federal GMO labeling law here. The GMO labeling law will effectively eliminate GMO food from our diet; at least, until more scientific research is done to ensure that GMO food is safe to eat."

"Also, I suspect that GMO food has an effect of lowering the humans' fertility rate. If that is true, Margaret Sanger would have been proud of the fine work that GMO's have played in the name of Eugenics."

"I have heard that some varieties of GMO corn have been created to create its own insecticide. When a bug eats the corn, his stomach explodes. I am just not convinced that this corn is safe for humans. Have you noticed over the last several years that more and more people are having trouble with their digestive systems and are advised to take what is called 'Pro-Biotics' to help alleviate the problems in their stomachs and Colons? I suspect that this GMO corn could possibly be causing the digestive problems, and there is the massive problem of honey bees dying. It is suspected that they are being affected by the GMO's."

Fluoride Poison Added to our Drinking Water

"One more thing that concerns me Jack, is that we have been poisoning our nation's water supply since the 1950's by adding sodium fluoride to our drinking water, allegedly to help prevent tooth decay. This may be a noble gesture with good intentions but forcibly medicating the public in mass in this way is not only unconstitutional but also immoral. Here, read this article I wrote for the local paper a few years ago and tell me what you think."

Houston Chronical
Water Fluoridation by Doctor Paul Ronan

When proponents of water fluoridation talk about putting Fluoride in your city's water treatment plant to help fight tooth decay, they invariably fail to tell you it is **not natural calcium fluoride** but rather is the **hazardous waste** byproduct of the aluminum and fertilizer industries called **sodium fluoride**. Typically a bag of sodium fluoride will carry the warning: "Danger! Poison-Toxic by Ingestion; Targets Organs- Heart,

Kidneys, Bones, Central Nervous System, Gastrointestinal and Teeth. Do not get in eyes or on skin-Do not ingest or inhale. Wear proper respirator." Do you really think this is good for your overall health even if it did help to prevent a few cavities?

Both proponents for and against water fluoridation are almost religious fanatics when it comes to explaining their position. The problem arises in that there are few published scientific studies proving either side's position. That is not to say that the studies don't exist but rather are either (1) classified for National Security reasons or (2) the controlling parties in the aluminum and fertilize industry makes it nearly impossible for them to be published. In reality those studies classified for National Security reasons are actually classified in order to cover up the crime of poisoning not only our drinking water but the air around the aluminum and fertilizers plants. In the past the fluorine gas killed farm animals, destroyed crops and even cost the lives of several humans. All of this had to be covered up to protect the government, industry leaders who were and are still polluting our environment, medical doctors, dentists and water companies from lawsuits.

Fluoridated water link to lower IQ

Harvard University researchers recently published a long term analysis that linked fluoridated water to lower IQ scores in children. The results were released in "Environmental Health Perspective" which is a publication of the "National Institute of Health." There are several sources that claim that Hitler and Stalin put fluoride in the prison camps water system to make the prisoners more docile and therefore easier to control. Here in the United States, we are putting fluoride in the drinking water of everyday citizens. Maybe that is why there is a problem with our students low test scores and why the average adult today is so apathetic to how our government is completely destroying our country. The Patriot Act and the National Defense Authorization Act, NDAA, with the inaction of our Congress, has completely destroyed our Bill Of Rights and who cares, besides a few right wing conservative patriots? Even if adding fluoride to our water systems reduces tooth decay, which it most likely does not, is it constitutional or for that matter ethical, to medicate the entire population with the same medicine or dose? Have you ever heard of a medication that is beneficial for everyone disregarding the person's age, weight, other health issues, the amount of water he drinks every day or how much of that medicine (fluoride) he receives from other sources like processed food, soft drinks, etc. This is ridiculous.

"The so called expert dentists and medical doctors that continue to endorse water fluoridation most likely solidified their opinions on this issue 25-30 years ago and have not updated their knowledge of what has been revealed the last few years. They will proudly show you a list of all the government agencies and professional organizations that approve of water fluoridation. Most of these people have not done any research of their own but rather are only endorsing the other endorsements. Also, several years ago, some of these same government agencies were the ones that remained quiet when doctors from all over the country were endorsing Camel Cigarettes because they were kinder to your T Zone, whatever that means. They already knew cigarettes caused cancer but failed to warn the public. The same thing happened with the government protecting those companies that had their employees breathing hazardous asbestos."

"No, I don't trust the various government agencies who tell us that adding poisonous fluoride to our drinking water is safe. Even fluoride tooth paste says," Do not Swallow, if swallowed call poison control immediately."

"You sure make a good case for removing fluoride from the peoples' drinking water. Once you arrest the traitors and we have access to all the classified studies on fluoride, we should be able to expose the truth of its harmful health effects even without the cost of any further research."

"Next week Jack, to promote fairness and reduce corruption, I'm going to address both the House and Senate to inform them that I will not sign any bill they present to me that includes more than one subject and is over 200 pages long. For example, a highway bill cannot include education appropriations. Also, the bill must have been presented to both houses at least 30 days prior to its passing in order that all concerned will have time to read it and discuss it. Any last minute additions or deletions will move the bill back 15 days."

"Paul you just solved the problem of allowing the President to have a line item veto. You just veto the entire bill by refusing to sign any bills which include more than one subject and are over 200 pages long. That is very clever Mr. President."

"Thanks Jack, I thought you would like that."

"Jack read this outline of a speech I plan to make to the nation after things settle down some. This is only a portion of the speech.

Abolish the Private Unconstitutional Federal Reserve and Reform Fractional Reserve Banking

The long term solution to our country's economic problems is to (1) abolish the private and unconstitutional "Federal Reserve System," and (2) reform "Fractional Reserve Banking.

Prior to 1913, when the Federal Reserve Act was passed, our country had periods of experiencing a booming economy and even had periods where the national debt was paid off. The Federal Reserve was supposedly established to keep our country from serious depressions and periods of inflation, eliminating the boom and bust business cycle. It hasn't worked. Since 1913 the purchasing value of the dollar has decreased over 90% and we have had a series of depressions and recessions. In the 1950's a silver dollar or paper dollar would buy four gallons of gas ($.25 per gallon). A silver dollar today (worth $18.00) will buy nine gallons of gas but a paper dollar won't even buy one gallon of gas which would be at least $2.00. The price of gas hasn't gone up; the purchasing power of the paper dollar has gone down due to the hidden inflation tax.

Now is the time to abolish the private Federal Reserve and allow the U.S. Treasury Department to issue and print our money supply interest free. The banking system we now have was bound to fail. It was only a matter of when. We can only print an amount of money that does not exceed the difference between the nations GDP and the amount of money in circulation which is referred to as the gap. We cannot print money to cover the expenses of the government without it being inflationary.

Our country is bankrupt. I am now proposing that the US Government declare bankruptcy and void all interest and payments to the Federal Reserve and start allowing the U.S. Treasury Department to print our money interest free. These write offs would be only a fraction of what the Federal Reserve has stolen from the American people since 1913.

Reform Fractional Reserve Banking

The banks, through fractional banking practices, create credit-not actual paper currency but it is referred to as money. The banks only create the money for the principal for a loan and do not create the money for the interest. There is always a shortage of money to pay the interest. The bank makes a good profit on these transactions because they weren't required to use any of their own money.

If the states, counties, and cities owned the banks (taxpayer owned) as I propose, the profits of the Fractional Reserve Banking would go to the taxpayer instead of the bank. The state, county and city could then use this profit to finance many of its public works projects interest free.
The private banks will still be allowed to operate but they will be required to loan out only their own money.

Stop Collecting an Income Tax on Our Citizen's Wages

Just think what a stimulus it will be to our economy and the citizens' well-being if they aren't required to pay income tax on their salaries! It is not only unconstitutional but immoral to require a person to pay a tax on his labor. A tax on your labor is a form of slavery since you are required to work every day a certain number of hours without pay just to pay the tax! Isn't working without getting paid, the same as slavery?

Most of the income tax we now pay on our salaries does not go to pay for government services but rather pays the private Federal Reserve for the interest it charges us for printing and loaning us our own money. If anyone other than a bank did this, it would be declared "fraud" and they would be charged with "counterfeiting." This interest paid to the Federal Reserve is actually theft from the American people and is completely unnecessary.

Colonial Script and Lincoln's Greenbacks

The paper money created by the colonists and the greenbacks created by Lincoln to pay for the Civil War worked just fine. Neither had any gold or silver backing. Many historians believe that Lincoln's action of bypassing the bank with his interest free "greenbacks" was one reason for his assassination.

I sometimes get a little depressed thinking our country is going to collapse due to our flawed monetary system. But then I remember that we still have millions of intelligent hard working people, natural resources, and an infrastructure to recoup what we have lost. Most people are willing to work to obtain the necessities of life. The only thing missing is enough money to make it possible to conduct commerce efficiently. Our government can create that money interest free on a printing press. It has worked in the past and it will work again.

This is the most important issue facing our country. Sadly the majority of the people in this country do not understand, and neither do the majority of our political leaders. It's the system they have known all of their lives and consequently the only system most of them know. Every citizen needs to diligently study this issue so they will support this sound money reform process.

Thank you my fellow citizens.

"Thanks for listening, Jack"
"Paul, that's probably going to be the most difficult task you have decided to tackle. Remember, some historians speculate that the bankers attempted to assassinate Andrew Jackson in 1835 because he had refused to re-new their National charter, and the B*anksters* were most likely also involved in the assassination of President Kennedy. Not only do we need to take extreme caution to protect you from harm but somehow we have to educate the public that abolishing the private Federal Reserve is the right thing to do."

"We won't even attempt to do this until we get rid of all the traitors within the shadow government. Once we do that they will be unable to plot their usual covert tactics to stop us. As part of my plea to Congress and the electorate, I will explain to them how the government pays for running the government and how it can create interest free money so our economy can run efficiently. Remember, money is only a measuring tool to keep track of a person's ability to add value to a product or service."

"Remember Jack, keep quiet about our upcoming meeting at Camp David. I'm still making a list of the most likely heads of the CIA, FBI, NSA, etc. whom I deem as possible unpatriotic conspirators according to the NDAA. (National Defense Authorization Act) This must be constitutional"Paul smiles.

Loss of electric power

"Jack, do you realize how vulnerable our country is when it comes to losing our electric power? You know how bad it is when you lose power for a day or two because of a huge storm but what if the power couldn't be restored for a year or so. This would be serious and could result in thousands of people dying if it were widespread."

"What do you mean? What on earth could cause something like that?"

Sun Solar Flares

"Actually there are two causes; one is natural and one is man-made. The sun provides light and warmth for the earth that helps sustain life here, but it also has temper tantrums every few years that create solar flares that have seriously damaging effects on our electronic equipment including the power grid."

Radiation from a Nuclear Electromagnetic Pulse.

"The other issue involves man-made radiation from a nuclear electromagnetic pulse. (EMP) Both of these examples explain how electronics can be damaged and how the power grid can be destroyed. Since our power companies are, for the most part, not prepared for this type of catastrophe, I have a solution. This is a fairly inexpensive and practical solution that would help alleviate the misery caused by losing power, as long as you could buy gasoline for your automobile.

Automobile Emergency AC Power Generator

"Each automobile manufactured after 2018 could be required to have a 12 volt inverter capable of producing a minimum of 3,000 watts of alternating current (AC). In other words your automobile would act like a 3,000 watt generator. There would be a power cord long enough to reach from your car to your home electrical sub panel. All new homes built after 2018 would be required to have a six circuit sub panel installed next to the main panel with a recessed male connecter to receive the auto power cord. Those owning older homes would get a tax credit for installing this sub panel. The circuits selected on the sub panel would be those most needed; refrigerator, TV, computer, a few over head lights, the blower on your gas or fuel oil furnace and receptacles above the kitchen counter. Each circuit on the sub panel would have a three position switch; up connects to the power company. Middle is neutral. And down connects to the receptacle connecting the circuit selected to the automobile generator. For little cost, the people could provide their basic electrical needs for quite some time as long as they could buy gasoline."

"Paul, how did you come up with such an ingenious idea?"

"Well Jack, years ago, I belonged to a Preppers group and we designed a few of these emergency power systems for just such emergencies, and I could not stop thinking how beneficial this would be for the entire country and at the same time, save billions of dollars for emergency government aid."

"I think it's an excellent idea, Paul. You could also use some of the car generators or truck generators to operate the gasoline pumps at service stations that have lost power. Great idea."

Jury Nullification

"Jack, another thing. I have been pondering the idea of making it compulsory, in all jury trials, that the judge inform the jury of their Constitutional right to engage in Jury Nullification. At first, I thought this should be handled just by the states but it is actually a federal issue also. Besides, I think New Hampshire is the only state that has passed such a law and it doesn't look like any other states are going to take New Hampshire's lead. The Constitution allows the jury to consider both the law itself and the facts in the case no matter what the judge tells them or doesn't tell them. Rarely will the judge inform the jury of this right and if the defense attorney mentions it in the company of the jury, he sometimes is found in Contempt of Court by the judge and fined. It is obvious how the judges feel about this issue. They want to keep it their little secret so they can convict a higher percentage of cases being tried in their courts. Whether this is true or not, it sure looks that way. Many times the Jury decides that the law, in a particular case, should not apply to the defendant at all. An example would be where a 90 year old man was being tried for murder for killing his 92 year old wife who was in constant severe pain and wanted to die but couldn't. Sure he broke the law but should the law really apply in this case? Should the jury sentence the 90 year old man to life in prison? Most sensible people would say 'Of course not.' The jury can and does make these kinds of decisions every day even if the court system is unaware of it. In many cases, jurors fail to convict a defendant in issues involving marijuana; possession and or distribution. When this happens over and over, it is an indication that the law may need to be abolished. It is simply not working and is assumed to be an unfair law.

Third Party candidates included in debates

"Jack, I barely got elected with some of my revolutionary ideas known, but third-party candidates with ideas outside the mainstream should also have the same chance of getting elected as a Republican or Democrat. What we have now is a *Two Party Dictatorship*. We must find a way to force the mainstream media to allow third party candidates to participate in the debates. The media reports the news about their favorite candidate and completely ignores or marginalizes those they deem are outside the mainstream."

Electoral College

"I agree Paul, and also, don't you think we need to get rid of the Electoral College and allow the popular vote to elect the President and Vice President? Should a candidate win the popular vote but then have the opposing candidate win the electoral vote? It seems like the people have been cheated out of their true choice. All of these caucuses and the election of electors is nothing but a gigantic dog and pony show that provides a few people a chance to party and appear important while not really adding anything of value to the election process."

"Jack, you've got it. The problem here is that it would take a Constitutional amendment to change the Electoral College and allow the popular vote to elect the President. I'm not sure though that the Electoral College should be done away with anyway. Actually it is another Check and Balance means to assure that states like California and New York are not represented more in an election simply because of their larger population. I'll need to give that some more thought.

"If it were changed Jack, where would all those elite delegates, electors and the people go who wave the signs and shout on the night of the convention?"

"Never mind about that now, Jack, we've got more important things to think about now. Let's save this issue for another time."

Patience and Perseverance Paid Off

It was tough going the first two years because President Ronan's views were so far outside the mainstream thinking that there was much education needed to explain to the electorate, both liberal and conservative, what needed to be done because of the years of neglect of not following the Constitution. Additionally, the lame stream media propagandists had convinced much of the public that anyone like President Ronan whose ideas were outside the mainstream was someone to avoid. The Constitution had been an almost perfect guide on how to run a government, but sadly the last few Presidents, had completely ignored it. One of the biggest issues was to educate the Liberals on how it was impossible to give billions of dollars of entitlements to one group without forcibly taking the money from others. This cannot be sustained indefinitely. Eventually the Producers will not be financially able or willing to provide the ever increasing entitlements that rob both the Producers and Non-producers of their freedom.

After President Ronan's revolutionary monetary reforms, the bankers who were losing billions of dollars due to the abolishing of the Federal Reserve System and the military industrial complex companies who were no longer making huge sums of money from all the unnecessary wars were understandably angry. The Israeli leaders were also upset because Congress had finally recognized that Israel was such a huge liability that no more money or military equipment could be given them. Israel was now on their own. It would take many years, if ever, for the Muslim countries to forgive the United States for assisting the Israelis' in their Holocaust against the Palestinians and other Muslims throughout the world.

As could be expected, President Ronan had created enemies but much of that threat was reduced when, with the help of the NDAA, he legally imprisoned both elected and unelected rogue leaders in our government who were engaged in covert actions to control the country. At the same time, he had created a multitude of supporters for saving the American economy. There were several attempts on the President's life but increased security by literally thousands of true patriots had been able to foil all of the attempts.

With the support of the newly elected far right conservative Congress, no longer was the United Nations directing the United States Military in unconstitutional wars, or as the traitors had referred to them, *Regime Change*. Once again a Declaration of War would have to be voted on by the Congress of the United States instead of the President sending troops around the world without authorization.

With the election of President Paul Ronan, the United States was again returned to a Constitutional Republic for the benefit of the citizens instead of special interest groups. Democracy had failed just as it was destined to fail. The idea of forcibly taking from the producers and giving to the non-producers could not be sustained any longer. Thanks to President Paul Ronan, we were no longer our brother's keeper but rather our brother's brother. Through proper monetary reform and the resulting job creation, nearly everyone was provided with the necessities of life including affordable healthcare.

The President's favorite quote was by Mark Twain. "It's easier to fool people than to convince them that they have been fooled." Fortunately millions of Americans were convinced that they had been fooled and voted for Doctor Ronan; whose great grandfather, Samuel Ronan, had immigrated to America from Ireland in 1858.

"May God help us to keep the NEW REPUBLIC by once again adhering to the U.S. Constitution" exclaimed the New President of the Republic. "The controlled mainstream media and the *One World Government* traitors had lost and the American people had won!

Chapter Twenty Four
Are you better Off Today than you Were Four Years Ago?

Are you better off today than you were four years ago? For once you could truthfully answer, "Yes absolutely, without a doubt." President Paul Ronan will go down in history as the President who returned the United States to a Constitutional Republic from a failed Democracy. Thomas Jefferson and Benjamin Franklin's philosophy of a small government with limited powers replaced Alexander Hamilton's brand of government consisting of a tyrannical powerful Federal government and an unconstitutional privately owned central bank.

President Ronan is credited with the following:

- Abolished the privately owned Federal Reserve banking system.

- Allowed fractional reserve banking for only those banks owned by the state (taxpayer). States, Counties and Cities now owned their own banks. Now the tax payers would benefit from the profits generated by fractional reserve banking instead of a privately owned bank. Fractional reserve banking was now considered a *Public Utility*.

- Since the United States government was effectively bankrupt with over 16 trillion dollars of national debt and with over one trillion dollars of a budget deficit, the President claimed bankruptcy. All principal and interest payments owed to the privately owned Federal Reserve Bank and other world banks connected to the Fed. were cancelled. Debts to other countries, individuals and private corporations were not cancelled. It was estimated the dollar amount owed the Federal Reserve was in excess of three trillion dollars but could not be confirmed because an audit of the Fed had never been done.

291

- Made the governors of each state, once again, Commander in Chief of their states National Guard units both in times of peace and times of war.

- Used the National Defense Authorization Act to legally arrest and incarcerate rogue leaders in the CIA, FBI, DIA, NSA, and the DHS who were engaged in illegal, unconstitutional and unethical covert actions that were not in the best interests of the American people.

- Stopped collecting an income tax on our citizen's salaries.

- Encouraged all states to adopt New Hampshire's Jury Nullification statute requiring that either the Judge or the defense attorney advise the jurors they have the constitutional right to judge the law as well as the facts in a case.

- Abolished unnecessary and unconstitutional federal government departments including the Department of Energy, Department of Education, and the Food and Drug Administration, etc. The states are capable of handling these issues much more efficiently.

- Released all studies, formally classified because of alleged national security issues, concerning the dangers of adding the hazardous waste fluoride to our drinking water. If the released documents fail to reveal the hazards, independent scientific studies will be conducted to determine if there are any dangers to our citizen's health.

- Stopped all farm subsidies and allowed the market place to decide the proper methods of control.

- Put the farmers in the lucrative energy business by allowing agricultural hemp to be grown legally.

292

- Stopped harassing the states that have legalized marijuana or who in the future may legalize other controlled substances. This is a state issue and not a federal issue.

- Allowed the states to handle the issue of abortion. This is not a federal issue.

- Made it clear to the public that the Constitution does not prohibit states from seceding.

- Encouraged all states to adopt GMO labeling laws.

- Wars and so called police actions and Regime Change, were almost non-existent now that transparent taxes were used to finance war instead of non-transparent debt financing.

- Any legislator who does not obey his oath to abide by the Constitution by voting for unconstitutional issues risked having impeachment proceedings brought against him.

- The Federal government is now financed through transparent taxes instead of non-transparent debt financing.

- Social Security and Medicare are now handled by private insurance companies at the state level leaving the Federal government to handle only the laws that govern payroll deductions to fund these programs.

- Congress voted to replace Alexander Hamilton's picture on the ten dollar bill with President Paul Ronan.

- Instead of attempting to get a *Line Item Veto* bill for the President, President Ronan simply advised Congress that he would return, without reading the bill, if it contained more than 200 pages and included more than one subject.

- The idea that the Constitution grants the Federal government unlimited implied powers, as believed by Alexander Hamilton and many of today's Liberals, is simply not true. Those now in power, agreed to fully respect the 10th Amendment to the Constitution; *"The powers not delegated to the United States by the Constitution, nor prohibited by it to the States, are reserved to the States, respectively, or to the people."*

Predator Eagle Should be a Peace Dove

In addition to the above, President Ronan modified the National Emblem from a predator eagle to a peace dove. The new president agreed with Benjamin Franklin.

Following is a letter Benjamin Franklin supposedly wrote to his daughter concerning his displeasure of the bald eagle being the symbol of our country.

"For my own part I wish the Bald Eagle had not been chosen the Representative of our Country. He is a Bird of bad moral Character. He does not get his Living honestly. You may have seen him perched on some dead Tree near the River, where, too lazy to fish for himself, he watches the Labour of the Fishing Hawk; and when that diligent Bird has at length taken a Fish, and is bearing it to his Nest for the Support of his Mate and young Ones, the Bald Eagle pursues him and takes it from him.

"I am on this account not displeased that the Figure is not known as a Bald Eagle, but looks more like a Turkey. For the Truth the Turkey is in Comparison a much more respectable Bird, and withal a true original Native of America... He is besides, though a little vain & silly, a Bird of Courage, and would not hesitate to attack a Grenadier of the British Guards who should presume to invade his Farm Yard with a red Coat on."

It should be pointed out that there are many more patriotic Americans than there are elitist bankers, industrial military complex company executives and special interest lobbyists. The question is, "Will you and the millions of other people in this country recognize your obligation in time and get involved in making the necessary changes to save America from economic ruin and the complete destruction of our Constitution by voting for a true patriot like Paul Ronan? Be on constant guard of the controlled corporate media telling you for whom to vote. They do not represent the electorate at large but rather the interests of their own media owners and their secret sponsors.

I implore you to vote for only those legislators that score 70% and above in voting for Constitutional issues.

You can Google the *'Congressional Score card'* to see how your particular representatives score. Reward those that consistently score 70% or above with your votes. Notice that many liberals rank below 30% while most conservatives rank 60-100%.

With the election of Paul Ronan, with few exceptions, the people can now afford their own medical insurance and other needs without government intervention. They are truly free at last!

Martial Law Under President Paul Ronan

When President Paul Ronan declared Martial Law in 2017 at Camp David and held the previous top CIA, FBI, NSA, Pentagon officials, the Joint Chiefs of Staff, etc. for investigation of subversion and war crimes, it only took six weeks to decide which to incarcerate until they could be tried in a court of law.

Naturally this action was only approved by approximately one half of the American people. Those who disapproved were the status quo politicians who had not abided by their oath to support the constitution, the internationals bankers who had cheated the American people, since 1913, by charging the tax payer interest for loaning them their own money, the war mongers including the military industrial complex companies that made billions of dollars in war profits and the Israeli lobbyist who had controlled much of America's foreign policy since 1948.

The new independent news network, TRBN- Truth Revealed Broadcasting Network, which was started by one of President Ronan's relative's, reported soon after the Camp David meeting that Mallory Fenton and her husband Phil were seen boarding a private jet heading for an undisclosed country in South America. It was later learned that the new attorney general had brought criminal charges against Mrs. Fenton for operating an illegal charity which was only a way for her to obtain millions of illicit donations which were in reality a fee to get insider favors if Mrs. Fenton had been elected president of the U.S.

America, was at last, returning to a Republic form of government as envision by our founding fathers and abolished the failed Democracy.

You can make a difference.
Get informed and get involved.

Encourage your friends and relatives to read this book and ask your local school board and libraries to make it freely available.

Even if you don't agree with 100% of the issues discussed in this book, remember the quote by Aristotle. *"It is the mark of a great mind to entertain a thought without necessarily accepting it.*

Larry Flinchpaugh

Prolog

*Author's note: The author spent almost every summer from 1945 to 1953 visiting his Uncle Clyde Tomlin and Aunt Winnie, Cousin Mike and Grandmother Monta Wilson in Breckenridge, Missouri. My mother would put me on the Burlington train in St. Joe about seven in the evening and I would arrive in Breckenridge, or as the conductor called it, **The Rock 40**, about midnight. I tried to time my visits with the annual carnival celebration in the city park. The next morning, after arrival, we were awakened by the crowing of the roosters announcing the sun was coming up. No need for an alarm clock on the farm.*

Being a city boy, it was a little hard for me to adjust to the rigors of farm life. Mike and I had to gather the eggs, weed the garden, slop the hogs and mow the grass with one of those iron wheel push mowers. Sometimes I would ride on the Ford tractor's fender, not to actually work but just to have fun. There was a nice cold water spring out in one of the fields where you could get a cold drink.

Every Friday morning we would fill a wash tub full of cold water from the hand cranked pump and drag it out into the center of the yard in the sun so it would be warm in the evening. Somehow that didn't work but it was still better than taking a bath in fresh cold water out of the well. We would get all cleaned up and Uncle Clyde would give us each four bits (fifty cents) to spend in town. Fifteen cents for a movie, five cents for popcorn, and five cents for a coke. That gave us twenty five cents left to blow at my Uncle Fritz Woolsey's and Aunt Alice's variety store on Main Street. (Broadway).

Aunt Winnie would bring into town things to trade at Place's Grocery, eggs, tomatoes, etc., and then purchase the rest of her groceries less the credit for her trading.

297

I especially remember the old livery stable at the East end of Broadway. I used to imagine the old timers coming to town and having their horses cared for there. It looked just like the ones in the Western movies we saw at the Electric Theater in St. Joe.

Many of my relatives are buried in the Trosper and Weldon cemeteries. It's sad to see that most of the historic buildings have been torn down, but I still have the fond memories of visiting Breckenridge in my youth.

Larry Flinchpaugh

Notable Quotes and Notes:

9-11 attack

Former Italian President Francesco Cossiga, who revealed the existence of Operation Gladio, has told Italy's oldest and most widely read newspaper that the 9-11 terrorist attacks were run by the CIA and Mossad, and that this was common knowledge among global intelligence agencies. In what translates awkwardly into English, Cossiga told the newspaper Corriere della Sera:
"All the [intelligence services] of America and Europe know well that the disastrous attack has been planned and realized from the Mossad, with the aid of the Zionist world in order to put under accusation the Arabic countries and in order to induce the western powers to take part in Iraq [And] Afghanistan." By http://www.americanfreepress.net/

First they ignore you, then they laugh at you, then they fight you, then you win. Quote Attributed to: **Mohandas Karamchand Gandhi**

World events do not occur by accident. They are made to happen, whether it is to do with national issues or commerce; most of them are staged and managed by those who hold the purse strings. " **Denis Healey, former British Secretary of Defense**

"Every Congressman, every Senator knows precisely what causes inflation...but can't, [won't] support the drastic reforms to stop it [repeal of the Federal Reserve Act] because it could cost him his job." **Robert A. Heinlein-Expanded Universe**

Illegal and Unconstitutional-*"The illegal we do immediately. The unconstitutional takes a little longer. "* **Henry Kissinger**, New York Times, Oct. 28, 1973

Suggested Documentaries

The Money Masters

The Money Masters is a fascinating documentary about the worldwide history of central banking and fractional reserve lending. It was made in 1998, but the information is still very relevant—even more so now than a decade ago. Despite being three and a half hours long and low-budget, it's an extremely gripping film. It opens by asking the following questions:

- What's going on in America today- why are we over our heads in debt?
- Why can't the politicians bring debt under control?
- Why are so many people working at low-paying, dead end jobs and still making do with less?
- What's the future of the American economy and way of life?
- Why does the government tell us that inflation is low when the buying power of our paychecks is declining at an alarming rate?
- Are we heading into an economic crash of unprecedented proportions? If so can we prevent it?
- What can we do to protect our families?

The entire film can be viewed on Google Video. (Running Time is 3 ½ hours)

9-11 Ripple Effect 96 minute documentary featuring Dave von Kleist- of "The Power Hour." Excellent presentation of the 9-11 attack questioning the government's explanation of events.
The Obama Deception and **The Fall of the Republic**, both by Alex Jones.

End Game by Alex Jones

Suggested Reading

The Declaration of Independence
The U.S. Constitution and Bill of Rights
The Law by Fredric Bastiat

And the Truth Will Set You Free—by David Icke
The Age of Reason-- by Thomas Paine
An Appeal To Reason-The Writings of Willis A. Carto
Attention Deficit Democracy-- by James Bovard
The Biggest Secret—by David Icke

Billions For The Bankers-Debts For The People, reprinted by JL Flinchpaugh Publishing Company April 2013. (94 pages) This original 1984 informative 37 page of Sheldon Emry's booklet will give the reader greater insight into our countries monetary system and explains why we must abolish the private Federal Reserve Banking cartel that has, from 1913, been in charge of printing our money and loaning it to the American government with interest. The U.S. Treasury Department can print our money "Interest Free." Forty Eight percent (48%) of our National debt is owed to the private Federal Reserve Bank.

Capitalism and Freedom--by Milton Friedman
The Christ Conspiracy-The Greatest Story Ever Sold-- by Archarya S

Common Sense-- by Thomas Paine

Constitutional Chaos: What Happens When the Government Breaks Its Own Laws –by Andrew P. Napolitano
Corporatism-The Secret Government of the New World Order by Jeffrey Grupp
Hamilton's Curse- How Jefferson's Arch Enemy Betrayed The American Revolution And What It Means For Americans Today. By: Thomas J. Dilorenzo

Letters Home From Civil War Soldier Charles W. Gamble to Family--**1862-1864** compiled by Mark Flinchpaugh, April 2011.
The Creature from Jekyll Island –by G. Edward Griffin
The David Icke Guide to Global Conspiracy (And How to End It.)
The Day After Roswell—by Philip J. Corso- A former Pentagon official reveals the United States government's shocking UFO cover-up.

The Deliberate Dumbing Down of America--by Charlotte Thompson Iserbyt
The Draft: A Handbook of Facts and Alternatives-- by Sol Tax
The Economic Hit Man-- by John Perkins
The End of America-- by Naomi Wolf
The New Babylon—Those Who Reign Supreme "Inside the Rothschild Empire: The Modern Day Pharisees
Freedom Under Siege--by Ron Paul

How to Win Friends and Influence People and Five Essential People Skills: How to Assert Yourself, Listen to Others, and Resolve Conflict—by Dale Carnegie
The Real Lincoln: A New Look at Abraham Lincoln, His Agenda, and an Unnecessary War- By: Thomas J. Dilorenzo
The Psychology of Winning—by Denis Waitley
The Revolution- A Manifesto-- by Ron Paul
Rothschild's Money Trust—by George Armstrong (Buy at Amazon.com or free on the internet)

Seeds of Destructions-The Hidden Agenda of Genetic Manipulation-by F. William Engdahl
The Terror Conspiracy—by Jim Marrs
Think and Grow Rich--by Napoleon Hill
The Tyranny of Good Intensions: *How Prosecutors and Bureaucrats are Trampling the Constitution in the Name of Justice*—by Paul Craig Roberts and Lawrence M. Stratton.
Vietnam-Why Did We Go-The Religious Beginning of an Unholy War-- by Avro Manhattan (1914-1990) the shocking story of the Catholic Church's role in starting the Vietnam War.
War Made Easy: How Presidents and Pundits Keep Spinning Us to Death—by Norman Solomon.
The Web of Debt—by Ellen Hodgson Brown, J.D.

Saving America Screenplay

Sam Ronan and His friend Kelsey O'Sullavan
Arrive in Philadelphia on May 25, 1858
They board the 26ᵗʰ Street Trolley to the Elmira Street
Boarding House

The author of this historical novel-
Against All Odds-President Paul Ronan
has written a screenplay entitled

Saving America **based on his book.**

It is available to be made into a five part TV mini-series.

For a Power Point slide presentation of the screenplay, go to:
http://www.larryflinchpaugh.com/more/saving-america-tv-mini-series/

For more information contact:
J L Flinchpaugh Publishing Company
5500 Cape Court
St. Joseph, Missouri 64503
816-676-2565 Email: lflinch@stjoelive.com

Additional Publications by
J L Flinchpaugh Publishing Company
St. Joseph, Missouri

lflinch@stjoelive.com
www.larryflinchpaugh.com
www.amazon.com/books/title

Secrets of Our Hidden Controllers Revealed

Author Larry Flinchpaugh
November 1, 2009
Paper Back 8.5 X 5.5

$15.00

Discover how the unelected controllers of our government control our lives and dictate what we do and think. I dare you to read this book. If it doesn't irritate you, I haven't accomplished my objective to get your attention. Unfortunately, most people are simply too apathetic and too busy to get involved with new thoughts and ideas that would drastically change their **outdated** opinions.

Most of the information presented in this book will more than likely be outside your *comfort zone.*

Perhaps you think you already know all you need to know about religion and the important political issues facing us today.

The ideas presented in this book may be shocking-but I sincerely hope it will open your eyes and expand your mind. This is more important than agreeing with the author on every issue.

Billions For The Bankers
Debts For The People

June 2009
Paper Back 8.5 X 5. 5 (93 Pages)

$6.00

This 1984 informative reprint of Sheldon Emry's booklet will give the reader greater insight into our country's monetary system and explains why we must abolish the privately owned Federal Reserve Banking cartel that has, from 1913, been in charge of printing our money and loaning it to the American government with interest. The U.S. Treasury Department can print our money "Interest Free," making it unnecessary to pay income tax on our citizen's wages.

Sheldon Emry's original book was not copyrighted and neither is this one. The publisher, Larry Flinchpaugh, has added two extra sections to help bring the booklet up to date a bit. Even though some of the information is a little outdated it is still relevant today.

Contrary to popular belief, the only reason our paper money should be backed by gold and silver is because that is what is required by the Constitution. Paper money is only a means to account for the value a person adds to the economy through his labor, investment and risk. That plus the government's willingness to accept it as payment of taxes is the only backing it needs.

It is imperative that the public understands are current flawed monetary system so that they will not be tricked into another Federal Reserve type deception when our economic system finally collapses.

Consider purchasing several at this low price and give to your friends and legislators.

304

Growing Up In a Zoo

February 2011

Paper Back 8.5 X 5.5 (166 Pages)

$15.00

This is a story of Larry Flinchpaugh growing up in St. Joseph, Missouri in the 1940's through the 1960's and working in his parents Pet Shop, Zoo, and Reptile Gardens. The facility was located at 3727 Frederick Avenue-old highway 36. (Now the home of The Citizens Bank and Trust Company)

The book is full of interesting and funny stories regarding his experience in training and handling their pet chimpanzee, Vicky Lynn. Vicky not only appeared regularly at the Krug Park Bowl, KFEQ TV, daily shows at the Zoo but even had a part in a Harvard Biology training film. Other stories include the part Larry played in the heroic Air Force flight from Homestead Air force base in Florida to Rosecrans Field in St. Joe. That flight saved the life of one of the Zoo's employees, Bill White, after he had been bitten by an Indian cobra. This story was carried by almost every major news outlet throughout the world.

There are many pictures and interesting stories included which should be of special interest to those who came from miles around to tour the facility and to be entertained and educated about a wide variety of animals, birds and reptiles. Even those people who never toured the Zoo but love animals and animal stories will find the stories entertaining and educational.

Vicky was one of the Flinchpaugh family Members. She ate with them in their private kitchen at the zoo facility and had her own sleeping cage. It was very sad when she reached the age of about eight and began to rebel; attacking the author, Larry Flinchpaugh.

Letters Home
(1862-1864)
Compiled by Mark Flinchpaugh, April 2011.

Paper Back 8.5 X 5.5 (124 Pages)

$15.00

These historic letters included in this book were written in the 1860's by Union soldier, Charles W. Gamble, to his wife and family during the Civil War. He bravely served with the 12th regiment, New Jersey volunteers, Company D.
A carpenter by trade, Charles joined the Union Army in August, 1862 to, as he stated, "to preserve the country and the Constitution." *Note: Not to free the slaves.* Several times in his letters he frankly wrote that he might not come back home alive, but he was serving for a just cause. This is a fascinating and personal account of a common soldier's life serving his country and fighting to keep the Union intact. Told from the intimate perspective of a typical volunteer soldier, you will glean interesting tidbits of historical information not usually found in books about the Civil War.

You will come to feel that you know Charles personally as you read his actual letters about his daily activities during the war. From mundane chores to the horrors of battle at Gettysburg, you will experience Civil War life through Charles' own words.

No matter how difficult the hardships became Charles courageously pressed on for the good of the country. History comes alive in these insightful, heartwarming letters written nearly one hundred fifty years ago by Charles W. Gamble.

This book is available on Amazon.com and at all the St. Joseph libraries, book stores, most local museums and various tourist locations.

Should I Start My Own Business?

Author Larry Flinchpaugh
January 20, 2013
Paper Back 8.5 X 5.5 (121 pages)

$12.00

This self-help 127 page paperback book follows the various business ventures that Larry Flinchpaugh has been involved in from 1963 to 2005.

It starts out by asking the question, "Why do you want to start your own business?" Sadly many people start a business for the wrong reasons and many lose a good portion of their life savings in the first year or two.

The book explains how to write a **"Business Plan"** and prepare a **"Break Even Analysis"** to help the reader predict their chance of success or failure.

Although, not intended to be an accounting book, it does explain basic accounting functions, how to calculate an individual's **"Net Worth"** and how to prepare a "Balance Sheet" and "Profit and Loss" statement.

This book is available on, Amazon.com/books and all St. Joseph, Missouri libraries. It can also be obtained at most local libraries thru their inter-library loan program.

Movie Documentary "This Is Our Town, St. Joseph, Missouri"
20.00

Filmed c. 1954. This movie was originally produced by "Robert M. Carson" productions on a 16MM film that was used as a promotional film for the city of St. Joe. It features several prominent businesses in St. Joe in the 1950's and shows nostalgic street scenes in a much different time.

The 16MM film was purchased by Mr. Flinchpaugh several years ago at a local estate sale from a former film collector. After retiring, Mr. Flinchpaugh re-discovered the long forgotten film in a box in his garage but noticed it had a strong odor smelling like bleach emitting from the metal film container. A quick check with "Accent Video" in Overland Park, Kansas confirmed that the film was rapidly deteriorating and needed to be restored immediately before it was entirely lost.

The film has been shown several times at the local libraries and civic organizations but anyone wishing to purchase a copy of the film may buy one at most of the local museums, the "St. Joseph Visitor Center" or at www.larryflinchpaugh.com.

Specific viewings for local civic groups, churches, and other clubs and organization can be arranged by calling Larry at 816-676-2565 or email him at lflinch@stjoelive.com.

The movie is approximately one hour long.

St. Joseph Missouri Memories-Personal Accounts-1915 to 1960
$15.00

Paperback 8.5 X 11– July 10, 2015
by Mr Larry Flinchpaugh (Author)

This book takes the reader on a journey down memory lane from 1826, when St. Joseph was founded by Joseph Robidoux to the 1960's.

A vivid picture is painted of what life was like in St. Joseph in the early 1900's to the 1960's with personal stories and photos by those who grew up in St. Joseph.

Not only is the book illustrated with numerous pictures of this period, there are also excerpts from other historical writings that give the reader a better understanding of St. Joseph's long history.

The "Illustrated London News" account in 1861 describes the people of St. Joe by claiming, "There is a wild look about the people of St. Joe. Nearly everybody carries a rifle…"

In addition to the personal stories and photographs, there are chapters describing notable events, notable people and special timelines to assist the reader in keeping St. Joe's history in perspective.

The personal stories are not only educational but also entertaining and sometimes humorous. This collection of stories, from those who lived it, will help the reader reminiscence a bit and will also be enjoyed by future generations wishing to discover more about their ancestors and what life was like in St. Joe in earlier times.

Story Contributors: Rick Drozd, John Larry Flinchpaugh, Margery Jean Flinchpaugh, Phyllis Ann Nelson Flinchpaugh, Rodney Eugene Keyes, George Barry Nelson, Truman Nelson, Sharon Louise Roberts Patching, Jack Quinn, Bob Slater, Denise Bartles Tapia, C J Vetter, Clyde Weeks, and Dennis Weiser

The book may be purchased on Amazon.com/books.

Paper Back
152 pages

Against All Odds
President Paul Ronan

Author Larry Flinchpaugh

January 3, 2017

Paper Back 8.5 X 5.5

$15.00

This exciting story follows the lives of four members of the Ronan family, from 1859-2016, as they influence the American political system to once again establish a Constitutional Republic.

In 1859, the protagonist, Sam Ronan comes to America from Ireland and becomes a telegraph operator in Philadelphia and shortly thereafter, he gets a job in Breckenridge, Missouri as a telegrapher for the Hannibal and St. Joseph Railroad

Samuel Ronan's long stagecoach trip to Hannibal Missouri permits him to see the interior of the country and meet some colorful characters. Because the Confederate bushwhackers had sabotaged the bridge over the Platt River, Sam almost loses his life while traveling to St. Joe on the Hannibal and St. Joseph Railroad.

Having graduated from Harvard, magna cum laude, Sam's son Jeff lands a job working for President Woodrow Wilson in Washington, D.C. Matt, Sam's grandson, meets the love of his life at the Frog Hop in St. Joseph and becomes a successful farmer and Federal Congressman. Graduating from Central High School in St. Joseph, Mo., Sam's great-grandson, Paul, obtains a medical degree from Baylor University in Texas and then joins the Navy and nearly loses his life when the Israelis attacked his reconnaissance ship, the USS Liberty in 1967.

Honorably discharged from the Navy, Paul becomes a Texas Congressman and after a ruthless campaign in 2016, he is overwhelmingly elected President of the United States.

Each one of the four generations of the Ronan family added greatly to the security and financial well-being of this country's citizens. You will learn how Paul Ronan obtained full employment, truly "affordable" health care, a balanced budget, a plan to totally "pay off" the national debt, all in a candid entertaining and educational story format. This historical novel will help you understand the issues and learn what you can do as an individual to help save our country from ruin.

This book is available on Amazon.com/books and all St. Joseph, Missouri libraries. It can also be obtained at most local libraries thru their inter-library loan program.

Be sure to check out the **J L Flinchpaugh Publishing Company** web site at www.larryflinchpaugh.com to read the "Flinchpaugh Gazette."

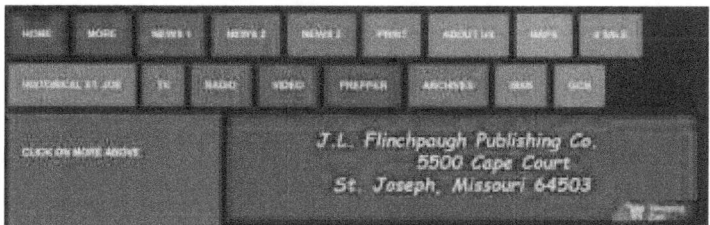

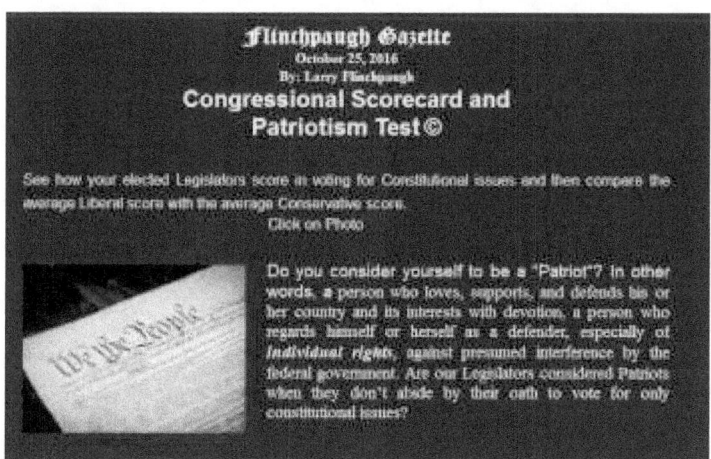

Notes:

Abercrombie Abe-89,90,92,93,103,113,120,145, 146
Acme Radio-195
Aeronca Champ-197
Afghanistan-230,242,246,265,274,298
Agrarian South-84
Agricultural hemp-167,193,292
Albert Pike-113,114
Alhambra-10,11,13,16,17,22,24,74,118
Aliens-79,224,253,277
Amateur radio-195
Anti-Semitic-212,237,238
Anti-Semitism-237
Apprentice-42,48,73,92,94
Articles of Confederation-50
Assets-206,207,231
Atheists-183
Aunt Mary-5-7,9-11,27,28,41,100
Baden Baden-182
Balanced budget-159,239,310
Bald Eagle-294
Ballew-120
Ballot Box-224
Bank of Montreal-97,98
Bastiat-90,92,300
Baylor University-198,200,311
Bible-18,21,22,73-75,109,125,130,182
Bixby Horace-73
Black Budget-254
Blacksnake Hills-67
Blackstone's Com. On the Law-35,90
Blakely Carol-206
Boarding house-26,28,32,35,65
Bolshevik Revolution-134,238
Bono Sonny-274
Boston Tea Party-115
Breckenridge Bulletin-146
Breckenridge Mo-39-47,55-100,104-195
Brown Ron-274
Buchanan. Cty–42, 63,79,83,89,171
Bull Moose Platform-133
Bernstein Bart.-47-50, 51,54,58,85

Bushwhackers-47,80,83,86,311
Cabin 64-66,68-70,84,120,136,243,251
Caldwell County-89,91
Calvin Barbara -168-181,184-190
Cambridge, Mass.-113,114,116
Cameron Simon-76,77
Camp David-3,224,277,285
Cartridge Box-224
Central High School-iii,195,311
Charles W. Gamble-300,305,87,102,118,186,187
Chippendale dining table-178
Christian-73,109,131,182,183,198,239
Christianity-73,183
Cincinnati, Ohio-44,182
Clark General Wesley-265,266
Clemens Orion-71,72,75
Clemens Samuel-vi,72-75,108
Coach Travel Rules-44
Coded message-253
Colorado-26,41,43
Commander In Chief-vi,292
Conductor-61,63,154,297
Confederate partisans-80
Confederate States-80,106,113
Confederates-vi,x,79,81,104
Conspiracy Nut-212,236,237,240-242
Coral Castle-253
Country Club-171-173,176
Cow bells-85
Credit as a Public Utility-217,271,272
Debt financing-v,vii132,215-218,270,293
Deist-109,131,181,182,
Delaney Maggie-81,90,100,146,
Denver-64,69,93
Deuteronomy -125
Dictator-78,84,107,133,231
DNA-253,278,279
Dog and pony show-288
Dorsey Jimmy-169
Dublin-6,7,9,10,13-15,20,28,29,42,47,71,118,145,
161,181
DuPont-167

Electoral College-249,262,288
Electromagnetic pulse-286
Emancipation Proclamation-88
Embalmed meat-66
Environmental Mod.-276
Eugenics-277,279
Exodus-125
Expense statement-207
Farmers and Exchange Bank-94,98
FBI directors-224
Federal Reserve-v,vii,viii,132-135,138-140,148,150,191,193,211-
213,215-220,223,225,226,234,238,267-271,282-
285,289,291,298,300,304
Ferry-9,11,55,56,60,72
Fluoride-279-281,292
Foo Ling Yu-180
Fort Sumter-76,80
Foster Vince-274
Fox Indians-66
Fractional Reserve Banking-
v,vii,127,212,216,217,222,223,225,272,282,283,298,291
Frankenstorm-275
Franklin Benjamin-iv,11,24,35,50,123,151,152,157,212,231,235,291,294
Free the Slaves-88,103,106,306
Frog Hop Ball Room-168,170-172,185,311
Gandhi-298
Gap-271,283
Garman Catherine-114-116,122,163,181
GDP-216,271,283
General store-31,58,66,67,69,99
Global Hawk-246
GMO-255,278,279,293
Golden Rule-109
Governor of Missouri-76,77,191
Grand River-109,112,153
Green Backs-267
HAARP-254
Habeas Corpus-84,107,230
Halliburton-232
Hamilton Alexander-xv,70,126,127,131,291,293,294,300
Hannibal & St. Jos. RR-vi,39,41,42,47,49,61,63,79,80,
89,99,114,145,161,181,195,311

Hannibal Gazette-73
Hannibal-39,42,43,44,58,60,61,63,70,71,145,146,311
Harvard-109-116,129,144,181,240,280,304,311
Hazardous Waste-279,292
Heating stove-61,152
Hemp-167,168,192,193,292
Higgins Mr.-33,35,37-41,43,45,46
Hijackers-241-247,254
Hitler-170,177,237,266,280
Holmes Oliver Wendell-115
Homosexuals-74
Honeymoon-100,101
House Edward Mandell-131
Immigration authorities-25
Impeachment-2,150,225,273,293
Incandescent light bulb-69,70
Indianapolis-40-44,47,48,55-60,69,85
Indians-30,40,41,45,47,56,57,63,66,67,72,120
Industrial North-51,72,84
International bankers-iv,xii,127,128,134,138,199,211,218,220,260
Inverter-286
Iran-265,266
Iraq-212,230,241,242,265,266,298
Irish immigrants-24
Israel-200-205,212,238,239,242,246,247,254,266,275,289,311
Itinerate preacher-182
Jackson Andrew-xiv,123,127,128,134,135,139,141,285
Jackson C.F.-76
James Jesse-vii,7,19,63,71,96,101,104,123,178,200,,178
Jefferson Thomas-vii,xiii,xv,11,102,109,123,211,235,291,301
Jesus stories-183
Jesus-20,74,75,182,183,239
Jews-120,237,238
Johnson Gary-150
Josephus-74
Josh-63-69,93,120
Juror-xiii,52,91,93,213,214,288,292
Jury Nullification-xiii,91,93,213,214,287,292
Katy, Texas-205
Kelsey-13-36,41,46,67,74,75,86-88,101-104,113-118
Kennedy Assassination-212

KFEQ TV-196,305
Khazarian Jews-238
Kingston, Missouri-79,91,92
Knights of the Golden Circle-vii,95,96,98
Kucinich Denis-150
Law books-35,69
Law practice-108
Lawyer's apprentice-48
Lawyer-26,35,42,43,48,50,85,89-94,103,108,112,120,144-
146,153,230,231
Lebanon-265
LeDroit Park-119
Lee Robert E.-105
Liberia-88
Libya-265
Lick Fork-98,99
Lincoln Abraham-xiv,30,35,40,50-54,72,76-81,84,88,92,103-
109,224,230,267,284,301
Longfellow Henry W-115
Manchurian Candidate-273
Marijuana-167,224,288,293
Martial Law-4,107,227,230,232,233,277
Martin Luther King, Jr-273
McFadden Act- 133
Militia-76,77
Mississippi River-39,40,44,45,60
Missouri Bar-107,145,146
Model T-145,162,193
Morse Samuel-34,37,97,195,202
Muslim fanatics-247
Napalm bombs-202
National debt-216,217,227,234,264,282,291
299,312
National Defense Auth. Act-4,226,230,231,276,280,285,292
Naturalization papers-42,76
Negro-51-54,72,88,119,120
Nelson Evelyn -168-170,174,185-187
New England Glass Co-115
New Jersey-24,86,87,113-117,305
Non-producers-289,290
North Dakota-v,217
Offensive military-221,265

One World Government-1,228,233,234,290
Osama Bin Laden-243,245
Parkside Hotel-115
Passenger Act of 1855-9
Patee House Hotel-40,82
Patriots-vii,ix,2,211,212,260,263,276,280,290
Paul Ron-vi,.vii,xiv,150,301
Pearl Harbor-238,240
Pennsylvania Railroad-40
Philadelphia Gazette-29
Philip Dru: Administrator-133
Pierce Arrow-168,170,172,177
Piper Apache-192,197
Place's Grocery-297
Planned Parenthood-277
Platte River-vi,x,79,81,85,89,90,96,100
PNAC-265
Poker players-49,55,57,58
Policeman of the world-194,212,221,239
Policy coup-265
Pony Express-40,47,80
Pray-162,182,183,184,190,224
Preppers-287
Preserve the Union-106
President Wilson-xi,112,129-134,138,148,149,191
Princeton-129
Pro-Biotics-279
Producers-289,290
Provost Marshal-100
Pullman car-114
Racial prejudice-181
Railroad Café-70,71
Regime Change-xiv,217,266,290,293
Revolution-xiv,134,224,238,301
RFID-
Rhodes Cecil -133
Robidoux Joseph-66,67,309
Rockefeller David-233,235
Rothschild-126,128,301
Rusk Dean-204
Saloon-62,66,70,175

Sanger Margaret-277,279
Scottish Rite-113
Secede-48,50,51,72,77,78,83,85,88,92,104,106,
Secretary of War-76,77
Silver City, Nevada-72
Slaves-53,88,103,106,141,149,235,306
Somalia-265
Sound Monetary Policies-161,194,212,220,225,239
Southern sympathizer-70,76,78,84,96,105
St. Joseph Gazette-80
St. Joseph, Missouri-iii,42,47,195,196,264,302,303,
304,306,307,311
Stagecoach-40,42,45,46,49,61,64,69,72,113114,181,311
States' Rights-51,54,78,92,211
Sudan-265
Tea Party-115,263
Telegraph- vi,ix,33-43,47,50,55,56,63,64,67-71,75,76,80,82,86-
93,97,144-146,161,181,195
Ten Commandments-109,147,148
Tennis elbow-208,209
Tillman Pat-274
Tom Sawyer-108
Tomlin Clyde-297
Top Secret-252,277
Trosper saloon-70
Trosper Cemetery-65,145,146
UFO's-224,277
Unholy war-77,84,237,302
Union Troops-78,84,86,90,118
United Brethren Church-82,182
USS Liberty-200-205,275,311
Usury-125,126,130
Vietnam-xiv,198,199,273,302
War Between the States-50,78,80,88,96,104,105,107,
149,195,230
War of Northern Aggression-83
War on Drugs-
Weldon-67,68,
Weldon Cemetery-298
Wilson Monta -296
Woodbury, NJ-86,87,113,115-117
Woolsey Fritz-297
A-AZ   02/03/17   12:25PM   DVD

Notes: